FIRE IN FLIGHT

Ariel Barbera

Gemini Valley
Publishing

Gemini Valley Publishing LLC

www.geminivalley.com

Book Cover and Illustrations by Isabel Barbera.

Book Design by Ariel Barbera.

Library of Congress Control Number: 2025928133

ISBN (paperback): 978-1-971214-00-9

ISBN (hardcover): 978-1-971214-01-6

ISBN (eBook): 978-1-971214-02-3

1st edition 2026.

To Isabel
This book would not have been possible without you.

"All that we see or seem is but a dream within a dream."
Edgar Allan Poe

Prologue

Darkness often harbored tragedies.

The murky streets of New Harbor welcomed the darkness, however. There was always room for sins and scandals in a city masquerading as a utopia. And the moon was the only witness to it all.

Beyond the fog stood the sniper upon the rooftops of southern Canton, masked in the moonlit night. The black-clad figure had their sights on a slow car several blocks down. They kneeled along the edge, then aligned their sleek rifle.

No one would suspect a thing, yet everyone would hear the sirens.

The gray vehicle rode along the bay at a leisurely pace. In the driver's seat sat a man in his late thirties. He grew a beard along his square jaw, and crow's feet wrinkles pinched his eyes. He stared ahead smugly. Beside him sat a woman in her early twenties. She released her blond hair from a braid, letting it fall against her pale shoulders.

"The moon is gorgeous tonight," the woman said.

The man chuckled. "Reminds me of someone I know." He rested his arm over the open car window and flicked his cigar.

The woman raised her brow and glanced his way. "Now, who would that be?"

The man smirked. He drove forward slowly and met her gaze. "I could be looking at her right now."

"Oh." The woman stared ahead and breathed in deeply.

The man returned the cigarette to his lips. He breathed in the smoke, then blew out smoothly.

"Is this why you offered to drive me home tonight?" she asked.

The man shrugged. "Well—"

"Noah," she sighed.

The man straightened. "Come on, Kylie."

"You know I'm engaged."

"Do I know?" he remarked. "I never see you wearing a ring around the office."

"I guess I should start wearing it, then." She met his eyes again. "But some secrets are better left in the dark. Are they not?"

The corner of Noah's lip lifted slightly. "I see what game you're playing here."

"Do you?" she said. "And what game are *you* playing?"

The man laughed again. "Find out, will you?" he teased. "I did something that'll earn me a whole lotta money."

"Oh, really?" she replied sarcastically. She leaned back against the seat and stared ahead. "Does this involve your private session with Jason Streak at all?"

Noah took one hand off the wheel and rubbed his thumb against his index finger. "I'm making all the money off that man. Just wait and see," he explained. "He gave me some confidential info on Streak Corp. And I sold the files to an associate of Sal-Tech. But don't be too worried. Mr. Streak can still benefit from this, too."

"And...? What's so confidential?"

"Look, I intend on keeping it *confidential* for now," Noah emphasized. "Secrets regarding illegal weapons used during the war with Optyma. Can't say what, but..." He lowered his voice, moving his hand back to the wheel. "Sal-Tech paid big money for the files. And if this info gets out, we can manipulate the story. We'll keep ruining the reputation of those island rats. I'm sure Jason Streak wouldn't mind in the long run. He'd probably give me a raise—"

Kylie scoffed, "And why are you telling me this?"

"You're still new, Kylie. Young blood," he said with a smirk. "You've been a manager for a couple of months now. But me? I've been in Streak's business for years. I know how it all goes down. So, I'm gonna offer you a proposal."

"A proposal," she muttered. "How ironic."

"Hey, now, come on," Noah said. "You join me, Kylie, and we can run off with the money together. We're talking *millions* at stake here. Between Streak Corp, Sal-Tech, and the Optymans, we'll be winning in the end."

Kylie huffed, "That is one hell of an offer."

Noah drove ahead, and his eyes flashed to her thighs under her black skirt. She turned her gaze to him, and he shifted his attention to the road.

"Well?" he continued. "What do you say? I've had my eyes on you since the day you joined the team."

"I know."

"And?" The man was desperate to reel her in. He didn't want to be alone in this endeavor—this scandal to steal millions of dollars from the leading weapons manufacturer in the world—and he wanted a partner.

"Sounds incredible. You'd turn my life around," Kylie yawned. "But I'd have to decline."

Noah's smile dropped. "Seriously?"

Kylie grinned. "I don't want money, Noah. I have dreams. But until you find someone who can give you what you need, you'll never be satisfied."

Noah inhaled sharply. "No offense, honey, but your man doesn't have what I have. I can buy you your dream. Just watch—"

A sudden gunshot ripped through the air, and a heavy bullet struck the front left tire of the car. Noah gripped the wheel as he lost control of the swerving vehicle. The car skidded into a dim streetlight, and airbags sprang out from the wheel, crushing him.

He shoved the door open as he gasped for breath, then crawled out of the car. He blew the smoke away from his face, turning to see the wreckage.

"Kylie?" he choked out.

"I'm fine," she coughed back in the passenger seat.

Noah shifted his gaze to the flat tire beside him. "What the hell—"

Another shot rang through the air. A bullet struck Noah's right shoulder, and he fell back onto the hood of his car. His head slammed against the metal, and he slumped to the pavement.

"Noah!" Kylie shrieked. She threw herself out of the car and ran to his side. She kneeled beside him, reaching for his shoulder. Blood dripped across her bare hands.

Noah shuddered and stared up at the rooftops. "Someone's there," he stuttered. He tried to lift his arm, but his shoulder sagged.

Kylie faced the structures across the street. Upon the nearest rooftop stood a slim figure cloaked in black attire. Hooded and masked, with a rifle strapped across their back, the sniper stepped away. A spiraling wind stormed the area, and Kylie caught her breath as her hair flew all around her. She let go of Noah, shielding herself from the sudden gust.

She opened her eyes and saw the sniper had disappeared. The mysterious shooter delved deeper into the city, vanishing with the wind.

ACT I

A NEW
WORLD'S FLAME

Chapter 1

PREDATOR AND PREY

Matthew Ellis was just another victim of a fancy thing called "fate." Change was his nemesis, and insomnia his malaise.

The masked vigilante stared out at the vast city of Miami from a rooftop, succumbing to the never-ending clutches of fate. Nothing could hinder his drive to do the right thing, even if this ironic action made a change in the world around him.

On this night, the streets remained quiet near the outskirts of the urban area. The local bar hosted people of all kinds, from lonely loiterers to passionate partygoers. Matt had his eyes set on one individual—the solitary stalker. The man waited outside the bar, smoking a joint with his car parked across the road. Reminiscent of a predator hunting its prey, the smoker watched the crowds of people enter and leave the bar.

Matt had searched for this man's whereabouts over the past three months, tracking him relentlessly to every corner of the city.

The smoker was a serial killer notorious for kidnapping drunk individuals. He would often prowl around the local bars and offer a ride to anyone in need. The authorities hardly investigated the matter, but this man had been Matt's mission for the past ninety days.

Tonight was the night his oppression would end.

Matt grabbed a pole attached to the building and slid down. He landed lightly on his feet, crouching to stay out of sight. His outfit matched the tone of the night—pitch black with a mask and a hood covering his face and hair. Usually, he would wear an orange shirt underneath his jacket, but tonight required a stealthy guise.

A lone woman exited the bar and stumbled slightly on her heels. Exhausted, she looked for a nearby taxi to take her home. Matt watched quietly from across the street, noticing the smoker had put his joint out. The stalker approached the woman casually. He gave her a friendly wave, introduced himself, and gestured to his vehicle. The woman insisted she needed no help, but the man continued to prod her.

As the smoker was distracted, Matt darted across the street. He pulled out a knife attached to his belt, flicked a switch that ignited the blade with fire, and sliced the car tires. In a flash, Matt disappeared behind the other side of the bar.

The woman finally caved and followed the man to his car. From her perspective, this was just a generous offer. The man opened the passenger door for the woman, and she crawled in. He then strolled toward his side of the vehicle and slid onto his seat. He started the engine, but as he did, all the air in the tires escaped.

While the man raged within seconds, Matt sprinted toward the vehicle. He ran to the driver's side of the car, smashed his fist through the window, and grabbed the man by the back of the head. The woman screamed and tried to escape the car but quickly found the door's inner handles were missing.

Matt forced the serial killer's forehead against the dashboard—

Thud! Thud! Thud!

The unconscious predator slumped forward against the wheel. Matt dusted his gloves off, then walked around the car to open the passenger door for the woman. She pushed herself out, trembling as she backed away.

"What the hell?" she screamed, gasping for air.

"Go inside and find security," Matt ordered. He pointed toward the bar's entrance.

"Who was that?" she demanded, still in shock.

"Herman Wild. Serial killer." He turned to look at the unconscious man. "Now, go."

"Wait, but who are you?"

"*Go.*"

The woman fell speechless and nodded. She backed away slowly, then ran into the bar. Meanwhile, Matt approached his target. He whipped a thick string from his pocket, tying the man's wrists behind his back and fastening his ankles together. He slammed the driver's door shut, then disappeared into the alley.

Matt climbed one of the buildings and returned to his perch on the rooftop. He stared at the clouded moon, noting the lack of stars through the hazy sky. His anonymous identity was all a part of his role as a vigilante.

None of the people he saved, nor the authorities, would know who he was. And he preferred to stay that way.

To be the anonymous hero of the state.

Tonight would be his last time overseeing the streets of Miami, however, and no one needed to know he was leaving. He could only hope he made a visible mark on this place.

Matt pulled himself over the balcony, slipped inside his bedroom, and shut the sliding door behind him. He dragged himself to his bed, then dove into the covers. His trek overnight was a desperate attempt to distract himself from the inevitable. Even after his successful capture of Herman Wild, the night still haunted him.

Matt stared up at the dismal gray ceiling in silence. The thought of living in a new city swelled him with anxiety.

He rolled over on his side, gazing through the window at the dreary sky. The seagulls chanted above, and the people below his apartment complex bustled around. The salty fumes of the sea crept into his room, and the rain clouds circled the city's spires. In the distance, foaming waves rushed onto the sandy beaches, and those same boisterous seagulls searched for any scraps of food they could eat.

Matt would not have it any other way. The view seemed average, but this was *his* view—the wonderful world of Miami. Even with all its flaws, he would miss this city dearly.

He was already missing it.

He ran his hand through his messy, dark brown hair and stretched his sore muscles as he turned to lay on his back. The colorless light shined against his fair skin, and he rubbed his weary eyes. This feeling was the norm for him almost every morning. He believed he could deal with his insomnia by taking his ceaseless energy to the streets overnight, yet it came with consequences.

Suitcases and bags leaned beside the gray walls of the vacant bedroom. Matt sank miserably into his bed. The whole atmosphere of his room felt barren and devoid of life.

"Matt! I hope you're awake!" his sister's sharp voice bellowed from the hallway. "Get your bags to the lobby!"

"I'm awake!" he called back. He huffed and slid out of bed, faced with his empty room.

Matt tore his jacket off and slipped into a casual blue hoodie. He kicked his shoes off, then threw the gear onto the middle of his bed. He covered his vigilante attire with a blanket before his sister could see the evidence that he had been out last night.

Madeline slammed Matt's door open as he rolled up the blankets on his bed. He turned around in a panic, then leaned against the mattress naturally. Her sea-blue eyes were usually welcoming in the morning, but not today. She stood there urgently with overflowing bags gripped in each of her hands.

"Clear your bed. I don't want to keep the helpers waiting," she ordered.

"Is the truck here already?" Matt gasped.

"No, but it'll be here any minute," she said. "Let's get going."

As Madeline left the room, her brown hair flowed gracefully behind her. He noticed she had dressed professionally this morning, with gray suit pants, a coordinated jacket, and a teal shirt tucked underneath.

Matt continued to pack his bed. He stuffed the sheets and blankets in cases, then leaned the mattress against the wall. All that remained was the bed frame. With everything packed and hidden away, Matt took his black pants off and slipped into a pair of dark jeans. He removed his fingerless gloves, grateful that Madeline hadn't noticed them, then glanced down at his right hand. Matt wore a black ring around his middle finger—something he hardly ever took off, even when fighting criminals late at night. He walked into the bathroom, brushed his teeth, then combed his messy hair. He noticed the dark circles under his azure eyes and grimaced.

After he gave his reflection a sour attitude, Matt packed his bathroom necessities, then returned his gaze to the window. The end of July often brought storms this time of the year, and moving was the last thing he wanted to do on the final day of his favorite month. Matt turned eighteen six days ago but hardly had the chance to celebrate his birthday. He also graduated high school in June, but since he was moving, he had no immediate college plans.

Madeline turned twenty-five back in May, and despite his indifferent opinions on her business life, he always admired her ambition. She had been his role model for as long as he could remember, and while he would follow her down every road, moving from Florida stressed him.

Madeline welcomed herself into his room again and grabbed a few bags. "You ready?" she asked with a grin.

Matt forced himself to smile back. "I'll be outside in a few minutes. I need a moment."

Her eyes moved to his bedside stand. "Don't forget your zolpidem."

"I won't."

Madeline nodded slowly, then returned to the hallway. "We'll talk more on the ride there, okay?" she mentioned on her way out.

His eyes dropped to the suitcases on the floor. Matt sighed. He knew what kind of talk they were going to have. Matt didn't want to leave, yet his sister needed to. Wherever life took her, he would follow. Their lives had been this way since their parents died almost a decade ago.

He was eight when they left to go to war. In the end, they never returned.

Instead, the War of Optyma changed the world forever.

Optyma was a country in the center of the northern Atlantic Ocean. What remained of the island was approximately two thousand miles east of New York City and over five hundred miles northwest of the Azores archipelago. The Optyman War started as a civil war between the island nation's president and a vocal senator who opposed him, yet the conflict reached the United States, who aided in the fight against the Optyman president's forces. The war devastated millions of innocent people, Matt and Madeline included. Now, Madeline intended to move to New Harbor, one of the largest cities on the East Coast, to receive a promotion from the company she worked for—Streak Corporation.

Whether he wanted to go or not, a new world awaited him.

Matt leaned against the side of the truck window and stared at the passing fields outside.

"This is going to be a *long* trip," Madeline sighed as they left Miami's borders. "It's a bit over a sixteen-hour drive. So, if we keep it up, we'll be there sometime before midnight."

"*Midnight*," Matt groaned. He let his head fall against the window again. "I hope that promotion is going to be worth it."

"Oh, lighten up," Madeline snapped at him. "You've been on longer trips than this."

"Have I?"

Madeline paused for a second. "Uh. I think so," she said, then checked the rearview mirror. "We've been to New Harbor before. You were seven."

Matt glanced at his sister, who focused on switching lanes to avoid the traffic. "It wasn't New Harbor," he told her.

His sister gasped. "Shoot. It was Baltimore back then," she muttered. "*Baltimore*. We visited Baltimore."

New Harbor was known as the most significant outcome of the Optyman War. After Optyma's forces demolished Baltimore during the war, the government began reconstructing the county into New Harbor. The lifelong citizens often refer to the autonomous city as Baltimore; some people will acknowledge its current identity as New Harbor, and others sometimes slip up and call it "New Baltimore."

Matt released another deep breath and closed his eyes as Madeline rambled on. He felt himself drifting off to sleep again, hoping to get away with a few minutes of shut-eye before his sister would jolt him awake. But she continued to mention their destination, and all he could see was the neo-metropolis.

Since his parents had died to bring this city to life, this place should have felt like a second home to him, but he wanted nothing to do with it. Every moment of his life in New Harbor would remind him of his parents' sacrifices, and he found no solace in that. He felt robbed, having lost them too soon, and maybe he was selfish for thinking that way, but he couldn't help it. All he wanted to see were his parents, happy and alive; not their so-called "legacy" from the war.

Of course, he would follow Madeline anywhere, but he wished he had his own path.

This path could very well be the "work" he did at night, which he would gladly continue in New Harbor.

Matt never gave himself an alias, and people hardly talked about the shady protector at night. Crime loitered the streets of every city, and in an age of wars that devastated entire nations, some extraordinary individuals struck a match and made a change.

This world was one of vigilantes and unseen justice, after all.

While Miami had a collection of felons, Matt had adapted to the issues of his hometown. New Harbor was a completely different territory for him. He hoped Madeline wouldn't chastise him for continuing this work. She frowned upon him being a vigilante, though she had done nothing to stop him. Her sighs of disapproval always hurt, regardless.

With New Harbor on his mind, he stared out at the vast road ahead of him, dreaming of the nights he would fight as one of the unseen justices of the world.

Chapter 2

Welcome to Utopia

Matt almost dozed off to sleep as darkness crept across the sky, but his eyes opened upon seeing the enormous city ahead. The urban area extended across the bay. Neon signs and lights flickered through the evening haze. Silver buildings waved flags of all kinds—from traditional cloth flags to holographic displays. Rows of cars loitered on the elongated black streets, and pedestrians walked across the stone-colored sidewalks. A salty gale drifted through Matt's open window, though it was nothing compared to the breeze down south.

A large metal sign stood alongside the highway, greeting hundreds of people into the city at once.

Utopia Awaits! Welcome to ~~New Harbor!~~

Black spray paint covered *New Harbor*, replacing the name with *Baltimore*. Someone had vandalized the sign a while ago. Instead of dwelling on the billboard, Matt focused on the silver city before him.

"It's huge," Matt whispered in awe.

"Say 'hello' to New Harbor, Matt," Madeline said as she watched her brother's face light up. "Our new home."

His heart dropped at the mention of *home*. "We shouldn't treat this place like a replacement," Matt said as he looked at his sister. "I can't."

"You'll get used to it. I promise," Madeline sighed.

"How?" Matt rested his gaze on the long highway. "Am I supposed to sit at home all day while you're making bank at Streak Corp? Or worse, I really don't want to go back to working fast food."

"Hey," Madeline snapped. "Stop acting like you're going to be a house pet. There's a reason I wanted you to follow me here."

"Yeah." He shuffled away from her. "I feel like I have nowhere else to go," he muttered.

Madeline's hands tightened around the wheel. "Is that really how you feel?"

Matt caught her gaze. "Uh, no—I mean...*no*," he replied weakly. "I...I don't know what my future is going to be like."

Aside from the vigilantism he planned to carry into New Harbor, he had no idea what he would do during the day. There was a distinguished university for artists in New Harbor—*The New Harbor School of Arts and Designs*. They could afford the education, but his sister had doubts that anyone could start a successful career around the fine arts.

"Well, I think you're in luck," Madeline said. The tone in her voice changed from mildly sour to optimistic. "I had a perfect idea for you, but I need to talk with Mr. Streak first."

"Really?"

"How does an apprenticeship at Streak Corp sound for you?"

Matt peered at her, dumbfounded.

"I did some research on it. Streak Corp offers paid internships and apprenticeships to undergraduates *and* young family members of current employees."

"But I'm not enrolled in school," Matt mentioned.

"What do you think I mean by *family*, Matt? You're eligible," she exclaimed. "It's a special program. They don't let just anyone in."

"Then what makes you think I have a chance? I have no clue what kind of work you do," Matt stuttered. "Streak Corp is a weapons manufacturer. I have no experience with stuff like that."

Even Madeline knew that was a blatant lie. He handled different weapons before on the streets late at night. But if he told the owner of the largest defense contractor in the world that he was a night-time vigilante, he would have no chance of getting the job.

"Don't worry. Interns get hands-on training," Madeline said. "I'd say your future in New Harbor already looks promising." She smiled at him. "And you might make some new friends here."

"I hardly had any friends back in Miami," he mumbled.

"Exactly. A new start means new friends. Look at the bright side." She prodded his shoulder.

Matt scoffed and folded his arms. He hardly made friends in school and preferred to remain outside the crowds, but he was an unashamed introvert—unlike his sister, who considered herself a social butterfly.

Madeline navigated the streets, and Matt stared at the silver skyscrapers. The city appeared clean with a patterned quality—radiant, reflective, and revolutionary. New Harbor was the "utopia" that the people of Baltimore desperately needed after the war with Optyma. But there was always corruption, even in cities as "perfect" as this one. And Matt liked to think of himself as someone who brought trouble to the trouble. He smiled, resting his head against the window as they passed the vivid streetlights.

Among the pedestrians walking along the sidewalks, Matt noticed the shadows of a few lone individuals huddling in the alleyways. Capes were wrapped around their shoulders, and other passersby didn't pay them any attention. His smile slowly dropped, and his eyes drifted to the skyscrapers instead of the people on the streets.

Only the Optyman refugees were known to wear cloaks nowadays.

They entered the neighborhood of Canton along the inner harbor and drove ahead on Boston Street. Madeline swerved into the Dockside Circle parking lot beside the pier, then slowed to a stop. Matt gasped as he stepped out and stared at the vast bay. He then turned around to face the tall building that stood along the harbor—a magnificent high-rise apartment. *Leo Towers*. Beside the condominium were smaller, low-rise apartments, though most of the space within Dockside Circle belonged to Leo Towers.

"We're staying *here?*" asked Matt.

"I knew you'd start warming up to this place," Madeline laughed. "Let's check in. We're on one of the top floors."

Matt sat on the edge of his bed and stared at his packing boxes. He needed to look on the bright side of a fresh start.

The apartment had two separate bedrooms and bathrooms, a living space, a kitchen, and a balcony that faced the harbor. The floor consisted of polished hardwood planks, which Matt had slid across a few times in his socks as he carried boxes to his room. The living room had enough space for a television, a couch, and a large coffee table. The kitchen on the right side of the apartment was small but had room for the essentials.

Madeline opened the door to Matt's room and waved. He beckoned her over, and she sat beside him.

"It's a beautiful apartment," she expressed as she stared at the white walls. "I was thinking of painting my room a light teal. Depends on how I'm feeling. But I might be a bit too busy to paint."

She laughed, and Matt smiled. The future was the one thing Madeline always set her sights on, and whether her thoughts were fantasies or ideal passions, they often diverted her attention away from her grief.

"Tomorrow is a big day for us," Madeline said. "It's all finally going our way."

"What do you mean?" he asked, confused.

"Oh, you know," she muttered. She tilted her head as she looked at the hardwood floor. "I don't think things have ever really gone how we wanted them to. But here we are. *Finally.*"

Matt caught a lot of irony in her statement. Things were going the way *she* wanted them to go. His opinions differed from hers, but he kept quiet and let her fantasize.

She grinned, then wrapped her arm around her brother. Matt faked a smile. "Anyway, there's a lot you'll have to get used to in New Harbor. The way of life and culture here is different."

"You mean the lawmakers here aren't as vile?" Matt replied.

"Okay, *yes*. But I was talking about the people," she chuckled. "A quarter of the population here is Optyman."

"Oh. Right." His shoulders sank.

"The Optyman refugees settled here after the war. I wonder if some people our parents knew back in the day are still around the area," Madeline pondered. "It'll be neat to know their history. I bet this place is full of lessons."

And there it was, the one thing that made Matt relentlessly uncomfortable—history lessons about the war that killed his parents. The war that made him an orphan.

"Also, I heard the city is hydro-powered," she added, which piqued his interest. "You know that one tech company? *Sal-Tech*?"

"I know people who have Sal-Tech phones," he replied, shrugging. "Isn't their mascot Miss Earth Day, or something like that?"

"Apparently, the company signed a deal with the city. They installed hydroelectric generators in the harbor. Isn't that neat?" Madeline nudged him, trying her best to lift his mood. He nodded back, and she stood up.

"I'm going to unpack some more. But take it easy. Don't feel the need to unload everything in one night."

She closed the door and left him behind in the dimly lit room. He walked over to the window, peering out at the harbor of Canton. At least the view was beautiful, from the docked ships to the endless waves.

Matt looked to his right, down toward the bustling street behind the apartments, where he found holographic signs hanging from the many buildings around the area. He then peered up at the sky, where the stars hid from the light pollution. He reached his arm out, pretending he could touch the clouds. It seemed so easy for him to fall.

Yet falling was the last thing he wanted to do.

Chapter 3

STREAK CORPORATION

Matt glowered at his reflection in the mirror. He wore a tight black business suit held together with two buttons and notch lapels. After he covered the white shirt underneath, he combed his hair as neatly as possible. Despite his efforts, his hair stuck out, appearing unkempt as usual. To him, it always looked like a windblown catastrophe.

He left his room and found Madeline standing close to the door. She wore a teal dress and tied her hair back into a single braid. A purse hung over her shoulder as she puckered her lips, applying a light pink balm.

"Are you ready? We should get going," she told him. She stuffed the lipstick in her bag and opened the door.

"Just about," Matt replied, then straightened his jacket. "How far is the office?"

"Um," Madeline pursed her lips as she held the door open for him, "about a two-minute drive. It's just down the street."

"Maddie," Matt sighed as he left the room, and she shut the door behind them. "You're not going to be late."

"It's better to be early. Seriously, this promotion is my future," Madeline exhaled. She guided Matt to the elevator, where they rode down to the lobby. "I must have been doing something right these past five years."

They left Leo Towers and started their westward trek. The main headquarters sat on the harbor in Fells Point, beside the boardwalk and the docks, and just a block west of the Canton neighborhood. In the distance, Matt saw several ships docked near the wall—some smaller and privately owned, and others owned by the government.

"So, how different do you think it will be working in New Harbor compared to Miami?" asked Matt.

"*Too* different," Madeline breathed out. "Look, I was an assistant manager for the Miami location. But Mr. Streak noticed my work and offered me the general manager position in New Harbor. This place is the home of the company."

Matt gaped at her, then glanced at the tall glass building ahead. "So, you're the general manager of the *entire* company now?"

"Well," Madeline shrugged, "I am the head of all the general managers."

Matt fell silent for a moment. He never realized how big this promotion was for his sister.

"I'm proud of you," he told her quietly.

Madeline beamed back at him, then turned to face the office. The structure consisted of dark gray stone and metal, with reflective glass windows and gray pillars along the edges.

Matt read the plaque near the entrance of the building.

Streak Corporation: Main Headquarters

"Beautiful building," Madeline whispered as she stared toward the sky. "The main headquarters has everything. There's a factory in the industrial area where they distribute the weapons. But here is where all the negotiations take place. And Jason Streak *himself* works in this very building."

"You always have so much to say about that man," Matt mentioned, crossing his arms.

"Matt, he's the CEO of the greatest defense contractor *in the world*." Madeline flushed red, then turned away. "There's a lot I can go on about. I'm just so excited."

Madeline started an internship at the Miami location five years ago while in college. She studied business with a passion for companies that aided the military. This pursuit allowed Madeline to dedicate her time and effort to helping the different military branches, which was her way of honoring her parents' memories.

As for Streak Corp, the defense contractor has existed for forty years. Jason Streak was the current chief executive officer of the business, having taken over for his parents, Jonathon Streak and Marissa Oleander-Streak, after they had retired. Jason Streak received fame as a young man because of his family's legacy, and his popularity skyrocketed after he took over as the corporation's leader. Over the past eight years, Jason had struck many great deals that expanded the corporation internationally, where he began manufacturing weapons and vehicles in nations other than the United States.

Matt knew everything about Jason Streak from his sister since she had researched the man and his career throughout college. During her studies, Matt was often the spectator of her practice presentations. She had taken on many projects centered around Streak Corp, and the company offered her an internship at the Miami location after she presented her efforts to the hiring managers.

As they entered the building, a lady in her late twenties with curly blond hair greeted them at the front desk. "Welcome to the main headquarters of Streak Corporation. You must be Ms. Madeline Ellis."

"Yes, that would be me," Madeline replied. "I have an appointment with Mr. Streak."

"His office is on the top floor," the lady said. "You may take the stairs or the elevator at your convenience. He will be waiting for you there."

"Thank you," Madeline said. "When I spoke with him before, I also mentioned my brother was interested in starting an apprenticeship here. And, uh, here he is." She patted Matt on the shoulder to show him off. "Is he good to go up?"

"Of course. Since he is not an employee here at Streak Corporation, he would need a guest card," the lady told her. She handed Matt a name tag and a pen. "Please write your name, sir."

"Thanks," Matt replied. He scribbled his name on the tag and clipped it to his suit.

"Also," the receptionist added, "Ms. Ellis, once you finish meeting with Mr. Streak, please report here to acquire your employee card. I will verify it for you during your conference, so it will be ready when you return."

"Of course. Thank you for your time," Madeline glanced down at the receptionist's name, Elaine Dusky, on the desk, "Elaine."

Matt and Madeline took the elevator up to the tenth floor. Once the doors departed, the two stepped off and walked down the hall. They approached the office with a golden plaque nailed to the door.

Jason Streak, CEO.

"This is it," Madeline breathed in sharply. She grasped Matt's hand for a second before she knocked on the door.

A muffled voice on the other side spoke up, "Come in."

Madeline held her breath and opened the door. Matt followed his sister in to see a man in a lavish gray suit seated at a desk. He read over several blueprints and papers, then peered toward them. He straightened himself as Madeline stopped a few feet from his desk.

"Madeline Ellis," Jason Streak greeted with a polite smile. "A pleasure to finally meet you in person."

So, this is the greatest CEO in the world, Matt thought. He felt his sister shaking more than he was; to be in the presence of someone world-renowned felt unnerving.

At thirty-eight years old, Jason Streak had light brown hair, neatly trimmed and combed, and fair skin with faint blemishes. His face had a sharp shape and a small goatee. Behind the reading glasses were ocean-blue eyes that shined even brighter when he took the spectacles off.

"Mr. Streak, the pleasure is the same," Madeline said. "I'm happy to work with you."

Streak stepped out from behind the desk and offered his hand to her. "You are exceptionally gifted in the art of business, Ms. Ellis. It's a privilege to have someone with your skills at my main headquarters."

Madeline took his hand, giving him a quick, firm handshake. Matt studied how the two acted professionally. Even the desk receptionist, Elaine, appeared so business casual. He felt like an imposter in a setting like this.

"As my general manager here at New Harbor, I expect great things from you," Streak mentioned.

"Of course. I've been preparing myself for this," Madeline replied. "Let me know everything I need to do."

"With pleasure," Streak continued. "You will be getting your own office, which is on the ninth floor. You will also manage the employees in this building and the workers in the Canton Industrial Area distribution center. I know it may sound like a handful, but it is your duty to ensure their tasks are up to speed."

"I understand."

"But given all that, you have a set of assistant managers who work under you," Streak informed her. "The department managers report directly to you. In return, you will then report to the chief operating officer. If my second-in-command is unavailable, you will report to me."

"The COO is here, too?" Madeline asked. "I wasn't sure if she would be at the New Harbor location."

"Madame Modisette makes her rounds to the other locations with me, but she works here primarily. Her office is also on the ninth floor." Streak cleared his throat. "I'll introduce you to the other managers today as well."

"Thank you so much for your time, Mr. Streak."

"No need to thank me, Ms. Ellis. I should be thanking you." Streak grinned. He then turned to Matt, who snapped back to reality and turned his gaze to the boss. "And you must be Madeline's younger brother. Matthew, is it?"

"Yes, sir," Matt replied quickly.

"Your sister mentioned that you were interested in starting an apprenticeship here. I would be glad to take you under my wing," Streak told him. Matt forced himself to smile. "I must say, the Ellis family has quite a lot of talent."

"I think we get it from our parents," Madeline added proudly.

"Ah, yes. Ethan and Eveline," Streak acknowledged. "I met them before they left for the Atlantic. Quite a shame what happened, but if not for their sacrifices, we wouldn't have had Baltimore's rebirth."

"That was so long ago," Madeline said as Matt shuffled back from his sister.

"Yes, I remember their visit to Baltimore back in the day...after what Optyma had done to us. My parents and I provided them with a unique set of tools for their mission," he recounted. "Now that I mention it, during one of my conferences with Eveline, she had a young boy with her."

Matt froze. He hardly remembered anything about his trip to Baltimore, but the one thing he did recall was that he had stuck to his mother like glue.

Another thing he remembered was the aftermath of the city's attack. Buildings were toppled, and the terrain was stained black. Nothing but ash had cluttered the air.

"Matt!" Madeline laughed. "You met Mr. Streak?"

"I'm so sorry," Matt said and stepped back. "Mr. Streak, I don't remember—"

"Dear boy, there is no need to apologize. You were so young," Streak assured him, then patted his shoulder. "But look how much you've grown since then. You couldn't let her hand go."

Matt's face flushed red.

"He was such a mama's boy," Madeline told Streak. "He hated leaving her side."

"Eveline was a kind soul," Streak mentioned. He paused as Matt looked down. "And it's nice to see you grew up to be a fine young man."

"Thank you, sir," Matt replied as he faced Streak again.

"There's a lot that I'm trying to recall from that day. I know what we discussed, but—oh! Matthew, I don't know if you remember my niece. You were so shy around everyone else, but you didn't mind talking to her."

Matt shook his head, then looked toward the window. "No, I don't remember."

"Should we meet with the other managers?" Madeline asked.

"Yes, let's go see them," Streak said. "And about that apprenticeship, Matthew, I will keep you informed. Perhaps we can start you off sooner than later."

Matt followed Streak and Madeline down the hall, hiding his bitterness. He never recalled *wanting* this apprenticeship. Madeline first mentioned the idea to him *yesterday*. But he had nothing good to say about it, so he kept quiet.

His contempt for New Harbor was only beginning to grow.

Chapter 4

MEET AND GREET

Matt followed Madeline and Streak off the elevator and onto the ninth floor. The level had several rooms, a long hallway, and the office of the chief operating officer.

Lorelei Modisette, COO

Streak opened the door and waved to the woman sitting at the desk. Lorelei had long brunette hair with bangs that rested against her warm skin. She sported a tailored purple shirt with a turquoise placket and a black pencil skirt.

"Do you need anything, Jason?" Lorelei inquired. Her voice sounded low with a thick French accent.

"I want you to meet our new general manager." Streak beckoned Madeline to his side. "Ms. Madeline Ellis."

"Hello, Madame," Madeline greeted with a wave.

"Oh, yes, Jason did tell me you were arriving today," Lorelei replied, standing. She walked over and shook hands with Madeline. "I look forward to working with you. There is so much to do after losing our last manager."

"I'm sorry to hear that," Madeline expressed. "Did he quit?"

Streak and Lorelei shared a glance. "Ah, it's a long story," Streak told her. He placed his hand on Madeline's shoulder. "He passed away a couple of weeks ago. But as we grieve, we look forward to seeing what you can bring to the position."

Madeline frowned. "If I have some big shoes to fill, I promise I'll do my best."

"Warms my heart to hear that," Streak replied with a grin. "Let's introduce you to our other managers and get you situated. Matthew, feel free to join us."

Matt stood by his sister's side as Streak turned to leave the room.

"I assumed the former manager retired," Madeline whispered to him. "This is heartbreaking."

"Hey," Matt nudged her lightly, "you'll do a good job helping these people."

"You think?"

Matt faked a smile and nodded. "Yeah," he assured her, yet he couldn't help but feel unnerved by the former manager's death.

Streak opened the door to the next room, and stacks of papers, boxes, and files cluttered the interior. A man stood on the other side of the room, pouring himself coffee.

"Hello there, Mr. Streak!" he hailed. He put the coffee pot down and waved over at him. "Sorry about the mess."

"It's no problem, Harold. I expect most rooms to look like this," Streak chuckled. "Here's the new general manager, Madeline Ellis. You will be responding directly to her."

Harold looked to be a young man in his mid-twenties. He had short black hair, dark brown skin, an oval-shaped face, and friendly ebony eyes. He had no right arm, and he held his left arm out to shake with Madeline.

Madeline grinned and shook his hand. "Nice to meet you, Harold."

"Please, ma'am, you can just call me 'Harry,'" he replied.

"Mr. Faresoul is in charge of overseeing designs, as well as scheduling meetings with military and government officials," Streak explained. "He always has a lot on his plate."

"Sounds like you can use some help," Madeline added. "I'll give you anything you need, Harry."

"I look forward to working with you, ma'am," Harry said with a nod. They smiled at each other as Streak strolled back to the door.

"Ms. Ellis, I'll introduce you to one more manager down on the eighth floor, and then we will get you an employee card," Streak announced. "A tour of the warehouse will be at another time."

"Alright." Madeline faced Matt as Streak departed. "This is so exciting," she breathed out.

"Yeah," Matt whispered plainly.

"Are you accompanying Ms. Madeline today?" Harry asked.

Matt glanced at him and nodded. "I'm her brother. Matt," he answered. "She's setting me up for an apprenticeship here...I think."

"That's great." Harry extended his arm to shake hands, and Matt returned the gesture. "We could always use some more help."

Matt shrugged. "I have no idea what kind of work I'll be doing, though."

"Whatever Mr. Streak needs," Harry laughed. "I'll see you around, Matt."

As Matt left, he smiled and waved back at Harry. He realized Lorelei had paid no attention to him, so it felt somewhat satisfying to be acknowledged by one of the higher-ups.

Streak beckoned the two onto the elevator with him and pressed the button to the eighth floor.

"So, which departments need the most focus?" Madeline asked him.

"I'd say all of them do in their own ways. Take Harold for example. He looks over two different aspects of the corporation here," Streak explained. "The manager here on the eighth floor is Kylie Kreene. She's been with us for a few months now, so she's still relatively new. But her experience with marketing, journalism, and social media has benefited the company tremendously."

They walked onto the floor and passed by a hall of cubicles. Several people tapped away at the keyboards on their desks and scrolled through different web pages.

"The workers here keep us updated on our social platforms and inform us of any news about the company," Streak told them. "Our social media accounts are also managed here. We tend to put a lot of focus into Oracle and VisionHive."

Streak led them further down the hall, where an enclosed office awaited them. A woman scrolled through the computer on her desk and peered up at them instantly.

"Ms. Kreene, I'd like to introduce you to Madeline Ellis," Streak greeted, then stepped aside for Madeline to come forward.

"Hello there," the woman replied ecstatically. "I am Kylie. Nice to meet you." Her voice had a sugary, ringing tone with a strong Mid-Atlantic accent. Kylie had light skin, and she had tied her ginger blond hair into a large braid.

"Nice to meet you as well. I like all the stuff going on here," Madeline noted, then looked around at the decorated room. Kylie had pictures all over the walls. One photo showed Kylie posing alongside a tall woman with long black hair and dark brown skin. They both wore deep purple dresses in the picture and stood in front of a seaside setting. Red blinds covered Kylie's window, matching the burgundy shirt and black jacket that she wore.

"Kylie is exceptionally skilled with handling social media. After months of searching for the perfect marketing manager, she came to my aid," Streak shared.

"I'm like a knight in shining armor here," Kylie exhaled with a sly grin. "Also, who's this?" Her baby-blue eyes darted to Matt.

"Matthew Ellis," Streak answered before Matt could say a word. "Madeline's younger brother. He is looking to start an apprentice-ship."

Kylie examined her nails, then glanced at Matt. "I could use more help down here, so send him my way."

Matt's mind drowned out their words. The apprenticeship, the work overload, the different positions—it all overwhelmed him. He needed a way out.

"Can I meet you in the lobby?" Matt asked his sister.

"Oh. Yeah, go ahead," Madeline said, unaware of her brother's sudden panic. "We'll meet up with you. This tour isn't something you need, anyway."

Matt stepped outside the room and turned around to rush toward the stairs. He passed several cubicles, but no one noticed he was in a hurry. He felt invisible, which was what he wanted to be—

WHAM!

Matt closed his eyes upon the collision and stumbled to the carpet. He rubbed his head, then saw a cluster of papers fall around him. A young woman landed on the floor beside him. She wore a ruffled maroon dress with thin straps and a red sash.

"Are you okay?" Matt stuttered.

He reached over to help her, but she pushed herself away.

"Don't," she snapped. She turned away and gathered the papers around her. Matt collected the folders beside him, then attempted to hand her the files. She stopped and stared at him again, and he did the same, albeit nervously.

Her emerald-green eyes cut right through him. She had a pale face coated in makeup and wavy auburn hair that fell against her shoulders.

"I'm sorry," he said as she took the papers.

"Just watch where you're going." Her voice sounded silvery with a soft-spoken tone, yet filled with frustration.

She stood up and continued toward the stairs. Matt grimaced, then proceeded to the elevator. He would have taken the stairs, but he was desperate to avoid the tension that followed her.

He was only looking for a way out now.

Chapter 5

SET IN STONES

Matt stood on the balcony and stared out at the harbor. Hundreds of lights reflected off the rippling water, and he admired what little of the stars he saw in the sky. At least the lack of stars was something New Harbor had in common with Miami, even if it wasn't that impressive.

"Matt, you alright?" Madeline cut in as she opened the balcony door. "I ordered some pizza."

"I'm fine."

"You can make dinner tomorrow if you want," Madeline said. "But what's going on? You've been out here for the past twenty minutes."

He sighed, "Just admiring the view."

Madeline rested her arms on the railing beside him. "It's a great view. Better than the one we had in Miami."

Matt wanted to argue against that, but after another peek, he found no complaints. Madeline picked out a luxury apartment close to her job. Everything was going her way.

He hesitated, then took a deep breath. "Am I really getting a job there? It sounds unbelievable."

"Why?" Madeline replied. "What's unbelievable about it?"

"I don't know," Matt shrugged, "it's just—I have no experience with that stuff."

"Matt, if anything, Mr. Streak will have you start in marketing. I don't think you'll be working with actual weapons," Madeline explained. "Plus, social media is important nowadays."

"My experience with social media is just looking through fan pages and shit on Oracle," Matt sighed, then rubbed his head. "I'm an artist, not a businessman."

"We've talked about this before," she told him. "You're getting a ticket into a full-time job without college. You've already got a future. Take advantage of it."

Matt remained silent, peering toward the bustling street below. He could still see the faint orange hue of the setting sun against the pavement as the salty scent of the bay drifted through the air.

"Okay," he muttered.

Madeline nudged his shoulder, then made her way back inside. Matt gripped the rails of the balcony and closed his eyes.

At least I have the nightlife, he thought bitterly.

He wanted to continue his secret vigilante life, yet he was unsure he could start again with his sister keeping him on a leash at Streak Corp. Vigilantism was a different kind of passion than art was for him. His night-time battles were necessary for the city—a desire to save lives through the art of fighting, just at the cost of his own sanity.

Matt took another breath, then followed his sister inside. Madeline had already seated herself on the couch, her eyes glued to the national news on the television screen.

He sat beside her, then pulled out his phone, though he didn't know why. The next thing he knew, he was scrolling through the countless threads of VisionHive. Post after post, and nothing piqued his interest.

"Oh no," Madeline gasped at the television.

"What?" he mumbled, dropping his phone on the couch.

"Someone stole one of the Core Stones," she mentioned.

"What? Really?" Matt fixed his focus on the news broadcast.

"General Peter Fren of the British Navy was critically injured last night by an unknown intruder. He was found by his stepdaughter, Cali Cavrien, with a large gash in his stomach," the woman on the screen reported. "According to the authorities, Cavrien had called the police upon finding her stepfather unconscious in his living room. Investigators discovered the intruder was most likely after the Core Stone Fren had possessed in secrecy for nine years. Once authorities arrived, the attacker and the stone were gone, and Fren was found in critical condition."

"Holy shit. Cali." Madeline covered her mouth. "I hope she's okay."

"Cali? Ms. Beth's daughter?" Matt asked.

"Yeah. I haven't seen her in ages," Madeline sighed. Matt hardly remembered her, but Cali Cavrien was Madeline's childhood best friend. He found it strange to see her name on the international news.

"Can't believe her stepdad had one of those stones," Madeline continued. "That's insane."

Matt knew the basics of the Core Stones. They were the most powerful relics in the world. The four stones originated from Optyma—named for being a "quartet" of stones—yet the Optyman settlers resorted to using the term *core* instead of *quart*. According to historical records and many eyewitnesses, these stones bestowed exceptional individuals with mysterious powers of the elements. The founder and first king of Optyma, Adam Dux, had come across the gems after settling on what would become the island nation. The stones had granted the explorer an unusual ability—the power to manipulate stone and earth. Tales of King Dux had spread worldwide, how he gained the ability to turn any mineral into gold. They called him the "present-day King Midas" when Optyma was a new nation in the early seventeenth century. But Adam Dux was not like King Midas; his touch had affected only the earth, and he could easily control it if he possessed one of the stones.

Over the years, the stones had remained within Optyma, overseen by each passing monarch—and then president—once the nation became a presidential republic in 1820. After the fall of Optyma, the American president gave the gems to four new keepers and ordered them to hide the stones.

"Who could be stealing the Core Stones?" Madeline panicked.

"Where are the other three stones?" Matt asked, even though he knew his sister was as clueless as he was.

"If I remember, one might be at the White House, but that was nine years ago. I don't know if they've given it to anyone else."

The reporter continued, "Due to leftover evidence, the culprit may be *Rare*, judging by the scorch marks left behind at the scene."

Rare—the term used to describe the unique individuals who inherited powers from the stones.

The short term originated from the Optyman phrase "Rare Soul." Only a few people in history wielded such powers, and the Optyman locals claimed that the stone users' souls spiritually aligned with the entity that created the gems. The Optymans believed "God" took the form of a mysterious female being named *Klypt*, who had molded the Core Stones long ago. People have allegedly encountered the entity in person and have witnessed her watching over the land. But the beliefs had become more abstract over time, and after the nation had fallen to war a decade ago, the rest of the world perceived this history as a mythical misunderstanding.

The term "*Rare*" has stuck around to describe anyone capable of possessing abilities from the stones. Even President Jake Agnes, the last leader of Optyma, had gained powers from the gems. But not even using the stones could have saved him or his nation.

The lone mid-Atlantic island remained desolate over the following decade. Government agencies from America quarantined the island after the war, claiming the air quality was too toxic after the bombings. Some people theorized other reasons why the fallen nation was closed to the public, as many tourists and explorers wished to scope out the ruins for relics. But authorities denied all access. People who snuck onto Optyma after the war had one of two fates. They were caught by the government and forced to sign an NDA, or they went missing on the island. Matt heard rumors about the "ghost island" over the years, yet he was disappointed in the quarantined state, as no one would be getting any answers regarding Klypt, the Core Stones, or the *Rare*.

"It's been almost a decade since someone was last able to use the stones," Madeline said uncomfortably.

Matt folded his arms and looked toward the window. "The last two people recorded were Optyma's president and his sister, right?"

Madeline frowned. "At least he's gone. If he had fire powers, that would have matched him well. A shame his sister was a pyrokinetic instead."

Matt glanced over at her. "You know it's a dream of mine to have fire powers."

"Oh, don't you start," she teased. "You know what I mean. Jake Agnes got stuck with manipulating light instead. That didn't really suit him."

"Maybe he was blinded by his ambitions," Matt remarked.

"Okay, fine." Madeline rolled her eyes. "Keep on dreaming of your fire powers. At least you don't have to associate them with President Agnes."

Matt reminisced on his early childhood—when it was fun to dream of fire. He would light up matches to stare at the little flames until his parents seized them from him. Matt still managed to find the matches hidden in the cabinets, as Madeline had let him climb on her shoulders. But after their parents died, Madeline was the one who took the fire away from him. He understood the dangers of fire at an early age, but he just wanted to be the one to control it. Perhaps one day, he could witness the elements. He knew he wasn't the only one who yearned to hold a Core Stone.

Matt turned to face the balcony again, watching the waves rippling along the harbor below.

Maybe this all felt like a fantasy.

In times like these, however, it was dangerous to mix fantasy with reality.

Chapter 6

The Crux of Common Knowledge

Matt and Madeline arrived at the Streak Corporation headquarters, loaded with boxes for her new office. Madeline brought a pair of turquoise curtains to brighten her room, and along with the new garnishments, she also packed a coffee maker for the kitchenette. Matt, meanwhile, played the role of her personal assistant, though this was a typical day in his life.

He struggled to squeeze his way onto the elevator with two large boxes stacked in his arms, while Madeline carried a bin, using her free hand to guide herself to the ninth floor.

"It would be great if you got a job as my assistant," Madeline joked as she opened her office door. "I'd be pretty generous with you."

Matt forced himself to smile, then set the boxes on the floor. "But you're the general manager. I might be an assistant for one of the sub-managers."

"True," Madeline said. "I did meet Mr. Streak's secretary yesterday. She might need an assistant." She paused, then opened her boxes. "Or maybe you can be Harry's assistant."

"He's a nice guy," Matt agreed and sat down. "But my apprenticeship probably won't start for another few weeks. They said I have a month to decide before they look for other potential candidates. And if I do want the job—"

"What do you mean *if?*"

Matt froze at his sister's skeptical glare. "I mean, they said that...uh, *hypothetically...*" The heat rose in his cheeks. "I don't know. I guess I can explore the building. Maybe Harry will tell me more about what to expect."

"Alright, go ahead." Madeline pulled a picture frame out from the bins.

Matt left the room swiftly. He closed the door behind him and took a deep breath.

Why is she like this? he thought hotly. *I say the wrong thing, and it's the end of the world.*

He returned to the hall and noticed Harry's door wide open. He peeked inside as Harry scooped up a few blueprints off his desk. The manager turned around, then spotted Matt in the doorway.

"Oh. Hello, Matt!" Harry greeted. "Whatcha doing?"

"Uh, I was just helping my sister bring some boxes in," Matt mentioned and stepped aside. "I might start that job soon, so I figured I'd explore the building."

"I can show you around," Harry offered, and Matt smiled. "Follow me down to the fifth floor. It's where we have a lot of our designers and consultants. I need to deliver these blueprints first, but I can give you a tour from there."

While they made a pit stop on the fifth floor, Matt witnessed many blueprints in the making. Workers cluttered around the rows of tables, gathering pieces of equipment for the next round of prototypes.

"So, when these workers finish with the blueprints," Harry explained as he pointed to several tables, "they take these to the consultants' offices, where they get reviewed. And after that, we send them down to the delivery room on the fourth floor. That is where our drivers pick them up and send them to the industrial area for manufacturing."

"This isn't what I expected Streak Corp to be like," Matt noted as two employees left a consultant's room with stacks of files.

"Inventing new weapons is our biggest priority," Harry said. "Mr. Streak laid out a system for us to follow. This is how he likes things done here. And with Ms. Madeline onboard, we should be more efficient than ever."

"So, the delivery floor is right below us?" asked Matt.

"Yep," Harry grinned, "and we always get shipments in. That's where most inexperienced employees start. They're either mail sorters or janitors. The janitorial offices are down on the fourth floor, too."

"Do you think I'll be working there?"

"Nah, I think Mr. Streak has bigger plans for you, considering you're Madeline's brother," Harry laughed.

"I was going to say," Matt sighed, then glanced at the floor, "I don't know how to drive yet."

"Hey, we have sorters too. Sorters don't do the delivering themselves," Harry told him. "Well, that's from what I know. I'm in charge of this floor. The sorting room is for one of the other managers to handle."

"So, are there any new inventions you're proud of?" Matt asked.

Harry's face lit up. "Actually, I gotta show you our best prototype yet," he replied, beckoning Matt to follow. He reached over a nearby table and lifted a rifle. "This bad boy is called the SK–08 sniper rifle. It fires over a thousand yards and holds a round of ten bullets at a time. It's quicker than other rifles, and it's also super lightweight. Feel it."

Harry lifted the sniper with the leather strap and handed it to Matt. As soon as Matt took it, his eyes widened. *It's so light.*

"Right?" Harry laughed. "It's only five pounds. One of the lightest snipers in the world right now."

Matt blinked. "Has anyone tried it yet?"

"Eh, sort of. This thing has been in development for over two years. And we've finally got something out of it." Harry took the sniper from Matt, setting it down. "Let's get going, though. I don't want to interrupt the other employees."

Matt followed Harry back to the elevator. He pressed the lobby button.

"I need to deliver something to Elaine," Harry told him. "And then I can show you where the cafeteria is. It's on the second floor."

Matt unconsciously glanced down at Harry's right shoulder stump. Before he could turn away, Harry caught him staring.

"Born with it," Harry mentioned smoothly. "That's all there is to it."

"Oh." Matt pressed his lips together and looked toward the door. "Sorry."

"Don't be. Almost everyone asks."

The doors opened, and Harry led Matt to the front desk, where Streak conversed with Elaine. Matt heard a piece of their conversation as they approached the desk.

"Reporters are visiting soon, so I need everyone in the building to be aware," Streak told her.

Harry stopped. "We've got the news people visiting?"

Streak turned around and held his hands behind his back. "Several local stations called and asked if they could interview me on the recent incident."

"What incident?" Matt asked.

"Oh, did you not hear the news last night?" Streak said. "The stolen Core Stone has gotten the public so worked up today. That's all anyone has been able to talk about."

"Well, yeah. But why do the news stations need to interview you?" Matt felt he asked too many questions, but the boss enjoyed the attention, judging by his smirk.

Streak chuckled, "My boy, I possess one of the Core Stones."

Matt froze as Streak turned to take the stairs to his office. "*What?*"

"Matt, you alright?" Harry shook him slightly. "What's wrong?"

"I didn't know Mr. Streak had one of those stones," Matt told him frantically.

"Ah, yeah," Harry said, "that's common knowledge around New Harbor. The government gave Mr. Streak one of the stones two years ago. Something about him being New Harbor's most beloved CEO made him the best keeper."

"The best keeper?" Matt said with disbelief. "Aren't they supposed to be hidden?"

"I guess you need to catch up on the Core Stone news to really know. But to be fair, there wasn't much news revolving around the stones until Mr. Streak became a new keeper two years back," Harry said. "Don't think much about it, though. The stone has been in safe hands."

Matt looked away. "Do you think we'll see the stone?"

"Doubt it," Harry sighed. "I suspect the news want to interview him because someone might want to steal it."

"Would anyone really try taking it from Streak?"

Harry put his hand under his chin as his eyes shifted to the ceiling. "Maybe? But Mr. Streak is so high-profile. No one could get away with robbing him."

"It can still happen, though," Matt pondered. He paused on the subject, wondering what else would qualify someone worthy enough of being a *keeper*. "Um. This might sound weird, but...is Mr. Streak *Rare?*"

"No," a soft voice spoke up behind them. Matt turned around to see the same girl he ran into yesterday, the one with the wavy, auburn hair. Today, she wore a black dress with matching flats.

"Hey, Christine," Harry spoke up with a wave. "How's it going?"

The girl shrugged. "Just another day."

"How are you feeling?" Matt asked. "I'm still sorry about yesterday—"

"Better. It's just a small bruise," she interrupted and rubbed her head.

Harry blinked. "You two met already?"

Matt glowered. "Kind of. I bumped into her."

"Christie, if you didn't know, this is Matt Ellis," Harry introduced heartily. "He's Madeline's younger brother."

"Oh." Christine glanced at Harry, then returned her cold gaze to Matt. "Is that why he's here?"

"Mr. Streak is considering me for an apprenticeship," Matt mentioned as he tried to avoid her glare.

"I'm Christine Elerare," she replied. "I'm his secretary."

Matt looked back over at her, confused. "Oh. You're the secretary?"

"Aside from being Madeline's brother, I don't know why he'd consider you for an apprenticeship," she mentioned, then crossed her arms.

Harry glanced back and forth between them, then looked away sheepishly.

"I'm sorry," Matt said again, this time with a flatter tone.

"Forget about that," she brushed him off, "why are you talking about his Core Stone?"

"Why do you want to know?" Matt mocked her as he folded his arms.

"Hey, Christine, you know it's a big deal right now," Harry cut in.

Christine scowled. "Too many people who just 'talk' about the stones always find a way to get closer to them."

"And what does it have to do with you? You heard Harry. Someone stole a stone yesterday, and your boss happens to have one. Sorry if I was curious," Matt snapped.

Christine straightened her posture and shot him another glare. "I have every right to be skeptical of anyone talking about my *uncle's* stone," she countered sharply.

Matt gaped, then took a small step back. She stood there stiffly, her face stern and bitter.

This girl was her—Jason Streak's niece.

A memory flashed in Matt's mind—a little girl his age in a soft red dress. She had a kind smile and a soft laugh. He tried to blink the memory away but came face-to-face with the coldest eyes he had ever seen.

"I'm sorry," he told her again quietly, "I didn't mean for it to come out that way."

"Too many people are 'curious' about the stone. That's always their excuse to get close to it," she said as her face softened. "Even employees have tried to take it before, and you and your sister are newcomers."

"Yeah, okay," Matt stuttered. He tried to shake off the brisk feeling. "I get it. If you don't trust me, that's fine. I'd never take your uncle's stone."

"Especially if you're trying to get a job here," added Harry.

Matt nodded, and Christine eased her stiff posture.

"Don't make me keep my eye on you." She left for the elevator, and Matt felt silenced.

"Hey, man," Harry nudged him, "so Christine's usually a total sweetheart. We get along really well."

Matt sighed, "I messed up."

"If you two end up working together, you'll sort it out," Harry assured him. "And you haven't done anything wrong. She's probably having a bad day."

"Harry, you heard her. Employees have tried to steal the stone from her uncle." He pondered General Fren, how he was found with a large gash. "Has anyone actually tried killing Mr. Streak for the stone?"

"Not that I've seen. But at the same time, Mr. Streak doesn't talk about the stone much."

Matt glanced toward the elevator, but Christine was already out of sight. Maybe it would be best to keep his distance.

Chapter 7

Nobody at Night

"They shouldn't be in there for too long," the girl said. "My uncle doesn't really like long meetings."

"But what does he want from her?" Matt asked as he peeked through the door crack. "Why can't I be in there?"

He pressed his forehead against the door, and the girl tapped his shoulder.

"It'll be okay," she told him. She took his hand, and they backed away from the room together.

"Sorry," he said as his gaze dropped to the floor. "I'm just scared."

"Don't be. You're not alone." He looked up, and the girl smiled. "We can just stick together until they finish talking."

Matt smiled back and nodded. "Okay."

"My name is Christine, by the way," she introduced herself, then held her hand out.

"Matt," he replied as he shook hands with her. They both giggled.

"I know what you're feeling. I travel a lot, too," she said.

"It's really different," Matt mentioned to her. "And my mum is leaving. I don't know what to do."

"Is she leaving for the war?"

Matt nodded silently, then wrapped his arms around himself.

"I hope she'll be okay," Christine replied. She glanced over at the door. "She'll come back—"

"Matt! Hey!"

Matt woke up from a daze with Madeline sitting on the couch beside him. He blinked a few times, then peered around the apartment.

"Were you saying something?" Matt mumbled while he rubbed his eyes. "Sorry."

"I was asking what you wanted to watch," she sighed. She put the remote down on the table. "Was it a long day for you?"

"Not really."

"Okay, liar," she said. "I'll head to my room and read for a bit. Get some sleep."

Madeline got up and walked over to her room. She closed the door behind her, turning the lights down low.

Matt glanced toward the balcony. He found that staying focused through a whole movie was a challenge. But that old memory with Christine felt different from his usual daydreaming.

Her bitter gaze from earlier unsettled him, and he couldn't understand why. Maybe it was because she was Jason Streak's niece, and she could get him banned from the office. Perhaps it was because she could also screw over his chances of getting any job at Streak Corporation, though that would upset his sister more than it would bother him.

Deep down, it was neither of those things. And it pained him to figure out why.

Matt prepared a quick cup of tea, then bundled up in his sheets. He thought about avoiding the Streak Corporation headquarters tomorrow just to take a day off to explore New Harbor.

Maybe he could decorate, rearrange some furniture, or unpack more boxes. His eyes settled on the nearly empty prescription bottle on his bedside table before drifting off to sleep.

"Matt."

Matt jolted awake. The voice sounded eerily familiar—a woman's voice with a sharp tone, yet one he couldn't distinguish.

He sat up and looked toward the black sky, where the city lights lit the surrounding clouds. He checked the time to see it was close to midnight. His heart raced.

Matt left his bed and found his vigilante suit in his closet. He changed his outfit, slipping on his black pants, orange shirt, and matching black jacket. He zippered up, then pulled out his mask.

He wrapped the covering around his face, then lifted the hood over his head.

Matt stalked the rooftops of Canton near the harbor, keeping an eye out for any suspicious activity. He peered into the distance and heard the engines of speeding cars, some honks from tired drivers, and the occasional yelling of pedestrians. Nothing crime-related.

Back in Miami, he knew the areas with the highest crime rates. This neo-city seemed more peaceful on the harbor. Perhaps he needed to dig deeper into the neighborhood, away from the water.

Matt stood up and sprinted for the other end of the roof. He leaped and landed on another ridge, then continued his race across as he dove deeper into the Canton neighborhood.

Before he could leap to another rooftop, he heard a muffled scream in the distance. The voice belonged to a young woman, her cries echoing around the area. He ran quietly to the alley, where two older men snapped at the girl.

Her scream sent chills down his spine, but he brushed the feeling away. The men tied her up and gagged her, then led her to a black van near the entrance to the alley.

"Quiet," one of the men lashed out at the young woman.

"Maybe we should knock her out," the other man said. "She's drawing too much attention."

The girl froze in place. Tears streamed down her face, and she shook her head. She breathed out in a stricken panic.

"That's it," muttered the taller man. He threw the woman to the ground and pulled out a baton.

Matt landed behind the three, catching their attention instantly. "That wasn't very nice," he said as he cracked his knuckles. "Care to tell me what's going on here?"

The woman screamed, then pushed herself away from her kidnappers. The shorter man in the ski mask grabbed her and shoved her aside.

"None of your business," the tall one spat with a glare. "Who do you think you are?"

"Nobody." Matt squinted and tilted his head playfully.

"Well, *Nobody*, I suggest you get lost," the man mocked. "Unless you want to end up in the van, too."

"Your threat sounds empty," Matt remarked as he paced closer. The man stepped back. "Almost as empty as your head."

"Alright, that does it," the man huffed, then pulled out a large knife. "Get lost, or else you're joining her."

The woman released another muffled cry, and the shorter man grabbed her as his partner faced Matt.

"Oh, we're playing this kind of game?" Matt laughed. He pulled out a knife from his belt.

The burly man chuckled and shook his head. "That thing is puny," he scoffed. He held up his hand to show off the large dagger he wielded. "It's nothing. Just like you're about to be."

"Really?" Matt gasped. "My knife is one-of-a-kind. I even made it myself."

As the men howled with laughter, Matt remained calm. He told the truth, albeit sarcastically. He crafted this knife when he was sixteen, just days after starting his vigilante gig. It was vital to him, and it had terrified many criminals on the streets of Miami.

"You should be afraid of it," Matt mentioned to him. "A lot of people are."

The tall man stopped laughing. "I've had enough," he grunted with a glare. He charged forward with his knife. Matt leaped against a nearby dumpster and kicked the man in the shoulder. The man flew into the side of a brick wall. A loud crack erupted from his left shoulder blade.

"Shit!" the other man yelled. He kept his grip tight around the girl's wrists.

"Damn, you're fast," the tall man spat. He shook his shoulder out, then winced. "That's still nothing."

The other man slid the girl away and stepped toward Matt.

"Alright," Matt sighed, holding out his dagger. "I can save you guys some pain. Turn yourselves in now and hand over the girl, or if you'd rather do it the hard way—"

"You really think you're winning this?" scorned the man in the mask. "We're just getting started."

That was all Matt needed to hear. He pressed a small button on the end of his knife's handle. The dagger burst into flames within seconds. The men's eyes widened, and they retreated backward. Matt swung the blade around, admiring the mesmerizing trail of flames it left for a second in the air.

"Still ready?" Matt mocked the two men, whose faces had paled.

The tall man sprung toward him, shaking. Matt ducked under his swing. He slid across the pavement, his dagger outstretched. He sliced the man's side, leaving a cauterized scar.

Matt jumped toward the other man. He kicked his chest, then sliced the man's back as he hit the wall. Matt landed on his feet and straightened his posture. Both men collapsed to the ground. The tall man clutched his hip while the other reached for his back.

Matt jogged over to the girl on the ground as mascara-stained tears covered her cheeks. He used the knife to cut the rope, then untied the gag around her mouth. She scrambled back.

"Hey, hey," he whispered. He brushed the hair away from her eyes. "It's okay. You're going to be okay."

She trembled and blinked her tears away. "Thank you!" she cried, falling into him.

He held onto her and patted her back. "We're going to call the police now. Do you have your phone?"

She pulled away and pointed toward the man in the ski mask. "He took it," she stammered.

Matt clutched the gag and walked over to the bruised man. He tied the criminal's hands behind his back with the rope, then searched his jacket and jeans until he found the phone stuffed in a pocket. He returned to the young woman, handing her the glittery phone.

"Here, I need you to call 9-1-1," he told her. "I'll make sure those guys don't get up. Their van is still outside."

The girl nodded and dialed for emergency services. Matt noticed she was around his age—maybe a year older. She had messy, short brunette hair, honey-brown eyes, warm beige skin, and a round face. Her voice cracked as she spoke to the emergency operator, but in between the singsong sobs, she sounded light and sweet.

"They're on their way," she mentioned.

"Okay." Matt turned to see the men struggling to get up, but the slices and bruises prevented them from making it too far. "They're finished."

"I don't know how I can thank you," the girl sobbed as she wiped another tear away.

"Were they stalking you?"

She nodded. "I was walking home from work, then their van pulled up."

"Where do you work?"

"It's a new place called the Jasmine Garden," she said. "I had the closing shift tonight. I'm a waitress, but I also wash dishes."

"I'm kind of new around here," Matt mentioned. He didn't want to say too much about himself, but if he gave her something to talk about, he could relieve her of some stress. "Is that a restaurant close by?"

"Yeah," she replied, "it's a nice place. It's a Chinese restaurant down on Fait Avenue."

"I might have to try it one day," he said warmly.

"I'd have to give you lunch or something. Please stop by," she insisted, then tensed. "*Wait.*" She stared at him for a moment, from head to toe. "I just realized...you're one of those vigilante people."

Matt tried to hold back his laughter. "How long was that going to take for you to realize?"

"Sorry," she laughed, flustered. "I should have figured." She smiled. "Um, do you have an alias? Or a street name? Like some of the other ones do?"

"A name? No." He shook his head. "I don't need anything like that."

"Really? You deserve some kind of credit," she said. "Once I tell my manager what happened tonight, he'll give you free lunch for life."

"No, really—" He blinked. "Wait, did you say 'free' lunch?"

"*Yes.*"

Free food, Matt pondered. *That might not be a bad idea—*

"No. *No*, I can't," he insisted, brushing the temptation away.

She clapped her hands together. "Okay," she begged. "If you want to be that way, fine. But can I at least know who you are? I want to stay in touch."

Matt fell silent. He didn't want to hurt her, but making new friends was not a part of what vigilantism entailed. And as sweet as this girl was, he had no intention of disclosing his identity.

"No, I'm sorry," he said quietly. "But I promise, I'll be around if you need anything."

The girl frowned, then looked toward the ground. As she did, Matt glanced back at the two men. The short one struggled to find a way out of the rope while the other clutched his side in pain.

"My name is Katelyn Crae-Zhao," the girl said. She held her hand out to him. "The least I can do is give my name. And if you stop by the Jasmine Garden for free lunch, please ask for me."

Matt sighed and shook her hand. "I'm glad I got here on time."

"Yeah, I'm glad you did too," she expressed. She paused again with a look of contemplation, then pulled out a small notepad from her back pocket. She scribbled on the pad and slipped Matt the paper.

"What's this for?" he asked. He noticed a phone number on the sheet.

"My number," she mentioned shyly. "Um, would it be okay if I get yours?"

"Why?"

She glanced at the street. "In case I have any more emergencies. I know it sounds weird, but..." She trailed off and swallowed.

He took the paper and pen from her, writing his number. "You need another emergency contact?" he finished for her.

She smiled and took the paper back from him. "Aside from my roommate, I don't really have any other contacts in the area. My parents live in Seattle."

"It's okay," he assured her. "I get it."

Katelyn stuffed the paper inside her pocket. As she did, several sirens entered the area, and three police cars pulled up outside the alleyway.

"And with that," Matt concluded as he took a stand, "I must bid you adieu."

"Thank you!" she shouted after him as he made his way toward a nearby fire escape.

The cops ran into the alley, and Matt glanced back to see them seize the criminals and question Katelyn. He stayed on the rooftop to eavesdrop.

"This guy came down, taking them out without breaking a sweat," Katelyn explained to the cops. "He was wicked fast, and he had this knife that lit on fire! If it weren't for him, I'd probably be dead."

"Another vigilante, I assume," the cop sighed. "Which one was it?"

"He doesn't have a name," Katelyn added, "and he said he didn't want one. But someone like him deserves one. It should be related to fire. Like, uh—*oh!* Something like *Speedfire.*"

Chapter 8

Mainstream Vigilantism

Matt entered the headquarters behind Madeline, exhausted from the long night. He hardly got any sleep, but the energy he spent saving that girl was worth it.

They passed through the lobby as Elaine and Harry talked with another man near the front desk. He had short blond hair and wore a heavy-duty leather jacket with jeans.

"I can't believe they were able to find that trafficking ring," the man expressed, which caused Matt to stop in his tracks. "They've been looking for those men for...what? At least a year now?"

"A real shame. All those poor people," Elaine replied solemnly.

"Yeah, at least this new guy showed up. I think they call him 'Speedfire' or something," the man continued. "One of those vigilantes."

Matt listened for a moment, then noticed Madeline perk up beside him.

"This place deals with vigilantism?" she asked. "I know we had people like that down in Miami."

Matt couldn't help but feel attacked by her last statement. She knew what she was saying.

"Yeah, there's a new hero in town," Harry said. Madeline glanced at Matt before she directed her attention back to the front desk. "He caught these two traffickers, and the police found the location of their underground ring."

"Oh, wow," Madeline gasped.

Elaine added, "The two men that Speedfire caught have been on the FBI's most wanted list for a year. No one could catch them."

They were so easy to beat, though, Matt thought nervously.

"That's impressive," Madeline said. Matt turned to hide his smile. "I guess this 'Speedfire' guy is something special."

"Hey, you're the new general manager, right?" the other man asked. He held out his hand. "I'm Jack Lainey, one of the warehouse managers. I work with product coordination."

Madeline shook his hand. "Madeline Ellis," she replied. "Nice meeting you."

"Likewise," said Jack.

"And this is my brother, Matt. He's discussing a potential apprenticeship with Mr. Streak later," she added as Matt nodded silently. "I'll probably be back down soon. I've got some rounds to make around the office."

"Yeah. I'm heading back to the distribution center. But it was great seeing you, Madeline," Jack told her.

"See ya, Jack," Harry said. He waved to Jack, then followed Madeline and Matt to the elevator. "Matt, I didn't even show you the breakroom yesterday."

"It's okay," Matt said. "You were busy."

"If you're waiting for that meeting with Mr. Streak, I could show you around if you'd like," Harry offered.

"Go for it," Madeline prodded her brother. "I'll be in my office if you need me."

Matt frowned as his sister left his side. He turned to Harry, who smiled warmly.

"Let's go. I kinda want to talk about that new vigilante," Harry said, leading the way to the stairs.

Matt rested on a couch across from Harry in the lounge. A kitchenette sat on the right side of the room, and the left room consisted of tables for gaming and reading.

"So, you wanted to talk about vigilantes?" Matt asked.

Harry nodded eagerly. "It's crazy. The streetfighters here hardly do anything that big. It's pretty refreshing to see."

"What do you mean?" The door to the lounge opened and closed, but Matt was too focused on receiving answers from Harry to notice anyone entering the room. "Does New Harbor have a lot of vigilantes?"

"Well, vigilantes are everywhere," Harry said. "But the ones here in New Harbor aren't that impressive, you know. They pop up in the news now and then. Like, someone gets mugged and saved. Or maybe there's a thief on the loose that gets caught. The usual good stuff. But this 'Speedfire' guy hit something huge."

Matt kept his smile to himself. "Sounds like it."

Matt always tried to find the riskiest crimes to solve. He had done his saving of the innocent on the dark streets, but he loved hitting what he called *the big ones*—the crimes that caused the most commotion. The bigger the crime, the bigger the score.

He still felt proud for making one final mark on Miami by ending the terror of Herman Wild. Catching a serial killer like him was one of his proudest wins.

Harry replied, "I can't think of anything impactful that the other New Harbor vigilantes do. I mean, a lot of them don't even save the victims on time."

"It's because most of the vigilantes here are attention-seekers," Christine said from the kitchenette. She placed a tea kettle on top of the small stove. "And when no one compensates them, they try to gain fame another way."

Her gaze met Matt, and he glared at her. "The New Harbor vigilantes sound different from the ones in Miami."

"I think they're all the same," she replied. "Harry, do you want anything?"

"Coffee, please." Harry beamed. "Matt, do you want some?"

"No." Matt turned around to face his back to Christine. "I'm more of a tea drinker."

"Tea's fine, too. But coffee gets me going," Harry said. "Anyway, I don't know what to say about the vigilantes. Like, they're good, but I think Christine has a point. Some of them do it for attention."

"How?" Matt glanced back as Christine poured a cup of coffee. "Vigilantes keep their identities a secret. It's a code they have. How would they be looking for fame?"

"That's interesting," Christine inferred. "How do *you* know they have a code?"

"Research," Matt uttered back.

"What kind of research?" Harry asked, intrigued.

Matt shrugged, yet he couldn't help but feel slighted by Christine's remark. "Do you know about Sky at all? I did a lot of school projects on her," he mentioned. If he talked about the legendary heroine, he hoped the conversation would keep his cover, especially from Christine.

"Yeah, Lady Stathis! She's like the original vigilante," Harry acknowledged. He reached over as Christine handed him a cup of coffee. "I'm guessing she had a code?"

"Maybe. I know she tried keeping her identity a secret for a long time. But many vigilantes base their codes on how she performed," Matt explained.

"Sky" was a young Greek woman named Jade Stathis who took to the streets of her hometown and punished the criminals that roamed at night. She had worn sky-blue attire and fought with ribbons, which was highly effective for someone as light on her feet as she was. Despite being a Greek native, other nations also acknowledged Sky as a heroine. English historians mentioned Sky's involvement during the First World War, where she helped save hundreds of civilians from aerial bombardments with her quick thinking and the shelters she founded.

As time passed, Sky became a notable figure—one of the world's greatest heroes—even if vigilantism was frowned upon by many public officials. Matt grew up with the stories of Sky before he lost his parents, and he was determined to follow in the legend's footsteps. He recognized her as his childhood hero, even in the darkest moments of his life, and his infatuation with vigilantism all started with the first steps Jade Stathis had taken to save her people.

"Yeah, the New Harbor ones aren't like that at all," said Harry. "This city is strange. Sometimes they try to outmatch each other. Vigilante competition, I guess."

"And then they think the law should remain in their hands," Christine finished as she walked over to hand Matt a mug of tea. "They see themselves as superheroes, yet they're too self-centered."

Matt stared at the honeyed green tea for a second before he took it from her. She then sat on the couch beside him and drank from her own mug.

"Why'd you make me a cup?" he asked. "I thought you didn't like me."

Christine drank her tea and stared at him. "Perhaps I poisoned it."

Matt raised an eyebrow, then sipped from his mug. "You know," he continued as he kept eye contact with her, "most vigilantes feel like they need to take it upon themselves to solve a problem the authorities refuse to handle.”

“Hm.” Christine took another sip. “But vigilantism has become so mainstream over the last decade. It’s lost its true meaning and purpose.”

“I totally get what you mean,” Harry commented. “As you said, it’s all about the fame.”

“There’s no fame and glory in vigilantism,” Matt remarked.

“Exactly,” said Christine.

“No, wait—” Matt scowled at Christine. “I mean, it shouldn’t be that way. Sky never sought any glory.”

At least...I don’t think she did, he pondered, his eyes following his tea’s steam.

“A legend from the past should not dictate the traditions of today,” Christine declared. “Her legacy has lost its meaning. People believe they can get away with anything.”

“Okay, then. Can you give me an example of a bad vigilante here in New Harbor?” Matt asked. He leaned back against the cushion.

“Ten-Fold,” Harry and Christine groaned simultaneously.

Matt blinked. “*Who?*”

“Ten-Fold,” Christine repeated. “He was a vigilante who would go out doing the usual deeds. Saving people from robberies, looking for fights with gang members. He claimed he was always ten times greater than any other vigilante in New Harbor, so people started calling him Ten-Fold.

“Well, Ten-Fold got a little greedy one day. He hired a gang of ten guys to act up and cause a ruckus in Downtown one night, all so he could put on a show. These guys had explosives, however, and several innocent bystanders died. Ten-Fold ‘stopped’ the criminals, but the police showed up too early for them to escape. So, one of the guys exposed Ten-Fold’s plan. And now, Ten-Fold is serving life in prison for manslaughter.”

Matt put his mug on the table beside him. “Are you kidding me? That’s not a vigilante.”

“He was,” Harry sighed.

“No, he became the very thing he stood against,” Matt muttered. “Are there any others?”

“Street-Style,” Christine answered. “She committed vigilantism to be famous. She revealed her identity to the public, though. Her name was Sara

Flynn. Someone ended up stalking her on VisionHive, found out where she lived, broke into her house, and shot her dead."

"Okay, okay, I get it," Matt exhaled sharply. "They aren't true vigilantes."

"None of them are," Christine murmured. "I don't have any personal vendettas against them, but not only do they endanger themselves, they get other people hurt. Like Ten-Fold."

"But what if the police aren't around to save people on time?" Matt mentioned.

"Alright, I'll give you that," Christine exhaled. "But most stories start as revenge missions. The system wronged them, and they weren't satisfied with how the government handled their issue, so they sought revenge on whoever hurt them. And most of the time, it ends in murder. Many vigilantes don't even get a chance at starting a 'career' around vigilantism because the police catch them."

"And then there are others like Sky. The people need another hero," Matt argued.

"Sky was from the nineteenth century," Harry said. "Things change."

"There has to be a good one, though," Matt pleaded. "If you can name one."

Christine drank more of her tea while Harry contemplated.

"I think the best vigilante will be whoever takes down the sniper," Harry proposed.

Matt perked. "The sniper?"

"Why are you mentioning the sniper?" Christine lowered her mug. "You'll scare him."

Matt shot her a quizzical look.

"Hey, I'm just making a point," Harry cited. "Okay, so there's this mysterious sniper in New Harbor who shoots people in the middle of the night. They could be walking down the street, in an alleyway, or even with friends, then *bam!* A shot comes from the rooftops, and the target always gets hit."

Matt remained silent as he listened to Harry intently.

"These shootings have been going on for the past two years. Biggest talk in the city. We don't know if it's just one person or a group of people," Harry explained. "But we know that most of these attacks have links to Streak Corp."

Matt spat out some tea. "*What?* How?"

Harry shook his head. "We don't know. Most victims either worked for Mr. Streak or had ties to the company. And I don't want to freak you out, Matt, but the sniper shot the former general manager. He died in the hospital the day after the shooting."

"The sniper killed him?" Matt gasped. "What about Maddie? Is she in trouble?"

Harry frowned with a shrug. "At this point, we're all in trouble."

Matt shuddered. *How can you people still work here?*

Christine set her mug down. "The sniper targets employees and acquaintances close to my uncle."

"Yep, but the reasons are still unknown," Harry continued. "Two years and counting, and Mr. Streak still has no leads on the killer."

"And you're saying that you hope a vigilante puts an end to the sniper?" Matt interrupted, dazed.

"That's what he's saying," Christine added. "But there's not enough evidence around the sniper for the authorities to use. No one's been able to do anything. So, as Harry said, it could be a whole group of assassins or just one person."

Harry whimpered. "If it's just one person, I'd be both impressed and terrified."

Matt held his tea close to him and breathed in the warm aroma of the jasmine scent. A sniper attacked anyone close to Streak Corp and struck fear among the residents of New Harbor. No wonder Jason Streak struggled to find a new general manager.

"I think I need some fresh air," Matt sighed as he stood up. He walked over to the kitchen and placed his cup on the counter. "I have a meeting with Streak, anyway."

"Don't get too worked up about it. These attacks don't happen often," Harry urged him. "I didn't mean to freak you out."

"No, it's okay. I'm fine," Matt lied as he stood in the doorway. He stopped and looked back at Christine. "Thanks for the tea."

She glanced at him before she looked toward the window. "Don't mention it."

Chapter 9

A Serpent in the Spotlight

Matt walked the long hallway to Streak's room alone. His stomach twisted as he approached the door of the esteemed tycoon. He knocked, then stared down at the knob hopelessly.

"Come on in," Streak said, raising his voice from the other side. Matt entered and approached Streak, who sat at his desk with a book in his hand. "Good morning."

"Do you want to speak with me now?" asked Matt.

Streak gave him a quick nod. "Have you made a decision on the offer?"

"It's been on my mind."

"Good." Streak smiled and took his glasses off. "So, any questions?"

"It feels like you're just handing the position to me on a silver platter," Matt said. "Why?"

"Let's make it a gold platter," Streak added with a smirk. "You and your sister bring so much potential to the team. With Madeline's experience, we could make the company represent New Harbor entirely."

"I thought it already did," Matt mumbled.

"That, my boy, is what I like to hear," Streak agreed. "Bigger is better."

"So, you think I'm the key to your company's success?"

"It's already successful, Matthew. But we could build on that. Streak Corp will remain unstoppable in the engineering industry as a whole."

"I don't mean any disrespect, sir, but I don't recall there being that much competition," Matt said. "I mean...that's what this all sounds like. You want to beat out some competition, right?"

"You're correct," Streak replied, "but Streak Corp currently has the tightest competition with Sal-Tech. They've become our greatest competitor worldwide."

Sal-Tech. Matt swore he and Madeline talked about the tech company a few days ago. Sal-Tech produced hydro-powered computers, tablets, phones, and vehicles called *hydroelectrics*—all revolutionary appliances in the world of engineering. As ecosystems slowly deteriorated, Sal-Tech was one of the only forces actively trying to save the world. Matt shifted in his chair when he realized Jason Streak led one of the corporations that rallied against hydroelectrics.

"Oh." Matt paused. "Um. Neat?"

Streak set his book down. "Now, Sal-Tech will not be the face of New Harbor, even if the company has forced its hydroelectric generators into the city. We will make sure of that."

"So, that's why you need help expanding your company?"

"Exactly. We don't need Sal-Tech crossing with Streak Corp. The company could take business away from us, as we mostly provide for the military, and that could be dangerous for our income. While we are strictly a defense contractor, Sal-Tech is much more than that."

Streak swerved his monitor around to show Matt a picture of an eight-foot-tall robot. The machine had a snake-like head with glowing blue eyes and two wing-shaped antennas. The center of the machine's chest displayed the Sal-Tech logo—an S-shaped serpent swimming in wavy water.

"What is that?" Matt gasped.

"Salbots," Streak answered. "Sal-Tech's next greatest invention. At Streak Corp, we don't create *robots*. But over there at Sal-Tech, that's their new craze. First-world governments have shown immense interest in them, so Sal-Tech is mass-producing these machines for when the time comes."

Matt stared at the image in disbelief. "How come I haven't heard of this yet? I don't think my sister even knows."

"It's been kept out of the media," Streak sighed. "But as an affiliate of the U.S. military, I know all about them."

"I can see where the competition lies now," Matt mentioned as he leaned back. "That's rough."

"It is." Streak exhaled sharply and turned the monitor around. "But Salus won't take New Harbor from me."

"Salus? Wait..." Matt pondered for a second. "Are you talking about the Earth Day girl?"

"Yes. Kiera Salus. Don't let her fool you. She is more than just a mascot. The young punk founded Sal-Tech three years ago. She's the youngest

CEO of a billion-dollar company right now. The fastest-growing business I've ever seen," Streak explained.

"How old is she now?" Matt asked.

"Twenty-three."

"She founded Sal-Tech when she was only twenty?" he gasped. Over the past year, he had heard all about Sal-Tech's devices but never a word about the company's founder. This whole time, he thought Kiera Salus was just a mascot for Sal-Tech. His heart deflated.

"She's slithered her way into the mainstream media," Streak muttered. "But once she reveals her Salbots to the public, they'll be all the talk. And *that* concerns me."

The door opened behind Matt, and a man wearing a military jacket walked forward. He had a U.S. Marines cap on and held a file in his hand.

"Mr. Streak, I am sorry for the intrusion, but we need to talk," the man said as he stopped behind Matt. The ceiling light flashed against the sergeant's badge on his jacket.

The sergeant looked young, with short brown hair and dark brown skin. Something about his features felt eerily familiar to Matt as he studied the man's russet-colored eyes. He also had a deep, soft-spoken voice as he talked, yet his tone was full of urgency.

"Sergeant Flyes, of course," Streak greeted. "Is it about your father?"

"Yes," the sergeant replied. He looked over at Matt and sighed. "Sir, I am so sorry. I need to speak with Mr. Streak privately."

"Uh, it's no problem," Matt said, then stood up.

"If you need to speak with him later, I won't be long," the sergeant continued.

"It's alright. This is Matthew Ellis, my new manager's brother. We were talking about his apprenticeship," said Streak.

The sergeant smiled and nodded. "I'm Billy. Good luck with every-thing."

"Thank you," Matt replied. "I'll see you later, Mr. Streak."

As Matt left the room, Billy's next words to Streak caught him off guard.

"So, about your Core Stone..." he heard Billy say before the door shut behind him.

Chapter 10

NEW HARBOR NIGHTS

Matt lay in bed, listening to the wailing sirens of the local harbor. Not a single cloud hovered in the sky, and the moon layered the city with a faint radiance. His eyes shot to the alarm clock beside his bed.

Midnight.

He exhaled softly, swallowed the rest of his zolpidem, then closed his eyes.

"*Matt.*"

He opened his eyes again. Two in the morning now. *Two hours.*

Matt turned over and pulled the pillow over his head. He hoped to block out the serenade of police sirens and car horns.

A few minutes passed by, or maybe an hour. The pills weren't working tonight.

Defeated, Matt opened his eyes. Instead of his room, he found himself surrounded by a yellow field of flowers. Hundreds of swaying blossoms scattered the open plain, and the drifting petals followed a ceaseless wind. He sat up, breathless. He plucked one of the flowers from the dry soil, examining the yellow petals that blended with its orange center.

A yellow chrysanthemum.

"Huh."

He stared ahead at the ambiguous space before him. Pearlescent clouds covered the sky, hovering before the frozen setting sun. Upon a distant hill stood a woman in a blue dress. Her dirty-blond hair flowed gracefully with the wind.

The woman faced him with her back to the sun. He locked eyes with her, and he refrained from taking another breath.

"*Matt,*" she spoke softly. The same voice that echoed his name tonight and the night before. She had a European accent, though Matt couldn't guess where she was from.

A transparent blue cape followed the wind behind her. He stared down at the yellow chrysanthemum in his grasp.

"Where am I?" he asked. "Why are these flowers here?"

She hummed. "*They were someone's favorite,*" she answered.

He held the booming bud close to his heart as he shifted his gaze to the field.

"I don't know if I even have a favorite flower," he said quietly.

"*Hm.*" She smiled. "*Just name one for me.*"

Matt contemplated as his eyes followed the swirl of colors in the fading sky. Everything began to fade. "I—"

Matt jolted awake as his sister shook him. "Ah!"

"About time you woke up," Madeline said. "Come on."

"What was that for?" he snapped.

"You slept through your alarm. I need your help at the office today," Madeline told him. "And when you're done, pick up our prescriptions from the pharmacy down the street. I already called to have them transferred."

He glared at her, then buried his face into his pillow. "I'm going back to sleep."

"Get up," Madeline ordered as she pulled the blankets off him. "This is important."

Matt groaned, "*No.*" Of course, he wasn't going to win this battle.

Matt napped on the couch with his arms wrapped around himself. He drifted in and out of a deep slumber, trying to reach that dream with the lady in blue again. The strange encounter somehow made him feel even more tired. But he spent countless nights with insomnia. That was why he usually took to the streets at night and not during the day.

Someone tapped his shoulder lightly, and he shoved his head back against the cushion in a panic. He opened his eyes, expecting Madeline, but instead, he came face-to-face with Christine.

"What?" he mumbled. He peered around to find himself in the breakroom of Streak Corp's headquarters.

"Are you alright?" Christine asked, leaning back.

Matt nodded slightly. "I guess." He saw no one else in the room.

"Sorry," she said quietly. "You just seemed...*off*."

Matt remembered now. He must have dropped himself off in the breakroom after he finished helping his sister, then fell asleep on the couch.

What the hell is my problem? He rubbed his eyes and sat up.

"I'm just tired," he muttered.

"Did you get any sleep last night?"

He rocked his head back and forth, then returned his attention to Christine. "I'm surprised you're concerned."

Christine gaped. "I don't know. Finding someone sleeping on the couch in the breakroom threw me off. Maybe I should give you a heads-up. Employees don't usually pass out on break."

Matt knew where this was going. Maybe they were both stubborn, but he wasn't letting himself back down.

"But I'm *not* on duty," he remarked. "I'm a *guest* here, and you should treat me as such."

Christine crossed her arms. "You're an ass, not a guest."

"And you're just inconsiderate."

"How? For waking you up?" she scoffed. "Leave while you can. You wouldn't even fit in with this company."

"You don't look like you belong here, either."

"Yet I'm still Jason Streak's secretary. You're not."

"Because you're his niece."

Christine glared at him. "Maybe," she said. "Like your sister, I'm filling in some big shoes." She cleared her throat. "Temporarily, at least."

"Yeah, well, Maddie worked hard for her position."

"Then there's you, who's in the same boat as me," she shot back. "But the difference is, I doubt you'd last long here."

"Why's that?"

"I just found you passed out on a company couch like a bum."

"If only you knew *why* I was so tired in the first place," he leaned back on the sofa, "you wouldn't be saying I'm a bum." As she blankly stared at him, he regretted his words immediately.

"Can I guess why?"

Matt's heart skipped a beat. *Why did I say that?*

"Uh." He let out a small, nervous laugh. "Gaming."

Christine huffed and rolled her eyes. "Sloth."

"Nepo baby."

They both heard the door open and turned to see Kylie walking in with a phone against her ear.

"Look, the job won't be open for long, and you know that," Kylie spoke into the phone. She ignored Matt and Christine, walking toward the kitchenette. "And it would be perfect for you. Get your ass out of London and apply. You said it yourself, love. If you want something done right, you ought to do it yourself."

Matt and Christine watched her, which reminded him to check his phone—several texts and a missed call from the girl he saved two nights ago.

Katelyn:

Hey!

Sorry if I'm interrupting anything!

I told the police all about you! And the news just interviewed me!

Did you hear they found a human trafficking ring because of you!!?

Anyway, thank you again! If you can come to JG, you get free lunch for life!!

I'm sorry if I sound like a broken record…

Tysm Speedy!

Matt noticed she had sent the messages ten minutes ago, which relieved him. He didn't want her to feel ignored.

Matt shoved his phone into his back pocket. He heard Kylie talking in the background still.

"Okay, I'll talk to you later," Kylie finished. "Love you. Bye." She ended the call and looked at Matt and Christine with a smirk. "I was sure you two were about to throw hands."

Christine buried her head in her palms as Kylie laughed and left the room.

"I'm leaving," Matt mentioned as he stood up.

"Okay." Christine rubbed her eyes and took a step back. "You sure you're alright?"

Matt stopped. "Yeah." He wanted to find the right words to say. Her concern still threw him off. "The nights just feel a bit longer here in New Harbor."

She smiled faintly. "They always do."

Matt smiled back at her. They agreed on something, at least.

The nights were long for everyone.

Chapter 11

Blue Jay

Matt strolled around Canton after he left the office, and the cleanliness of the neighborhood caught him by surprise. Community workers tidied up the road, and most people kept their distance from each other. Despite the crime rates at night, the city felt oddly secure to Matt.

He shook the feeling away, however, and kept his guard up. This area was part of the inner city, after all.

Matt entered the local pharmacy, which was branched with a convenience store. As he waited for the current customer to finish, he picked up a drink, settling for a soda and a bag of chips. He then approached the counter as another patient argued with the pharmacist.

"I need it just in case," the customer demanded. "What if—"

"The doctor is telling you to cut the blood-thinners *temporarily*," the pharmacist emphasized. "You don't want to take them right now. It can take weeks to recover from internal bleeding."

Matt shuffled in line uncomfortably. The topic of internal bleeding always unsettled him, even if he never experienced it. Matt had bled from scars and scrapes before, but never internally. And he would hate to ever inflict an injury like that on someone else.

Now that his mind was stuck on the thought, he felt sick to his stomach. What if he ever found himself in a situation like that? What if something happened at night, and he was alone on the streets—

"I can help whoever's next!"

The pharmacist waved to him as the previous customer left in a hurry, and Matt snapped out of his thoughts.

"Hey," he said, setting his items on the counter. The pharmacist reached over to ring up the snacks for him. "My sister and I had our prescriptions transferred here. Ellis. Matthew and Madeline."

The pharmacist returned to her computer. "Do you have your insurance card?"

"Yeah." Matt pulled out the card from his wallet, then handed it to the pharmacist. As she updated his information, a hooded individual got in line behind him. Matt picked at his nails, then glanced to the side as he waited. He didn't want to be here, but he would rather not tamper with his sister's temper.

The pharmacist returned the card to him, then pulled out two separate bags from under the counter. "Zolpidem for you, and Seroquel for Madeline. You don't owe anything today."

Matt nodded as he took the bags and paid for the snacks. "Thank you," he stammered, then moved out of the way. He clenched the bags tightly, already thinking of ways he could hide or dispose of the zolpidem without his sister noticing.

Before he could push through the doors, the hooded man screamed.

"Empty the vault. *Now!*" he demanded with a gun aimed at the pharmacist.

She froze, staring at the barrel with her hand under the desk. She glanced at her assistant, then nodded. The technician backed away to the vault, then scrambled for the medications.

Matt ran behind one of the aisles. He threw his bags down, lifted his jacket's hood over his head, then snuck around toward the middle aisle.

"All of it!" the man ordered, gripping the gun tighter. The weapon jittered in his hand.

The pharmacist slid the bottles toward the robber. Matt had a feeling she had already hit the panic button below the counter, judging by her collected demeanor. The thief returned the gun to his belt and piled the drugs into a bag. He zippered the satchel but left himself no time to dodge. Matt struck the side of the thief's head with his elbow. The man collided with the counter, lurching to the floor. Matt made his advance, then kicked his chest. The man slid across the floor, his head slamming into the wall. He lay there limply, knocked out cold.

Matt recovered his balance, grabbed the bag, and handed it to the pharmacist.

"The police are on their way," she said as her technician approached the counter.

"Good." Matt took a nearby rope from the utility aisle, then tied the thief's arms back. "Don't hesitate to knock him down again."

"Are you one of those vigilantes?" the assistant asked breathlessly.

Matt paused for a few seconds. "No." He backed away. "But if anyone asks, can I be anonymous?"

The pharmacist nodded, and Matt grabbed his bags down the aisle, leaving without another word.

Matt sat on the couch, sketching a landscape of his bayside view. He took a sip from his soda, then flinched when the door opened. He turned to see Madeline close it behind her. She threw her purse on the dining chair and met him in the living room.

"We need to talk," she said.

Matt put his sketchbook down and sat up. "About what?"

"The news," Madeline replied. She pulled a chair over and sat down across from him. "So, what's going on?"

"What do you mean?"

"Don't play dumb with me," she snapped. She grabbed the remote, turned the television on, then switched to the news channel. The broadcast addressed a recent incident with New Harbor vigilantes.

"The vigilante chose to remain anonymous, but with his help, the armed robber was apprehended," the reporter announced. A video showcased the "hooded hero" striking down the gunman with his back to the camera. Matt glanced over at his sister, who watched intently.

Madeline muted the television and turned to face her brother. "So, when Elaine, Harry, and Jack were talking about *Speedfire*, I was hoping it wasn't you."

"That's...I'm not even *Speedfire* there," Matt argued. "How did you find out?"

"I'm not stupid, Matt! You'd come home bruised from fighting like *that* back in Miami. I know your damn fighting style. And I would know what my brother looks like, even with his back to the camera."

Matt grimaced and turned away.

"*Why?*" she demanded.

"I don't want to give it up," he muttered.

"Considering you're making a new life here, I think it's better that you give it up. I heard this city already has plenty of vigilantes."

"They do it for fame," he argued. "I don't."

"Well, it's not really your right to do anything about it, period," she sighed. "Look, it's great that you uncovered that trafficking ring, but can you leave it at that? You've already done enough. Focus on that job you're getting."

"I *can't*." He threw his face into his hands. "I'd rather be out there at night."

"Matt, this isn't normal," Madeline insisted. "Do you need any help?"

He shot her a glare. "No."

"I'm just thinking. I swear, insomnia eats you alive. You're taking your medicine like you're supposed to, right?"

"Well..."

"*Matt.*"

"I don't need it."

"Don't get snappy with me. I want what's best for you."

"And maybe I want what's best for the world," he mumbled.

"Just tell me what's wrong. Why do you need to be out there?" Madeline demanded. "Does it get you worked up or excited? Do you get a 'kick' out of beating people up? It's not *right*."

"Damn it, I know it's not," he snapped. "I'm not hurting anyone that doesn't deserve it."

"Maybe I do need to get you serious help. A therapist? Psychiatrist?"

"Please, no psychiatrists," he begged.

She paused as he refused to keep his gaze on her. "Then let this 'Speed-fire' thing go. It's dangerous."

"I can't sleep at night."

"Can you at least try to?"

"I do! I just—I *can't*," he repeated.

"Because you're not taking your pills."

"*No.* I am," he groaned. "It just calls to me."

Madeline muttered something to herself and shook her head. "Bullshit. Why?"

"I'm not kidding," Matt said. "Why don't you believe me?"

"Explain how it 'calls' to you, then," she demanded.

Matt shrugged and looked away. "I hear her."

"Who?"

"This voice." He exhaled. "There's this lady in blue. She appeared in my dream last night. Or I thought it was a dream. I think she wants me to keep going."

"Matt." Madeline waited until he looked her in the eyes. "Hey. You need help."

"I don't—"

"Matt, that sounds like Blue Jay," she said.

"Maybe." He pressed his lips together. "She's not bad."

"You're eighteen," Madeline groaned. "You need to let this go."

When Matt was a kid, he had an imaginary friend named Blue Jay—this girl his age dressed in blue and full of energy. Well, everyone else had called her an imaginary friend. She always felt real to Matt.

"I'm sorry." He folded his arms and glanced toward the balcony.

Maybe this woman in blue was different from his imaginary friend in the past. Blue Jay was his best friend, someone he could always count on when he needed company. But ever since his parents died, Blue Jay disappeared.

"Okay, let's make a deal," Madeline offered. "If you stop being Speed-fire, I won't send you to a psychiatrist. Alright?"

"Why?"

"Because this vigilante life is going to kill you."

Matt sighed and nodded quietly. He knew he would never give up the nightlife. He needed to be better at hiding. That was all.

Matt trailed behind his sister as they entered the office. He hoped there would be a day when he could visit this place without facing the pressure of an apprenticeship. So many people had their eyes set on that job at Streak Corporation. He couldn't understand how Streak would waste this opportunity on someone like him, who wanted nothing to do with it.

No one else knows I don't want this, though, he thought dismally.

Matt spotted Harry and Christine near the stairway. With Madeline in a frustrated mood, he didn't want to follow her up the elevator.

"Hey, I'm going to talk with Harry," he mentioned. "I have some questions for him."

"Go ahead," Madeline said. As she continued toward the lift, Matt made his way over to Harry and Christine.

"Your uncle is talking to him right now, but it's so weird," Harry said as Matt stopped nearby. "I don't understand why the design deliveries have been off this past week."

Christine shrugged. "Someone could have messed with the warehouse's coordination."

"What's going on?" Matt spoke up.

"Hey, Matt," Harry greeted him. "We were just talking about Jack."

"Oh." Matt frowned. "Is everything okay?"

"Not really," Christine told him. "We've been missing a few blueprints. And Jack manages the transportation of products at the warehouse. So, we don't know if he's aware of the situation."

"Ah...I hope it gets resolved." Matt had no idea what else to say.

"Eh, I might go check on Jack in a few minutes," Harry mentioned. "Oh. Have you guys heard about what Speedfire did yesterday?"

Following that statement, Matt was ready to leave. He didn't need another reminder of the "infamous" Speedfire, especially after the fiasco with his sister.

"He saved a pharmacy, right?" Christine asked. Matt tensed and shifted his gaze elsewhere.

"Yeah, I'm surprised he hasn't shown his face in the news yet," Harry added. "I hope he shines a good light on vigilantes here."

Christine looked away. "I guess we'll have to see."

"How are you certain that was even Speedfire?" Matt asked warily.

"Come on. He's the new hero around Canton," Harry expressed. "But it's just my theory. I could be wrong. The camera didn't catch his face."

"And he's staying anonymous," Christine mentioned.

"Anyway, I'm going to find Jack," Harry said. "See ya!"

Matt and Christine both waved as Harry left toward the stairs. Silence filled the air between them.

"So," Matt said slowly, "what do you think of Speedfire?"

"Harry's excited, but I doubt the new guy has any potential," she sighed.

"Why?" he asked, unsure whether he wanted to hear her answer or not.

"You know how vigilantes are in New Harbor. Their egos skyrocket the second they're on the news. And Speedfire made national headlines," Christine stated. "He's going to end up like the others. He won't last long."

Her last words struck him. The reason he wouldn't last long was because of Madeline.

Christine continued, "I admire what he did, though. He managed to do something that took the authorities months to solve."

Matt curled his lips and nodded.

"But I'm worried his ego will catch up to him. It always does," she said.

"I don't think it will," he assured her.

"Sure," Christine scoffed. She rolled her eyes playfully. "You're still new here. You don't know."

"Well, at least have some faith."

Christine smiled softly. She gazed around the room and exhaled. "His ego isn't the only problem. It's still dangerous out there. Vigilantes aren't invincible."

Matt's smile dropped. Christine had a point, but her statement threw him for a loop. Even if she despised vigilantes, she showed concern for them. And though she had yet to realize it, she was concerned for him.

Chapter 12

WIND ON THE WATER

Matt left the headquarters hours before Madeline, already scheming of ways to sneak out as Speedfire. He opened the window of his room and peered down the apartment complex. The balconies aligned perfectly along the side of the building.

He heard the door to the apartment room shut, then dragged his upper body back through the window. He leaped onto his bed and pretended to scroll on his phone as Madeline entered his bedroom.

"I was wondering where you went," she spoke up. "Did you talk to Mr. Streak?"

Matt shook his head and leaned against his pillow. "I was feeling light-headed, and he was too busy today."

"Oh, yeah, rumors were spreading around the office," she muttered.

"What rumors?"

She sat down on the edge of his bed. "Have you heard about what Jack Lainey did?"

"Harry and Christine mentioned a few blueprints went missing."

"Yep. Last I saw, Harry was talking to him. And Mr. Streak isn't happy."

"Well, yeah, those are his supplies."

"It gets worse," Madeline added. "Mr. Streak looked into the situation this afternoon. He believes someone stole the blueprints and sold them to Sal-Tech."

He shot her with a confused look. "Who would sell those designs to Sal-Tech?"

"Don't know, but some conspiracies are floating around."

"Like...?"

"A few of us believe Jack did it," she confessed.

Matt stared at her blankly. "What if he's getting framed?"

She shrugged. "It's just a rumor, but it makes sense. Sal-Tech probably paid big money for those blueprints."

"Well," Matt mumbled, "do *you* believe Jack sold those designs?"

"I can't say. I haven't even been here for a week," Madeline said. "Harry believes there could have been a few employees involved. Possibly someone outside the company, too."

Matt shifted his attention back to his phone. "Is Streak okay?"

"I guess," she said. "But I can't blame him for panicking a bit."

She stayed on his bed for another minute, and when she realized he had nothing else to say about the matter, she left his room. He continued scrolling through the endless feeds of Oracle until he heard Madeline shut the door to her bedroom. After the lights went out, he threw himself out of bed and scrambled for his vigilante suit in the closet. He pulled out the jacket, the pants, the shirt, the mask, the fingerless gloves, and the belt. He even double-checked to see if his dagger was attached. Once he acquired his gear, he undressed and put his suit on, then headed for the window. As he rehearsed earlier, he opened the window. The wind blew his hood off, and he reached back to grab it.

Here we go, he breathed in.

He stretched out, hanging from the window. He sucked his breath in, then pushed his legs against the wall. The balcony was a few meters away, but he knew he could reach it. Taking a leap of faith, he pushed himself from the window. He nearly slipped, then grabbed the railings, saving himself with his upper arm strength. He gazed down at the street as the cars and streetwalkers bustled through the neighborhood, crowded as ever.

Matt lowered himself onto the roof of the next balcony, and onward. He scaled the building to the lobby window, dropped to the ground, and heard his knees crack.

Shit.

Matt lost balance for a second but threw his arms out to the wall, catching himself from the fall. He stretched his legs out and exhaled. After warming up, Matt dusted off his jacket and zipped across the street toward an alley. He found a fire escape to the top floor, then reached for the roof. The starless sky called to him as he rolled onto his back.

"Beautiful," Matt whispered with a grin.

These silver buildings were different from the ones he used to climb in Miami. He needed more practice if he wanted to traverse them quickly.

He sat up to stare at the harbor, then rested against the edge of the roof, letting his legs dangle as he lowered his mask. Fresh air blew in from the east. He could get used to this view and the serene feeling that came with it. To Matt, this was a form of living.

After his moment with the wind, he stood up and charted a parkour course for himself. He leaped from one roof to the next, perfecting his landings. When he came across a taller building, he pinpointed a fire escape. And when there was no ladder, he took a chance and jumped.

Matt climbed up a tall building, finding himself in western Canton. His mind wandered to the other vigilantes of New Harbor, and he wondered if they performed stunts like this. Stalking the area for crime from below sounded risky, but it was easier than parkouring across the rooftops.

The headquarters of Streak Corp stood a couple of blocks to the west in Fells Point. Matt spotted two silhouettes walking away from it and toward Boston Street.

As they got closer, he recognized the two men as Harry and Jack. He could even distinguish their voices, though their words sounded jumbled in the distance.

Matt figured since there was no crime in sight, he could return to his post and watch the waves on the harbor. He imagined sitting at the edge, with his mask lowered and legs stretched out.

Maybe he could even return to that field of yellow mums out here—

BOOM!

The crack of a gunshot interrupted his thoughts.

"*Jack!*" Harry's voice. "Help!"

Matt jumped up, then ran toward the noise. He peered down to find Jack on the ground, bleeding from the shoulder. Harry knelt with him and held onto Jack as he looked around frantically.

"Shit..." Matt whispered.

He peered down at the nearby alley and saw no traces of anyone, but when he looked up toward the rooftops, he noticed another figure nearby with a rifle. He broke into a sprint, leaping across the building to reach them.

The sniper rifle caught his eye. He recalled the one conversation he had with Harry and Christine.

The Sniper.

When he reached the building, he climbed up, already out of breath, then saw the shooter wrapping the rifle around their back with a strap. The sniper's figure was thin, and they wore a black suit with a zippered jacket. Two pistols and a pouch were locked onto their belt. Black feathers fluttered across their torn cape and hooded cowl, following the passing breeze.

The sniper turned around, ready to depart, then stopped upon seeing him. Pale skin hid under a purple mask covering the bottom half of their face, and smoky eyeshadow clouded their eyes. Matt pulled out his knife and pointed it toward the sniper.

"You're not going anywhere," he murmured. He clicked the switch and ignited the dagger with flames. The sniper's dark eyes widened, yet they remained fearless toward his fire, shifting into a defensive stance.

All the rumors about a shooter targeting affiliates of Streak Corporation were true. Whether the sniper was planning to attack Harry or not, Matt was determined to stop them.

He charged across the rooftop, keeping his dagger low. The sniper swiftly dodged, kicking him in the side. He lost balance and fell back on the roof, inches from the edge. He shot himself back up, and the sniper took the same stance. This time, they came for him. He raised his arms to block their attacks, then sent the sniper sliding back with a kick to the stomach.

The sniper came back around, leaping toward his head. Matt ducked. He rolled toward the corner of the roof. He got up, throwing his fiery blade.

Clang!

The sniper deflected his knife with a metal wristlet. The dagger propelled it into an alley below.

Damn it. Matt stood warily and got back into position. He noticed an odd symbol on the sniper's belt—an open semicircle with two arrows on the ends.

The sniper made their way to the other side of the roof, away from the harbor. Matt followed the sniper's steps as they circled each other in a dance-like rhythm. He stood with his back to the pier, holding the sniper's gaze. As he got a steadier look of their eyes, he found their irises were purple.

"You're wasting your time," the sniper hissed. The voice sounded husky, low, and feminine, like a loud whisper—enough to send a chill through him.

His gaze fell over the sniper's slim figure as the hoarse voice echoed inside his head.

The sniper's a woman...

Matt took a defensive stance. "As if I'm going to leave you," he countered.

The sniper breathed in as she stepped forward, then placed the tips of her gloved fingers together. Matt took a breath as well, then sprinted ahead, focused on finding a weak spot. Instead of fighting back, the sniper shot her arm out and waved her other hand around. The wind swirled around the rooftop. Before Matt could react, the sniper shot her fist forward.

A powerful gust stormed toward him, blowing him off the roof. He gasped, voiceless, as he fell toward the street below. Another blast of wind struck him, forcing him over the water. As Matt splashed into the bay, he closed his eyes, waving his arms around to push himself to the surface. He pulled his mask down, breathing in the swirling air. His gaze locked onto the building as the sniper escaped.

Matt swam to a nearby dock, pulled himself up, and coughed out some water he swallowed. His arms quivered, feeling numb. Speechless and stunned, he couldn't stop trembling.

The wind. The sniper. He felt like his life had flashed before his eyes at that first gust.

She controlled the wind.

The sniper manipulating an element like the wind meant only one thing. She was *Rare*. And she possessed one of the Core Stones. He didn't see the sniper holding the stone, but he thought he noticed a pouch attached to her belt.

He needed to get back to Harry and Jack immediately.

Matt climbed the stairs, raised his mask, and ran toward where he last saw them. Jack's limp figure lay on the ground while Harry called for help. He sprinted across the street, then knelt before Jack.

"I saw what happened," Matt told Harry, breathless. "I saw the sniper."

Harry's eyes widened as he lowered the phone. "You...you're Speedfire!"

"Did you call an ambulance?" Matt asked as he put pressure on Jack's shoulder.

Harry nodded quickly. "They're coming. I don't know what happened," he stuttered. "We were just walking, then suddenly—" He lost his voice.

"It's okay," Matt assured him. "I'll tell you what I saw later. We need to get him help first."

He heard the sirens down the block and saw the flashing lights. Matt debated on whether he should reveal his identity to Harry.

Moments before, Matt didn't know whether to believe the sniper was a real threat. He had nearly forgotten about the rumors until tonight. But his last fight told him otherwise.

He could even say the sniper took the breath out of him.

Chapter 13

Rare in the Dark

Harry had a small apartment with two rooms, a bathroom, and a kitchen. Matt and Madeline sat down together on the couch as Harry prepared the three of them something to drink. After last night, Matt was desperate to check up on Harry and had persuaded Madeline to join him.

Harry handed Madeline her tea first, then returned from the kitchen to give Matt his mug. "Thank you for stopping by. I've been a wreck since last night."

"After what happened, we need to be here," Madeline assured him. "We want to make sure you're okay."

"Well, *I'm* okay," Harry mentioned. "But Jack has me worried. He could have died."

When Matt came here with Madeline today, he planned to reveal his identity as Speedfire. He kept his mask tucked in his pocket until the right moment came.

"At least you weren't hurt," Madeline told him. "And since Jack's in the hospital, he should be okay. He was shot in the shoulder, right?"

"Yeah. It probably hurts a ton," Harry stammered. "I don't know what to do right now. I'm glad that vigilante was there, at least."

"Vigilante?" Madeline questioned.

"Speedfire showed up and said he saw the sniper."

Madeline snuck a glare at Matt, then returned her attention to Harry. "Really?"

"Harry, I need to tell you something," Matt interrupted.

Harry perked. "Okay?"

Matt glanced at Madeline, then pulled out the mask he wore the night before. "That was me. I'm Speedfire."

Harry gasped, staring down at the mask with disbelief. "No way."

"There's a lot I need to tell you. I didn't want to keep you in the dark, but we need to get to the bottom of this," Matt continued.

Harry looked over at Madeline. "Did you know?"

"Of course," she mentioned, then crossed her arms. "And I told him he should *not* be out there like that, but he didn't listen."

"But he saved Jack's life," Harry pleaded. "He's brilliant out there."

"Yeah, I know," she mumbled. Her gaze shifted to the floor.

He looked back at Matt. "So, you saw the shooter?"

"Yes," Matt assured him. "I fought the sniper after I heard the gunshot."

Harry gasped, "And you won?"

Matt winced. "No...I don't know. I didn't win," he said bitterly. "Remember how I was soaking wet last night? The sniper blew me into the water."

"He *what*—?" Madeline spoke up, puzzled.

"Like, he kicked you?" Harry added.

"Um." Matt shrugged nervously. "No. I don't know how to put it. The sniper used the wind."

Madeline and Harry stared at him, speechless. Matt clapped his hands together and took a quick breath.

"Okay, so the sniper *controlled* the wind and used it to blow me off the roof. Into the water. Boom. There we go. The sniper is *Rare*."

"*Rare*?" Harry stammered. "How? He would need one of the Core Stones to have powers like that."

"Harry, I'm not lying," Matt argued.

"What did he look like?" Madeline demanded. "Maybe we can get this info to the police."

"Um..." Matt rubbed his head. "So, I don't think *he* is the best way to describe them. The sniper is a woman..."

Harry blinked. "*What?*"

Matt frowned. "Her voice. It was cold and...I don't know," he winced. "I don't want to make assumptions, but I have very few traits to use. So, I'm going to use them."

"Okay, well, how would you describe her?" Madeline pestered him.

"Uh, black suit, pale skin, really thin. She wore a mask and a lot of eyeshadow. Kind of looked like a raccoon...or a raven," he described. "And she had a feathery cape. But aside from that, I don't have much on who she is."

"So, you're certain she is *Rare*?" Madeline continued.

Matt nodded. "No one else can control the wind like that." He reminisced about the fight last night. The sniper's martial prowess was better than his own, so she was an expert fighter and most likely an assassin. She also wielded a rifle, but she only used the gun to attack Jack Lainey. The Core Stone was a unique asset, however. "Another notable thing about her. Her eyes were purple."

"Purple?" Harry repeated uncertainly.

"Yeah. A deep purple," he continued. "Do *Rare* people have purple eyes?"

Madeline raised her brows while Harry tilted his head. "I couldn't say," he said.

"I don't recall President Agnes having purple eyes in any of his pictures," Madeline muttered.

"But he wore purple clothes, right?" Harry added.

"Eh, true. Purple is Optyma's color, though," she sighed.

"Hm." Matt's gaze flickered to the floor in contemplation. "I have a theory."

"What?" Harry asked.

"So, you know how someone stole a Core Stone a few days ago?" Matt said. "What if this sniper happens to be the culprit? And maybe the stone turned her eyes purple?"

"How?" Madeline argued. "The thief stole it from General Fren in England. And weren't there *scorch* marks left behind? You're telling us this sniper has wind powers, not fire."

"Maybe those marks were caused by something else," Matt noted. "She probably traveled overnight after discovering the identity of one of the stone keepers, got it, came back here, and continued attacking Jason Streak's employees. I think she wants his stone."

"This doesn't make any sense," Madeline muttered, facepalming. "Why would she attack random people?"

"I don't know that, Maddie," Matt remarked. He looked back at Harry. "So, did no one else know the sniper was *Rare*?"

"No one even knew the sniper was a woman," he pointed out. "This information is *huge*."

Matt held his hand to his chin. "Did the police already question you?"

"Yeah, but I can give them all the stuff you gave me," Harry said. "I already told them that Speedfire saved me, though. I can keep your identity a secret if you want."

"Please."

"So, how do we even get to the bottom of this? A psychotic sniper has been killing people, and Matt just happens to come across her?" Madeline asked frantically.

"It's a miracle. These attacks have been going on for two years," Harry added. "Not even New Harbor's best detective has been able to crack the case yet. We're hoping someone finally stops the sniper."

"We talked about the sniper the other day with Christine. You two told me what I needed to know," Matt recalled. "Leave it to me."

"Hey," Madeline spoke up with a glare, "don't go running into danger like that. You don't know what you're up against."

"Actually, I kind of do."

"Oh, yeah. Someone who could make you fall to your death. Gotcha," Madeline remarked. "Just be careful."

"I will." Matt rolled his eyes. "Harry, when was the last attack before Jack's incident? I need to know."

Harry fell silent for a moment, struggling with a response. "Almost a month ago. It, uh, it was the former general manager, remember?"

"*What?*" Madeline shrieked.

"I'm sorry!" Harry whimpered.

"I remember you telling me," Matt said quietly. "Maddie, don't freak out. You're not a target."

"I better not be!" she yelled. "What am I signing myself up for?"

"Nothing dangerous!" Harry pleaded with her. "Not everyone in Streak Corp is a target."

Madeline uncrossed her arms and looked away. "Okay."

"His name was Noah Mallory. Kylie witnessed the shooting a few weeks ago, too," Harry added.

"She did?" asked Matt.

"Yeah, she said Noah was giving her a ride home that night. But then the sniper came out and shot him," Harry explained. "She won't say anything else about it, though. I don't blame her. It's traumatizing."

"So, did the sniper shoot Noah on the street?" Matt continued.

"Yes, but he survived that first shooting," Harry replied. "He died in the hospital."

Madeline winced. "And Jack's still in the hospital, right?"

Harry grimaced. "Yeah, but Jack's fine right now. When Noah died, the sniper had shot him through the hospital window."

"I hate to say it, but maybe we need to talk to Kylie about this," Matt suggested. "We need all the clues we can get."

"Why is the sniper even a thing?" Madeline groaned.

"Maddie, I promise I won't let anything happen to you," Matt assured her. He placed his hand on her shoulder. "Okay?"

Madeline huffed, then looked back at her brother.

"So, is there anything else I should tell the police tomorrow?" Harry asked.

Matt thought for a moment. The public needed to be aware of the sniper's power. Now that Matt knew she was *Rare*, he could help the detective find a possible identity. Her wind powers and access to the Core Stone made her a unique opponent. He had never fought anyone like her before.

"The *Rare* Sniper," he murmured. He directed his attention back to Harry. "She needs a proper name."

"The Rare Sniper?" Harry repeated.

Matt nodded. "I think it's distinct enough. And everyone deserves to know our enemy is *Rare*." He pondered her violet gaze, and his stomach twisted at his sudden revelation.

Purple...Optyma's colors...The stolen Core Stone...

"What if...the sniper is Optyman?" Matt proposed.

Harry tensed. "Oh, shit."

"And if Streak Corp supplied our military during the war," Matt continued, "what if she's a survivor? And she's looking for revenge..."

"You might be onto something," Harry gasped. "She's *Rare*, too. And Optymans have a higher chance of being *Rare*."

"Guys, guys, guys," Madeline hissed. "We can't go around assuming things. Not all Optymans are bad—"

"We know," Matt groaned. "But this gives us a lead, Maddie."

"Okay, but don't go around thinking every Optyman has a vendetta against Streak Corp," she mumbled. Matt crossed his arms, and she glared at him. "I taught you better than that."

Harry's phone buzzed in his pocket. He stood up and stared at it for a lengthy moment.

"Give me a second. It's Mr. Streak," he said before he turned away. "Hello, sir?"

Madeline sighed beside Matt, and he put his arm around her. He didn't know what else to say.

"What?" Harry shouted, dropping the phone. He turned to face Matt and Madeline again. He locked eyes with them anxiously. "Jack is dead!"

ACT II
FATED CHAINS
OR DESTINY

Chapter 14

A Scandal and a Sniper

Someone poisoned Jack Lainey in his hospital bed overnight. Several hundred visitors had entered the hospital that day, but the nurses and investigators failed to find a culprit. There would have been thousands of innocent people in the vicinity, many of whom were doctors and nurses on the front lines. No one had time for questions.

Matt wondered if any visitors resembled the sniper, but a thin, light-skinned woman matched too many profiles. Her purple eyes were his only lead.

Over the next week, Matt kept his speculations to himself, Madeline, and Harry. When Harry returned to the police after Jack was declared dead, he gave them all the information "Speedfire" had provided.

The city of New Harbor agreed to call her the "Rare Sniper" after hearing about her wind powers and Optyman connection. Even the claim that she was a woman shocked a lot of people.

As of now, the threat of the sniper loomed over everyone at Streak Corp. There was no guessing who she would target next, and why.

After a weeklong break, Matt returned to the headquarters. He entered with his guest card, then waited in the lobby for Harry to join him. Elaine waved to him from the desk, and Matt waved back with a smile.

"Hey, man!" Harry greeted as he stepped off the elevator. "How's it going?"

Matt whistled. "Better than last week."

"Tell me about it," Harry sighed. "People have been driving me nuts. But I have some interesting stuff to share. Things I do *not* want to talk about here."

"I don't blame you. Maddie said everyone keeps asking about the incident."

Harry shook his head with a scowl. "Some people can't respect any privacy here."

"Do you think we should talk to Kylie?" Matt suggested.

Harry gasped, "That's right. Let's head up while she's still in her office."

After they rode the elevator to the eighth floor, Harry opened Kylie's door, then walked inside with Matt. Kylie stood beside the bookcase in her room, dusting her shelves.

"Kylie?" Harry spoke up.

"Huh?" Kylie turned around, confused. "What do you two need?"

"We need to talk," Harry said. Kylie frowned. "If that's okay with you?"

Kylie set the duster down, then strode to the front of her desk. "Is this about Jack Lainey?"

Harry shared a glance with Matt. "Uh, yeah," Harry stuttered, then faced Kylie again. "How'd you know?"

"I figured," Kylie sighed. "You witnessed the shooting."

"We heard you were there when Noah Mallory got shot," Matt added.

Kylie raised an inquisitive brow. "Is that so?"

Matt bit his lip lightly, hoping Harry would carry on with the conversation. Even after spending the past two years as a vigilante, he hated questioning people.

Harry continued, "We're trying to get to the bottom of this. We need your help."

Kylie crossed her arms. "My help?" she repeated. "How can I help with any of this?"

"Well, you witnessed one of the shootings," Harry pleaded. "We just want to know what you saw."

"Hm. Good question," Kylie said. "It was very windy and foggy that night. The sniper shot Noah's tire, and once he stepped out of the car, they shot him in the shoulder. And when I got out, I saw the sniper. They were standing on the rooftop, dressed in black, and carrying a rifle." She pursed her lips. "Then they left. Just like that."

"That's all you saw?" Matt asked.

"Harry probably saw more than I did. Or Speedfire? I heard that was who fought the sniper," she added.

"Yeah, Speedfire," Harry mentioned. "That probably explains why it was windy for you."

Kylie checked her nails. "Yep. I guess so."

Harry stiffened, and Matt glanced over to check on him. Jack's death left Harry devastated this past week. Kylie, meanwhile, was undisturbed with the matter of Noah Mallory's demise.

"Kylie?" Matt spoke up, catching her attention. "Were you close with Noah at all?"

"Nope."

"But you saw what happened to him," he continued. Kylie glared at him. "I figured you'd be a little more...I don't know. Upset?"

"What happened to Noah is sad, but it's not the end of the world for me," Kylie snapped. Harry and Matt tensed. "Noah was a scandalous pig. He didn't deserve what happened, though he wasn't completely inno-cent."

"What do you mean?" Matt questioned. "Did he do something?"

"Can't really say what was going on inside his mind. He thought he could get away with screwing over the Optyman population using stolen info from Streak Corp. That much I do know," Kylie explained. She leaned closer, lowering her voice. "And he wanted me to help him."

"That doesn't sound like Noah," Harry gasped. "You didn't help him, right?" She scowled. "Did...you?"

"No." She ran her hand across her blond hair, then flicked some strands over her shoulder. "I think he wanted a companion. Someone he could throw under the bus. And he had eyes for *me*, of course. The bastard even tried putting the moves on me, as if," Kylie scoffed. "I prefer to see myself as *immovable*."

"Uh...sorry he was trying that with you," Harry replied, rubbing his head.

"Eh, I know the signs all too well. He tried reeling me in with all these promises. Called me *young blood* and all, thinking 'fake love' and money would get me to fold," Kylie said. Her gaze flickered to the side as she smirked. "If you pretend to love someone long enough, you may find yourself winning a slave." She dropped her grin as she met Matt's eyes. "That's why I wouldn't run off with someone like Noah Mallory. It's also why I don't really have the energy to care. I've witnessed worse things, boys."

"Worse things?" Harry asked. "Like what?"

"Well, let's see," Kylie rambled as she counted on her fingers. "I watched a building fall on my parents, I became an orphan at thirteen, and I've witnessed people get burned alive over where they come from. And no, I won't elaborate. So please, for the love of...*God*, leave me out of this." She grabbed a set of files from her desk and stormed past them. She shoved her office door open, turning toward the stairwell.

Matt and Harry watched her in stunned silence.

"Wow," Harry exhaled.

"At least we know her perspective now," Matt sighed. "It matches what I saw. Unfortunately."

"Well, let's rendezvous at the lobby," Harry suggested. "I'd still like to get something to eat. We can talk more over lunch."

Matt waited several minutes in the lobby for Harry. He pondered his latest conversation with Kylie and wondered what she meant to convey by listing all her grievances. There was more to Kylie Kreene than he expected, but he needed to focus on solving the mystery behind the Rare Sniper. Any other anomalies in this city would have to wait.

He looked up as Harry approached him. "We should get going. You said you want lunch at this Jasmine Garden place?" Harry asked.

"I haven't been there yet, but I want to try it," Matt mentioned. "I want to take Maddie one day when she's not busy—"

"What are you guys up to?" a light voice interrupted from behind.

Matt and Harry turned around to Christine standing there, wearing her casual red dress.

"We were just about to get lunch at this Chinese place," Harry answered.

"Really? I love Chinese food," she gasped.

Oh no. Matt glanced at Harry nervously.

"Do you want to join us?" Harry offered.

No. Matt shuddered.

He looked back at Christine, and they locked eyes for a moment.

"I mean...if it's okay," she said as her voice dropped. She bit her lip and glanced toward the wall. "Never mind...I can skip out."

"No, you can come," Matt forced himself to say. "We're leaving in a few minutes."

"Okay, let me get my purse. I can pay for it," she offered, then turned toward the stairs.

"Aw, Christie, no!" Harry called after her. "We can pay for ourselves!"

"I'm paying!" she shot back playfully.

Matt took Harry's shoulder and turned him around. "Hey," he whispered.

"What?" Harry asked, confused. His eyes widened. "I probably shouldn't have invited her..."

"Yeah, no shit," Matt muttered. "I don't want her to know about any of this."

"Aw, come on. Christine's fine. She won't tell a soul."

"Are you sure? She is Streak's *niece*," Matt hissed. "And this all deals with his business."

"We're talking about the Rare Sniper and the incident," Harry said. "Besides, Christine can keep a secret. She's the sweetest girl in New Harbor."

"I know," Matt huffed restlessly, although he doubted that last statement. Perhaps Christine was sweet to everyone but him. "But there's another thing..." His voice dropped, and he glimpsed the area. Elaine occupied herself by talking to a client over the phone, and no one else lingered in the lobby. "Christine doesn't like vigilantes."

"Yeah?"

"Yeah. You know that," Matt pointed out. "I don't want her knowing about...you know..." He put his fingers together. "*Me.*"

"You?"

"Yes. Me. Speedfire."

"I think she'd be cool with it."

Matt shook his head. "She doesn't like Speedfire. I talked to her about *me* one day, and she went on this whole rant," he explained. "If you want to talk about the Rare Sniper, that's fine. Maybe she can even give us her own theories. But please, I *beg* of you. Do not bring up Speedfire."

"Matt, I have to mention Speedfire. You're all over the news," Harry sighed. "Besides, everyone believes that Speedfire will take care of the Rare Sniper. Christine might think so, too."

"And I *will*," Matt promised, holding his finger up, "but that's not the point. You and Maddie are the only ones who can know I'm Speedfire. I don't want anyone else to find out. Especially *her*."

"I'm ready," Christine announced as she flung her purse over her shoulder.

"Great!" Matt turned around in a hurry. "Do you like Chinese food?"

Christine gave him a confused look. "I told you that already."

Matt paused blankly. "Yeah, you did," he said, then turned toward the doors awkwardly. "Let's just go."

A stone exterior garnished the small restaurant, and a path of bushes led the way to the entrance. The interior had white walls with a green tile floor, and the aroma of freshly brewed green tea lingered in the air.

Matt peered over at Christine, who sat across from him and admired the nearby sunset paintings on the wall. He wondered what she was thinking about as she looked around the room. When she glanced his way, he quickly shifted his gaze to the menu in front of him.

"Welcome to the Jasmine Garden!" a familiar voice piped up. Katelyn stood before them with a notepad and a jade apron tied around her clothes. "May I start you all off with some drinks?"

"Uh, what do you two want?" Harry asked. "I was thinking of getting some tea with the meal. They offer us a whole teapot."

"Sure," Christine replied. "We can get tea and water if that's fine." She looked at Matt, who nodded.

"Alright, coming right up. I'll be back with the drinks," Katelyn said and turned away.

Harry cleared his throat and slid his menu aside. "So, we're going to talk about some things today."

"As you do," Christine remarked.

"Like, some serious things," he continued. "Uh, you know...the incident?"

"Jack Lainey?" she finished for him.

Harry nodded. "Matt and I have been speculating."

"About what?" she asked.

"Uh." Harry fell silent, trying to find his words.

"The Rare Sniper," Matt continued. "And what happened to Jack Lainey in the hospital."

"The fact that someone crossed the sniper is incredible," Christine said. "My uncle was quite surprised."

"He's been trying to investigate the whole 'sniper mystery' for ages," Harry added. "But not just anyone found the Rare Sniper." Matt shot him a quick glare, which Harry caught immediately. He smiled anxiously. "Speedfire did."

Christine nodded. "I heard about that."

"Did you hear about what happened?" Matt asked. "He was blown off the rooftop."

"That's why he's calling her the *Rare* Sniper," she sighed.

"I think it's better than just calling her *the sniper*," he pointed out. "At least it gives everyone some sort of lead."

She slid her menu away. "Harry, you actually talked to Speedfire about this?"

Harry bowed his head, and Matt leaned back into his seat. An awkward feeling overcame him.

"He's cool," Harry told her, then faked a smile.

"How cool?" she questioned.

"Like, really cool."

"What was he even doing there that night?" she asked. "Sounds kinda suspicious to me."

"Hey," Matt argued, "he happened to be in the area and saved Harry's life. Who knows what the Rare Sniper would have done if he hadn't intervened?"

Christine shrugged. "I don't know." She noticed Katelyn walking back with the drinks. "I guess vigilantes like him just patrol certain areas. Maybe it was a coincidence."

"Probably," Matt agreed in a low voice as Katelyn placed the teapot in front of them.

Stuck-up and ignorant. He side-eyed Christine through the steaming tea as he faced Katelyn. *Why did she have to come along?*

"Anything to eat?" Katelyn asked with a wide grin.

"Vegetarian fried rice," Christine spoke up.

"Uh, shrimp lo mein," added Harry.

"Same as him," Matt mentioned.

"Easy!" Katelyn jotted their orders down. "Coming right up!"

As she left them for a second time, Harry continued, "So, anyway, I have a weird theory."

"Okay?" Matt and Christine said simultaneously.

"Jack was selling blueprints to Sal-Tech," Harry explained. "But I looked into it more, and Jack showed me what he was stealing. He took blueprints of Optyman-inspired weapons."

Matt raised a brow. "*Optyman-inspired?*" he echoed. "Like what?"

"Optyma was more advanced in its time. Just look at what the refugees have done with New Harbor," Christine explained. "But I know what Harry means. He's talking about electromagnetic railguns and energy-beam-based weapons. They're supposed to be directly inspired by Jake Agnes' light abilities, but it's confidential."

Matt gaped. "And you just told me?"

She rolled her eyes. "Well, you *asked*. And it's not like I'm handing you a step-by-step blueprint on how to make an energy railgun. Besides, your sister is the manager of the headquarters."

"Yeah. Now, get this," Harry continued. "Most targets of the sniper have stolen something from Streak Corp *for* Sal-Tech. And it's usually related to Optyma. You heard Kylie earlier. Even Noah Mallory was intending to target the Optymans with whatever intel he stole from Mr. Streak."

"This sort of ties into our theory from earlier," Matt mumbled.

Christine tilted her head. "What theory?"

Harry scratched the back of his head. "Speedfire...believes the Rare Sniper is Optyman," he confessed. "An Optyman has been targeting your uncle's company. And she just-so happens to be a Rare Soul. The odds are insane."

Christine muttered, "The Optymans don't think very highly of my uncle."

"So, what are you thinking?" asked Matt. "Is Sal-Tech behind all this? Or is the Rare Sniper on a revenge mission against Streak Corp?"

Harry's phone buzzed. "Ah, shit. Hold on."

Matt watched him scramble for his phone, then glanced at Christine. She stared at the tea uncomfortably, her gaze darting to him for a moment.

"Damn it," Harry groaned, then stood up, "your uncle needs me back at the office. With Jack gone, I've got a lot to organize at the warehouse."

"Oh." Christine gazed at him sympathetically. "Do you want us to make your order to-go?"

Harry feigned a smile. "Yeah, that'd be nice. Thanks," he said. "Sorry to leave you two, but we can talk later."

Harry bolted out the door and into the city streets. Matt turned to look back at Christine, and she did the same with him. He didn't know how to feel being left alone with her.

"So..." he spoke up. He felt his voice drifting away.

"Interesting topic," she pointed out.

"Yeah."

"Judging by your interest in vigilantes, it doesn't surprise me that you'd jump on these theories," she said.

"Oh." Matt laughed nervously, then glanced away. "I just want to help as much as I can. And I want to make sure Maddie is okay."

She smiled slightly. "That's sweet."

He peered back at her, catching the sudden warmth in her gaze. For once, she didn't seem cold toward him.

Katelyn returned with their meals, then looked puzzled upon noticing Harry's empty seat. "Did he go to the restroom?"

"He had to leave for work," Christine told her. "But can we get his lo mein in a box?"

"Sure thing," Katelyn replied, taking back Harry's plate. "Enjoy your meal!"

Katelyn returned to the kitchen to prepare Harry's lunch as carry-out. Matt could have gotten a free meal if he revealed himself as Speedfire to her. He sometimes wished he could tell anyone what he did at night. Maybe he could get away with telling Katelyn one day, but he would need to know her more.

Matt shifted his attention to his food, then glanced at Christine, who stopped and locked eyes with him again. He had no idea what was on her mind, but she suddenly smiled at him.

Her smile was quite contagious.

Chapter 15

When History Has a Name

Matt and Christine traveled the long road to the bayside. An earthy scent followed the light rain; the smell of petrichor often kept him at ease.

Matt's grip tightened around the carry-out bag. His eyes flickered to Christine, who watched him quietly.

"Um." She curled her lips, then stared ahead. "I want to say something, but I don't know how to put it."

"What is it?"

She brushed a lock of hair behind her ear. "I want to apologize."

Matt raised a brow, confused. "For what?"

"I guess for the way I've been treating you," she said.

"Oh." He rubbed the back of his head, still puzzled. "I practically bull-dozed you—"

"No, it's not just that," she added. "I've been acting petty."

"It's okay," he assured her. "I said some rude things, too."

Christine rubbed her arm. "No, you hardly did anything."

"Hey." They stopped, and he exhaled. "Look, I understand. You're usually skeptical."

"And I'm sorry for that." She looked away. Her auburn hair glistened in the rain.

"You caught me asking a hundred questions about your uncle's Core Stone. And his company will probably fall into your hands one day," he said. Her frown deepened. "I was saying the wrong things at the wrong time."

"You don't have to justify my actions." She faced him with a grin. "But I can't stop you if you do."

He returned the smile, then strolled with her toward the waterfront. "I'm guessing you were raised to be skeptical."

"Of course," she replied. "But you're one to talk, Mr. Detective."

"I think anyone with ties to Streak Corp should be a little cynical right now," he pointed out.

"True." She watched two seagulls synchronize their flight over the water. "My uncle raised me to think a lot like him after my mother passed away."

Matt held his breath, taking in her words. "I'm sorry to hear that," he mentioned quietly. "What happened to her?"

"A car accident. I was seven." Christine closed her arms around herself. "She and my uncle were twins. He would say it felt like losing his other half."

Matt learned about Jason Streak's sister when Madeline was studying the company. Amelia Streak was supposed to be the original successor of the enterprise, but after her death, Jason had taken on the responsibility for his parents.

"And what happened to your father?" Matt asked.

"He went missing when I was six. So, when my mother died, my uncle took me in."

"Your father's missing? Was he ever found?" Matt gasped.

Christine shook her head. "No...he just...I'm sorry," she sighed. "I don't know why I'm sharing all this. It's a lot."

"Don't be sorry." He knew what it was like to get lost in a conversation. To make her feel better, he figured the best thing he could do was to keep it going. "Maybe he's still out there."

"If he is, he'd have come back by now." She released her arms. "My uncle believes he returned to Holland or Optyma. Back home. Maybe being with my mother didn't feel like home to him anymore."

"Wait...you're Optyman?"

She nodded quietly.

Matt stared at her for a moment, speechless. His only experience with Optymans was listening to what everyone else had to say about them. A handful of Optymans had migrated to Miami, but they were persecuted after the war. Matt never knew them, but he always remembered what everyone had to say to him.

The Optymans killed your parents. Never forget what they did.

There were many days Matt would cry to Madeline after school, and despite the harsh reality of what happened to their parents overseas, she always told him to ignore the hate.

"Their leaders killed our parents. Don't let anyone tell you to hate those innocent people."

Eventually, everyone around him stopped mentioning his dead parents. They found other things to talk about, and Matt could finally hide in peace.

But *Optyma* always came back to haunt him.

The niece of Jason Streak didn't strike him as someone who would be from the Atlantic island nation, but he was surprised.

"We were just talking about how an Optyman could be the sniper, and you didn't even say anything," he stammered. "I'm so sorry—"

"No, don't be. I'm not a full-blooded Optyman. As the people say, you must be born on the island to truly be an Optyman, or an immigrant who treats the soil as their home. I'm neither, so..." she sighed. "I'm not really anything."

"Was your father born on Optyma?"

"Yes." She feigned a smile, then looked toward the vast bay. "My father wanted to move to Optyma with me. So, it makes me wonder why he left us alone. He disappeared, my mom died in the crash, and then the war happened. I never got any answers."

Matt kept his eyes on her as they crossed the road. He flipped his hood up before the rain could drench him.

"We're back." Christine walked toward the pier and grabbed the railing.

"What's it like being Optyman?" he asked her.

She narrowed her eyes with contemplation and breathed in the bayside breeze. "It makes me feel like I belong here," she replied, smiling. She turned to stare at the rest of the city. "I lived in Baltimore before the war. But after the bombing, I grew up in a mansion outside the area. I got to witness its rebirth."

"Have you ever visited Optyma? Before the war..."

Everyone was aware of Optyma's quarantined state. Even if Christine tried to visit today, the trip would be too dangerous due to the toxic air quality. Yet Matt often wondered what the nation was like before the war—before President Jake Agnes took control.

"Never had the chance. I would have if I knew any relatives there, though," she mentioned. "Relatives on my father's side."

Christine flipped a loose strand of wet hair across her shoulder. Matt glanced at the take-out bag, grateful that Harry's lunch wasn't soaked.

"So, does everyone else know you're Optyman?" Matt asked. "Or is it kind of a secret?"

She shrugged. "Most people are aware. But I try to hide it. I mean, I don't really flaunt my Optyman heritage." She gazed back at him. "Especially not in this city. Any Optymans who still wear their capes are pretty brave around here."

Matt recalled how the Optyman people were known for wearing capes with their attire. Shrouds were a dominant fashion trend on the island, but after the war, refugees were shunned for donning their cloaks. Even the Rare Sniper wore a black cape made of feathers, further feeding his theory.

"I actually...um..." Christine coughed. "I bought myself a cape years ago." She blushed when Matt tilted his head. "It's this little white cape. Nothing special. It was more-or-less an impulse buy."

Matt smiled slightly. "Have you worn it?"

"Only at home." She rolled her eyes. "I'm too chicken to wear it. People give the Optymans enough dirty looks as it is. Capes are just beacons, you know." She sagged against the railing. "But it's a cute cape. I thought it would look nice with my red dress. I just don't know who I'd wear it around."

"Well," Matt leaned into the railing, "you can wear it around me. And I'd make sure no one gives you shit for it."

Christine gaped. "Really?"

"If you're that desperate."

She smiled softly, then twirled her hair. "I might take you up on the offer..."

They spent another few minutes together and watched the seagulls circle the pier. Through the fog, Matt found the building where he had encountered the Rare Sniper a week ago. He still couldn't believe he had flown into the water that night.

"Are you going back in or heading home?" Christine interrupted his thoughts.

Matt jolted. "I think I might head home." He returned his attention to her. "I'll stop by another time."

"I can take Harry's food to him," she offered. He nodded, and she took the handles of the bag. Her hand brushed against his as she slipped the plastic from his grasp, and she glanced down at the black ring around his finger. She stepped back and looked up at him again with a small smile. "Thanks again for letting me join you."

He grinned. "Thanks for talking."

"It was a good talk." Christine turned away. "There's not a lot of people I can really connect with, you know."

Matt stepped aside. "Is it because of your family?"

Christine sighed, "Always is."

With that, she returned to the headquarters. Matt watched her for a minute before he turned his attention to the harbor. He breathed in the earthy air, then walked back to his apartment.

Matt found himself back at the Streak Corp headquarters in two days. He entered the building with Madeline and rode the elevator to Streak's office. Even if he felt unprepared, he was giving his final answer on the offer.

Matt knocked on the door, and Streak opened it within seconds.

"Matthew, what brings you here?" asked Streak.

"I want to talk about the opportunity," Matt replied as he entered the room.

"Take a seat." Streak beckoned Matt to a chair in front of his desk. "I have an interview scheduled in a few minutes, but do you have questions about the offer?"

Matt nodded. "So, there's an open position in the marketing department, right?"

"Yes, Ms. Kreene is looking for help down there," Streak mentioned. "You are not in school, correct?"

"No." Matt frowned. "Does that affect anything?"

"It shouldn't," Streak assured him, contemplating. "Though most of my interns and apprentices currently attend school."

"If you want to wait a year, I can go to school first," Matt told him. He didn't know why he was coming up with this idea. He had no interest in working for Streak Corp, nor did he have any secondary education plans aside from art school, and he did *not* want to hear Streak's opinion on that.

"Hmm, well," Streak mumbled as he mulled it over, "that's all up to you. The offer is still open, but if you wish to do part-time while attending a community college, I can arrange for that."

The door swung open, and another individual entered the room. Streak straightened in his seat and smiled warmly toward the guest behind Matt.

"Hello," Streak greeted, then took a stand. Matt turned toward the man, who he assumed was the interviewee Streak mentioned a moment ago. "You must be James Salamar."

"Yes, sorry," the man replied as he tripped on his words slightly. "I did not mean to interrupt. The lady at the desk told me to come up here."

"That's not a problem," Streak assured him. "You're right on time."

Matt assumed he was sitting in the seat Streak had planned for James and stood up. "I can get going," he stuttered.

"Wait," Streak said as James stood beside Matt. "Actually...Matthew, I had an idea."

"What?" he asked cautiously.

Streak glanced back and forth at Matt and James. Matt tried to pay no attention to the future employee beside him. He felt that being here during his scheduled interview made things more awkward than they should be.

"James, I recall you are also applying for a position under Ms. Kreene," Streak added. "She might find it easier to train two new employees at once. One as an apprentice, one with former experience. That's if you don't mind, of course."

"If it's convenient for everyone, I don't mind at all," James answered casually. His voice sounded soft and smooth with an English accent.

Matt nodded regrettably. He glimpsed James, who stood two inches taller than him. James wore a black suit fit for an interview and a pair of rectangular glasses. He had tied his black hair in a bun with a few loose bangs drooping above his eyes. His skin was olive-tan, and his eyebrows were angled. James turned his head to glance at Matt and smirked. His sapphire blue eyes caught Matt's attention the most. He never had an incentive to comment on the beauty of other people's eyes, but James' eyes left him speechless.

"Matthew, if you could give us some time, I'd still like to interview Mr. Salamar," Streak's voice pierced through his thoughts.

"Oh, yeah." Matt took a step back and headed for the door. "Thanks for the opportunity."

He closed the door and leaned against the hallway wall. He could only feel weights on his chest.

Matt explored the bookshelf in the breakroom while he waited for Streak to call him back. As expected, nothing caught his interest.

The door opened behind him, and someone walked toward the kitchenette. Matt turned around and caught James pouring himself a cup of tea.

That was a quick interview...

Matt felt obliged to start a conversation with him since they would be training together—if only he didn't have social anxiety.

Just do it.

Matt walked over quietly and opened the cabinet to pull a mug out. James steeped his tea, then brought the cup to his lips.

"What kind of tea do you like?" Matt asked abruptly.

James flinched and coughed, then put his mug down. "Damn," he cleared his throat and glanced at Matt, "I hope I wasn't ignoring you. I'm sorry."

"Oh, no, you weren't," Matt replied. "I didn't mean to scare you."

"What? No," James scoffed. He cleared his throat again and pushed his mug aside. "I should be the one apologizing. I interrupted your meeting with Mr. Streak earlier. You're Matthew, right?"

Matt nodded. "James?"

He smiled and held out his hand. "I suppose we'll be working together," he said as he shook hands with Matt. "Hm. *Matthew*...I like that name."

"Uh," Matt forced himself to smile, "thanks?"

"It's not really unique. Quite common. But there's something about it," James mumbled. He looked toward the ceiling. "It sounds saintly. Like one of the apostles."

"I guess." Matt subconsciously picked at his nails. He urged himself to go with the flow of the conversation.

"It's nice," James continued. "Are you Catholic?"

"Yeah. I mean, I don't go to church, but..."

"It's a part of your identity," James remarked. "You're not openly religious, but you still treat it as an important piece of your history. You have your beliefs, but you value your own ideologies above what others preach."

"I—" Matt paused and nodded slowly. "That's a good way of putting it." Small talk was not his forte, nor did he excel in keeping eye contact with others. But James' eyes held his gaze, and his nonchalant talking eased Matt's mood. "What about you?"

"I'm not quite sure," James answered. "But I like to be open-minded. I study a lot of religions."

"I see," Matt said, trying to hide his awkward tone. "Why do you study it?"

"Why not study religion? It's everywhere. And you can learn so much about the way the world works from it," James replied, then sipped his tea. "Religion will always be a crucial part of our lives. Just look at how many wars were caused by the concept of creed. Think of all the lives lost over conflicting faiths. I'd say it has left its own stain on society."

Matt froze uncomfortably. Political discussions were simultaneously his fascination and his bane. At this thought, he wondered if Optyma's religion had anything to do with its fall.

"So, why do you want to work at Streak Corp?" Matt decided to ask instead.

"It pays great," James said. "And I know a few people who work here."

"Me too. My sister is the general manager."

"I'm supposed to meet her in a few minutes, actually. If she's anything like you, I already have a good impression of her," James told him.

Matt blinked, and his cheeks reddened.

"I look forward to working with you, Matthew."

James waved goodbye as he departed. Matt waved back, then glanced at the mug his new coworker left behind. He pondered James' previous words reluctantly, yet as much as he wished to stray from the subject, it always came back to him.

Nothing could convince him that history wasn't just another name for war.

Chapter 16

THE KNIGHT IN SHINING ARMOR

Matt found himself in the field of yellow chrysanthemums. He followed the direction of the breeze and came face-to-face with the lady in blue.

Blue Jay.

"Why am I here?" he demanded, watching the loose threads of her dress blow through the wind.

"*You need to wake up.*"

"Why?"

"*The night is calling,*" her voice echoed. A smirk crept from the corner of her lips. "*And questions remain unanswered.*"

"I need to find the sniper," he muttered, "but I don't know what to do."

"*Maybe 'you' don't.*" She grinned. "*But 'Speedfire' might.*"

Matt jolted out of his slumber, his heart racing. He threw his sheets off him, then faced the closet. He crouched in front of the doors, shuffling through his gear. He pulled his jacket, belt, pants, and mask out. He dug around his laundry and realized what he was missing.

His fire dagger.

Matt had crafted his weapon nearly two years ago. The fire-based dagger required a piezoelectric crystal, a compressed liquid form of methane, fire-resistant steel, and a leather handle. Within the handle was a compacted quartz stone, and with a click of the mechanical button, the quartz would ignite the weapon's blade as soon as the methane touched it. He *needed* to get it back.

The apartment hallways were usually quiet at this time of night. He descended the dim stairway and passed through the lobby. A man and a woman stood beside the elevator, deep in conversation. They paid no attention to Speedfire as he sped through the foyer and out through the doors.

He sprinted down the street, close to where the shooting had occurred. His stomach twisted as he crossed the road and looked out toward the bay. He still wondered if luck had been on his side that night.

Matt took a turn and entered the uncanny alley. A cat digging through the dumpster for scraps caught his attention. Perhaps his dagger had fallen in with the trash. The dark gray cat twitched, then jumped away as he approached it. Matt reluctantly shoved his hands through the scraps, scavenging like the cat had moments ago. He pushed through to the bottom of the dumpster, then paused to peer around the area.

Nothing.

The cat meowed, eyeing him with its pupils dilated.

"What?" he asked it.

The cat approached him slowly, then batted at a half-eaten fish. It stuck its nose out, sniffing the area for food.

"I wish I had something. I'm sorry," Matt whispered. He took his fingerless glove off and held his hand out to the cat. It sniffed his fingers, gazing at him with its piercing green eyes. "If I find what I'm looking for, I'll come back."

The cat hopped onto his lap and purred against him. He sat there, motionless.

Shit, Matt panicked.

The cat squeaked and closed her eyes. Matt sighed, defeated. He stroked the cat's black-spotted back.

"Okay, fine."

He stood up with the cat, then helped it onto his shoulders. She wrapped herself around the back of his neck and purred lightly.

"Hang on," Matt muttered, then grabbed onto the nearby fire escape. He pulled himself up, and the cat clutched onto his shoulder. Maybe he needed to get a better view of the area. He could have been searching in the wrong alley.

He hauled himself up the roof, careful not to roll over. He stood and glanced at the piers, then peered toward the north. The cat perched herself upon his right shoulder, taking over half his view.

Matt reached to take his mask off but stopped as he heard sudden footsteps behind him. He turned around while the cat clung to his shoulder. A dark figure lingered on the other side of the roof.

Same black suit and violet eyes; the sniper stood still, then tilted her head.

Matt's heart skipped a beat. "Don't shoot!" he shouted, holding his hands up. "I'm not here to fight."

The Rare Sniper stayed silent, locking eyes with him. Her hand hovered over one of her pistols.

"I'm looking for something. Don't...blow me off," he begged. He felt more concerned for the cat's safety.

The sniper held up a knife by the handle, where it dangled in her grip. Even in the dark, he recognized the weapon as his own.

Matt caught his breath. "How'd you find it?"

She refused to speak. He glared at her as she dropped the dagger, then she kicked it over to him. The knife slid across the roof and skidded into his boots. He bent over to pick it up, keeping his eyes on the sniper.

"Why did you give it back?" Still, he garnered no response from her. "You have better weapons, right?" he mocked. "Where's your rifle? Who are you attacking tonight?"

She took a few steps toward the edge, then sat down. "Nobody." Her hoarse voice echoed in the air.

Once Matt clipped the knife to his belt, the cat hopped into his arms. He stood there for a moment and watched the sniper. The breeze ruffled through the feathers of her cape.

"Then what are you doing?" he asked.

The Rare Sniper ignored him as she watched the waves wash upon the harbor wall. Matt shot another glare at her, even though she refused to look at him. Maybe this was why he experienced the dream earlier with the lady in blue. This encounter could give him answers.

"Why did you kill Jack Lainey?"

She drummed her fingers against the rooftop.

"Did you poison him in the hospital?" he continued, cradling the cat. "Were you going to attack Harry Faresoul, too?"

The conversation remained one-sided as the sniper paid him no attention, and he despised her more for it.

"*Answer me*," he demanded.

"You want to save the day, right?" she said, then shifted her gaze back to him. "You want to be New Harbor's knight in shining armor?"

Matt stood there silently, dropping his shoulders.

"Go on…" She spread her arms out. "*End me.*"

His eyes fell to the pistols attached to her belt. He kept silent.

The Rare Sniper lowered her arms, then resumed her viewing of the harbor. "Coward."

"I don't kill people," he mentioned bitterly.

"Good. Once the blood is on your hands, you'll never be the same." Her guttural tone plagued him.

Matt got his knife back. He did what he set out to accomplish.

He could end her, however. He could take her down before anyone else gets hurt.

But *she* wanted to spend this night watching the harbor instead.

Matt left quietly and lowered himself down the fire escape with the young cat. He landed softly, then walked out of the alley, back toward his familiar street.

The wind drifted against his hood, fluttering across his bangs. It felt too unnatural.

He turned around to face the building. The sniper was already gone.

Matt slept undisturbed as the morning sun drifted through his curtains. He felt a lump on his chest, then fluttered his eyes open to see the kitten from last night curled on top of him. After he stared at it for a solid minute, he realized he was still wearing his Speedfire gear.

He smelled coffee outside his room and heard Madeline humming to herself as she walked through the kitchen. His heart raced.

Speedfire. Lost kitten. Rare Sniper.

"I'm so stupid," he hissed.

Madeline swung the door open with a mug and a great smile. She froze upon seeing him, and her smile dropped into a panicked gape.

"Matt, what the hell is *that?*" she shrieked.

The cat perked its ears and glanced over at her.

"What the hell is what?" he replied.

"That!" She pointed at the cat. "Where'd you get that cat? And why are you sleeping in... *that?*" She gestured toward his suit.

"Maddie, you won't believe it," he said as he stroked the kitten. "I'm a cat whisperer."

"Where were you last night? Did you just randomly adopt a cat as Speedfire?"

The cat stared at her as Matt propped himself up on his headrest. "She chose me, Maddie."

"Okay, but did you get cat food? A litter box?"

"I will," Matt assured her. "I had a weird night."

Madeline shook her head and walked away. "Mr. Streak told me about your new job, by the way," she called out. "When do you start?"

"I don't know!" he yelled back.

"You should stop by today and ask!"

Matt huffed as the cat crawled off him. He would rather spend the day with his new companion, but Madeline was right. This job was his responsibility now. He groaned and rolled out of bed.

"You'll be starting next week," Streak told him.

Matt stood across from Streak's desk with his new employee card. "Already?"

Streak nodded. "With James. You will be working under Ms. Kreene."

Later that day, Matt caught up with Harry in his office.

"Matt," Harry stuttered, "you're going to think I'm crazy, but I have an idea."

"What?" Matt held back the temptation to tell Harry about his encounter with the Rare Sniper last night. He didn't know how to explain anything without Harry freaking out.

"I'm going to try something," Harry continued. "Uh, with Sal-Tech and Streak Corp."

Matt tilted his head, confused. "Try what?"

"Okay. So, I checked Jack's emails today. Someone from Sal-Tech bribed him into selling Streak's blueprints," Harry explained.

"Who bribed him?"

"I dunno," Harry mumbled. "Their email had no IDs linked to it. They only signed their messages off as 'Whip-Master.' But that's who Jack sent the blueprints to."

Whip-Master. The sound of this Sal-Tech alias vexed Matt already.

"And I have another possible lead on the sniper," Harry continued. "The more I think about it, the more I believe she's Optyman."

"Yeah…" Matt said quietly, his gaze moving to the side. He thought of her feathered cape, and his mind drifted to the discussion he had with Christine about her Optyman ancestry. "Without a doubt…"

He wondered if relentlessly accusing the Rare Sniper of being Optyman would further hurt the population in the city. She was just one criminal—New Harbor's most-feared felon—but even one person could ruin the reputation of a whole community.

And the masses loved to hate.

"Now, get this. Optyma has a long history of assassins," Harry explained. "One of their leaders even hailed from a lineage of assassins. The Arch-Ambassador."

Matt leaned back in his seat, curious. "Go on."

"Ambassador Alazne Fatalis was the right-hand of President Jake Agnes," Harry said. "And I heard she was brutal during the war. Aside from the president himself, she had the highest body count on the battlefield. Slaughtered *hundreds*." He tapped his hand against the desk. "Granted, any war details are fuzzy, but it's believable. Assassin and all, right? Well, Ambassador Fatalis has no known surviving family members. But there were a lot of people who went missing during the war. Even a decade later, and not everyone who survived has been accounted for."

Matt rubbed his thumb against his index finger, then glanced at the window. "So…do you believe the Rare Sniper is an Optyman assassin? Maybe even someone who fought in the war?" he asked. Harry nodded. "What if she's a Fatalis?"

"Possibly," Harry agreed. "That's what I'm saying. So, we take *that*, and now let's look at this *Whip-Master*. Someone has been coaxing Mr. Streak's employees into giving away intel related to Optyma."

Matt rested his hands under his chin. "Basically, we're dealing with an Optyman assassin who has a vendetta against Streak Corp. But why?"

"That's what I'm trying to figure out," Harry said. "So, what if I try something like that? Sell information to this Whip-Master, get caught, then see what happens. I've already got their email on file."

"*What?*" Matt gasped. "You're going to risk your job!"

"I am."

"And your *life*, maybe," Matt argued. "Are you crazy?"

"Look, this isn't my dream job. And I...I just want this all to be over."

"You're at a breaking point..."

"Yeah. And, well, it's worth the risk," Harry said. "If this gets us closer to stopping the Rare Sniper, then I'm willing to try."

"You're still crazy."

"It's worth it," Harry repeated. "It will take me a few days, but when I do, will you have my back?"

Harry's eyes watered pleadingly. Matt sighed and nodded.

"Fine," he said. "I'll be there." He placed his hand on Harry's shoulder. "But you need to look out for yourself, too."

"Oh, please," Harry mentioned with a shy grin, "I've been doing that my whole life."

Chapter 17

Meeting a Ghost

Matt stayed occupied over the next few days as Harry launched his plan. His free time dwindled with each passing day, yet he considered the benefits of working at Streak Corp. He could get closer to the scandal as an official "employee."

Jack Lainey was not the first victim caught in these corporate crosshairs. And he would not be the last.

In the meantime, Matt cared for his new cat. He named her "Kiwi" for her dark gray fur, black spots, and small size. She was less than a year old, so he had no idea how much more she would grow.

At night, he pursued more criminals as Speedfire. He had yet to run into other vigilantes, though he heard that most "heroes" in New Harbor performed in broad daylight. As Matt recalled, they liked the publicity.

The news captured more stories about Speedfire as he saved innocents from local thieves and home intruders. Matt kept his eyes locked on the nighttime streets of Canton, Fells Point, and the Inner Harbor. Muggers, kidnappers, and gangsters who threatened the locals—he could not even count the number of felons he caught on his fingers this past week. He felt unstoppable.

One thing threatened this relentless feeling, however. Matt received an inevitable text from Harry.

Harry:

Matt, I got in touch with Whip-Master.

I'll send you the screenshots, but this is crazy!

> Mr. Streak has so much hidden on Optyma. I never realized.

Harry had collected confidential emails from nearly a decade ago, which discussed the discontinuation of weapons used during the Op- tyman War. According to the screenshots, Harry sold the info to the Whip-Master alias.

Matt:

> Ok, just be careful. Let me know if you need anything else.

Harry must have been working through the evening to hack into the emails.

For Matt, however, the beginning of the night was the dawn of his day. He had work to do as Speedfire.

As he texted Harry, he also watched the streets for trouble. Matt sat upon a tall building across the street from Streak Corp. The main headquarters shined like a beacon through the night, even with its tinted windows. He noticed someone leaving the building, and he would usually question late-night work, but this was Streak Corp. Some employees didn't return home until the next morning.

He checked the time after reading Harry's texts again. *Quarter to midnight.* Matt shrugged, then glossed over the emails. He was con- cerned about this "Whip-Master" more than anything else. Everyone seemed to have an alias in this whole scandal, including Matt himself.

"Up ahead. Look," a man's gruff voice whispered below.

"Careful. We're still too close to the office," a woman hushed back.

Matt glanced down. Two pedestrians dressed in gray hoodies stalked the sidewalk together. The man pointed ahead at the person who had left the headquarters.

"Wait until we're farther away," the woman mentioned. "Then you can jump her."

"How much do you reckon Jason Streak would pay to get his niece back?" the man chuckled.

Matt froze. He turned his attention to the sidewalk leading west into Fells Point. The small figure was shrouded in a light jacket and wore a simple black dress.

"Shit..." he muttered.

Matt stood up and stretched his arms. He pulled his mask up and darted across the rooftops, heading west. Christine didn't hear the two stalkers whispering from behind. But fortunately for her, Matt did.

The criminals slowed, quieting their steps as they crept closer to Christine. Before the man could jump her, Matt swung from a pipe screwed into the side of a building. He landed on the man, knocking him to the stone sidewalk. The woman jumped back in shock, and Christine turned around.

Matt swiped out his fire dagger, ignited the blade, then charged toward the woman. She balled her fists, swinging at him. He swerved under her hit, then rammed into her abdomen. She flew into the metal building and slumped to the ground. Matt stepped back, turning to face the man, who stumbled as he stood up. His eyes darted to Christine, who watched from a few feet away, stunned.

The man grunted, then paused. He eyed the fire dagger and shook his head. "Wait!" he gasped, backing up. He glanced at Christine, then returned his shocked gaze to Speedfire. "Don't—"

Matt gave the man no time to react. He ran forward, slamming the hilt of his dagger against the back of his head. The criminal collided with the sidewalk in seconds.

With both stalkers knocked out, Matt faced Christine. Her mouth hung open, and her eyes rested on his flaming dagger.

Matt held her gaze briefly, then went about his routine. He extinguished his blade, returned it to his belt, then pulled out his string. The wind howled restlessly, and he peered toward the harbor. A storm blew in from the horizon. He never enjoyed fighting in the rain.

Christine watched as Matt dragged the man over to his partner. He tied their wrists and legs, then left them leaning against the building. Once he finished, he faced Christine again.

"I overheard them planning to kidnap you," Matt told her, lowering his voice. She said nothing and stared at him, dazed. "So...I'll leave calling 9-1-1 up to you. Have a good night." He bowed, then backtracked into the nearest alley.

Matt blended in with the shadows, but he stayed behind until he knew she was safe. Christine didn't call out for him, didn't chase him. Instead, she stayed silent and did what she was told.

As soon as the sirens neared, Matt left the scene.

Matt had no energy to keep himself awake through the day. He found himself in the breakroom, where he planned to talk with Harry later. After a quick nap, he lifted his head. Christine sat on the other side of the couch with a book in her hand.

"I didn't mean to disturb you," she said as her eyes flickered to him. She set the novel aside.

"Sorry," he mumbled, then rubbed his eyes. "You could just wake me up."

"I didn't want to." She leaned back. "Are you alright?"

Matt nodded. "Just tired."

"Are you going to be like this when you start working?" Christine asked, concerned.

"No. I hope not." He scratched the back of his head. "I just have trouble sleeping."

Christine brushed a strand of hair behind her ear. "Maybe you need to go to bed earlier."

Matt faced her, already tempted to share his secret identity. *Hi, it's me. I'm Speedfire. I stopped those people last night from hurting you. You're welcome!* Something urged him to tell her, but at the same time, she was Jason Streak's niece.

Two other people knew who Speedfire was. And that was enough.

"I have insomnia," he said.

Christine blinked. "You could have said that sooner. Last time, your excuse was gaming."

He shrugged lightly. "I don't really like talking about it."

She sighed. "Now I feel bad. I'm sorry."

"Wait, don't be. It's okay," he stuttered. "I, uh...I take meds for it. My mom had insomnia, too. I guess it's hereditary. But I try to fight it."

Speedfire fights it, he thought smugly.

"Do your meds help?" she asked.

"Eh. Even if they did, I'm still a light sleeper."

"Oh." Christine wrinkled her nose. "Me too."

"What usually wakes you up?" he asked. He might as well shift the attention away from himself. Maybe Christine had trouble sleeping too, but if she did, she knew how to hide it.

"Weird noises, or my uncle working in the middle of the night."

"Strange dreams wake me up," he mentioned, leaning back.

"What kind of dreams?"

Matt held his breath with regret. Madeline was the only other person who knew about his dreams, and even she thought he was crazy.

"Well," he said, sinking into the couch, "someone visits me in my dreams."

"Who?" Christine asked curiously.

"This lady in a blue dress," he answered. "And we're always standing in a field of yellow mums." He held onto his arm, drifting off for a moment. Christine was patient and kept quiet. "She's young, always in blue. She's also got these bright blue eyes, like the sky."

Christine smiled. "Your mind sounds wild."

"That's what Maddie would say," he sighed. "She thinks I need therapy."

"No, not in a bad way," Christine replied. "It's cute. But I'm sorry it's keeping you awake."

"It's just a dream. I don't mind," Matt laughed. "But Maddie thinks I'm nuts."

"Well, you could be," she teased. "I wouldn't say that, though. You're not the only one who has dreams like that."

"I doubt it," Matt huffed.

"I've been visited in dreams, too. You know, dreams that feel so *real*. It's like meeting a ghost," Christine explained.

Matt paused as her words sent a chill through him.

Meeting a ghost.

"So, you've had dreams like that?" he asked quietly.

"Well, there's this boy. Maybe close to my age, I don't know," she started. "He dresses in black and wears a hood. When he appears, we're in a barren desert. And every time, there is an oasis we can never reach. Perhaps it's a mirage or just a futile destination."

Christine stopped and looked up with contemplation. Matt stared at her for a moment as he processed everything.

"That—" He inhaled lightly. "That sounds even weirder than my dreams."

"*Stop*," she remarked. "It *is* weird, but I don't see him every night."

"How often do you see him?"

"I saw him recently." She shrugged, then frowned. "But he's quiet. He hardly says a word."

"The lady in my dreams talks to me," Matt mentioned. "Sometimes."

"You see, they're still different."

Matt and Christine sat on the couch in silence for the next minute. Even if the dreams were drastically different, he didn't feel alone in his head.

"Um...speaking of different," Christine added, drawing his attention.

"Yeah?"

She frowned. "Something happened last night."

Matt gaped. *Speedfire*. Judging by how she looked away, she was thinking about the stalkers.

"What happened?" Matt asked, sounding as clueless as possible.

"I...I saw Speedfire," she stammered, fixing her eyes on him.

"You did...?"

"Yes. He kind of...fought some bad guys," Christine continued sheepishly. She rubbed her arm. "He really does focus on Canton and Fells Point, I guess."

Matt hid his smile and nodded slowly. "That's what I've heard."

Christine rolled her eyes. "Yeah, duh. You're all caught up on the vigilante news," she said. "But this was like a first for me."

"First what?"

"I don't know." Her shoulders sank, and she sighed. "Those people were after me...and he just..."

Matt leaned forward. "He just...?"

"He just *spawned*." She picked at a piece of fuzz from her dress. "I...whatever. Promise you won't tell anyone else. I called the police, and Detective Hu said he'd keep the whole thing in the dark."

"Is there a reason why?" Matt asked, confused. "I mean, I don't blame you—"

"My uncle hates vigilantes. And I'm not about to go bragging about meeting the new one," Christine exhaled, crossing her arms. "Besides, if

New Harbor finds out that Speedfire saved Jason Streak's niece, I doubt anyone would leave him alone."

"Leave who alone? Your uncle?"

"Speedfire."

Matt leaned back slightly. "Oh."

The door opened behind them, and Harry stepped into the room with an awkward grin.

"Hey, Christie," he spoke up and waved. "Mind if I talk to Matt privately?"

Christine scowled. "I should get back to work, anyway." She stood up and left the room without another word. Matt watched her go quietly. He didn't know why he wanted her to stay.

"Alrighty," Harry cleared his throat and sat beside Matt, "so, Whip-Master has the files. They want to see if the weapons have actually been discontinued or if they're just hidden underground."

"I still can't believe this," Matt groaned and buried his head into his knees. "I'm not liking this *Whip-Master*."

"They make me queasy too, but that's the whole point. And if anyone finds out about the hacks, all evidence will be pointing at me," Harry continued. "Man, I feel like a criminal."

"Yeah, what you did was a *little* illegal," Matt scoffed.

"I feel bad. Mr. Streak didn't deserve that," Harry sighed. "But I hope we can get some answers."

"When do you need me to watch over you?"

"Uh, cover me at night?" Harry said nervously. "Thank you, by the way."

"Don't thank me yet," Matt told him. He glanced at the door, which had closed behind Christine a moment ago. "We haven't even gotten to the hard part yet."

Chapter 18

Enigmas at Dusk

Matt sat in Madeline's office as he waited for her to finish her work. He wondered if she knew about Harry's plan, but on the chance that Harry had kept his lips sealed, Matt chose to say nothing of it.

"Matt, I'm sorry," Madeline muttered as her head fell into her hands. "I've got a lot to catch up on. How about you start heading back. I'll see you later before bed."

Matt frowned. "Are you sure? I can try helping."

"You wouldn't know what to do," she brushed him off, then sorted a few files.

Matt took that as if she wanted him gone. At this rate, he felt like a liability.

One of her many burdens.

The sun disappeared under the horizon as he left the headquarters. He walked further down the sidewalk, where he saw a pale man nearby with a large sign gripped in his hands.

STREAK BRINGS THE END!

Behind the protester sat two women huddled beside each other as they faced the headquarters. The older of the two women glared at Matt while the man continued holding his sign.

"Do you want something?" the older woman asked as she stood up. "Or will you report us to the police?"

"What? No," Matt replied, stopping abruptly. "I was just reading the sign."

The man lowered the poster. "And?" he said with a croaky tone.

"Can you tell me what that's about?" Matt asked, then pointed at the sign.

"As if it isn't obvious," the woman murmured. "You people are all ignorant."

"Wait," Matt stuttered, "I'm new here. I don't know everything about this city yet."

"You'll know what *they* want you to know," the woman seethed. "But nothing more. Nothing about us."

Matt sagged his shoulders. "Well, tell me something, at least. I don't want to come off as ignorant."

The protester nodded toward the headquarters. "Jason Streak and his company have too much control," he mentioned with a Mid-Atlantic accent.

"Too much control over *Baltimore*. And the military," the younger woman emphasized. She stepped forward and met Matt with a sour gaze. She was shrouded in tattered black clothes and a gray cloak. "Their power is a problem."

The man gripped his sign. "That family fueled the destruction of Optyma."

Matt glanced over his shoulder, then faced the activists again. "Are you all Optyman?"

The older woman nodded. "We were."

"I'm sorry," Matt said quietly. His gaze fell to the ground. "I don't think Jason Streak wanted to see a nation fall like that."

She scoffed, "He is a prodigy. He continued what his parents started."

The man faced Matt. "Do you work for him?"

"Uh." Matt paused. "My sister does." He didn't want to admit that he was working for Streak soon. That was the last thing these people probably wanted to hear.

"So, she supports it," the protester continued breathlessly. "She supports what happened to us." He raised the sign higher as the older woman held his shoulder.

Matt tensed. "She would never support a war."

"Then why does she work for a weapons manufacturer?" the girl seethed. "She works for the people who brought East Optyma to its knees."

Matt stepped back. "You three were East Optymans..."

Silence followed the group. The Optyman War was a civil war, one started by President Jake Agnes and his sister, Senator Kayla Agnes. From Matt's understanding, the nation had politically split in two once the war was waged. While Kayla Agnes rallied her people in West Optyma, Jake Agnes held control over East Optyma with his followers. Yet after the war, anyone who was "Optyman" struggled as a refugee, whether they were an Easterner or a Westerner.

Regardless of the outcome, Optyma had fallen, and both sides had sought refuge in the remains of Baltimore.

The history of New Harbor and Baltimore fascinated Matt, but as he feared when he first moved to this city, it was a constant reminder of his parents.

"If it's not too much to ask," Matt said as the younger woman turned her head to him, "what do you think of New Harbor?" He wanted to ease the tension. "Didn't your president cause the war?"

"There is a reason for every war," she told him. "None of us would be here now if we never lost our homes."

"But New Harbor—"

"Optymans built New Harbor," the girl interrupted. "And according to men like Jason Streak, *we* destroyed what remained of Baltimore, even if this city stands because of us."

Matt fell silent as the people continued ranting. They had every right to lament.

"Jason Streak has New Harbor wrapped around his finger. Don't trust a single word from that man's mouth," the woman snapped.

"I understand. But he cares about the city," Matt pointed out. "He donates a lot—"

"He gives nothing to the Optyman people," the man rebuked. "He lets us suffer. Even though he has one of *our* stones."

The Core Stones.

Matt understood now why Christine was cynical toward anyone who mentioned it. Everyone had eyes on Jason Streak's Core Stone—especially the Optyman people.

"Would you take it back if you could?" Matt asked cautiously. Perhaps the Core Stone pilfered from General Fren was stolen by an Optyman. He would take any leads on the stones or the Rare Sniper.

The Rare Sniper is Optyman, he reminded himself. *Just like these people.*

"It belonged to our leader. All four of those stones should have rested in his hands. But that's not for me to decide," the man mourned.

The world referred to President Jake Agnes of Optyma as a madman. Matt despised the president himself for killing his parents, but someone from Optyma had spoken of the late tyrant with dignity and grief. He wondered if all East Optymans still admired their fallen leader.

"Those stones should be nowhere near Jason Streak," the girl added with disdain. "The fate of those stones should lie in the hands of our Lady. Only she should decide."

"Your god?" Matt said.

"She is the closest thing we have to 'God' in this world," the man assessed. "Klypt and her stones. Optyma was the closest land to eternity. To Paradise. Though now it is a land that belongs to the dead." He lowered his sign again. "You believe in the stones but don't believe in her?"

"What? No, I didn't mean—" Matt cut himself off and shuffled back a few steps. "I mean, I guess I do. I don't know."

"Everyone interprets religion differently," Christine interrupted from behind. Matt turned around as she approached them. "And to the rest of the world, Lapaism is rather outlandish. But not in a bad way. Just...different."

Lapaism—the Optyman religion. The practice focused on worshiping Klypt and the Core Stones. Matt hardly knew much about the dying religion, though it still had an influence over the world.

"As *his* niece, you would say that." The man scowled at her. "Our ancestors have encountered her. We hold those beliefs deep in our hearts."

"I like having an open mind," Christine said with a smile.

"Sure. Says the nepo baby. Your 'open mind' is a lie," the girl countered. "You completely disregard your Optyman ties, *Elerare*."

Christine's smile dropped. "It's a bit hard to express anything around my uncle."

"Well, whatever *Rare* ancestor you had in the past would be ashamed of you," the girl hissed, then turned away. "Shame on you for even keeping your name. You're a Streak. Nothing more."

Matt backed up quietly as Christine took all the attention away from him. He was speechless.

"You don't know me personally," Christine argued calmly. "I wish I could convince my uncle to help you—"

"Yet he still holds a Core Stone," the older woman cut her off. "Go and be the peacekeeper somewhere else. You're not Optyman."

Christine swallowed hard as she watched the three protesters walk away. She released a sigh, then sealed her lips.

"What was that about?" Matt asked, baffled. "I just saw them, and—"

"The Optymans in New Harbor don't like my uncle." She walked toward the water, and Matt followed her to the bench nearby. "And my uncle doesn't like them."

"I could tell."

"They've had it hard over this last decade," she said. "The Optyman refugees are still mistreated, even after they rebuilt New Harbor."

"But the war wasn't their fault."

"I know. It's because the world despises President Agnes. And everyone blames the Optyman people for letting their president and his sister cause the war, even if it was far beyond their control." Christine tilted her head as she eyed the pavement. "I'm guessing there weren't a lot of Optymans in Miami."

"I hardly knew any," he admitted.

"Well, it's different here. New Harbor is the home they built, and it's where most of them stay. But the whole world discriminates against the Optymans. Maybe it's because the war was recent history, and it's still affecting people today." She exhaled deeply. "Reasons why I'm too scared to wear a cape. I might get more than just dirty looks."

"Would people really do that?" he asked. "Do they just attack Optymans out of nowhere?"

Christine grimaced. "Seven years ago, a man slaughtered an Optyman family in Riverside. He was upset because he lost his son to the war. But when the man was on trial, he claimed that the family 'worshiped' Jake Agnes. He's on probation today."

"What?" Matt gasped. He glimpsed the headquarters. "If your uncle has power in this city, he should do something about it. He needs to help those people."

"He's not happy with the Optymans. Besides," she lowered her voice, glaring at the ground, "an *Optyman* is targeting his business." She glanced his way. "Isn't that right? So, why would he help them?"

Christine's eyes watered under the streetlamp nearby. Matt faced the ground in regret.

I'm sorry. I'm sorry. I'm sorry.

He couldn't tell if Christine was upset with the theory behind the sniper being an Optyman. She didn't seem too bothered during their talk at the Jasmine Garden, but maybe she tried to hide her feelings in front of Harry.

"Even if the sniper is Optyman, one person doesn't define a whole demographic," Matt said, lowering his shoulders. "The same goes for how people talk about Jake Agnes. The president and the sniper don't represent the Optymans."

"No." Christine brushed her hair across her shoulders and breathed in the humid air. "But they do define the Rare Souls."

"They mentioned your name…" he said quietly. "Elerare."

"I use it for my father, and that's it." She cast a disheartened gaze at the water. "Not for Optyma. Not for my supposed *Rare* ancestors."

"Okay, but that's kinda cool," Matt laughed slightly.

Christine raised a brow. "What is?"

"Having *Rare* ancestors," he said. "So many people wish they could be *Rare*."

"Eh, not everyone," she exhaled, then glanced at him. "But are you one of those people?"

Matt blushed. "Not really," he coughed. "But I guess…I don't know. Maybe fire powers would be neat."

"What? Like Speedfire or something?" she scoffed.

Matt tensed. "He's not *Rare*."

"I'm teasing," she said with a smirk. "You and your vigilante obsession."

"I'm not *that* obsessed." He held his breath, knowing he was spilling flat-out lies. "But what about you? If you were *Rare*, what powers would you want?"

Christine shook her head. "It doesn't even matter. I've held my uncle's Core Stone before, and whatever I wish for won't change reality," she muttered, staring down at the water. "Besides, people who dream of being *Rare* will never get the powers they want. You'll end up with something different, or maybe not. But you will be hated by society. You get epic powers, but at what cost?"

Matt's heart sank. "I never thought of it that way."

"The world will never see the *Rare* in a good light ever again. Thanks to President Jake Agnes," Christine explained, then sagged her posture. "And…the Rare Sniper now."

They remained silent and watched the colors of the sunset fade in the distance. The horizon stole the remaining hues of the fire.

"This is so weird. I'm sorry," Christine spoke up as she folded her arms.

"What—"

"I feel like we keep talking about personal things. And I'm not used to that," she admitted. "I just—I don't mean to seem strange."

"Wait, what? Christine, you're not the weird one," he joked.

"Maybe. You'd have to know me more," she laughed. "But it feels nice having someone to talk to."

"About anything?"

"Yes." She exhaled softly and smiled. "I don't know if you feel the same. You have your sister."

"I do. But I can't say everything around her."

"Because she thinks you're crazy?"

Matt shrugged, then nodded slightly. "She doesn't mean to be harsh. She wants what's best for me, and I get that. She just doesn't understand me as much."

"Oh. I see."

"And she has bipolar disorder," he continued. "She hides it a lot. But she goes through mood swings."

"I wouldn't have guessed," Christine said. "She's usually sweet."

"She is. I'm not saying it's a bad thing. She doesn't have control over it, so I try my best to support her," Matt admitted. "Some weeks, she's upbeat, ready-to-go, and appreciates everything around her. But then there are other times when she's..." He wrapped his arms around himself.

"I think that shows how much you love her," Christine expressed. She shared a soft gaze with him. "Her flaws don't define her, just as your flaws don't define you."

Matt closed his eyes and let the breeze guide his feelings. He never realized how much he needed to hear that.

Matt and Christine admired the rest of the evening sun and the gentle wind against the edge of the harbor. From the corner of his eye, Matt spotted a figure across the street—a young blond man in a sweatshirt. The mysterious figure stood in the distance and watched the headquarters. Matt glanced at Christine, and she also caught sight of the individual.

They had no idea how long he was standing there. He blended in perfectly with the streetwalkers, and after a long moment, the blond man strode further into the neo-city.

Enigmas from all over New Harbor seemed drawn to Jason Streak.

Chapter 19

Salvation Has its Call

Matt returned to his apartment to suit up, then patrolled the streets again as Speedfire. He stopped a couple of bullies from harassing a pair of teenagers near the outskirts of Canton, then kept an eye out for the mysterious stalker he saw earlier. Before Madeline came home, Matt settled in bed around midnight, then pretended to be asleep when she opened the door to check on him. After she had gone to bed, he snuck out of the apartment to do more patrolling.

He eventually crawled back into his sheets before sunrise. Sleep never came to him, even with his eyes closed. Matt rolled out of bed, caught his balance, then walked to the living room. He rubbed his eyes and noticed Madeline's door wide open.

He peeked inside, finding Kiwi perched on Madeline's bed. Her dusty paws left litter crumbs on the sheets as she licked her legs.

"Hey!" Matt ran over to his sister's bed.

The cat's ears perked. She meowed as he scooped her up in his arms.

"You're not allowed over here," he scolded playfully. Kiwi licked her chops, and he winced at her fishy breath. "Maddie doesn't want your stinky paws on her bed."

"What are you doing?" his sister asked outside the room.

Matt and Kiwi turned their heads. Madeline stood there with a grocery bag and a blank expression.

"You left your bedroom door open," he said.

"Do I have to keep it closed now?" she scoffed.

Before Matt could answer, Kiwi shoved her paw over his lips. "Mmhmm."

"Whatever. I got breakfast. Also, I might have to go down to the office today," Madeline mentioned as she walked over to the kitchen.

Matt left the room with Kiwi and set her on the sofa. "Why?"

Madeline huffed as she threw the bag on the countertop. "Mr. Streak said he's having more issues with Sal-Tech."

Matt stood there, frozen.

Harry. Sal-Tech. Whip-Master.

"Oh?"

"There was an email hack," Madeline continued. "He thinks he caught the culprit, so I might have to come in and cover some work for him."

"Maddie—" Matt stopped, then noticed his phone on his bedside table. He moved to grab it, then saw a missed call and several texts from Harry.

Harry:

> Mr. Streak caught me. I'm talking to him in a few minutes.

> I'm so nervous, dude.

> Call or text me back when you can. I know it's early!

"What's going on?" Madeline interrupted as she stood behind the couch.

"Do you know?" he stammered.

"Know what?"

"About Harry."

"Matt, can you calm—"

"Harry hacked the emails," Matt confessed.

Confusion clouded her face. "Why the hell would he do that?"

"He's trying to retrace Jack's steps so that he might be a target of the Rare Sniper. And if he does this, he can help *me* find her."

"When were you two going to tell me?" she shrieked.

"I thought Harry did," Matt groaned. "Please, just listen." Madeline crossed her arms and lifted an eyebrow. "These shootings have been going on for two years. Harry wants to end it."

"And what if the Rare Sniper kills him?"

"I won't let that happen," Matt snapped back. "*Trust me.*"

"I don't," she seethed. His heart dropped. She caught the look on his face immediately, then sighed. "Look, I do...I just..." She trailed off and shook her head. "I'm sorry. This is crazy."

"Yeah, I know you think I am," he muttered.

"Are you sure about this? What if I lose you?" she said.

"I've been doing work like this for years, Maddie."

"That's not what I mean," she countered.

"Then I don't care what you mean. I'm catching the Rare Sniper," he told her. "You can't stop me."

"I'm not." Madeline sat on the couch and rubbed her forehead. "What am I going to do? Harry just blew his job."

"He had a big reason to."

"I know. But also, I *don't* know. I wouldn't do something like that. What if he gets nothing out of this?"

"I tried warning him," Matt mentioned quietly.

"So?" Madeline shot him a glare. "You two are conspiring behind my back."

"As if you haven't done that to me," he bickered. "You dragged me to New Harbor with you."

Kiwi hopped down from the sofa and trotted over to her food bowl. Matt watched her briefly as Madeline looked at him, even more befuddled.

"What is *that* supposed to mean?" she yelled.

"You've been planning my whole life behind my back," he argued, then leaned back.

"Well, someone has to. And that's not what I did. You chose to come here, too."

"Did I really have a choice? Or was I pressured to?"

"Goddamn it, Matt. I've been taking care of you even before Aunt Lizzie died. Cut me some slack," she said harshly. "Sorry you feel like you don't have a lot of choices, but I've fought so hard to give you a decent life. And you just want to throw it all away."

Matt lowered his arms. He didn't need to hear his aunt's name at this second. She had passed away from breast cancer shortly after Madeline turned eighteen, and since then, the two have only had each other.

"Someone else could have fostered you," Madeline admitted, then peered toward the television. "But I didn't want that for you."

"I don't want to talk about it," he mumbled.

"Then why'd you bring it up?"

"You're the one fighting me on saving Harry's life."

"I'm not!" she groaned. "Save him! I'm not saying you shouldn't. I just hate being left in the dark. What is with you?"

"*Forget it.*" Matt turned away. "I'm going for a walk."

"Okay." Madeline threw her hands up, then reached for the remote.

Matt shut his bedroom door behind him. He breathed in and leaned against the wall. All he needed to do was prepare for tonight.

Matt switched into a casual blue hoodie and jeans, then left to stroll through the Inner Harbor. He walked from Canton and all through Fells Point to explore the most famous area of what had been Baltimore. The Inner Harbor was a spectacle, with ships docked along the silver piers and holographic displays hanging from the tall towers. He wanted to explore the historic sights of New Harbor with his sister, but they needed time away from each other.

Another day, another fight. But they would be talking again the next morning.

Matt drifted his gaze to the historic ships ahead. The maritime museum included vessels from as far back as the nineteenth century. He even spotted a few modern crafts that had partaken in the Optyman War.

Maddie would love it here, he pondered, shoving his hands into his pockets. His sister was always obsessed with war history.

He passed the museum, trying to distract his thoughts. Matt glanced up at the skyscrapers across the street. Holographic screens flashed a variety of advertisements, including ones dedicated to Sal-Tech.

Welcome to the Inner Harbor!

A smaller sign greeted tourists entering the most popular neighborhood of New Harbor, showing a cartoon boat riding the bay's waves.

"*Here in New Harbor, we utilize hydropower from Sal-Tech,*" a robotic, feminine voice echoed from the speakers. Matt walked along while some tourists stopped to watch. "*Directly beneath this harbor are hydroelectric power plants that draw water from the bay and generate electricity for the city. The flowing water runs through our rust-resistant pipes, bringing power to the city's generators. The water is then released back into the harbor, restarting the cycle safely and resourcefully. But do not be afraid for the fish, as Sal-Tech's safety nets keep the wildlife at bay!"*

Matt paused as the tallest screen changed to another Sal-Tech advertisement. A striking woman with long black hair and olive-tan skin waved to the crowds from the screen. She wore a navy-blue sleeveless top with a light blue hem and a matching split skirt—the notable colors of Sal-Tech. Matt eyed the screen, pressing his lips together. He recognized her from the various Sal-Tech commercials. This young woman was Kiera Salus herself.

"New Harbor is a pioneering city of change!" the hologram of Kiera announced. "Whether you live here or simply like to visit, your support for this city helps the environment."

Matt caught a few tourists out of the corner of his eye as they applauded the screen. Everyone seemed captivated by the tech company's CEO on-screen.

Kiera's advertisement continued, "Here at Sal-Tech, we invest in using renewable resources, and so should you. Switch to a Sal-Tech device today and find out what you can do to help the ecosystem. After all, every action makes a difference." She placed a hand on her hip, smirking as she pointed at the crowd. "Only *you* can save the world!"

Matt felt glued to the concrete as the holographic version of Kiera Salus pointed at him. While she was spewing a simple promotion for her company, he couldn't help but linger on her words.

He would never reach Sky's level of success in saving thousands of lives across the globe. No vigilante could, for that matter. Yet he did his part as *Speedfire*, focusing on helping the people of Canton, Fells Point, and the Inner Harbor. And he was intent on saving New Harbor, one scandal at a time.

Kiera's commercial faded into a different promotion for New Harbor's hydro-themed hotels. Matt took a deep breath, then turned around. Anxiety was building up inside him, but he needed to move forward. And perhaps Kiera's corny message was enough to make him pull his Speedfire gear out already.

He was intent on saving *his* world.

The night fell quicker than Matt had anticipated. Aside from the pickpocket he caught, he didn't deal with too much crime.

He remained seated on the edge of a rooftop and watched the head-quarters. Through several texts, Harry mentioned he was leaving the building not long after sunset.

Minutes after dark, Matt spotted Harry walking along the sidewalk. He grabbed onto a nearby pole, sliding down the side of the building.

"Hey," Matt exhaled, jogging across the street.

Harry faced him with disappointment. "Hey," he replied quietly. "Thanks for being here."

"Fill me in. What happened?"

"Mr. Streak's upset," Harry mumbled, then scratched his head.

"That's obvious," Matt said.

"I feel bad." Harry slapped his forehead. "I lost my job. And I don't know if I did anything right."

"What do you mean?"

"Well, after he found my employee ID linked to the email hack, he organized a one-on-one conference with me," Harry explained. "And I confessed everything, you know. I made it sound like I was secretly conspiring with Jack. And I lied. I told him I even helped sell the blueprints."

"And?" Matt gasped.

"Well...Mr. Streak believed it. He already consulted 'Whip-Master' about the issue," Harry continued. "But I'm a clear culprit now. And I don't know what to do."

"So, what next?"

"Ah. That's not all," Harry pointed out. "I offered to help Mr. Streak get the emails back, and we discussed things with Whip-Master over text. They wanted money and access to upcoming designs, or else they would leak the 'discontinued' weapons. Mr. Streak was pissed, man."

"And did he pay them?"

"No." Harry rubbed his nose. "Mr. Streak threatened to file a lawsuit against Sal-Tech *and* me instead. I...I fumbled and just spilled it all right after that."

"Spilled what?" Matt asked cautiously. He remembered why they were out here in the first place. He glimpsed the nearby rooftops—no figure in sight.

"I told him the truth and why I did it," Harry confessed. "I was trying to find the Rare Sniper. But I didn't say a word about you or Speedfire."

Matt stared at him, shocked. "So, what did he say?"

"He thought it was a bit *out there*. You know?"

"Oh yeah, I know."

"But he was nice about it. He knew why. He said he was still firing me, which was fair," Harry sighed, then looked up at the sky. "He hopes I find something if anything happens. But he doubted anything would come of it. Oh, but he said he would keep everything under wraps."

"How come?" Matt asked. He felt he was asking a million questions at this rate.

"Well, because I was trying to find a way to save his business, or at least save him from the Rare Sniper, he let me go off easy. He wasn't going to file anything against me or give me a bad name," Harry said. "Which was nice of him. I was scared for my future. But..."

Harry fell quiet, then started walking away from the area. He continued further down the street in silence. Matt kept up with his pace.

"But what?" Matt pestered on.

"I don't know," Harry mumbled. "Do you remember the news headlines when Jack died?"

Matt recalled the reporters had covered the incident around the Rare Sniper, such as her ability to manipulate the wind. They also investigated Jack Lainey's death in the hospital.

"I sort of do. Why?" Matt replied.

"Something was off about them."

"What?"

"His reputation," Harry admitted. "None of those articles or headlines mentioned anything about Jack betraying Streak Corp."

"They were probably focused on his death more than anything. I don't think they wanted to dishonor him."

"That's not my point," Harry argued. "He was a target because he stole those designs. I understand giving everyone their time to mourn, but doesn't the public deserve a *hint* of what the attacker's motives were? If the sniper is Optyman, and Jack was stealing Optyman designs, shouldn't that line up at all?"

"I...I don't know."

"It just seemed odd. Like, what if *I* died out of the blue? And even after a week or two, the media doesn't cover the scandal? Not even *once*? I was just thinking about that, and..."

Harry continued his rant. Meanwhile, Matt's focus began to stray. A pitted feeling in his stomach formed. He kept his eyes on any passerby across the street—dark figures ahead of them, behind them, across the road. His eyes wandered everywhere.

The sky shifted to black, the clouds covered every star in the sky, and the streetlamps were not bright enough to light the foggy street. His heart raced.

He realized the fog had spread slowly, swirling in the air unnaturally. Matt caught the movement in the corner of his eye—a figure amongst the rooftops. The layers of fog clouded the space around them. Even the streetwalkers nearby appeared dazed.

"Everybody, run!" Matt screamed. He threw himself in front of Harry. "Get down. *Now.*"

Harry ducked behind Matt as he stood guard. He realized this was how she had gotten away without being seen most nights. She found a way to use the wind to force the fog up from the water.

The patter of footsteps echoed across the street as several pedestrians ran. The fewer people that got hurt, the better.

Matt stood before Harry like a statue, peering up through the fog. The spectral figure stood on the roof with a rifle in one hand. Her feathered hood fluttered with the breeze as she stared at them, then she stepped off the building. She landed lightly on the other side of the road, flicking her hand to blow the fog away. No one remained on the street aside from the three of them.

The Rare Sniper strapped the rifle across her back, then watched them. Harry trembled uncontrollably behind Matt.

"Move," she hissed.

"Make me," Matt shot back with a glare.

She pulled out a pistol, aiming it at Matt. His eyes widened.

"*Move,*" she repeated.

His mind raced at a viable way out of this.

"No wind this time?" he taunted. "You have a Core Stone, yet you prefer the sound of gunfire."

She lowered the gun. Harry whimpered and covered his head with his arm.

"He's innocent," Matt continued. "Leave him alone."

"Make your move first," the sniper said, then stepped back. She returned the gun to her belt and spread her arms out. "Go on."

End me. Her words echoed in his head from that other night.

Matt took this opportunity to pull out his knife. He pressed the button, and the metal blade seared with flames. Harry gawked at it, then glanced at the Rare Sniper.

The sniper reached for her pouch and pulled out a luminous purple stone. The crystal resembled a transparent opal with a violet hue—something most people would only see in pictures nowadays.

The Core Stone.

The violet gem matched her purple irises perfectly.

"You've got a beautiful weapon, Fire," she uttered as she held out the stone. "I wonder *how* you got it back."

Her sarcasm aggravated him. He wondered why she gave him his dagger the other night only to taunt him now. He wanted to defend Harry and save him. He wanted everyone out of this mess alive.

"I wonder what it's like to have no empathy," he countered. "Maybe New Harbor's Reaper can fill me in."

The Rare Sniper lowered her hand with the stone. "I can tell you one thing."

"Really?"

"Your words mean nothing to me."

"Then why haven't you killed me yet?"

She swung her arm with a scream, sending a gust of wind into his side. She blew Matt further down the street, and he lost his breath. He landed on his back sharply, paralyzed. He forced himself to roll over, throwing himself up in time to see the sniper aiming her pistol at Harry.

"No!" Matt screamed as the shot rang out.

He stopped in his tracks. Harry grasped his bleeding leg as the Rare Sniper fled the scene. Matt gripped his knife, aimed, then threw it at her.

The dagger cut through the air. The sniper peeked over her shoulder, then tripped as she dodged. Once she got up, Matt ambushed her, slamming her back down. She took his arm, then twisted him around. She kicked him away as she pushed herself up—hardly a tussle.

Matt rolled on his back, groaning. He held his breath. She kicked his dagger away, then aimed her gun at him.

Harry screamed in agony behind him, but Matt continued staring at the pistol. That was all he could focus on.

"You have a choice," she muttered coldly.

The Rare Sniper glanced at Harry, then back at Matt. As she clipped the gun to her belt, she turned away. She summoned several strong gusts, blew herself onto one of the buildings, then glided into the city's depths.

Matt held his arm, spotting his knife on fire in the middle of the road. He crawled over to it, extinguished the flame with a click of a button, then ran over to Harry.

"I...I'm not dead," Harry cried out.

"You're okay," Matt assured him. He pulled Harry's phone out of his pocket and handed it to him. "Call for help."

"What are we going to do?" Harry stuttered. Tears streamed down his cheeks. "You should've gone after her."

Matt put pressure on Harry's lower leg.

"I'm not leaving you," he told him. "I made a promise to protect you. That's what I'm doing."

Chapter 20

THE SILVER WINGS

Harry was tucked in a hospital bed with his ankle wrapped in bandages when Matt and Madeline arrived. The nurse pulled over two seats beside Harry's bed and left to give the three of them a moment alone.

Harry leaned against his pillow. "Thanks for visiting."

"Of course," Madeline replied as she took his hand. "You doing alright?"

"Could be a lot worse right now." Harry glanced over at Matt. "Thanks, man."

"You don't have to thank me," Matt told him.

"Don't even start. I'm lucky to be alive because of you," Harry said. "I can't believe the Rare Sniper didn't finish me off."

Matt stared at Harry's bandaged ankle. "She shot your leg, but that was it."

"I thought she was going to blow my head off," Harry stuttered. Madeline gripped his hand a bit tighter. "Maybe she didn't do it because you were there, Matt."

"No, she did something similar with Jack. She shot his shoulder before she knew I was even in the area," Matt mentioned. "Did all her victims end up in the hospital? Did any end up dead on the streets?"

Harry looked ahead with a stern look of contemplation. "I think so...but most die in the hospital."

"Someone poisoned Jack," added Madeline.

Harry nodded. "The sniper raids the hospital to finish them off. Those victims would be alive today if security gave them better protection."

"But you said *most* of them end up dead?" Madeline asked.

"Yeah. I think three survived. I'm pretty sure they all left the state," said Harry. "One went out west to Utah. Another moved to some old Pennsylvanian town. I dunno where the last one hid. But I don't blame them for hiding."

"I'm sorry I couldn't catch her," Matt sighed.

"Hey, don't apologize. You made your choice."

Matt pressed his lips together and nodded quietly.

"I hope no one comes after me, though," Harry mentioned. "My family is visiting me tomorrow. They're all from New York. My ma and sisters."

"That's nice," replied Madeline. "I bet they're worried."

"I have too much to tell them," Harry laughed.

A light knock came from the door. The nurse opened it and peeked her head around the corner. "Mr. Faresoul, you have two more visitors."

"Who?" Harry asked, confused.

"Jason Streak and his niece."

"Oh, my God." Harry tried to sit up, careful not to move his ankle.

The nurse stepped aside. Streak and Christine walked in, and the nurse closed the door. Matt got up from his seat and stood closer to the wall to give them space.

"Mr. Streak?" Harry looked up and smiled slightly. "Hi. I wasn't expecting you to visit."

"I want to make sure you're going to be alright," Streak replied as he stood on the other side of his bed. "I heard something down the street as I left the office last night. A gunshot."

"Oh, yeah." Harry pointed to his bandaged ankle. "It was the Rare Sniper."

"What happened? You were fixing those emails with me just before you left," sighed Streak.

"Mr. Streak, I swear, the Rare Sniper is after you," Harry exclaimed. "I don't think she's done with me yet."

Christine took a spot beside Matt and folded her arms. He glanced at her for a second before he turned his attention to Harry and Streak's conversation.

"You're right," Streak muttered. He took his glasses off and put them in his pocket. "I'm so sorry this happened to you. I wish I could prevent these attacks."

"Maybe hire bodyguards?" Madeline suggested.

"What are bodyguards going to do against a sniper?" Christine spoke up as she lowered her arms. "They have lives, too. Human shields would just add to the body count."

Harry exhaled, "She has a point. I was just lucky to have Speedfire with me. The Rare Sniper ambushed us from a rooftop."

"Speedfire?" Streak looked back at Harry. Christine tensed. "You're talking about that vigilante, right?"

Harry nodded again. "He even interfered with Jack's incident. So, no bodyguards. We need someone to stop the sniper, period."

"Speedfire is the only one who's gotten close enough to her, apparently," Madeline mumbled, then let go of Harry's hand. She snuck a glimpse at Matt.

"What are you implying?" asked Streak. His eyes flickered to Christine. "Are you saying we should contact this 'Speedfire' and see what he can do for us?"

Harry and Madeline locked eyes before they returned their attention to Streak. "Yeah? Maybe we should," Harry said. He looked over at Matt sheepishly.

"I don't know if I could trust any vigilante. I have a friend in the police department that will help me with the investigation," Streak mentioned coldly.

"Mr. Streak," Matt spoke up. He took a step forward and glanced at his sister. "Your best workers are in danger. They have been for the past two years. The police haven't gotten anywhere."

"Then I will start a proper investigation myself," Streak told him. "I'm not placing my company in the hands of a vigilante."

Matt stiffened. Despite coming across the Rare Sniper more than once, he still needed to find a way to have "Speedfire" earn Streak's trust.

"Not even New Harbor's greatest detective can figure anything out," Matt argued. "What makes you think a private investigator will?"

"Is that not what Speedfire already does?" Streak's expression turned sour. "It's my company. I will decide what is—"

"Uncle Jason, what would you do if the sniper killed me?" Christine interrupted. All eyes shifted to her. "I feel like there's been a target on my back for two years now. I'm just wondering. What would you do?"

Streak stared at her for a long moment. "What do you think I would do?"

"I can't answer that," she said.

Matt was so focused on what could happen to his sister that he had not even thought about Christine. She could potentially be the most personal target of the sniper. If two random criminals could consider kidnapping Christine for money, there was no doubt the Rare Sniper would have her eyes on Streak's niece.

"What if the sniper is trying to send a message to you, sir?" Matt said. "She's picking off the employees that are closest to you. What if this becomes even more personal? The sniper is most likely Optyman—"

"She *is* Optyman," Streak insisted.

"Then answer her. What are you going to do?" Matt asserted.

"You think she would really target my niece?" Streak asked sternly.

I won't let her. Matt thought about what he wanted to say more than anything right now.

"What would you have me do? Beg Speedfire to watch over her?" Streak continued.

Christine's face flushed red. "*No,*" she coughed.

"Well, clearly, Speedfire is already watching over the area," Matt muttered. "I doubt you'd even have to ask him."

"At this rate, anything could happen," Harry added. "If you come across the sniper, you're ending up in the hospital one way or another."

"I'll look into it, but I came here to offer you your position back," Streak said. "I apologize for how I reacted yesterday, Harold. I understand what your intentions were."

Harry stared at him with a frown. "Thank you for the offer, but I don't think I'm going back."

Streak sighed. "I see." He straightened his posture and took a step back. "If you have second thoughts, my doors are still open, Mr. Faresoul." He walked toward the door and beckoned for his niece to follow. "I wish you the best of luck. Get well soon."

"Thank you, sir."

Streak opened the door and stepped out. Christine started to follow him until Matt grabbed her hand.

"Hey, sorry," he whispered. "Are you okay?"

"No." She turned back to him. "I need to go."

"Do you think we can talk later?" he asked urgently.

She scowled. "Maybe."

He let her go, and she left the room without another word. Matt turned back to face Harry and Madeline.

"So much to take in," Madeline groaned as she rubbed her eyes. "We're all targets."

"I doubt I am," Matt muttered.

"Dude, the Rare Sniper beat the shit out of you last night," said Harry.

"She didn't kill me, though."

"She almost did."

Madeline's eyes widened, and she glared at her brother. "This is getting out of hand."

"It was already out of hand before we moved here, Maddie," Matt hissed, then walked over to the window.

He glimpsed the city below; the endless traffic, the walkers who continued their daily routines, and the bay full of ships in the distance. The sniper lurked in the shadows of this city, no matter the time of day. She could be anywhere. And Matt had to stop her.

The people of New Harbor already knew about the Rare Sniper attack from last night. Matt lay in bed and scrolled through his phone with Kiwi in his lap. While she purred contently, he was feeling the opposite of relieved as he studied the recent articles posted on Oracle, including a segment from the city's local newspaper, *The New Harbor Sun*.

Speedfire Fends Off Rare Sniper in Canton Shooting
By: Natalie Tray

The harbor was surrounded by fog, and several locals were walking along the docks of Canton when they heard bouts of screaming and a single gunshot. In another surprise attack, the Rare Sniper had targeted yet another employee of Streak Corporation, but for the second time, newcomer vigilante "Speedfire" swooped in to save the day.

Harold Faresoul, 24, was walking along Boston St. when he encountered Speedfire. According to eyewitnesses, the sniper had approached the two from the rooftops, and after a quick fight with the vigilante, shot Faresoul in the ankle. Faresoul is now getting treatment at the

> Mercy Medical Center, and Speedfire has yet to give a statement on
> the incident—

Matt pulled up the pictures attached to the article. The area was covered in fog, but even through the mist, he could see himself standing against the sniper. The silhouettes were undeniably theirs, and even if none of the locals captured a clear shot of the sniper, he could still see the feathers poking out from her cape. She looked like a walking nightmare in the fog.

While he browsed through the other articles on Oracle, a text from Christine popped up on his screen.

Christine:

Do you still want to meet up?

Matt stared at her message for a minute, shocked.

Matt:

Sure. When?

Christine:

Now. Which apartment is yours?

Matt:

Leo Towers. In Canton.

Christine:

Give me a few minutes.

Matt put his phone down and continued petting Kiwi. He considered changing his clothes, so he got up and explored the options in his closet. Black shirt, black jacket, and cuffed jeans—the usual for him.

He left the apartment and waited underneath the canopy. In another minute, a motorcycle pulled up to the curb, and the rider climbed off steadily. Christine removed the helmet and shook out her tied-up hair. She wore a jean jacket, a purple hooded shirt, black pants, and brown boots.

Matt gawked at her bike. "*What?*"

"I have a spare helmet." She beckoned him over as she opened the seat. She pulled out an extra gray helmet and handed it to him. "Mind joining me?"

Matt tried his best not to shake with excitement. He climbed on the back, then held onto her waist.

"Where are we going?" he asked as she started the engine.

"Somewhere special!" she shouted back. She waited for a car to pass before she merged onto the road.

The lights illuminated the silver city at night; the perfect time for an evening ride as they soared past the streets of New Harbor. They rode beside the drifting water below. He took in the view and the crisp breeze against his face. Christine swerved from the harbor, and Matt stared at the evening sky. He admired the faint outline of the moon beside the incoming rain clouds. His face lit up at the array of sparkling lights in the night, from the city's rays to the few twinkling stars. They rode toward an intersection, stopping at the red light.

Matt's gaze wandered to an alley nearby. Two people huddled together under their cloaks, hiding from the impending rain. He didn't need to guess if they were Optyman. Their capes and tattered purple garments had said enough. He tried to keep his mood from drowning, and as the light turned green, they were on the move again. The rest of the ride would distract him, but this city's poverty lingered in his mind. He would check on those two people later as Speedfire. That was the least he could do.

They hit a small bump, and Matt held onto Christine even tighter to keep his balance.

He closed his eyes, imagining the sites around him as they flew by turns and glided down the straight lanes. The motorcycle slowed, and Matt opened his eyes as they approached a large park in northern Canton. The two-story townhouses that once crowded the neighborhood before the Optyman War had been replaced with apartments and expensive condominiums. Many buildings even belonged to businesses, including a tall museum across the street from the park.

The bike stopped in the quiet parking lot, and Christine hopped off. She helped Matt climb down, then hid his helmet in the seat again. She locked her helmet around the handles and put the keys in her pocket.

"What's this place?" he asked as they walked under the archway.

"Scintilla Park," she answered, guiding him toward the hill. "It used to be Patterson Park before the war, but they named it after an Optyman gulf."

Flowering bushes and leafy trees shaded the stone path before them. Upon the center hill stood a white marble monument of a woman in a long dress and a feathery masquerade mask. One hand of the statue clutched her chest, and the other hand held up a flame. A pair of dragon-like wings grew from her back.

Matt walked up to the bronze plaque in front of the monument.

> *In Honor and Memory of Senator Kayla Agnes*
> *June 15, 2010 - September 8, 2038*
> *This statue honors Senator Kayla Agnes for her efforts in the Optyman Civil War. As she led the forces of West Optyma against President Jake Agnes, she saved countless lives along the way. Thanks to her actions, the nation's legacy lives on in the heart of New Harbor.*
> *Her flame of guidance was not in vain, and the silver wings will remain.*

"What do the silver wings represent?" Matt asked.

"Optyma's symbol," Christine replied. "I'll show you. Over here."

She guided him over to the hill. From a distance, he assumed the flag had been an American flag but was surprised when he saw a purple flag with silver angelic wings instead.

"The refugees rebuilt the park to honor their nation's fall," Christine explained. "They call it the heart of the city. And the wings represent their goddess, Klypt."

Christine sat on the grass below the flag. He took a moment to watch the cloth flickering in the wind, then sat beside her.

"If my dad is still around, I wonder if he ever visits this park," she sighed.

"You said you were half-Optyman, right?"

"Well, he is half-Optyman. He used to live in Amsterdam. So, I guess that makes me quarter-Optyman." She grimaced. "But I might as well not even say that. Either I'm not Optyman, or that's all I am."

Matt thought about those protesters the other night. Even if she was related to Jason Streak, she had no control over her uncle's choices, nor did she get to decide her heritage. Regardless, Christine's ancestry intrigued him.

"Issac Elerare," she muttered her father's name, then huddled her knees to her chest. "Sometimes I come here hoping that he'll show up."

"I'm sorry," he said quietly. He could empathize with Christine. There were days he dreamed of his mother opening the door. He had dreams of being wrapped in her arms, dreams that he had yearned for so long now to be a reality. He found that he had wrapped his arms around himself.

She sighed, "I hope he just disappeared. I want him to come back so badly."

"Are you mad at him for leaving?"

Christine shook her head. "He probably couldn't stand the corporate life. Besides, I was too young to remember what my parents fought about," she said, wiping a tear away. "But I remember how he held me. How he poked my nose and would let me ride on his shoulders." She huddled her knees closer. "He and my mother yelled at each other a lot. I don't know why. But they would argue in front of me *all the time.*"

Christine looked up at the sky with a glower.

"I hope he's out there," Matt said quietly.

Christine glanced at Matt, then scooted closer to him. "Maybe he can take me away if he comes back. Not to Optyma, but maybe to the Netherlands."

"Do you want to leave?"

She nodded. "I do." She stared at the city, at its marvelous towers that lit the night sky. "I love this city, though. Baltimore...New Harbor is my home."

"I feel that way about Miami," he exhaled.

"Maybe you can run away back home, too," she added. "Back to *your* beach."

"My beach," he laughed and smiled slightly at the dream. "I never spent that much time on the beach. But I did love it."

"How come?"

"It was hard to go back after my parents passed," he told her. "My mom and I always hung out together in the shade while Maddie and Dad played in the water." The smile dropped from his face. "It's not the same without them."

Christine put her hand on his shoulder, and Matt turned to face her again. Even for a moment, he admired how the moonlight twinkled against her emerald eyes.

"It's like going to Amsterdam won't be the same without my dad," she added.

"Maybe your uncle can take you on a trip," he suggested. "Even if it's for the business."

"Uh. Yeah." She choked a bit on her words and nodded. "I guess he could do that." She got up. "Do you think my dad would have taken me if he knew I wanted to leave with him?"

Matt stood up beside her as she turned toward the parking lot. "I don't know," he said. He wished his mother had taken him with her. He knew that would have been impossible, but he could still dream. "I wish I knew him, though. He sounds like a good guy."

"He is." Christine stepped down the hill carefully. She paused to help Matt as well. She took his hand but let him go once they returned to the stone path. "I wish my uncle would acknowledge that, too."

She turned away in silence and continued back to the parking lot. Matt trailed behind her, struck by her words. Her voice sounded like ice with that last statement.

Matt decided to keep quiet as they returned to her bike. She pulled the helmet out and handed it to him. "Let's get you home before it rains," she said.

They left the park and rode through the swarming gusts of wind. The harsh breezes of the coming storm reminded him of the sniper's chilling guise. Anything that dealt with the dark assassin twisted his stomach in knots. To stay distracted, he locked his eyes on the foggy road ahead.

She stopped the bike in the parking lot of Leo Towers. Matt unclipped his helmet while Christine slid off the motorcycle to lift the seat.

"Thanks again for the ride," he said while she took off her helmet.

"No problem," Christine replied. She lifted her face to the sky and smiled as the rain washed through her hair. "I needed to clear my mind."

"Me too." He realized they didn't talk about the scandals or Harry. But Christine needed company, and Matt could give that to her.

Christine put her helmet back on, letting the sudden shower wash her worries away.

"You stay safe, alright?" Matt said. "Be careful riding home."

"I've ridden in the rain before. It's not as hard as it seems." Christine hopped back on her motorcycle. "Will I see you tomorrow?"

Matt huffed, "The day after tomorrow. I have one more day of freedom."

Christine snickered, "I bet you're thrilled. I'll stop by your department every hour just to bug you." She pulled out of the parking lot and sped off into the night, disappearing from his sight as the rain fogged the neighborhood.

He wished he could enjoy the wind and rain as much as she did. Maybe one day, he could again. Just in a world without the sniper. He slipped inside the apartment, leaving the night behind him.

Chapter 21

No Limits in the Dark

Matt spent his last day catering to himself by taking naps and calling Harry while he was still in the hospital. Harry had already read the articles about the Rare Sniper attack, and since the assassin hadn't come for him yet, dozens of reporters arrived at the hospital to get an even deeper scoop on the incident.

As Matt ended the call with Harry, he received a text.

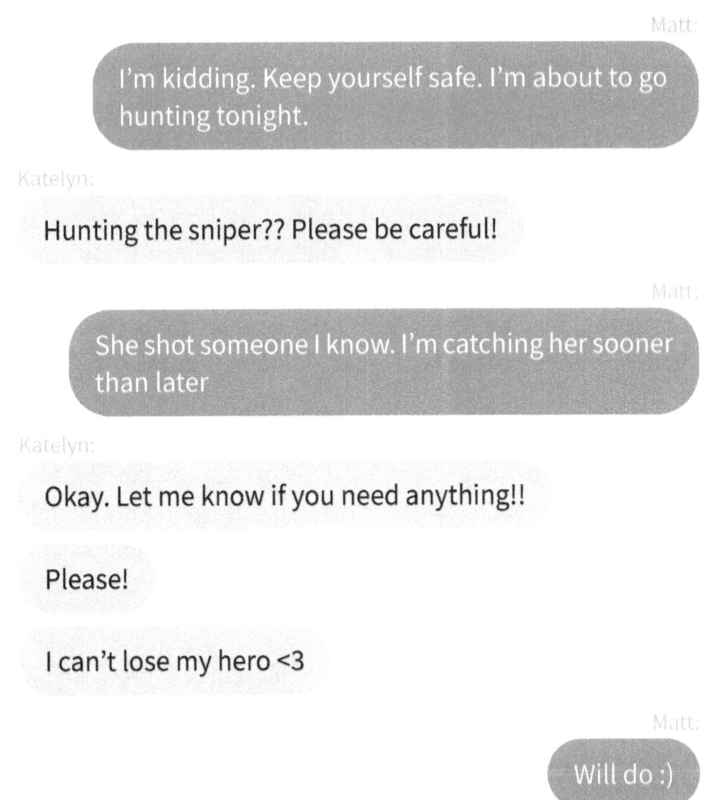

He sent his last text message, still guilt-stricken over Harry's situation. Harry shouldn't be stuck in the hospital. He shouldn't have been shot at all. There was one thing Matt needed to do tonight, and that was to make amends for his failure.

Once his sister returned home in the evening, Matt was off hunting for the Rare Sniper.

He knew she lingered in the neighborhood, stalking the innocents from above. But she wasn't defending them as he did. She was a monster under the moonlight, and Matt feared she was picking her next victim with each passing hour.

Even if the sniper had no targets tonight, he could still catch her. And he wouldn't let her slip through his fingers this time.

Matt scaled the walls of Leo Towers, then eyed Streak Corp down the street. He moved westward at first, keeping close to the alleys as he prepared to lift himself to the rooftops. The silver towers of the city twinkled with the rising moon, illuminating the whole harbor. As he observed New Harbor's architecture in the night, a sudden figure caught his eye. A hooded man lingered outside of the headquarters, and after another minute passed, he started walking away in Matt's direction.

The man shoved his hands into the pockets of his sweatshirt, skulking about and avoiding eye contact with the other passersby. He reminded Matt of that one individual from the other night. When he was outside with Christine, speaking with those Optymans, he noticed a young man stalking the perimeter of the headquarters. Perhaps this was the same person.

Matt crept into the alley and waited for the individual to pass. The hooded man walked along the sidewalk, closer to the harbor. He then looked both ways before crossing the street, blending into the night like an ordinary citizen. Matt stepped out from the alley, ready to follow him, then froze. Madeline stood there with her hands on her hips, glaring at him.

"Maddie!" he gasped. "Hey—"

"Where the hell are you going?" she lectured. "*Really?* Speedfire? Tonight?"

"There's a guy—"

"You're starting that job tomorrow," she cut him off. Matt winced, looking past his sister. *Gray hood. Black pants.* "Get back inside. I'm not having you do this again. Not after what happened with Harry."

"I thought we agreed that I should be out here," Matt argued.

Madeline looked over her shoulder, trying to catch what Matt was watching. "Hey." She snapped at him. "Can you do this another night?"

"No," Matt hissed. "I need to follow that guy." He walked around his sister, and she huffed. "He's been stalking the office. I've seen him out here before."

"Okay? And?"

"I don't know. Something's up," Matt said. "Here. I'll climb on the rooftops. Can you keep your distance and follow him from behind? Maybe cross the street. Don't make it obvious."

Madeline blinked. "Excuse me?"

"Thank you!" Matt called after her as he reached for the nearest fire escape. He hauled himself up as he heard his sister yelling from below. After a few seconds, she was quiet.

Matt rolled his shoulders, stretching as he watched Madeline crossing the street with a bitter look in her eyes. He smirked, then turned eastward to follow the hooded individual.

"I see him up there! Speedfire!" a woman cheered from the streets. Matt snuck a glance over his shoulder to see a group of three friends whipping out their phones. He rolled his eyes, then continued his trek inward to avoid the riverside.

Madeline kept a safe distance from the figure, wrapping her arms around herself as she followed him on the other side of the road. She observed her brother from below, avoiding any contact with the other pedestrians who joined in on the Speedfire parade.

The wind howled the further he traveled. The man quickened his pace and stayed on Boston Street, though his destination remained a mystery. Matt was prepared in case he took a sudden turn. As long as the individual didn't catch Madeline following him, this plan should work out.

Matt watched from above, leaping from roof to roof. He landed softly, then climbed up to a higher structure. He halted as he noticed another silhouette lurking three blocks across from him. The wind blew stronger here. His heart hammered as the feathers ruffled along the sniper's cloak, but he stayed put. He steadied his breathing when he realized she had yet to see him.

Instead, the Rare Sniper shadowed southern Canton. Matt didn't know her routine, but she was out tonight. And she was stalking someone.

He couldn't tell if she was pursuing the same individual he was, or if she was after a different target. Her rifle was left behind, as she only bore her dual pistols and the Core Stone on her hips. Regardless, he had his eyes set on her now. His sister was in the area, and he was taking no risks tonight.

The Rare Sniper stepped toward the edge of the roof, peering down as the rain started to fall. She remained unsuspecting of Speedfire as he crept closer. His mind still buzzed with endless questions, and he never felt more determined to get to the bottom of this case after what she did to Harry.

This is for him, Matt assured himself. *Do it for Harry.*

Matt sped forward as the gravel kicked up under his boots. The sniper turned around, caught unaware—

WHACK!

Matt struck the side of her head with his knuckles. She stumbled back, then caught her balance. Before he could strike again, she whipped around, kicking his stomach. The rain grew intense, and the surface became slippery in seconds. He reached for her, his fingers nearly grabbing her mask. As the sniper drew back, she slipped across the edge, and they plummeted toward the street together.

Matt closed his eyes as she pulled him into her, and a swarm of gusts swirled around them.

THUD!

He landed on the sniper. Madeline screamed across the street. The hooded man turned around in a panic when they hit the ground behind him. He bolted in seconds, slipping on the sidewalk as he disappeared behind a nearby alley.

"No…" Matt grunted, rolling over as the Rare Sniper shot herself up. He followed her, slamming into her before she could recover.

The sniper caught his elbow and twisted his arm around. He yelped as she lifted his arm, then kicked him away. Matt landed on his knees. He peered up at the crowd forming across the street. Madeline stood among the onlookers, her face petrified with worry.

He couldn't lose. *Not again.*

Matt forced himself back up, swiping his dagger out in the process. The sniper was already trying to flee. His boots splashed against the puddles on the street as he sped up to her. Matt clutched his fire dagger, keeping it low as he approached her. She turned around to catch his next act, but he swerved to the side, avoiding her block. Matt rammed into her again, then drove his blade toward her shoulder.

The sniper jumped back. She swung her fist upward, striking his chin. He fell backward as he lost his grip on the dagger. For a mere second, he saw stars through the cloud-covered sky. He staggered, standing back up. The Rare Sniper stood across from him, clutching his dagger. She clicked the button on the end of the handle, and the dagger burst into flames. Her gaze darkened, and Matt froze in shock.

"Speedfire!" one of the onlookers called out.

"You can do it!"

"Take her down!"

The voices drowned in the thunder as soon as the sniper bolted toward him. He couldn't deny she had murder in her eyes as she swung the blade. This was all a dance, the same as it was the night they first fought. He leaned back, swerving under her fiery swings. The rain doused some of the flames, and the longer he kept up with this dance, the sooner the fire would die.

More people joined the audience. Matt had no idea what he was getting himself into as this fight became public. He tripped over the curb, and he lost all balance. His back slammed against the street, and the sniper kicked him over. He grunted as she landed on top of him, and he lay still when the warm metal grazed the skin of his neck.

It was over.

The Rare Sniper held the doused blade against his throat, and he stared into her violet eyes with fear. He shuddered under her grip as she clenched the handle, breathing raggedly.

The sudden flashing of news cameras ignited the street, and police cars swarmed into the scene. The Rare Sniper looked at the incoming crowd, then glared back at Speedfire. She pushed herself off him, then darted further down the street.

Matt scrambled to sit up as he struggled to breathe. He turned to the crowd. Reporters waved to him, beckoning him over. The onlookers turned from a small gathering to dozens of watchers in minutes. And Madeline stood at the forefront, with her arms still wrapped around herself as she met her brother's gaze.

Nothing but tears of concern filled her eyes.

This fight would have been over any other night. But the sniper took his dagger with her.

"Damn it," he hissed. He ignored the calls as he turned toward the piers. The sniper leaped down the stairs, then landed against the docks with the dagger still clutched in her hand.

Matt followed her down, reaching the piers, yet landing roughly. Lightning blazed the sky, and the rapid waves of the bay crashed into the harbor wall. He pursued her, and she looked over her shoulder. She exhaled, then swung her arm back.

Matt lost his breath as the wind smacked him, and the gust threw him against the dock rails. All he heard was the ringing of metal as his head and back collided with the railing, and the Rare Sniper skidded to a stop when Speedfire fell into the Patapsco River.

Matt shot his eyes open. He leaned against the wall of a crammed, dark alley, drenched from the bay. A small ray crept into the space. The rain had stopped temporarily. Matt trembled, then looked at the faint light emanating from outside the alley. His heart stopped as the sniper sat there, glaring at him in the dark. She held the dagger in one hand, and in the other, he saw a bright glow from the purple stone.

He sat up, slipping slightly. "What happened?" he stammered.

The sniper remained silent as she twirled his dagger. Her cape was soaked.

He reached for his face. He felt the mask beneath his fingers but kept his eyes on her. "Did you—"

"No." She tilted her head, her eyes still narrowed. "I was just about to lift your mask, though." She dropped the dagger toward him. "Want to fight for your secret instead?"

Matt tensed as he glared back at her. "Is that why you pulled me out of the water? You couldn't let me go without knowing my face, right?"

She gave him dead silence.

Matt eyed the fireless dagger. If the Rare Sniper discovered his identity, she could link his actions back to Madeline. That would undoubtedly put his sister in the line of fire.

His back was sore from the impact, and his head throbbed. He didn't even know where the sniper had taken him.

"You started the fight," she uttered. "Now, *finish it.*"

Matt swallowed hard. He crawled toward his doused blade, then clutched it. In return, she whipped out a pistol and aimed it at him.

"Make your move first," she demanded.

He held his breath as he stared into death's eyes. A strand of her dark, plum-colored hair escaped her hood, resting against her shoulder.

"You're a cold-blooded murderer," he murmured. The sniper glanced to the side, watching what remained of the rain slither down a pipe. "You're never going to find peace."

The sniper rested her finger on the trigger. "I know."

Matt scowled. The only weapon he had was his voice at this point. The dagger would do nothing for him against her pistol. "You know? You're heartless. You put an innocent man in the hospital," he remarked, sitting up straighter. "You murdered another man just weeks ago. And that's all you have been doing. Targeting innocent people just to kill them when they're at their weakest." His glare deepened. "And that's all you have to say? You *know?*"

She tilted her head to the other side. "A monster understands its reflection." The sniper stood up swiftly. She stepped forward, eyeing him intently as he shuddered. "And it also knows its limits," she whispered. Her husky voice echoed across the walls, following the wind.

"Then do what you have to do. I lost," he admitted. "You got me."

Her scoff surprised him. "This poor, reckless boy has met his match," the sniper mocked. "Oh, Speedfire. This city looks to *you* to defeat me. I hear the people singing your praises. Imagine if I had left you in the Patapsco, or if I had slit your throat with your own blade. What if your body fell into *their* hands? And after all that, you're just going to admit defeat?"

"You have a *gun* pointed at my *head*."

"Oh." Her eyes fluttered to the pistol. "I do." Her finger returned to the trigger, and before he could react, she pulled it.

He closed his eyes, wincing.

Click.

Matt peeked his eyes open to find the sniper showing him an empty barrel.

"You're lucky," she said.

He shivered. "Why?"

"I only shoot my bounties." She stepped back, returning the pistol to her belt. "And you aren't my target."

"Yet," he countered.

"*Yet*," she echoed. She ran her empty hand along the wall, brushing her fingers through the remaining raindrops.

Matt leaned back, taking a deep breath. A gut feeling assured him that he would live to see another day. Tonight was not his last on this earth.

"Wow," he breathed out, and she returned a glance to him. "An assassin with *morals*. Who knew those existed?"

Her gaze turned sour. "Keep it up, Fire," the sniper threatened. She lowered her hand with the Core Stone, dropping her glare to the damp ground. "Someone with a brain should know better than to fight a *Rare Soul*."

Matt shook his head. "Sorry to disappoint you, but even the most lethal powers in the world can't keep me from coming back." Perhaps he did lack a brain, but he still had two fists and a beating heart.

"A cursed thing about being *Rare* is that you will never reach your full potential," she shared. "You're always finding something *new* about your abilities. And...I feel as if I make a new discovery every time I touch this stone." She opened her palm, letting the gem bask in the darkness. "You've become my test dummy the more you come after me. Did you know that?"

Matt fixed his silent gaze on her, listening warily.

"I noticed in the beginning that if I let my emotions run loose, I lose control of my powers. And you were frustrating me to no end. The wind can take your life if I let it," she said, clenching the stone. "So...let's see who catches who first."

Matt noticed a playful but bitter look in her eyes. Perhaps he was setting himself up for a trap, but this challenge was one he couldn't decline.

"That depends. Who would want my head?" he demanded.

The Rare Sniper stared down at him, balling the Core Stone in her hand. "Only the worst of the worst," she murmured. Without another word, she turned away, leaving him alone in the alley as the rain softly returned.

The hunt was far from over.

Chapter 22

Doomed Desire

Matt sat on his bed the next morning as Madeline covered his bruises with makeup. He closed his eyes, letting her brush the powder along his cheeks. He felt ridiculous, but he had this coming.

When he returned home after the Rare Sniper dragged him out of the river, Madeline was already waiting for him. The news had questioned everyone at the scene, including her.

SPEEDFIRE VS THE RARE SNIPER!

Their fiery fight ensues!

The public now had a clear image of the Rare Sniper, as the mix of onlookers and reporters caught enough pictures of her fighting Speedfire.

Madeline was forced to watch the sniper savagely beat her brother last night. She didn't even want to help him track the strange individual who stalked the Streak Corporation campus. Yet she still followed him, she still berated him, and she still tended to his wounds.

She avoided talking about the events last night and instead focused on covering the dark bruises along his head with a third coating. Her silence was more deafening than her lectures.

Less than an hour later, Matt walked with Madeline to the headquarters. When they entered the building, she patted his shoulder, then left to climb the stairs to her room. Still, she said nothing. As Matt approached Elaine at the front desk, James was already standing there with an employee card.

"Perfect timing," greeted Elaine. "I have some news for the both of you."

Matt grimaced. "What is it?"

"Due to a recent incident, Mr. Streak has pushed your positions back," she told them. "Starting next week, you will be training under Ms. Kreene."

The tightness in Matt's chest unraveled with her words. He had another week to himself.

"Why?" James demanded with an eyebrow raised.

Elaine's smile faded. "Ms. Kreene will be covering Mr. Faresoul's duties, so she won't have time to train today."

"This is ridiculous," James muttered. He shoved the card in his jacket and turned away. "He could have told us sooner."

"James, I think he's just concerned," Matt said. "Did you hear about what happened?"

"The shootings?" James looked back at Matt. "I don't live under a rock."

"The sniper is targeting people who work for Streak," Matt mentioned.

"Are you saying she'll go after us next?" James remarked. "I still don't see how holding off our jobs will help his cause."

Matt frowned. "You don't get it. He's worried about our safety. And Elaine just said Kylie is too busy to train us."

James removed his glasses, then narrowed his eyes. He took Matt's shoulder and guided him away from the front desk.

"I know what it is," James said, then crossed his arms. "You don't want to work here."

Matt froze. "Um. I do."

James tilted his head. "Your sister is the sole reason you're here."

"I'm just following in her footsteps," he stuttered.

"You don't have to lie." James stepped back and gave Matt some space. "Not to me."

Matt's posture sagged. "How do you know?"

"I could read your eyes. You're thrilled to have your job delayed," James said. "But I'm not."

The elevator doors opened down the hall, and Streak and Christine stepped off. While he wore a black suit with a gold tie, Christine sported her red dress today. She held a clipboard and rushed to her uncle's side, keeping up with his long strides. Matt turned back to James and saw his eyes locked on them.

"Great timing," murmured James.

"He looks busy," Matt pointed out.

"What a shame," James sighed. "He still wasted our time this morning."

James stepped toward Streak and Christine to meet them. Matt trailed behind him with uncertainty.

"Mr. Streak," James called over to him. "I was told you pushed our start date back a whole week."

Streak stopped in his tracks, and Christine nearly bumped into him. "I hope it isn't too much of a bother," replied Streak. "With losing two managers this month, we're a bit tight on schedule."

"See?" Matt nudged James.

James scowled at Matt, then turned his attention back to Streak. "Of course," he expressed with a fake smile. "I would have liked to help Kylie out with the workload, but I understand."

"Since you two are now off the schedule, I'm hosting a public rally outside of Scintilla Park at noon. Regarding all these attacks, I want to assure the people of New Harbor their safety," Streak mentioned. "You two are welcome to come, of course."

Matt gaped, then looked over at Christine. "Will you be there?"

She nodded. "I helped him schedule it."

"What's the rally about?" James questioned, dropping the feign grin.

"An update regarding the Rare Sniper and the Core Stone," Streak told him. "I'm certain you saw the news last night, just following what happened to Mr. Faresoul."

"I saw snippets. We finally have some clear shots of the sniper," James replied. Matt stood beside him uneasily. Even if the makeup covered the bruises left on his face, his whole body felt stiff and sore. "She's terrifying, isn't she? Dresses like a crow, can blow her victims across the city..."

"And the presence of a monster like the sniper is exactly why I must make a public appearance," Streak stated.

A monster understands its reflection. Her words haunted Matt, day and night. Even as Speedfire himself, he had nothing to contribute to this conversation. He wanted to slip away and hide in his sister's office.

James nodded as he turned his gaze to Christine. "What about you?" he asked with a smirk, catching her attention. "What did you think of the fight last night?"

"Oh..." Christine lowered the clipboard in her hands. "I actually saw some of it." Matt tensed as he looked to the side, avoiding eye contact with her. "When I left work, I heard a lot of commotion. And everyone was shouting at something down the street."

Matt should have known Christine was among the many faces in that crowd last night. Possibly a few employees of Streak Corp had also followed her toward the suspense. He hadn't even noticed her, although the surrounding faces blurred in that moment. His focus had only been on Madeline and the Rare Sniper.

"It was intense," Christine continued, glancing at her uncle. "I guess it was only a matter of time until New Harbor got to witness a fight between Speedfire and the Rare Sniper."

"At least you kept your distance. You didn't get hurt, and neither did anyone else besides...those two," Streak mentioned as he patted Christine's shoulder, and her gaze dropped to her clipboard.

"But what was it like?" James asked. "Seeing New Harbor's most deadly felon in action. Knowing you were safe in the crowd, witnessing something like that must have been exciting."

"I...I wouldn't say that," she said sheepishly as she stepped aside. "It was brutal." She breathed deeply. Her eyes flickered to Matt with concern. "I hope Speedfire is okay. No one's seen him since he disappeared with her last night."

"I'm sure someone like him is fine," Matt replied quietly. "He's come out alive every other time. He'll do it again. Right?"

"Time will tell," said Streak as he checked his watch. "James, if you are interested, I suggest you stop by the rally. And you as well, Matthew. If Speedfire is missing, I'm certain New Harbor could use a good boost in morale. After all, this city looks to me for assurance."

"They idolize you," muttered James. "I suppose I'll watch."

Streak lifted a brow and smirked at him. "I highly encourage it. If you wish to be more acquainted with me, that is. Oh, and Mr. Salamar..." He made a gesture to wipe his nose. "You have something...there."

Streak continued on his way as Christine shadowed her uncle. Matt glanced over at James and saw a drop of blood under his nose.

"*Shit*," James hissed, then covered his nose with his hand.

"There are tissues on Elaine's desk," Matt mentioned.

"Ignore it." He wiped his nose with the sleeve of his jacket. "I get spastic nosebleeds."

"Are you okay?"

"I said ignore it."

Matt silenced himself as James wiped away the rest of the blood.

"So, um...did you just get snarky with him?" Matt stammered.

"Maybe."

"He's going to be your boss."

James smiled at Matt. "Boss of Streak Corp? Sure. However, Matthew, I am my own boss," he replied, then turned toward the stairs. "If you need a ride to the park, let me know."

Matt was unsure what else to say or even do as he waited for the public rally. Speedfire was "missing," the city was in a panic with the sniper's recent appearance, and Matt had to keep this all to himself.

He rode the lift to the ninth floor, then entered Madeline's room. She glanced at him.

"What's up?" she asked.

"Streak pushed my job back another week."

"Oh, for heaven's sake," she groaned. "I guess just wait it out. Maybe your face won't look as bad by then."

"Uh, did you hear about the rally?" he mentioned.

"Yep."

"Are you going?"

"Nope."

Matt frowned. "I'm sorry."

"Don't be. I've got work. Besides, it'll be on national news," she told him. "I'll still watch it. But you should go. It sounds fun."

"What if I went as Speedfire?" he joked. She glared at him. "I'll just get a ride."

"No Speedfire," she snapped.

"No Speedfire," he sighed.

Matt stared out the window of the black car and took in the city view. He then gazed at James in the driver's seat, who concentrated on the road ahead. His glasses sat abandoned in the cup holder.

When the car stopped at an intersection, James glanced at him, and Matt turned away instantly.

"Funny," James spoke up with a smirk.

Matt looked back at him. "What?"

James faced the road again. "You must do that a lot."

"Do what?"

"You don't want people to catch you staring at them," James mentioned. "The second they see you, you look away."

"I don't..." Matt sighed. "Sorry."

"Don't apologize," James told him. "It's cute."

Matt tensed, then faced the front window with a frown. "It's a habit. I don't mean to stare..."

James chuckled. "Don't be afraid to look someone in the eye, even if they think it's weird." He turned to Matt with determination. "Assert your dominance."

"What?" Matt gasped. "No, that's..." He sank into the seat. "I'm just weird."

"I am too, Matthew. It's nothing to be ashamed of."

Matt spotted the city park up ahead. A large crowd stood in front of a stage near the parking lot. "Why are you driving without your glasses?"

"Oh." James scowled. "Is that why you were staring?"

"What? No, I'm just wondering. Sorry."

James' glower turned into a smile as he pulled into the parking lot. "You say that a bit too much." He rubbed his eyes, then unlocked the car doors. "*Sorry.*"

"Do I?"

"At least to me." James slipped out of the car with Matt and locked the doors. "I don't need the glasses."

"Then why do you wear them?" asked Matt.

James shrugged. "For work." He reached up and fixed his messy bun. "I've also got a headache right now. I'd rather not make it worse." He faced Matt and smirked. "You didn't look away this time."

"No shit," Matt huffed and walked toward the crowd.

He folded his arms and found his way to the front of the stage. He looked around the area for Streak or Christine, then spotted them nearby with a reporter. They stood side-by-side and smiled with their heads tilted toward each other. Once the small session with the photographers ended, their smiles dropped, and they shuffled away from each other. Christine noticed Matt instantly and pushed through the audience to reach him.

"Hey," she breathed out. "You made it."

"Well, you said you'd be here," he replied with a smile.

"Didn't your uncle mention this was just a publicity stunt?" James spoke up beside them.

Christine paused, then stared at him. "Excuse me?"

James crossed his arms and exhaled. "Anything to make himself look better, right?"

"He's just a little bitter," Matt whispered to her. "About the delay."

"Oh." She frowned and looked away. "I'm sorry, I don't have control over that."

James muttered, "I'm not upset at you, don't worry."

The chatter died down as Jason Streak stepped onto the stage. The audience filled the entire intersection.

"Citizens of New Harbor, welcome," Streak announced as he put his hand over his chest. "I know how hard these past few months have been regarding the sniper attacks. And I fear this city will lose its spirit because of her." Streak waited for a moment as the crowd clapped for him. "But first, I want to remind you all that the Core Stones are still in safe hands." He pulled a gem from the pocket of his gray jacket, then showed the purple stone off to the gasping crowd.

To Matt, it looked no different than the Rare Sniper's stone, though he had learned that all four Core Stones looked the same.

"With my protection, this stone will not fall into the wrong hands. It will continue to be a prized symbol of our sacred harbor," Streak continued. "And no one, not even the Optyman assassin who has been targeting my company, will have it."

Someone scoffed beside Matt. His eyes darted to James, who crossed his arms again. He then looked over at Christine, who watched her uncle intently. Two bodyguards eyed the crowd as Streak continued his speech.

Matt. He heard the lady in blue's voice, and he stepped back, facing the ground anxiously.

Matt's heart raced, and the hundreds of voices around him drowned out his thoughts. He felt a hand on his shoulder.

"Are you okay?" Christine asked. Matt could hardly hear her voice.

He nodded, then took a step forward. *Inhale. Exhale.* He saw Streak depart the stage. His speech must have ended, his words overwhelmed by the audience.

"Come on," Christine said. She took Matt's hand and dragged him through the surrounding crowd. He followed her to Streak, who was already holed up by a group of reporters. The two bodyguards allowed Christine to pass through with Matt and James.

"This city is home to me. I was born and raised in Baltimore, and I've witnessed its evolution," Streak mentioned to one of the reporters. The short woman had chin-length brown hair, tan skin, and a round face. She flashed her long lashes at Streak as she felt touched by his response. She wore a silver nametag on her gray jacket—Natalie Tray, lead reporter of *The New Harbor Sun*. "My goal is to see it prosper. A well-protected city has the faith of its people, after all."

Natalie nodded with a wide grin. "Perfectly said, Jason."

"That was a good speech." Christine caught her uncle's attention. "You hyped everyone up out there."

"I'm surprised you're complimenting it," Streak replied tiredly. He noticed Matt and James, then smiled. "Ah, I see you two showed up."

"How could we not?" James sighed. His eyes fell to the stone. "I didn't realize you were bringing *it* with you."

"I do, on occasion." Streak grinned. "Don't look at it for too long, now."

"What? Afraid someone will take it?" James joked with him.

Matt understood it was just a jest, but Christine tensed beside him. Meanwhile, the crowd swarmed in, pressing against the guards. He wondered how many of those people secretly wanted to hold the stone.

"People have attempted to take it before," Streak added. He strode toward James to pat his shoulder. "Even those closest to me. Some of my best employees turned out to be frauds."

"I can imagine. You hold the rarest gem in your hand—"

A scream from the crowd interrupted James. They turned around to see one of the bodyguards on the ground while another individual advanced toward them.

A blond-haired man wielded a bloody knife and sprinted toward Streak. The other bodyguard attempted to chase him but tripped on the ground.

Streak took several steps back and hardly had any time to react. James threw his arms out quickly, putting himself between Matt, Christine, and the attacker to shield them.

The masked thief caught up to Streak, attempting to take the stone from his hand. Streak saw the raised knife and let the gem go. Despite his latest speech, he was taking no risks on his life today. The thief scooped the Core Stone off the street, then shoved Streak to the ground, fleeing from the area.

"He's getting away!" Streak yelled, wincing as he held his bruised arm.

"I can catch up to him. Just give me something to throw," Matt hissed at Christine and James.

Christine took one of her heels off, then handed it to Matt. Meanwhile, the bodyguards were too occupied with helping Streak.

With a silent prayer, Matt ran forward, then hurled the shoe at the thief. The heel hit the back of his head, and he lost balance, skidding onto the concrete. As he scrambled to get back up, Matt jumped on him. He gripped the thief's wrist, then reached for the stone.

The thief pushed Matt away, whipping the blood-stained knife toward him.

"Don't make me!" the thief cried out. His brows furrowed fearfully.

Matt held his hands up. "Drop the knife. This doesn't have to—"

"Get him!" Streak demanded, ushering the bodyguards forward.

The thief stumbled as he stood. He held the stone close to his heart, staring down at Matt, then catching Streak's glare in the distance. He turned around and ran.

"Matt!" Christine kneeled beside him, then took his arm. "Are you alright?"

"I'm fine," he grunted as she helped him up. "He's getting away."

Sirens filled the air, and the crowd dispersed to make room for the cops.

Matt and Christine rushed after the thief until several police cars blocked the road near the intersection. The thief stopped and turned hurriedly. Matt paused with Christine as the attacker lifted his knife toward them.

His blond, leftover swept hair had brown roots, and his gray eyes glinted against the shade of his hood. His tan skin and mysterious aura felt familiar—the enigmatic figure who had stalked the headquarters late in the evening. Matt was just tracking him down yesterday before the sniper sidetracked him. Perhaps stealing the Core Stone had been the stalker's mission.

"Give it back," Christine demanded. She took a step forward and held her hand out. "No one else has to get hurt."

James caught up, and he rested beside Matt. The guards and Streak paused behind them, and others from the audience crept closer to watch the scuffle.

The thief trembled. His gaze darted from Streak to Matt and Christine. He rested his eyes on James. A look of concern overcame him.

A sudden spark erupted from the stone. The thief gasped. Another flash struck the air, crackling like lightning. The Core Stone sputtered incessantly, its sudden lights reflecting against the eyes of everyone in the vicinity.

"*Help!*" the thief cried, dropping the stone. "No, no—"

A final spark shaped like fractured lightning struck the thief, and he was gone. A luminescent blue ring lingered on the pavement where the thief stood. Within seconds, it disappeared, leaving behind a black stain and the Core Stone.

Silence filled the air.

Christine took a few small steps toward the stone. She picked it up gingerly and cupped the glowing gem in her hands. She turned back to Matt, James, and the rest. A look of confusion clouded her face.

"What was that about?" Streak demanded. He walked over to Christine and held his hand out.

"I...I don't know," Christine stuttered. She handed her uncle the stone, stepping back to look at the mark on the ground. The glow faded from the gem as it rested in Streak's palm. "He's gone."

The vision of the blue ring never fled from Matt's mind. Every time he blinked, it was there.

The authorities arrived at the scene. Half of the crowd stayed behind, eager for answers.

"He has to be a Rare Soul," added Streak. He glared at the black, ring-shaped stain on the pavement.

An officer approached Streak. "Jason, we're putting out an arrest warrant for the thief. We'll find him."

Streak nodded. "Thank you, Chief Grand." He looked down at the stone in his hand and took a deep breath. "I want a name."

Chapter 23

Damien Surtair.

Jason Streak found the thief's name within a day.

No one saw any signs of the boy after he vanished from the park, but they had a lead through his name.

Twenty-one years old, lower class, and a high school dropout. After investigators reviewed the footage taken from the event, they found Damien lurking around the crowd. He had put the mask on before he stabbed one of the guards.

He was raised in California by a single father and left home when he turned eighteen. He kept a journal, which he had left behind at his apartment in southern New Harbor. His last entry focused on his plan to steal the Core Stone. Someone had paid him to take it during any of Streak's public speeches.

Along with the journals, Detective Hu Chen of the New Harbor police reported findings of mythological memorabilia. Ornaments and trinkets of the Egyptian deity, Anubis, were hidden among Damien's personal belongings.

The news was all the talk for the following days. And Damien Surtair wasn't even the only topic of discussion.

Young hero steps up to save the Core Stone!

Jason Streak: "A brave soul. He'll be working at Streak Corporation soon."

Matt watched the footage of himself tackling Damien. Fortunately, no one had linked any ties between the "brave young man" and "Speedfire," thanks to Jason Streak informing the reporters that the boy just so happened to be his new manager's brother.

No one had mentioned Speedfire at all, which was fine by him.

Without any distractions, he could focus on Surtair. The fearful look in Damien's eyes, the shattered strike that sent him to the unknown—all of it left Matt in a daze.

He was *Rare*. And he was gone.

A picture popped up on the screen of Damien Surtair—blond hair with brown roots and a leftover haircut, gray eyes, golden tan skin, a curved nose, and a soft frown. Damien's eyes had remained gray after he took the stone. Nothing changed in his irises, but Matt was desperate to find a connection between the sniper's purple gaze and Damien's eventful disappearance.

In the meantime, Matt stopped by the headquarters and asked Christine if she wanted to join him in visiting Harry on his last day in the hospital. When they made their way up to Harry's room, they were greeted with a pleasant surprise.

Madeline was already there beside his bed. She looked over at them, startled. "I didn't know you two were coming to visit."

"You didn't mention it, either," Matt said.

"I'm almost out of here," Harry sighed with relief, then leaned back. "I still need to figure out what I'm going to do next."

"Hey, you need to take it easy," Madeline reminded him. "Try staying out of all that sniper business."

"Maddie, aren't you supposed to be at work?" Matt asked her, confused.

"I'm on my lunch break," she replied. She glanced over at Christine. "I'm guessing you're on break, too?"

"Not really," Christine mumbled. "I wanted to visit him, though."

"Aw, Christie." Harry beamed. "Just 'cus I quit doesn't mean I'll stop seeing you all."

"Working with you has been a pleasure. I'm going to miss you," Madeline mentioned. "But I understand why."

"I'll still be around," Harry assured her. "Streak Corp will be fine without me, too. You're the most hard-working woman I know."

Madeline blushed, then looked away.

"On another note," Harry faced Matt and Christine, "I heard about the Core Stone fiasco. What's up with that Damien Surtair guy?"

"It's still a mystery. No one can piece his story together," Matt replied. "He hardly had any trouble getting the stone, though. Something about it all felt...*staged*?"

"Did it?" Christine said. "Damien stabbed one of the bodyguards. And he threatened to kill my uncle. How was that staged?"

"Okay, maybe 'staged' isn't the right word," Matt huffed.

"I'm glad you two are alright," Madeline said. "Considering he's *Rare*, he could have done some serious damage."

Christine's arm brushed against him. "You were really brave out there, Matt."

Matt flushed slightly. "It was nothing." He glanced her way, and she smiled softly. "He was going to get away. And...he did."

"Not with the Core Stone. You still saved it," Christine said. "Thank you..."

Madeline shook her head. "Stop putting yourself in danger," she lectured, sneaking Matt a glare. "I don't want you being like Speedfire."

"That was a one-time thing," Matt clarified.

His attention returned to Christine, who moved closer to him. He understood her tension when it came to the Core Stone. He witnessed something she had probably seen multiple times over the past couple years.

Her life could be on the line for that stone, too, Matt pondered.

Anyone would steal the stone for the chance of being *Rare*.

Matt continued his sprees as Speedfire over the week, receiving the occasional text from Katelyn regarding suspicious activity near upper Canton or Fells Point. Alongside his work at night, he spent the evenings watching over the harbor in Canton. He found Christine walking home alone again, and he had no desire to leave her. As she walked the short way to her apartment, Matt found a perfect spot among the rooftops between the main headquarters and Streak's apartment. He would park himself there every night until he knew she was home safe. As soon as Christine entered the complex, he would join Katelyn or get caught up in another scuffle. But watching over Christine became a new yet small part of his nightly practice. No stalkers would be targeting her, and neither would the Rare Sniper.

During the day, Matt stayed home with Kiwi to catch up with the news. There was no new evidence of the individual who hired Damien to steal the stone. Investigators kept their eyes out for similar blue rings and black markings on the ground, however, but only one remained outside Scintilla Park from the initial incident.

Maybe everyone was right when they said Damien disappeared off the face of the earth.

Could the Core Stones really do that to people? Matt pondered anxiously.

Matt eventually found himself back in the headquarters of Streak Corporation.

"So, you two will be monitoring articles written about Jason Streak, Streak Corp, or anything dealing with the company," Kylie said as she guided James and Matt through a tutorial in her office. She showed them the homepage of *The New Harbor Sun*. "Keep track of *everything* written about the company. Take notes, save the links, and report everything to me."

"Doesn't seem too hard." James leaned back in his seat and flashed a grin. "But it's important, right?"

Kylie nodded and smiled at James. "It's related to our SEO. Mr. Streak wants to keep track of his company's traffic," she explained. "Because of that incident last week with Damien Surtair, Streak is all over the news."

"Of course," Matt muttered, then crossed his arms. "I'm guessing that's a ton more articles to keep track of?"

"Exactly," Kylie sang as she stood up. "Follow me. You two will catch each other up on the content you find."

"What do we do with social media, though?" Matt asked. He followed her and James into the hall. She led them straight to their shared cubicle. "Do we catch any mentions of Streak Corp on Oracle?"

"Oracle sucks," James coughed.

Matt snuck a glare at James. "Or VisionHive?" he added blankly.

"We already have employees running the social accounts. It's their responsibility to keep track of the company's reputation on all the platforms, so that's something you don't need to worry about," Kylie replied. She gestured to their desks and smiled again. "Check out *The New Harbor Sun* first, then look at other national headlines. Monitor anything that seemingly deals with Jason Streak or the company."

"Sounds feasible," said James. "Thank you, Kylie."

She winked at him and strolled back to her office.

Matt sat in his cubicle and visited *The New Harbor Sun*'s website. He scrolled through the front page and found several new articles on Streak

Corporation. Damien Surtair's face took over the front page, followed by Streak's stock market numbers, recent trades, and even comparisons to Sal-Tech.

He rubbed his eyes and looked down at his keyboard. This was going to be a long day.

Matt needed a break from work. His mind tired from navigating dozens of websites. Fortunately, he had James beside him. While Matt worked on *The New Harbor Sun*, James explored *The Times*. They shared a document, jotted down all their notes, and formed a list of links to the articles mentioning Streak Corporation and Jason Streak. Half of these articles focused on the story of Damien Surtair, however. A week after the incident, the boy was a household name in New Harbor.

The Core Stones would always be at the center of the world's news. This reality was something that not even the evanescent Damien Surtair could escape from.

Matt descended the stairs, and just as he turned the corner to the breakroom, he heard Streak talking with Madame Modisette in the hallway. Lorelei stood beside the boss with her hands on her hips and a stern expression. Matt hardly interacted with her much. Even Madeline mentioned that it was a challenge to talk to Madame Modisette. He peeked his head around the corner to eavesdrop.

"I don't understand why the search is taking this long," Streak muttered. "Chief Grand has given me everything they found on him, yet we're no closer to finding that scoundrel."

"Give it time, Jason," she assured him. "I'm still surprised how quickly that all went down."

"No one has ever tried to steal the stone from me in public," Streak mentioned. "And a complete stranger, no less. Damien Surtair is just a kid from California. He's nothing."

"He's going to have nothing after this," added Lorelei.

"I'll make sure of it." His gaze dropped to the floor. "He deserves a life sentence for what he did."

"Too many strange figures in this city nowadays," Madame Modisette sighed. "Including that new vigilante."

"Speedfire," Streak muttered. Matt stiffened. "His motives confuse me."

Lorelei raised a brow. "You're worried about your assets, right?"

"Always."

Streak glanced toward the end of the hall, and Matt shot himself backward. His heart raced immensely. He retreated to the stairs.

There was no doubt that Streak wanted revenge against Damien Surtair. The thief held a knife to him, and the stone could have cost him his life.

But little did Streak know that Speedfire had been the one to stall Damien.

He had saved Streak's greatest asset of all—the Core Stone itself.

Chapter 24

ALWAYS VIGILANT

Matt fixed his mind on the disappearance of Damien Surtair over the next two weeks. Almost every article he came across mentioned the missing thief, and still, no one had any leads on him. Matt was even more bothered by the sudden lack of interest in the Rare Sniper. The journalists hardly mentioned her, so it was only a matter of time before another shooting would bring the public's attention back to her.

Regardless, Jason Streak was at the front and center of it all.

On top of chasing leads, Matt could hardly get any sleep at night. As opposed to suffering in bed, he searched the streets for Damien Surtair and kept himself near Scintilla Park. Matt protected a woman from a mugger, then saved a jaywalker from a speeding car. All in another night's work.

During the day, he continued his research for Streak Corporation. Matt laid his head down for a few minutes to rest, but he woke up an hour later to see James had done his work for him.

"I think you should take a longer break," James mentioned. "Go out for some lunch. You look wasted."

"I had a few rough nights," Matt mumbled, then rubbed his eyes. "I'll be fine."

"No." James put his hand on Matt's shoulder. "Get some rest. Clear your mind. It's just scrolling through news feeds. I can handle it."

Matt nodded quietly. He cleaned up his desk, then got up from his seat. "I'm sorry."

"Don't be," replied James. "Take care of yourself."

Matt and Christine sat across from each other at the Jasmine Garden, each with a bowl of fried rice. When Matt was on his way out to get some fresh air, he found Christine delivering paperwork to the front desk and offered to let her join him.

"You look tired," she mentioned. Matt glanced at her and frowned. She bit her bottom lip. "I'm sorry...I just want to make sure you're okay."

He took a bite of his rice. "I'm fine."

"Is anything bothering you? How's work going?" she asked.

"I'm still thinking about Damien Surtair."

Christine sighed and looked down at her steaming food. "Me too."

"How's your uncle holding up?"

"Fine, as usual," she mumbled. "He's not too worried. But he wants to see Surtair behind bars."

"Is he worried about Damien coming back for him?" Matt asked.

"Nope." Christine dabbed her mouth with a napkin. "Core Stone thieves are usually one and done for him. My uncle manages to get them locked up. Sometimes for up to twenty years."

"I don't blame him," Matt exhaled. "I hope we get some leads on Damien."

Christine shrugged. "I don't know if we will. It's been over two weeks. Damien hasn't even returned to his apartment. He's just...gone."

Active members on Oracle claimed the thief had disappeared off the face of the earth. Some even believed that his *Rare* powers had caused his death, theorizing that everyone in the vicinity had witnessed Damien's incineration.

Matt felt too uncomfortable with those theories to believe in them. Waiting for the truth was better than assuming nonsense.

"Anyway..." Christine changed the subject with a smile. "We should do this more often."

He laughed. "Going out for lunch?"

"Why not? We see each other every day," she teased. "Let's hang out after work, too. I'll take you on more rides."

"Whatever you want. I'm not doing much."

Aside from Speedfire, he thought. He put the mask on late at night, however. He was content with spending his daylight hours alongside Christine if she truly wanted that.

"I could use some more time out, anyway." She rested her hands on her lap. "A break from the business."

"You don't look like you've ever had a break," Matt pointed out. "You need to find more people to get out with more."

"Well, I've never really had a friend like you." She paused and blushed slightly. He watched her, speechless. "I mean, I have 'friends.' It's just..." She waved her hand and sighed. "We're coworkers now, so it's easy to hang out."

"Hey, it's okay," he assured her. He had to find a way to stop Christine from getting herself all flustered. She seemed to be good at doing that. "Do you want to stop by my place after work? I can cook dinner."

Her eyes dropped to the table again, and she nodded. "That would be nice."

Matt waited on the pier outside his apartment. Before he left the headquarters, he noticed Madeline's office lights were out, so he assumed she was already home. He rested against the railing until a pair of footsteps approached him from behind.

"Matt?" Christine spoke up.

He turned around, and his jaw dropped. Around her red dress, she wore a sparkling white cape.

"You're wearing it!" he gasped.

Her face turned red as she shrugged. "Your place is probably the safest I'll ever feel wearing it, so..." She forced a smile. "Does it look okay?"

"It's so cute." He reached around her, letting it drape across her shoulder. "I doubt anyone would pick a bone with you if you did wear it in public."

"Are you sure?"

"Who's really going to mess with Jason Streak's niece?" he said.

"Well," she shuffled, "besides stalkers, I guess. Still, I'm like a beacon out here."

"Okay, fine," Matt huffed. He beckoned her to follow him inside, catching a glint of the cape as it swayed behind her. "But if you want to wear it when I'm around, that offer is still open."

She smiled as she followed him to the elevator. "And you wouldn't be embarrassed?"

"Now, why would I be embarrassed?"

"People act weird with anything Optyman-related…"

"Does the cape make you happy?" he asked. She nodded quietly as he closed the elevator doors. "Okay. Then that's what matters." He leaned against the wall as she lingered near the button panel. "Let's just relax tonight. Dinner and a movie. Maddie can join us if she's in the mood."

"What kind of movies are you into?" Christine asked.

"Uh, I don't really watch much," he replied. "Maybe action flicks."

"My uncle makes me watch all the 'prestigious' stuff," she joked. "I've never seen superhero movies."

"Like old-timey classics?"

"Movies about millionaires. Some based on true stories. Others about corporate romance. The usual boring jumbo."

"*Corporate romance?*" Matt laughed. "I didn't know that was a genre."

"It is," she scoffed. "I think my uncle wants a movie made about him. Maybe about his parents, too."

"Sounds like him," noted Matt.

She lifted an eyebrow. "You know, mister, I can tell you that *everyone* in this damn city would love to see a film about Jason Streak. And I bet your sister would go crazy for it, too."

"*Stop*," he groaned with a grin. "I would not want to sit through a three-hour movie about your uncle."

"Now you have me curious," she said as the doors opened. "Do you not like my uncle?"

"I mean…he's fine," Matt stuttered, then led the way down the hall.

She shrugged. "Loads of people adore him."

"It sounds like you have a different opinion," he said, pausing in front of the door. She stopped beside him, and they locked eyes. "Do you?"

"I do." She stared up at him. The smile dropped from her face slowly. "I don't have to idolize him, even if he's family."

"Does this have anything to do with your father?"

She exhaled softly and looked toward the door. "We can talk about movies again if you want." She glanced back at Matt and frowned. "I don't want to drop the mood."

"No, you're not. It's okay," he replied. He took his keys out and opened the door. When they stepped inside, they found Madeline and Harry on the couch. Their laughter filled the room, but they stopped and turned to face Matt and Christine. An awkward silence split the air.

"Hey," Madeline greeted after a long minute. "Finally made it home, I see. How was work?"

"It was fine," Matt answered. Christine stayed behind him and peered around the apartment. "What's up?"

Harry waved over at him. "Just catching up."

Matt forced a smile out, then locked eyes with his sister. Madeline stared at him for a moment. Her eyes darted over to Christine before she rested her gaze back on her brother.

"Uh, we were going to watch a movie, but we can go somewhere else," Matt said, breaking the silence.

"Aw, stop," Harry replied. "Don't let me ruin your plans."

"Harry, it's no problem. I can show Matt the movie theater instead," Christine assured him. "I don't mind."

Madeline frowned and took a stand with Harry. "Matt, can I talk with you for a second?" She nodded toward her room.

"Sure," Matt sighed, then followed her lead. He entered the room, and Madeline closed the door behind them.

"So, what's up?" she asked, then bit her lower lip.

"What do you mean?"

Her eyes peeped at the door. "Christine?" She gazed back at him. "Here?"

"She wants to hang out," he replied, then crossed his arms.

Madeline facepalmed. "Okay, I didn't want to tell you this," she muttered. She caught her breath and stared at the ceiling for a second. "Mr. Streak isn't very fond of Speedfire. He hates vigilantes in general. But *Speedfire* specifically gets on his nerves."

"I never would have guessed," Matt muttered. He let his arms fall to his side. "And?"

"And I hope you aren't revealing anything to his niece," said Madeline. "Streak mentioned it to me earlier this week. He thinks 'Speedfire' will get in the way of the investigation, and I didn't know what to say. So, I lied and agreed with him."

"Maddie, it's okay. I don't plan on saying anything to Christine," he promised her. "I even saved her before. And she still doesn't know it was me."

"You *what?*"

"There were these two thugs. They wanted to—"

"Matt, please, just be careful," Madeline interrupted. "Look, I'm glad she's alright, but you shouldn't parade that close to the headquarters. And especially not around *her*. I have no idea what she would tell her uncle if she found out you were Speedfire."

Matt frowned. "I hope nothing bad..."

"But you don't *know*."

"Maddie, it's not a big deal."

"Don't argue with me," Madeline exhaled. "Just keep that in mind, okay? I don't want Mr. Streak taking advantage of you by knowing your identity."

"In what way—"

"Like suing you. Or possibly getting you *and* me fired."

Matt paused as her words sunk into his heart.

Fired.

He took a step back and grimaced. "Okay," he murmured, then turned away. "I get it now."

"You two can have fun at your movie or whatever. But don't say anything," she mentioned, oblivious to his expression. Madeline opened the door and waved over at Harry.

Matt followed her silently. He put on a fake smile when he faced Christine.

"I hope something good is showing at the theater," Christine said with a grin.

Matt nodded, then glanced at Madeline and Harry. Whatever Harry said seconds ago made her laugh. Matt breathed in anxiously as he faced Christine. Just like she said a few minutes ago outside, he would hate to drop the mood again.

"Oh, hold on," Christine said as she turned back to Madeline and Harry. "I don't think my uncle mentioned it yet, but he's holding a party on October third. It's the fortieth anniversary of Streak Corp."

Madeline gasped with excitement. "*Really?*"

Christine nodded. "You're welcome to come, considering you've done so much for the company over the past few years. And guests are allowed, too."

"Did your uncle put you up to telling everyone?" Matt joked.

Christine peeked back at him and rolled her eyes. "We have a party every year. It'll be on the top floor of The Oleandris."

"The Oleandris?" he repeated.

"Tallest skyscraper in New Harbor, named after my grandmother. My uncle gets first dibs on reservations all the time." She pressed her lips together. "Anyway, you're all invited."

"She said guests," Madeline whispered and prodded Harry.

"As long as there's no sniper, I'll go," muttered Harry. He looked back at Madeline and smiled. "Mr. Streak and I are still on good terms."

"You two should head out to your movie before it gets too late," Madeline added, eyeing Matt and Christine.

"Oh. Yeah." Matt backed away as he noticed Madeline holding Harry's hand. "See you later..."

Christine winced as she reached for her cape. "Can I leave this here? Since we'll be back after—"

Matt held his hand on her shoulder. "Keep it on."

She blinked, then lowered her arm. "Okay."

Matt waved back at Madeline as Christine led him out to the hallway. She closed the door and smiled at him, then noticed the solemn look in his eyes.

"Hey..." she spoke up and stepped closer. "Are you alright? I don't mind going to the theater. You can make dinner another night."

"I'll be okay. It's nothing," he lied, then walked down the hall. They stepped back onto the elevator.

"Did she say anything to you?"

Matt shook his head, then gazed at the concerned look in her eyes. She wanted to spend time away from work-related hassles tonight, and he would hate to ruin this evening for her.

"Thanks for hanging out with me tonight," he told her, forcing himself to smile.

"You're the one who let me," she laughed.

Matt nodded and closed his eyes before he stepped off the elevator. The thought of sharing his identity with Christine had crossed his mind before, but everything about his alias suddenly made him feel guilty. Keeping his involvement in the sniper's scandal a secret from her did not feel right to him, yet he understood his sister's concern.

He would hate to hurt either one of them over his actions as Speedfire.

Chapter 25

The following night, Matt continued his patrol around New Harbor as Speedfire. The movie he and Christine had watched was a romantic comedy, and although he hardly remembered much about the film, it made him think of Madeline and Harry.

Her words stung him. Everything had to be a secret. And not just for his sake, but for Madeline's as well.

Matt lingered around Scintilla Park for a while longer, still getting nowhere in his search for Damien Surtair. A girl's sudden scream echoed across the buildings nearby. He turned his attention to the noise—another mugging.

Matt ran across the rooftops and took the fire escape down. He peeked around the corner, ready to jump the mugger. Before he could act, another figure darted across the street, taking the criminal head-on.

The victim scrambled away. Matt sprang out from around the corner as another vigilante jumped the mugger. She pummeled the man, leaving him limp as a slug on the ground.

Matt helped the trembling victim up and handed her the wallet.

The other vigilante walked over and placed her hands on her hip. She had her purple hair tied back, wore a black mask over her eyes and mouth, and covered herself with a black jacket and shorts. She also wore long boots and had nun-chucks attached to her belt.

"Well, well, look who it is," her muffled voice spoke up. "You must be the new kid. Speedfire, right?"

He lifted his mask slightly higher and fixed his hood. "Who are you?"

"Trix," she replied and pulled her phone out.

He eyed her carefully as she put her phone away and placed her hand on her hip again. "You're another one of the vigilantes here, I'm guessing."

She scoffed. "If you're trying to take after us, you should have at least bothered to recognize me."

"I've been doing this for two years now," he replied, then crossed his arms. "I'm not taking after anyone."

"Really? I guess we'll have to see. You're all the public wants to talk about right now," Trix scorned. "Hope you can live up to our ranks."

"You keep talking as if you're part of some club."

"If there is a club, you're not invited," she added. "I've noticed you patrolling northern Canton. I hope you know this is my zone."

"*Your* zone?"

"And now that you know, you may go on your merry way, Speedfire," Trix shot back. She walked over to the quivering girl, then offered her hand, guiding her away from Matt.

"I'm not here to invade your space. I've been searching for someone," he said.

Trix turned around. "Who?"

Damien Surtair.

"None of your business," Matt muttered. He needed to get back to the docks.

Trix gave him a different perspective on the vigilantes in New Harbor. They did things their own way, and even if they clashed at times, they fought for the same ideals.

Individuals like Jason Streak, however, despised vigilantes, despite how much they could help him.

Within the next half hour, Matt found himself back at his usual spot along the southern harbor and gazed toward the headquarters.

In no time, he would be back at his cubicle. He would be conducting more repetitive research, stuck in place.

Jason Streak. Streak Corporation. Streak. Streak. Streak—

"I thought he'd be around this area," a voice groaned nearby. A group of five men in black masks and jackets loitered a block down on the harbor.

Matt got up and slid down the side of the building.

"He might be. We'll catch him," another man replied.

Without a sound, Matt kept his distance and hid behind a dumpster.

"This is a waste of time, Victor," a burly man spat. "We searched this street every night for the past week and have found *nothing*."

Maybe they're looking for Damien, Matt pondered.

"*Quiet*," snapped Victor. He appeared different from the rest, having spikes on his leather jacket and a white skull printed on his mask. Perhaps he was the leader. "Maybe we need to cause some commotion. Speedfire will show his face, then."

Matt sank behind the dumpster. He covered his mouth with his hand.

His mind ran all over the place. These men wanted *him*. He didn't even know who they were.

These men had the looks of a gang, however, and he wasn't letting anyone get hurt on his behalf.

Matt stepped out, then snuck over to a nearby building across from the guys. For a touch of confidence, he leaned against the wall and rested his foot behind him.

Stay calm.

Matt cleared his throat. "Evening, gentlemen."

All eyes darted to him in an instant. The men got into a defensive stance, and the leader stepped forward. "We were thinking you retired," Victor said. "You haven't been around for the past week."

"Just patrolling other areas," Matt replied, then pushed himself away from the wall. He took a slow step across the street. "Anything I can do for you?"

Victor laughed. "You're a bold one. Care to hand yourself over?"

"For what?" Matt feigned. This fight would be five against one, but he didn't want to appear afraid. He could take them. "Or should I ask...for whom?"

Victor crossed his arms. "You really think I'm gonna answer that?" he chuckled. "Look, kid, no need to drag this out. You can come with us and make yourself cozy for a bit. Or we can drag you back, barely breathing."

"Hm. Sorry to disappoint you," Matt unclipped the dagger from his belt and lit it on fire, "but 'Option Two' sounds more exciting."

The eyes on Victor's mask widened. "That shit really works?" he mentioned as he gestured to the knife.

"Wait, what?"

"Forget it," he spat. He pulled out a gun. "Bringing a knife to a gunfight ain't the brightest way to go. For someone with your skills, I thought you would've known that."

"I do." Matt stood there, uncertain. A soft breeze blew along the street, and his hood shuddered. The other men pulled out their guns.

"Good," Victor whistled. He strutted over to Matt with his gun held firmly. Before Matt could back away, the leader seized his neck. Victor tightened his grip, then slammed Matt to the ground. His head rang as he gasped for breath. Victor held him down, putting the gun to his head. "Drop the knife."

Matt's grip tensed around his weapon. He had seconds to think of an escape plan.

"Put your weapons down. *Now*," a cold voice echoed around them. The other men glanced up at the roof behind Matt. He and Victor turned around to see the Rare Sniper above them. She stared down from the rooftop.

"What the hell?" Victor whispered. He let Matt drop to the ground and backed away.

The sniper leaped off the roof and landed effortlessly. A light breeze swirled around her, nearly knocking Matt's hood off as he crawled away from her. His heart raced even faster.

"Put them away," she hissed and raised her hand.

Victor and his gang returned the guns to their holsters. The Rare Sniper shot a glare toward Matt. Her eyes flickered to his knife, then back to his face. He extinguished the fire and clipped the dagger back to his belt.

"You're not supposed to be out tonight," Victor told her. Another breeze swept the area.

"I'm on a mission," she snapped back at him. "*Leave*."

"You can't make us," he said bitterly.

Another gust blew the men back a few steps. Victor receded with a huff.

"I'm saying something," he threatened. "Boss wants him dead. You know that."

She stepped in between Victor and Matt. "Maybe *I* want to be the one to finish him."

"Considering you haven't been doing your job right, I don't think that's a good idea," Victor argued. The sniper's hands tightened into fists, and he took another step back. "I can shoot him right here, and I'll give you the honor of cleaning up the mess. Hell, you can even take the credit."

Matt trembled as he lay there helplessly. He was at the mercy of his greatest enemy, and he had a sickening feeling that he wouldn't be seeing tomorrow's sunrise.

Maddie, I'm sorry—

"I'm not looking for a big mess," she uttered. "I'll take care of him. Let me have this, and you won't see him again."

"And why do you want him so bad?"

She narrowed her eyes. "He's *my* nemesis. Not yours."

Victor scowled as he glared at her. "Fine," he spat. "We keep this between us. Then you can tell the boss yourself. Let this be a test, whelp."

"A *test*," she taunted as she lifted her hand again. "Sure."

The men shuffled their way back, further down the harbor. Victor shot another glare at her before he followed the rest of his gang.

Matt lay there behind the sniper, shocked.

I only shoot my bounties, her words echoed in his head. *So...let's see who catches who first.*

And he was undeniably a target now.

The Rare Sniper turned around quietly and stared at him. She unclenched her fists, then tilted her head.

Matt gazed up at her, trembling from the sharp pain in his head. "Are you going to kill me?"

She answered with silence.

Please...

He struggled to sit up, only to land on his arm.

Her eyes fell to the few drops of blood beside him. "Those men have been waiting for you," she spoke up.

"You knew?" he whispered.

He touched the side of his head and felt the liquid stain his fingertips. He brought his hand forward, and his blood glistened under the moonlight.

His eyes darted back to her as she crouched in front of him. "They almost got you. Like predator and prey."

"I'm not prey," he murmured.

"I'm not either." She glared at him with another head-tilt. Her husky voice filled him with dread.

"Who are those guys?" he asked, confused. "You sound like you work with them."

"They call themselves *The Reapers*," she mentioned. "They're bounty hunters."

All her snide comments from the night she pulled him from the river continued to haunt him. She was an assassin, after all.

What have I gotten myself into? he cursed himself.

"Will you finish me off?" Matt stuttered. "You told them—"

"That's why I'm here," she silenced him. He froze. "You're dead after tonight."

"Wait—"

Matt struggled to get up, yet his head spun. He nearly fell back over until he felt her arm under his. She pulled him up, guiding him away from the street. She took him into the nearby alley and sat him beside a ladder. He remained silent as she softly touched the side of his head. He pushed her hand away and fixed his hood.

"You have a concussion," she said.

"Doesn't matter," he mumbled. "I'm dead after tonight."

"You've done this to yourself. They were hired to kill you," she snapped. "And it's all because you keep getting in my way."

Matt blinked. "What?" he breathed.

She kneeled beside him. "And they don't do mercy shots."

"But you do?"

She glared at him, then glanced over her shoulder toward the road. "Your stalking ends tonight."

"We've only seen each other four times. By chance." A sheer lie, but maybe she wouldn't catch onto it. "I'm not stalking you."

"Harold Faresoul survived. Everyone in the city knows Speedfire saved him from me," she mentioned. "It's clear to The Reapers that Speedfire has become a problem."

"You're really one of them?" he whispered, dazed. "I was right, then. You're literally New Harbor's Reaper."

She stared at the blood soaking the side of his head.

"Who are you?" he seethed.

Are The Reapers Optymans, too?

The question rang through his sore head.

"Such bold words for a dead man," she murmured.

The Rare Sniper stood and walked to the other end of the alley. His heart pounded.

"Sniper," he called to her quietly. She stopped and turned around. "Can you at least give me one answer?"

Before I die.

She slowly pulled out one of her pistols. Her cold gaze stunned him as she raised her arm, aiming at him in the dark.

"This city is a masquerade," she said, her finger landing on the trigger. "Everything is a lie."

Their gazes locked. The dark circles she had painted around her eyes were as ominous as before, yet he could not read her emotions. At this rate, he never would.

The Rare Sniper pulled the trigger, and the sound of gunfire echoed all the way down the street. The bullet grazed his arm, and Matt screamed out.

He cried, clutching his arm as it started to bleed. His head throbbed, and tears swarmed his vision.

Matt pushed himself forward, then turned to face the Rare Sniper as he gritted his teeth. She was nowhere to be seen, having left him alone to dig his own grave.

Chapter 26

THREE STRINGS

The cold water soaked through Matt's hair as he stood under the shower-head. His blood mixed with the water, sinking into the drain as his head continued to bleed. Matt did what he could to still the bleeding in his arm. While he showered, he cleaned the wound, then wrapped it in bandage tape. The graze would scar up, but it was better than dealing with a bullet inside his arm.

Such bold words for a dead man.

Matt already harbored enough resentment for the sniper, but now she truly wouldn't leave his mind.

Once he stopped bleeding, he slipped out of the shower, then returned to bed. He had work to deal with the next day, and as much as he desired to linger on these mysteries, his mind wouldn't let him.

To sleep was harrowing bliss.

Matt tried to keep his head straight. Vertigo overwhelmed him as he sat at his desk, and the world looped around him. He could feel nausea inching its way up his throat.

James had gone to speak with Kylie about a half-hour ago. Matt attempted to read the words on his screen, but his head continued to throb.

The Reapers. The Rare Sniper. The Boss.

His concentration feigned. His eyelids fluttered. He felt he could pass out at his station.

"Are you alright, Matthew?" James crouched beside him. He used the back of his hand to feel Matt's forehead. "You don't look so good."

"I think I have a concussion," Matt murmured. He closed his eyes and turned away. "I'll be fine."

"You need rest," James told him. "Come on. I can give you a ride home."

"*What?*" Matt faced him again. "No. You've given me enough rides already."

"One ride is enough?" James remarked. "Just get up."

"I look pathetic," Matt groaned. James put his hand on his shoulder and helped him gain balance.

"Don't hesitate to lean on me," James muttered as he guided him toward Kylie's office. He knocked on her door, and within seconds, she answered.

Kylie raised an eyebrow as she noticed James' arm wrapped around Matt. "What's wrong?"

"He has a concussion," James replied. "I'm giving him a ride home."

"It's walking distance," Matt said.

"Then I'll walk you back." James looked at Kylie and frowned. "He needs rest."

Kylie shrugged. "Take care. I'll let Mr. Streak know."

James guided Matt down the hall and toward the elevator. A sudden wave of heat struck Matt, and he couldn't tell if his head was making him hot, or if James was just that warm.

"Does your sister not realize you have a concussion?" James asked with concern. "When did this happen?"

Matt shook his head, then flinched at the pain. He touched the side of his head and grimaced. "I'm good at hiding stuff from her." That was partially true. He could hide stuff from his sister temporarily. "It happened last night."

"You should have called off this morning—"

"I'll be fine," Matt repeated.

"Well, take it easy. You don't have to move that much," James reminded him. He offered his arm to help Matt keep his balance on the elevator.

"I was trying to hide it. I'm sorry," Matt confessed as his gaze dropped to the floor.

"No need to apologize. I don't want you suffering."

Matt gazed up at James speechlessly. His care somewhat startled him. He never expected this kind of attention from people he hardly knew.

The elevator doors opened, and they stepped off together. Matt saw Streak conversing with Elaine at the front desk, and his heart stopped.

No, no, no, no, no.

Streak turned his concerned gaze toward James and Matt. "Is there a problem?"

"He's not feeling well," James replied. "I need to take him home. Kylie could tell you more."

Streak glanced at Matt and nodded. "Take all the time you need. Your department has been quite productive this past week, anyway."

Matt's sight blurred. Was he afraid of looking weak in front of Jason Streak? Or perhaps he didn't want to make his sister look bad by ditching his work.

Regardless, he was free to go.

The thought of returning home to his apartment and getting comfortable with a cat in his lap was enough to heal his mind. Before he knew it, James had already escorted him back. He lay on his couch as James picked up the remote from the coffee table nearby.

"Last night," James muttered. "You need to be more careful."

Matt sank into the couch. "I try to."

"Do you, now?"

"I slipped and banged my head," Matt huffed, praying James would not catch the lie. "It happens."

"It does. And it could have been worse," James sighed. "You're lucky it's just a concussion. I've been in a coma before."

Matt blinked. "You were in a coma?"

"Years ago. One of the worst experiences I've ever had," James replied, playing with the remote. "Wouldn't recommend it."

"What was it like?" Matt asked cautiously.

James exhaled, "It's hard to describe." His eyes lingered on the remote. "I felt stuck in place. I could hear everything and everyone around me, but I couldn't move. I was trapped in this long shadow, and I couldn't do a thing about it."

"I've heard that before," Matt mentioned, biting his lip. "People in comas can still hear things, almost like they're awake...but they're not."

James grimaced. "It's scary. I almost died, apparently."

"It was that bad?" Matt gasped.

James loosened his shoulders. "Maybe..." he murmured. "When I woke up, I didn't feel the same. I think that was the worst part about it."

"What do you mean?"

"I dunno. I felt...bitter." James breathed out, then shrugged. "I think I'm okay now. It happened when I was sixteen. I've had plenty of time to recover."

Matt frowned. "How did it even happen?"

James stared at the floor, contemplating. "Head injury."

Matt leaned back. "Okay...so, what kind of head injury? Nothing like mine, right?"

James chuckled. "Everyone told me I fell down the stairs." He faced Matt with a grin. "That's what being reckless does to you."

Matt glanced at the cushion. He never meant for the conversation to take an awkward turn. He wondered if James told him the truth, or perhaps he was eager to turn the topic away from his coma. With an experience that traumatic, Matt could not blame him.

"Want something to watch in the background?" James offered. "When my sister had a concussion, she preferred having something on, like a nature documentary or music."

Matt eyed the television, careful not to move his head too much. "You never told me you had a sister."

James inspected the remote. "Well, I do," he said. "She means the world to me."

Matt exhaled softly. "My sister means the world to me, too."

"You two seem close," James mentioned. He sat beside Matt on the couch and browsed through the different channels. "Working at the same place and all. How old is she again?"

"Twenty-five."

"Oh. She's my age," James laughed. "My sister is twenty-three."

"Are you two close?"

James glanced back at the screen. "Sort of. We still talk." He took his glasses off, then put them on the table. "We just...went down different paths in life."

Matt stared at James with somewhat of an understanding. That was what he and Madeline both feared at some point. The idea of going down different paths was something they couldn't handle.

"At least you still talk," Matt said quietly.

"Not like we used to," James sighed. He passed a channel every couple of seconds. "It's never going to be the same."

His words stung Matt with a truth he never wanted to hear.

"You remind me of her," James spoke up again. "My sister."

"How come?"

"You have this secret passion in you," he added, smiling faintly. "You both want to do things *your* way. But something always held you back...or is holding you back."

Matt's face dropped. James already knew he didn't want to work at Streak Corp. Perhaps he saw too much of his sister in Matt.

"What is she doing now?" he asked, curious yet hopeful.

"Running the whole damn world," James muttered under his breath. He glanced at Matt. "I should be helping you. Need some tea?"

Matt nodded carefully. "Thank you."

James set the remote down and made his way to the kitchen. He then proceeded to take the tie out of his hair. Matt had never seen him without a bun, and he looked different without the glasses as well. His bangs parted down the middle, framing his face perfectly, and his hair rested an inch above his shoulders.

Matt's attention shifted to the news on the television. James must have forgotten to find a documentary.

"Detective Hu Chen of New Harbor's police recently found a discarded letter hidden within the walls of Damien Surtair's apartment," Natalie announced. "While Surtair's journal had already confirmed he was hired to steal the stone from Jason Streak, this letter gives us a new possible lead on his employer."

"What?" Matt breathed. A sharp pain shot through the side of his head, but he ignored it.

"According to Surtair, a figure he refers to as 'The Tyrant' is responsible for organizing the incident," Natalie continued. "Authorities from London are now on the case, as this may deal with the stolen stone from Peter Fren.

"The Tyrant supposedly persuaded Surtair into raiding Jason Streak's rally for the stone. Here is a snippet of the letter Surtair supposedly wrote to himself."

Matt skimmed through the words as best as he could.

I'm scared. I'm alone. I've always been alone. I don't know what I'm getting myself into. These people, they just came. And they found me starving on the streets. New Harbor was advertised as this city of peace. It was always supposed to be this haven. But I was wrong. I thought running away from

Dad would have given me a chance. But it never mattered. Because then they came. The acolytes. I was led into a trap with a promise of shelter and food. And then their leader arrived. The Tyrant. He was so kind. Too kind. He wanted to help me. But he was a bit too generous. The Tyrant showed me a Core Stone. He said we are both Rare. *And I couldn't believe it. If I was* Rare, *I wouldn't be living like this. But the Tyrant didn't hand me the stone. Instead, he promised me that I was* Rare. *I just need to do one thing to prove it. He wants me to steal Jason Streak's Core Stone. No one will listen. But I'll have a future if I do this, even if that future is scary. Because that's all I feel. Fear. The Tyrant is too kind for this dream that he is chasing, and I am terrified of him.*

Matt's eyes stayed glued to the television until he noticed James standing beside the couch. He held a small mug of tea.

"Sorry," James interrupted and handed Matt the cup. "I can turn it off."

"I wanted to know more about Damien. It's fine," Matt assured him. "That's..." He glanced at the screen again. "It's interesting."

"Crazy kid," James mumbled as he sat on the couch. "You're right, though. It is interesting." He scowled. "*The Tyrant.*"

"So," Matt rubbed the side of his head, "a guy with a cult-following is trying to steal the Core Stones? That's what I'm getting from all this?"

James switched the channel again. "A shame we won't be getting answers from Damien anytime soon." He landed on a dolphin documentary. "That also means more work for me back at the office."

Matt pondered for a moment longer and watched the dolphins as they splashed in the waves. He could hardly focus on the narrator's voice.

The Tyrant. Cult. His mind wandered, and his eyes widened. *Optyma...The Reapers.*

Perhaps The Reapers and the Rare Sniper were all tied to the Tyrant and Damien Surtair's disappearance. And Jason Streak was at the center of it all—the target.

Streak and his Core Stone.

"I should get back to work." James took a stand. "If there's anything you need, shoot me a text."

"I'll be fine. You did enough."

"I insist."

They locked eyes for a moment. Matt still didn't know how to thank him properly. He hardly had anyone go out of their way to help him.

"Thank you," he said. Kiwi trotted out of his bedroom and hopped on the sofa. James watched the cat crawl onto Matt's lap.

"I'll let your sister know," James mentioned as he stepped back. "Take care, Matthew."

A sudden push jolted Matt awake, and his eyes shot open. He came face-to-face with Madeline.

"Are you okay?" she gasped, trembling. "Why didn't you tell me you had a concussion?"

"I'm sorry," he whispered. "I didn't want to worry you."

"How did it happen?" she demanded. She inspected the side of his head. "Did you fall? Did you do it at work?"

"Did James tell you?"

"He told me, but he didn't say how."

She stared at him until she got an answer. His heart raced. *Speedfire.*

"It happened last night," he mumbled.

"*Last night?*"

"But I got rest—"

"You should have told me!" Madeline shrieked. She took a deep breath. "Okay...what else happened?"

"There was this group of guys..."

"Matt!" Her palm collided with her forehead.

"I'm okay," he assured her. "I'm alive, right?"

Madeline cast a glare at him. "I can't believe you didn't tell me first. You told James, at least. But still."

"He found out on his own," Matt huffed.

James was the most perceptive man Matt knew at this point. He wondered if he could uncover anything, including Speedfire's identity.

"He was very nice about it," Madeline told him. "Not going to lie, he is hot."

"Maddie, no." Matt wanted to cover his face with a pillow.

"Where did Mr. Streak find someone like him?" she teased. Matt sunk into the couch even more. "I wonder if he's single. I didn't see a ring." She laughed as Matt frowned. "I'm kidding. Don't look at me like that."

"I'm judging you."

"Alright, Mr. Concussion, go ahead. I'm not into James. I'm actually..." She pursed her lips as she glanced at Matt, who raised an eyebrow. "Never mind."

"What?" he asked. "Actually, *what*?"

"Actually..." she repeated with a mumble. "Yeah."

"*Maddie.*"

"Okay, okay," she huffed, then sat beside him. "I should probably tell you."

"While I have a concussion, whatever it is," he muttered. "Maybe I'll forget about it."

"Really?" she asked, intrigued. "Alright, so...I've been going on a few dates..."

"With Harry?"

"What?" She flushed red and stared at him. "How do you...I mean..." She rambled on, flustered. "Maybe."

"It's okay," he exhaled. "I figured. When are you two making it official?"

"We're attending Mr. Streak's anniversary party as a couple."

"Ah, but you still have the hots for James?" Matt mocked playfully.

"That was a joke, you stinker," Madeline shot back. "You looked so red when I said that."

"Sure. Act like you weren't a tomato when you mentioned Harry." Matt forced himself to smile as Kiwi jumped on his lap. "You didn't have to hide it, Maddie."

"You didn't have to hide that concussion either, Matt," she remarked. She brought out a genuine smile from him. "Maybe we just suck at hiding things from each other."

"We honestly do," he groaned.

"Come here," Madeline said, wrapping him in a hug. She checked to make sure his head was not in any discomfort. She then leaned back on the couch and linked her arm with his. "We should watch something. Does your head feel alright enough for that?"

"I might doze off," Matt replied as Kiwi snuggled into his leg.

Madeline flicked through the streaming channels, and Matt paid no attention. His eyes drifted to the balcony door, toward the radiant moon above the harbor. With Madeline beside him, his mind was at rest.

He closed his eyes slowly and tightened his arm around hers.

Going down different paths...It's never going to be the same...

Chapter 27

The Protocol

Matt's concussion could take up to two weeks to heal, which meant he was now a designated couch potato. As he lay in bed, Kiwi purred against his stomach, flicking her tail against his arms. He was grateful to at least have her company.

His phone buzzed on the bedside table. He picked it up to find an urgent message from Katelyn.

Katelyn:

> Hey Speedy! Sorry if this is sudden!

> There's a sketchy guy following me on O'Donnel St.

> I'm kinda staying near some crowds, but I could tell he's still following me. Has been for the past 5 blocks.

> If you're not busy, can you help??

> So sorry again, I don't want to be a burden.

Matt sighed with frustration. He could tell her about the concussion. But if he didn't do something, she could get hurt.

He lifted his phone.

Matt:

On my way.

Matt hadn't put his gear on since he got the concussion. He flipped up the hood, swiped his neck gaiter, and headed for O'Donnel Street. The road was just north of Leo Towers, so Katelyn should be close by.

Matt:

Where are you?

Katelyn:

By the club.

Matt peered ahead, noticing a group of people outside a small building decorated with neon lights. Katelyn stood outside and typed away at her phone.

Katelyn:

The guy is camping in an alley.

Matt:

Stay there. I'm coming

Matt jogged across the street when the cars cleared out. Katelyn waved at him excitedly.

"Thank you so much!" she shouted. She ran over and hugged Matt, nearly throwing him off balance. "He's in that alley." Katelyn pointed to the backstreet behind Matt.

He snuck a peek over his shoulder. "I can draw him out."

"Oh. I was hoping I could play the bait, and then you can jump him," she suggested. "We can be a team!"

"Are you sure?" he asked, concerned. "What if he hurts you?"

"Pish-posh. I'll be fine," she scoffed. "It's better than taking him on alone."

"Okay...so, why didn't you call the police?"

"I felt safer asking you," she admitted. "Because you're always there."

Am I really? he wondered, blinking.

"Fine. We'll go with your plan, but be careful," Matt ordered, then stepped back. "I'm sure he'll try pulling you into the alley."

"I'm always careful." Katelyn closed her eyes smugly as she walked toward the narrow passage.

Matt kept his distance, then followed her slowly. Suddenly, the man sprang out from the alley and grabbed Katelyn. She screamed, and Matt broke off into a sprint. He turned the corner as Katelyn pushed the man away. The criminal had a knife, and that was all Matt had to see. He leaped toward the guy and kicked him away. The man rolled over to a dumpster, dropping the knife.

Matt fell to the pavement and flinched. His vision blurred from the impact.

"I've got him!" Katelyn called out.

"Kate, wait—"

Katelyn was already on top of the guy, smacking his head. For a small girl like her, she wasn't doing much damage. Fortunately, Matt's kick had already impaired him.

Matt scrambled over and held the guy's hands behind his back. The man cowered as Katelyn slapped him one last time. She then backed away to let Speedfire finish the job. Matt pulled out a thick string from his pocket, tying the criminal's wrists together.

"You know the protocol," Matt mentioned to her. "Police. Now."

"On it," she sang, grabbing her phone. "We make a good team!"

"You didn't have to pummel him like that," Matt sighed.

The man glared at him but did nothing to escape. "You're some kind of stalker, huh," he spat.

"You could say that," Matt huffed, rubbing his head to ease the throbbing. "Takes being one to know one."

"The police are on the way," Katelyn interrupted, then sat beside Matt. "I owe you big time."

Matt shook his head. "No need."

Katelyn's cheeks turned pink. "I really want to, though."

"And I insist that you don't."

"Maybe I can be your sidekick or something." She grinned.

Matt tried his best not to laugh. He looked away, but at least she could tell his eyes smiled.

"I don't need a sidekick."

"Okay, I was joking. But maybe not," Katelyn snickered. "If you need anything, I've got your back."

"And I've got yours." Matt stood up as the sirens closed in. "See you next time, Kate."

"You do you, Speedy," she teased.

The police officers entered the alley, and Katelyn waved them down as Matt sped to the other entrance. He could rest now.

Matt returned to the apartment within the next hour after he took a gentle stroll around Canton. As he passed some late-night walkers, they recognized him immediately. Some snapped pictures, and others stopped to ask him about his rivalry with the Rare Sniper. He was in no mood to talk with fans, especially as his head throbbed from the concussion, but he allowed them to approach him. He wanted them to feel safe, and if engaging them was the way to do it, then so be it.

"So, you think all Optymans pose a threat to this city?" a fan asked.

Matt shot him a quizzical look. "Since when did I say that?"

"You fight an Optyman villain."

"We agree with you, Speedfire. It's okay," another fan added.

Matt eventually pushed past them. He didn't have time for their remarks.

Before he entered the apartment building, he stared out toward the harbor. His stomach twisted when he gazed toward the rooftops. A gentle wind followed the silence.

He closed his eyes when his vision began to blur again.

As he returned home, his eyelids felt heavy, but he found his focus again. Madeline stood in the living room with her hands on her hips and a glare in her gaze.

"Matthew Ethan Ellis," she lectured. "What the hell is your problem?"

"Someone was in trouble," he mumbled, then tried to avoid her. She stepped in his way, preventing him from escaping to his room. "My head hurts."

"I wonder why."

"I need to lay down," he groaned. He wiped his eyes again.

"Maybe take the mask off?" she suggested. "Were you after the Rare Sniper?"

"No."

"Then why were you out there? If someone was in trouble, I'm sure the police could handle it. Or maybe another one of those vigilantes."

"They don't do shit," he sighed, then nudged her aside. He opened the door, seeing Kiwi stretched out in the middle of his mattress. He turned the lights on and rolled his eyes.

"I'm sure they did plenty of shit before you got here," Madeline told him. Matt turned around and squinted. "*Pretty* sure."

"'Shit' could be interpreted differently," he remarked. "They like doing publicity stunts. That's the kind of shit they're into."

"And you're not, *Speedfire*?"

"*No.*"

"I've seen the news, Matt. They treat you like a celebrity. A superhero."

Matt faked a laugh. "That's bullshit, too." He slumped down on the edge of his bed as his sister lingered in the doorway. "I never asked to be seen as one. In fact, I *love* the mask."

He pulled the neck gaiter off his face, then threw it in the closet.

"You have a concussion. That's all I'm trying to tell you."

"I know I have one, Maddie. It's *my* head." He crawled his way to the other end of his bed. He avoided Kiwi and curled up along the side of the mattress. "I'm sleeping in this, by the way."

"Whatever," she muttered, then shut the door behind her.

Matt exhaled and closed his eyes. The lady in blue had not visited his dreams since he got the concussion, but that was for the better.

He drifted off to sleep within minutes—

A sudden chirp woke him. Kiwi then perched herself on top of his shoulder.

Friday.

Matt hated being in bed on a Friday night, of all days. People ran rampant in clubs and bars, and traffic was always a disaster. The fifth day of the week always called to action, and Speedfire loved Fridays for that.

However, Matt had to spend the whole day resting. He didn't want to risk Madeline lecturing him again, but she was away at work the entire time. He had nothing to lose, yet he stayed put. Sleeping and drinking water were his new hobbies. Kiwi would constantly wake him up by playing in her litter box. Matt sat up and watched as she dug through the pellets. His jaw dropped when she kicked the litter out of the box.

"Kiwi!" he yelled.

The cat chirped as she met his gaze, then started scooping out her own litter. Matt groaned and leaned back on his pillow. He could get Madeline to clean up the mess for him later.

By evening, Matt lay awake, watching the sunset. Madeline wasn't home yet. Matt huffed, then turned over on his other side, facing his open closet. His Speedfire gear tempted him, yet he needed to rest.

Stop thinking about it, he scolded himself.

Matt closed his eyes tightly. His heart hammered inside his chest. All he saw was Christine. She could be walking home alone again. Those men—The Reapers—could be causing chaos to lure Speedfire out. And the Rare Sniper...she could be looking for her next target.

His mind drifted back to Christine. Her safety was a good enough reason to push him out of bed.

Matt geared up, preparing for a short night on the harbor. That was all he planned to do that evening. Find a spot along the rooftops, look over the bayside, and then call it a night.

After the sun vanished, Matt paused on a building across from the headquarters. He sat down, breathing in for a minute as he waited for any sign of Christine. She could be home already, but he decided to wait. Even if she had left work early, Matt didn't mind watching out for any other crime. Many people walked along the harbor this time of night, including criminals.

He sat up suddenly when he heard footsteps passing by. His gaze flickered to the street below, and he spotted Christine huddling in her red dress. He stood slowly, stretched his arms, then followed her from the rooftop.

Just a gentle stroll. Matt leaped carefully from one building to the next. He kept up with Christine's pace, bracing himself for anything. *The Reapers. The Rare Sniper.*

Anyone could be stalking these alleys. Anything could come out and—

"*Shit!*" Matt lost his footing and slipped into an alley. He reached for the fire escape, slamming into the side of a brick building.

Matt looked down, and Christine was already staring up at him. He hung there like a limp fish, gazing back at her awkwardly. His arm throbbed from the impact, but not as much as his head.

He wanted to smack himself, though that would only make things worse.

Matt coughed, then lowered himself. He slipped again—

Thump!

He landed roughly on his knees.

Christine gasped, and he scrambled up, dusting off his jacket as if nothing happened.

"Uh..." He cleared his throat, stumbling forward. "Hi."

Christine scowled. "Hello..."

"That, um..." Matt pointed to the roof, then faced her. "It's a bit slippery..."

Christine raised a brow. "Are you following me?"

"What?" Matt stammered. "No—"

"Just so you know, I don't need your protection," she cut him off. "That was just *one* time."

"Yeah. One time. It still counts as something," he said.

"At this point, most criminals are going to realize *Speedfire* patrols southern Canton," Christine added. "So, I see no use in you following me around." She eyed him, head-to-toe. "And you're not looking so well."

"I'm fine," Matt mumbled.

"Really?" She smirked and crossed her arms. "You just fell a minute ago."

"Slippery roof," he argued. "And I'm just looking over the area. You say most criminals already know I'm here, but that doesn't stop the sniper from coming back."

Christine grimaced. "Uh-huh."

"On top of other things," Matt mentioned, "I found a new gang lurking around the eastern side of Canton. Can never be too careful."

"That, or maybe you're wondering why the general public has no clue you saved me," she proposed.

Matt glared at her. "I'm not doing this for attention."

Christine glanced at the sky. "Yet..."

"I'm not."

She returned her gaze to him. "So, you've come to save me again?" she asked, tilting her head. "Are you sure you're not the damsel in distress this time?"

Matt scoffed, "I...don't need saving."

Christine smiled slightly, glancing at the ground. "Okay."

"And this isn't a search and rescue mission. I already told you why I'm here," he said. "So, if you don't mind...that's what I'm going to do."

"Oh, yes. Don't mind *you*," she emphasized, stepping back. "You're just...hanging around."

Matt scowled at her. He glanced back at the fire escape for a second. "I know how to save myself, at least."

"From falling? Good to know." Christine turned around. She paused, staring across the street at the harbor. The full moon shined across the pavement, igniting the silver city.

"That's beautiful," Matt commented, stepping beside her.

"You don't get a moon like that every night," Christine uttered. She strolled along the street, making her way to the docks.

Matt watched her until she looked over her shoulder. She beckoned him, and he followed her across the road. Christine found a quiet spot at the end of the pier. She lowered herself against the edge, letting her legs hang above the water. She left an open space beside her, and Matt sat down.

"So..." she spoke up, glancing at him. "Are you sure you're okay?"

Matt fixed the hood over his head and nodded. "Don't worry about me."

"I'm asking in general," she said, snagging his attention away from the moon. "I don't know how you do it."

"Do what?"

"*This*." She gestured at his attire. "You're up all night, I assume. You probably take countless beatings from countless criminals. And you can say you're alright, but..." She drifted off for a second, taking a deep breath. "What if you don't get up one day?"

Matt turned to gaze down at the water. The white reflection of the moon mesmerized him, but it didn't distract him from her statement.

"I'll keep getting up," he answered, resting his eyes on her. "That's all I can say."

Her lips parted as she studied him. She turned away with a sudden smile. He noted the blush in her cheeks.

"So, is that what it takes?" she asked, watching the water. "To be a vigilante? You have this invincible mentality."

Matt bit his lip, then shrugged. "It's different for everyone." He turned to her. "Why?"

Christine froze, turning more red. "Why?" she stuttered.

"I mean, why do you ask?"

"Oh." She pursed her lips. "You just...have me curious now." She exhaled roughly. "If you...uh...know about my uncle. He's not—"

"Fond of vigilantes," he finished for her.

Christine faced him and frowned. "And...I'm not sure..."

"Oh *no*," he sighed dramatically. "Don't tell me *I* could possibly be changing your feelings toward vigilantes."

"Hey!" she snapped, turning her nose up at him. "I'm not saying *that*. It's just...you're different."

"I get that a lot," he said, closing his eyes and facing the bay. "But why am I different?"

"You just are."

"Hm."

"Well...you can tell me what it's like," she continued. She rubbed her arm and looked away. "If it's exciting, or..."

"It's invigorating but also deteriorating," he muttered.

"Oh." Christine paused, and her eyes glistened in the moonlight. "Is that how it feels?"

"Uh, it depends," Matt said, resting his hands against the dock. "Some nights, I feel great. Other nights...I guess it matters who I face." He breathed out lightly. "Like that gang I mentioned...they took a lot out of me. And the Rare Sniper..."

Christine's gaze followed the horizon. She stared across the bay solemnly.

"But no matter what, I need to be out here," Matt expressed, tilting his head as he stared at the starless sky. "Every night, I'm doing *something*. And if you want to know what it feels like, it's this long climb. I'm always climbing, reaching for something greater than myself. Though no matter how high I go, I remember where I come from. I eventually have to go back down, right?"

Christine watched him silently, then nodded.

"Climbing takes a lot out of me, too," he huffed, sitting up. "But at the end of the day, it leads me here."

She returned her gaze to the moon. "You get to enjoy views like this."

Matt sighed. "Always."

They sat along the bayside, drowning in the moonlight. Matt was usually keen on spending time with anyone in his vigilante guise. But tonight felt different. Something had told him to be here.

"In the moonlight," Christine whispered, closing her eyes, "we can let it all go."

The breeze drifted through her hair as she blushed faintly. She let the light cascade across her, and he couldn't help but find peace in this moment.

To spend the whole night out on the pier with her would have been a privilege.

"This was nice," Christine said, standing up. She offered her hand to Matt. "I should get going. It's late."

"You don't say?" he said, and she laughed as she pulled him up.

"It is," she emphasized. "And...I don't need you coming with me. Climb somewhere else and save someone who needs it. Whatever it is you do."

"So, you don't need saving?" Matt reiterated, crossing his arms.

"Not now." She wrinkled her nose, then turned around. "You should save yourself more often, Speedfire."

"Whatever you say, Miss Elerare," he replied as she walked away.

Christine glanced to the side. Her face reddened. She waited for the wind to die down before speaking. "Thank you," she said quietly. Without another word, she strolled further into the night, finding her way back down her usual path home.

Matt strolled across the pier slowly, looking after her as she returned to her uncle's apartment. As soon as she was safe inside, Matt turned the other way. He didn't realize until now that his headache had eased off.

The clock became Matt's best friend with each passing day.

He found himself texting Christine just to have her company, even from afar. He didn't share the truth about his concussion and told her he had a fever. Something he feared was this head injury outing his secret identity. *Matthew Ellis and Speedfire both have concussions at the same time? Way to make it obvious!* He wanted Madeline, James, and Kylie to be the only people to know about his condition. He didn't want anyone to pester him with questions about how or why he got a head injury. He found it easier to explain a fever.

Christine wished him well and offered to check on him. The gesture made him smile, but he declined since he didn't want to take up too much of her time.

"I still can't believe you get the flu right after I planned a whole itinerary for you," she said during their latest phone call.

"My immune system sucks. I might be allergic to Streak Corp," he replied, throwing in a fake cough.

"Or you're allergic to James," she suggested.

Besides Christine, Harry also texted him often.

Matt told Harry about The Reapers and his recent encounter with the Rare Sniper, but he left out the part about the concussion. Harry, in return, told Matt that he and Madeline planned to go shopping for dresses and suits to wear for Streak's anniversary party. They would be able to catch up at the gala instead of over the phone.

Matt waited patiently for the day to come. When his head started feeling slightly better, he watched more than documentaries, and he found he could enjoy some light novels again. Matt had the news on in the background, and occasionally he saw his fellow vigilantes being interviewed. Even Trix appeared, the woman who scolded him about patrolling northern Canton. She stood beside Natalie Tray and another vigilante known as Slide.

Slide wore all black clothes and a metallic helmet with a visor. The helmet left his nose and mouth uncovered, and he appeared to have fair skin and a light stubble. He stood beside Trix, arms crossed with a smug grin. They were talking about a recent bank robbery Downtown, but Matt couldn't care less until Trix mentioned his alias.

"New vigilantes in the area like Speedfire still don't know what they're doing," Trix said. "He doesn't have a clue what it's like here."

"Agreed. I know the people think highly of him, but come on," Slide sighed. "I've seen pics of him. He's just a kid thinking he can get with the big leagues."

"And by *big leagues*, you mean with you two?" Natalie inquired.

Trix laughed. "If he could stop a bank robbery, then maybe."

Matt glared at her through the screen. He met her once by chance, and she made sure the whole world knew she detested him. Little did Trix know that Matt stopped plenty of robberies back in Miami.

"Eh, that kid's still got a lot to prove," Slide argued. "I wonder if he'd bother showing his face more on the northern end of the harbor."

"Speedfire has done some incredible work along the docks," Natalie said with a sly smile. "Don't forget about the Rare Sniper now."

"Could be a whole scam," Trix scoffed and turned away.

"If he's as great as he thinks he is, he would've caught the sniper by now," Slide added, then fixed his visor.

I'm trying, Matt fumed. *What is their problem?*

"Whatever. Streak's got every right to be concerned. But I think the 'sniper' figure is just some made-up act," Trix argued. "Like *really?* That fight on the harbor had to be staged. Speedfire *wishes* he had a real rivalry. If he wants competition, I dare him to challenge Hot-Shot."

Matt ignored the news for the rest of his time at home. The last thing he needed to hear was someone calling him a liar.

When his head finally cleared of any pain, he got out of bed without tripping. He cried with joy. For thirteen days, Matt *mostly* stayed indoors.

As he munched on some toast, he heard a knock on the door, and Madeline greeted Harry inside.

"How are you feeling, man?" Harry asked with a wide grin. "You look great!"

"So much better," Matt replied. "I can probably go back to Streak Corp next week."

"As you should," Madeline mentioned. "Your partner has been do-ing double the work."

"James?"

The guilt struck him. If it weren't for James, Matt would have passed out at the headquarters, and everyone would have known about his severe concussion by then.

"Kylie helped him out a ton. I'm sure he'll be happy to see you back," Madeline continued. "Anyway, I'm getting my hair done for the party tonight. Harry, want to join me?"

"Wait. It's *tonight?*" Matt spat out his orange juice.

"Matt, it's October."

Matt leaned back in his chair, defeated. "I lost so much time," he whispered.

"That's what fevers do. It's all fine." Harry patted his back, then strolled over to Madeline. "Before we head out, I brought you something."

"Oh?" Madeline stopped as Harry grabbed a small jewelry box from his pocket. He pulled out a silver necklace with a turquoise gemstone in the middle.

"Just for you," he told her with a soft smile.

Madeline's eyes swelled with tears. She took the necklace in her hands. "Harry," she stuttered. She unclipped the chain and wrapped it around her neck. Her eyes met his as her lips quivered. "You didn't have to."

"Of course I did. You deserve to stand out tonight," he insisted with a blush.

Madeline stepped over to him and kissed his cheek. "I'll get you back one day," she teased.

As Madeline hugged Harry, Matt stepped out onto the veranda to give them a moment. He often had mixed feelings toward relationships after witnessing his sister go through her fair share of heartbreaks during school. As those years passed, Matt wondered if most relationships ended in pain. His sister escaped toxic boyfriends time after time, and the fear of ending up with an abusive partner eventually had them both feeling the same way about love.

It's not worth it.

But time changed everything, as it always did.

Chapter 28

FORTY YEARS OF LEGACIES

The Oleandris towered above the rest of the Inner Harbor, its silver beams glinting under the moonlight. Many guests were ushered through the entrance, where security guards checked for invites and sent the attendees to the top floor.

Madeline donned a sleeveless teal dress for the event, while Matt found a simple black and blue tuxedo tucked away in his closet. He had even combed his hair back, and Madeline helped him gel it. The two approached The Oleandris with Harry, and within minutes, they caught an elevator ride to the top floor.

The doors opened, revealing a spacious room made for events. A wrap-around balcony, crowded with guests, presented a vast view of the city, and a set of stairs led up to the roof. Golden ribbons and pictures of the Streak family hung from the walls, which included Jason, Amelia, and their parents, Jonathon and Marissa. The nearby tables consisted of punch bowls, glasses of wine, and platters of sliders and cheese. Chairs and couches, already occupied by eccentric partygoers, were set up against the walls and near the windows.

"This place is nice," Madeline spoke up and held Harry's hand. "I wonder where Mr. Streak's at."

As she peered around the rest of the crowd, Matt turned to see if he could find anybody he recognized at the party. Before he could move away, Madeline tapped his shoulder, pointing toward the tables.

"I see your friend," she said, and he tensed as he spotted James and Kylie. "Want to tell him you're doing better?"

Matt frowned. "I don't know—"

"Come on." Madeline took his hand, then dragged him and Harry toward the wine. "Hey, James!"

James stopped sipping his punch. "Yes?" He turned to face them, noticing Matt instantly. He blinked. "*Oh.*"

Matt bit his lip, then waved once. "Hey..." His eyes glossed over James' black and red suit. His hair was even styled differently, having been combed back neatly instead of thrown together into a messy bun.

"Aw, Matthew. You survived," James laughed.

Matt flushed red as Madeline patted his shoulder. "He's a trooper. Thank you again for helping him. I don't know how long he was going to hide *it* from me."

"The fever?" Harry mentioned, confused. "How in the world do you *hide* a *fever?*"

Madeline leaned close to Harry. "It was a concussion but we're keeping that a secret."

Harry facepalmed. "*Dude.*"

"The department's been busy," Kylie mentioned, holding a glass of wine as she smirked at James. Her blue dress sparkled under the lights. "This one here couldn't stop talking about having you back."

"Well, I've been doing all the work," James remarked. "Glad to see you're doing better now, Matthew. Stop hiding things from your sister."

"I don't hide *too* much from her," Matt replied, and Madeline rolled her eyes.

"But when you do, at least James is around to catch you," she said, then shifted her gaze to James. "I can't watch him every minute of the day, unfortunately."

Matt tensed. "*Maddie.*"

James smirked. "He's stuck with me all day, so no worries." He winked at her. "I've got him covered."

"Well, promise me one thing," Madeline added, holding her hand out to James. "Watch his back when I'm not around. He clearly needs it."

James shook her hand. "I grew up with a wild sister," he mentioned. "Years of experience here."

Matt knew Madeline and James were jesting, but his feelings sank. His sister watched over him relentlessly, and no matter what path he would take, he was always going to cause her grief.

"Hold on, I see Lorelei," Madeline said, glancing to the left. Matt followed her gaze, where Madame Modisette spoke with a few patrons near the stairwell. She wore a long purple gown with a skirt that dragged along the floor. "I'll be right back."

"I'll come with you," Harry offered, joining her as they left Matt behind with James and Kylie.

Matt stepped closer to James. He wasn't in the mood to talk to many other people tonight.

"Try this," Kylie spoke up behind him. She handed James her wine glass. "It's forty years old."

James eyed the glass uncomfortably. "I think I'll pass..."

"Seriously?" Kylie took another sip. "Don't take this stuff for granted. It's a rarity."

James scowled. "I'm your ride home tonight."

Kylie raised her eyes to the ceiling. "And? It's just a sip." She glanced at Matt with a smirk. "Nothing wrong with getting a little tipsy, either."

"Is it good?" Matt asked as she filled another glass to the brim with the burgundy wine.

Kylie handed him the wineglass. "You tell me."

"Oh." Matt took the cup, catching a side-eye from James. "Are you sure?"

"It's fine," Kylie sighed as she reached back for her own glass. "No one here is going to care. Besides, the drinking age in Optyma was eighteen. And don't some people say New Harbor is an Optyman city? I mean, it's nothing compared to Port Haven, but still."

Matt caught the aroma of fresh berries and vanilla as he brought the glass to his lips. He took a large sip, and he started coughing as the wine burned down his throat.

"Kylie," James groaned as she laughed.

"You'll get used to it," Kylie said, patting Matt's shoulder. "At least someone here can appreciate fine wine with me."

Matt didn't say anything. He stared at the swirling liquid in his wineglass, wondering if he should drink the rest of it or set it aside.

"My father owned a vineyard years back," Kylie mentioned as she passed her glass to James again. "He was very successful, too. I can't help but wonder if I'd have taken it over. But here I am instead."

"Being tipsy." James set the wine down on the table while Matt finished off his glass. "Let's not overdo it."

"You should let yourself unwind," Kylie uttered, swatting his shoulder lightly. "Even Matt's more fun than you."

"Hey," James snapped.

Matt cleared his throat. "That stuff was strong…"

"She gave you port wine."

Matt stared at him, confused. "Okay?"

"And you've had enough," James said, taking Matt's empty glass. Kylie snickered. "Go find your sister before I'm stuck driving you home, too."

Matt winced, then turned away from Kylie and James. He would rather sit by them the whole evening just to avoid other people. Instead, he sauntered to Madeline's side as she spoke with Lorelei.

"Jason is by the balcony," he overheard Madame Modisette say as he stopped next to Harry. "Do feel free to converse with some of our clients here. I'm sure they'd love to meet you."

"Definitely," Madeline said. "I wonder if—oh…hi, Matt. I wonder if some of the other district managers are here."

"I'm certain you'll see a few familiar faces from Miami," Lorelei mentioned. "But have fun. I'll be here the whole night if you need me."

"Thank you." Madeline turned to Matt and Harry, then motioned them toward the balcony entrance.

Jason Streak stood near the glass doors, chatting with several other men. He wore an elegant black suit with a golden trim, and a gold-dusted, black tie. Beside him stood Christine, who wore a long black dress with her hair tied back in a waterfall braid.

"Not even the recent incidents have halted my progress," Streak said as they entered the vicinity.

"That is always good to hear, Jason," an older man replied warmly.

The man wore a dark gray suit and a black tie. He had gray hair, a handlebar mustache, and gripped a cane. Beside the older gentleman stood a younger man who looked like him, with light brown hair and a fancy dark brown suit.

"Hello, Mr. Streak," Madeline greeted. "I didn't expect to see so many people here. The Oleandris is beautiful."

"Madeline," Streak opened his arms, "I'm glad you're enjoying the gala so far." He gestured to the older gentleman with a smile. "This is Richard Edinburgh, one of my most trusted friends and sharcholders. He holds thirty percent of the shares in Streak Corporation. He also owns Edinburgh Towers, the largest hotel chain along the East Coast."

"Pleasure to meet you," Madeline said, then shook hands with Richard.

"Likewise," Richard replied. "I've heard a lot about you."

She grinned. "How do you and Mr. Streak know each other?"

Streak chuckled as he leaned closer to Mr. Edinburgh. "He's been a family friend for ages," he added. "I'll let you in on a secret, Madeline. Richard is quite an expert on lobbying."

Madeline straightened. "Oh."

"Ah, you know I was a former politician in Washington," Mr. Edinburgh prodded Streak. "I retired from being a representative to focus on my company again."

"That's...wonderful." She glanced at Streak. "Harry came too."

Harry waved at Streak shyly and continued to stand behind Madeline.

"Glad to see you're doing well, Harold," added Streak. "Also, Mr. Edinburgh brought his son to join us. This is Edward." He gestured to the younger gentleman beside Richard, who smiled at them. "He's following in his father's footsteps."

"I'm currently expanding the business across the West Coast," Edward added, shaking hands with Madeline. "I'll be staying in New Harbor for a couple of months, though. The gala gave me a perfect reason to come back."

Matt scooted his way beside Christine, who crossed her arms.

"It's great meeting two of our most trusted stockholders," mentioned Madeline.

"Sadly, there aren't many people I can trust nowadays," Streak sighed. "Especially with Sal-Tech intruding New Harbor, and the whole Core Stone ordeal."

"I have to say," said Richard, "despite the struggles, Streak Corp has grown faster than ever."

Streak put his arm around Christine. "I've done the best I could to raise this company," he told them. "And with years to come, I hope to see that legacy continue with our children."

He gripped her shoulder, and Christine's face dropped. Edward glanced at her with a smile.

"Still preparing your niece for that responsibility, eh?" Richard laughed. "I think she and Edward will do an incredible job with both companies."

"I know we will," Edward added. "And since I'll be in the area for a few months, we should plan some time out."

Christine shrugged her uncle's hand off her shoulder. "Yeah…"

"Here. How about you two chat, and I'll introduce Madeline to the Norfolk managers," Streak mentioned.

Matt stared at the floor, trying to blink his eyes into focus. Meanwhile, Madeline and Harry left with Streak and Richard to find another group of attendees.

Why did she give me port wine? He glanced back at Kylie and James, who moved to the couches near the wine. His vision spun slightly. *Shit…*

Edward stepped toward Christine. "So, I had made some reservations," he said. "It would be pretty wise to start seeing each other in public sooner than later."

Christine's face remained passive. "Sure."

"So, a few dates here and there. We can get to know each other a bit better," Edward continued. "It's what your uncle suggested—"

"Wait," Matt turned around to face them, "since when did you two start dating?"

Christine's face turned red. "We're not." She stared at him, concerned. "Why didn't you follow your sister?"

"What…? I don't know." Matt rubbed his eyes. "I think I need to step outside."

Edward gave him a sour look, then turned back to Christine. "Let's talk in private later."

"Okay." She nodded, and Edward left to join his father. Matt stared at the lights reflecting against the window until he felt her hand around his wrist. "Come with me."

"Shit, sorry," he stammered. He nearly stumbled as she dragged him through the crowd.

Christine paused before the stairs to the rooftop, hesitating for a moment. After a quick breath, she pulled Matt up with her. They climbed to the roof, finding it was lit with lanterns but empty.

She sighed. "It's so hot in there."

Matt bit his bottom lip. "So…"

"I didn't want to come out here alone," she said quietly.

"Oh."

Christine straightened herself and took a step toward him. She smiled at his suit. "You look nice."

"So do you," he replied with a grin.

"At least you're feeling better," she exhaled. "I missed seeing you around."

"I'll be back tomorrow." He still didn't want to mention anything about the concussion. At this point, he wished he could forget he even had one. "I missed you, too."

"Texting isn't the same, you know?" she laughed. She stepped forward, hugging him. He wrapped his arms around her as a breeze drifted by them.

"So, what was that all about?" he asked as they pulled apart. "The whole Edinburgh thing."

"Uh." Her voice dropped. "I don't know what to say about it."

Matt frowned. "Sorry for eavesdropping..."

"No, that's not your fault. I guess Edward didn't think you were there," she huffed. "You looked like you were staring off into space, anyway."

"Yeah, actually, I was."

She nodded. "A signature Matt Ellis move."

"Shush. Let me play in space," he teased. "I'm just feeling a little...light-headed." He held his breath, then looked around. "Look at this view, though." Matt walked across the roof, resting his hands on the railing. "You can see the whole city up here." His grin widened as a faint breeze drifted against his skin. "I can see Streak Corp. And my apartment."

He looked over his shoulder to find Christine hesitating. She stared at the edge anxiously, clutching her hands against her chest. Without a word, she pressed her lips together, then slowly joined his side.

"Best part of the gala right here," he joked. He glanced at her again, and she stared down the side of the skyscraper, her fists still curled. "Christine?"

She breathed deeply. The wind fluttered through her hair, and her brows furrowed.

Matt gazed down at the street. He wondered if the height worried her.

"Are you scared of heights?" he asked. "We can go back inside."

She said nothing. Matt caught her staring down at the city again. Perhaps the building reminded her of her late grandmother. Too much was on her mind, and Matt felt like he wasn't helping her situation.

"Last time I was up here, I was sixteen." Christine lowered her hands, gripping the railing in front of her. "At least this time, I'm not alone." She shared a quick gaze with him before turning her attention to the distant water.

Matt slid his hand closer to hers. "You know, you can talk to me about anything," he offered. She continued to stare off into the distance. "Hey." He waited for her to meet his eyes again. "I get it, okay?"

She scowled. "So, you want to know about the Edinburgh thing?"

"I mean...only if you're comfortable sharing," he said. "Sorry again...about..."

"What? Interrupting the dating plans?" she scoffed.

Matt swallowed. "Was he asking you out?"

Her gaze moved to the street again. "My uncle's been trying to set us up. And Edward wants to move forward with it."

Matt rubbed the railing. "Why...?"

"He wants Edward to take over Streak Corp one day. We're talking about something years from now. But keep in mind, Uncle Jason also wants to retire young. Before my mom died, he didn't plan on taking over the business," she explained. "So, to avoid public suspicion, he wants Edward to *inherit* the company, if you get what I mean."

Matt gaped. "*Why?*" he repeated.

She crossed her arms as her eyes moved to the west. "He doesn't trust me to take it over," she muttered. "But the public can't know how he feels about his niece, right? So, this whole 'thing' exists to save his own reputation."

"And...you're going through with it?"

Christine grimaced. "I have to. My uncle's already looking for another secretary," she said. "He's pushing us to start 'publicly' dating, or whatever."

"That's..." His shoulders sagged. He didn't know what to say or how to comfort her. "I hope Edward's not a complete ass."

"Yeah." Christine wrapped her arms around herself. "Me too."

"And the dates," he continued, and she glanced his way. "I bet they'll be awkward."

She forced a smile. "I can tell you all about it."

"Only if you want to."

"No..." Her lips quivered as she turned away from him. "I think I'll need to."

Matt could hear the crowds of people inside. His mind still felt foggy, his gaze slightly spinning. The stupor only got worse with each passing minute, and he tried to recall how much wine Kylie had given him.

One glass? he pondered. *Full? Half-full?*

The music grew louder, and the smell of delicacies wafted from the open door. A sudden gust blew around them, and he noticed her shivering from the cold.

"Hey," he whispered, moving closer to her, "if there's anything you need, let me know."

She winced. "I don't want to burden you..."

Christine turned toward the edge. She stared down at the waves of the inner harbor and wiped a tear from her cheek.

Matt watched her tears fall. "Are you okay?"

"No. I don't care," she cried. "And why should I?" She rubbed her eyes. "I don't even own myself."

Matt frowned. "But what if you left? No one can stop you."

"There's nowhere else to go." She gripped the railings in front of her. "Imagine just...flying. Setting yourself free with no more strings."

Matt wanted to feel the same way—to be free without the pressure of owing his life to someone else. He felt this way with Madeline, but he wanted to find a way to make his sister understand his pain and guilt without her feeling terrible about it. Christine's situation felt even more complicated, however. Her future was set in stone by Streak, and she was running out of time.

"If you teach me how to climb, I will show you how to fly," she lamented. *"So when the world decides to test us, we can save ourselves from the fall."*

Matt glanced at her. "What was that?"

She breathed in deeply. "A poem I've been working on," she replied. "I think it fits my mood right now."

"I didn't know you wrote poetry," he said in awe.

"I like songwriting," Christine added. Her gaze flickered to him. "I've never shared my poetry with anyone else. Ever."

The corner of his lips lifted. "Did you write that for anyone in mind?"

Christine looked back toward the water. "I can't say." She tried her best to hide her growing smile. Her cheeks turned red, and she closed her eyes.

If you teach me how to climb...

Those words were all it took to make him blush as well. He held his breath, turning his head.

There's no way, he thought, focusing on the cool air.

Matt glanced at her face, and she looked the same as she did on the pier with him—with Speedfire.

He placed his hand over hers, and her gaze returned to him. "I need to tell you something," he said.

Her lips parted. "Okay?"

Matt stared into her questioning gaze. He started shaking, still feeling her hand grasped in his. The emotions overwhelmed him in seconds. The vertigo spun his brain into every direction possible. His heart raced rapidly, crushing his chest.

I'm Speedfire.

And just like that, he could make or break her whole night.

He opened his mouth, but his sister's words came back to haunt him. Even as light-headed as he was right now, he wondered if taking a gamble was worth the risk tonight.

"You're my best friend," Matt confessed instead. "I...I just want you to know nothing will change that."

"Matt..." Christine let his hand go as she moved toward him. She wrapped him in another hug, then rested her head against his shoulder. "You'll always have me, too."

He held her gently and rubbed her back as the wind softened. Despite his words, he felt like the greatest coward in the world.

"Shit," Christine whispered. She pulled away, then faced the door. "We still have a party to get back to. And I have so many guests to take care of—"

"Or so many guests to watch and judge," he suggested slyly.

Christine snickered. "If you insist. I'd love to do that. Judge them all."

"Judge them all for liking Jason Streak?"

Christine took his hand and guided him back inside The Oleandris. "You don't like *Jason Streak*?" she gasped. "How could you?"

They leaned against the wall and gazed at the crowd of fanciful attendees—all with their glasses of wine and spectacles. Matt could barely hear himself think with all this constant chatter.

"Look at them all," Christine said loudly. "They're like ants."

Matt glanced at her to follow her gaze. "To be honest, I feel like a sore thumb."

"Stop. You look great."

"I'm a mess," he claimed sarcastically.

She laughed, "Then I'm the bigger mess."

"Okay, so be it. But I think the biggest mess goes to that gentleman over there who spilled wine on his date's dress," he pointed out.

Christine gasped as she noticed the lady's white dress soaked in red wine. The lady angrily pointed her finger at the man in a blue tuxedo beside her.

"That could be us, but we're not old enough to drink yet," she mentioned, nudging him with her elbow.

His face flushed red. "Ha...yeah..." He found the wine station, where Kylie had returned with James glued to her side. "I might have had a bit to drink tonight..."

"Oh." She smirked. "So, that's why you're feeling light-headed."

He grinned. "Perchance."

"I'm so telling your sister—"

"*No.*" He locked his arm around hers, and she laughed. "I can't let you go. Sorry."

"And that's a bad thing?" she teased, scooting closer to him.

Matt had not expected to spend the night as a wallflower with Christine, but he loved every second of it. The various shenanigans of the partygoers entertained him. One woman stepped on a man's foot, and he hollered loudly, which called attention to the pair for a good minute as they bickered. Another man demanded to see the "prestigious" Jason Streak and interrupted several conversations. This one made Christine laugh more than usual.

As time passed on, the music grew, and more people joined each other on the dance floor. Matt swayed his head back and forth slightly, letting the tipsiness overcome him, until Christine dragged him away from the wall. At this point in the night, he hadn't a care in the world. He was tired, slightly drunk, and on the verge of spacing out again, but Christine's energy lit up the room for him. She placed his hands on her hips, then threw her arms across his shoulders. Step after step, back and forth. They blended in with the rest of the attendees, taking in the symphony. The music drowned out the chatter in the background, and the golden space around him became a blur. All Matt could focus on was the genuine joy in Christine's eyes. Her smile only widened, and her softening gaze moved up to his eyes as he joined her in this slow dance.

After hearing all her grievances, the least he could do was keep her smiling.

"Matt!" Madeline called out, pushing herself through the crowd. She waved over at him while holding Harry's hand. Matt and Christine pulled apart from each other. His mind still felt like it was in a daze. "Mr. Streak's about to make an announcement. The party's almost over."

"Oh, good," Christine huffed. Madeline shot her with a confused look. "I mean, good...as in...I'm tired."

Within a few minutes, Streak lifted a wine glass and tapped it with a spoon to produce a light ring. The whole party's attention turned to him.

"Thank you all for coming to celebrate the fortieth anniversary of Streak Corporation. It has been a pleasure hosting for you all," he announced. "As you can see, Streak Corp is far from losing any battle we find ourselves in.

"Our sales and designs are increasing at incredible rates, all thanks to Madeline Ellis here at New Harbor," continued Streak. He gestured toward Madeline on the other side of the room. All eyes were on her, and her face flushed red from the attention. She smiled and waved. "With this statement, I also want to mention that our loyalty has been wavering. Several affiliates have stolen from me in support of Sal-Tech, and you all know Salus is currently setting up a distribution house in the Inner Harbor. Seeing your loyal faces here warms my heart, however, and I am thankful to meet with you all today.

"Sal-Tech has been scheming with inside agents, but despite these incidents, Streak Corporation will remain at the top of the industry." He paused as the audience burst into applause. "Sal-Tech prefers to *cheat* their way to the top. Trust me. They will not be getting away with it. I will stunt their growth myself."

Before Streak could turn away, a loud voice called out for him in the crowd, "Kiera Salus is a *genius!*"

The look on Streak's face dropped as he scanned the crowd. All eyes were now on the speaker. James had his arms crossed with a smug look on his face.

"And what are you implying?" Streak replied as he raised an eyebrow.

"She's a genius. That's a fact," James claimed. "Her inventions have made her successful, and you have no proof that she cheats."

"My proof lies in the workers who exploited my company through hacks and theft," Streak remarked. "Through this *Whip-Master*." He shot a glance at Harry as the crowd watched the argument with interest. Kylie lingered back, narrowing her eyes at James. "Besides, Kiera Salus seems more like a mascot than a CEO. Whoever funded her company, along with the *mascot* herself, should be held accountable for their illegal actions against me."

"But you can't deny her intellect, Mr. Streak," James continued. "Sal-Tech is successful because of Kiera. Your sole success comes from your parents."

Gasps broke out from the audience. Matt shrunk back against the wall with Christine, concerned.

"Kiera Salus is a cunning, deceitful girl who has used her charm to climb the ranks of this industry. I know how people like her work," Streak countered.

"But you don't truly *know* her," James told him. His face dropped to a glower. "I stand by my word. She's a genius. If you want to beat your enemy, you must know them best. False accusations will get you nowhere."

Streak paused as he took in his words. He gazed toward the crowd for a moment.

"I suppose you are right." Streak smiled, then turned away. "I conclude my statement, however. Salus will not outlive me."

The cheerful atmosphere of the celebration was gone.

Matt tried to find James in the middle of the crowd once Streak was done, but to no avail. He and Kylie had already vanished.

Chapter 29

NIGHT-RAVEN

Three days had passed since the gala, and Matt sat at his desk, overwhelmed with articles. The news didn't cover James' remarks about Sal-Tech, however, even though those reporters had to have witnessed the dispute.

Maybe it would have made Streak look bad. Matt tapped his pen against the desk. *He did say some rude things about Salus.*

"After leading an expedition finding the remains of what she believes to be a *horned* serpent, Dr. Macha Storm retires at seventy," a journalist announced from James' screen.

James smiled. "Here, check this out," he said, swerving his monitor to show Matt.

"The Lakota archeologist is known for studying lost fossils and finding proof of old indigenous myths," the reporter explained. She showed a picture of a serpent's enormous skeleton along a northeastern coastline. "After fifty years in the field, Dr. Storm is ready to retire."

"That woman is incredible," James exhaled. "I love her research."

"She researches myths?" asked Matt.

James nodded. "She finds fossils of creatures from Native American folklore. Just look at the size of that thing."

Matt fixed his eyes on the serpentine skeleton. "Do you believe in that stuff?"

James shrugged. "My sister does. She was always obsessed with snakes. Even thinks dragons were real. She got me interested in Dr. Storm, actually."

Matt swiveled his chair to face his own computer. The thought of myths existing excited him, but his eagerness ran dry as soon as his eyes returned to the gala article.

"Wait," he gasped, turning around. "I was going to ask you about the—"

James was already gone, and his screen was black.

Matt grimaced. "Never mind."

After ten minutes, James returned to his desk and leaned back in his chair.

"Everything okay?" Matt spoke up. He caught James' attention immediately.

James peered over at him with a blank face. "Yes. Why?"

"I don't know." Matt attempted to scramble a question together. "I saw what happened at the party, and you've hardly gone through any articles this week. Instead, you're showing me videos of fossils."

James took the glasses off his face. "How'd you enjoy the gala? Besides Kylie giving you wine, at least."

"It was fine." He cared more about his time with Christine than the actual event. "What about you?"

"There was this moment, you know," James scooted his chair closer to Matt as he lowered his voice, "to get at Streak."

"To *get at* him?"

James peeked around the corner, making sure no one eavesdropped. "He has an ego. I'm sure you've seen it."

"I would expect that he has one, yeah."

"He thinks he's better than Kiera Salus. Granted, he's been around longer than she has, but you would think he'd at least have some humility."

"Wait, wait, wait." Matt raised his hands. "No offense, but I've never met Kiera Salus."

"She makes her rounds. If you stick around in the industry, you probably will," James said.

Matt felt dumbfounded. "Okay? What are you getting at?"

"Do you trust Streak?" James asked him abruptly.

Matt gaped. "I...think so? All of New Harbor trusts him."

"But do you trust him personally? Put aside the Core Stone, his business, and his public image. Do you trust his character?"

Matt frowned as his sapphire eyes stared deeply through his own.

James squinted with a smile. "Follow me."

He stood up, beckoned Matt to Kylie's office, then stepped inside. James closed the door, and Kylie glanced at them from her desk.

"What's wrong this time?" she asked, then eyed Matt.

"We were talking about Streak," James informed her. He crossed his arms and sat in a chair across from her desk. Matt walked over but stood beside him, unsure whether to take a seat.

"Oh, about the gala?" she added. "That was quite a show you put on."

"I know," James replied, then pretended to check his nails. "Matthew, you said that you *maybe* trust Streak?"

Everything that Matt knew of Kiera Salus, Sal-Tech, and the involvement of the Rare Sniper and The Reapers disturbed him. It didn't help that Streak Corp was under fire by Sal-Tech.

"Matthew," James repeated.

"I..." Matt lost his voice. He wanted to say he trusted Streak over Salus. He wanted to trust the man who offered his sister a position for life, who motivated and inspired Madeline to follow her ambitions in honoring her parents. He wanted to say many great things about Jason Streak, just like everyone else would. Yet Streak would do anything to keep his business and legacy alive, and Christine was the key to ensuring its longevity. "I don't know."

"How could you *not* know? Streak has something Kiera doesn't have, right?" James replied, stretching his arms.

Matt's face dropped even more as his mind clouded with confusion. His brows furrowed as he faced James. "What does the Core Stone have to do with anything?"

James smiled at him. "The Core Stone *is* everything."

"As it always has been," added Kylie.

Matt glanced back and forth between them. "Streak has trust issues because of it."

"I don't blame him. Everyone wants it," sighed Kylie. "When Streak happens to have it with him, they like to strike."

"But why do you two sound like you'd try to take it?" asked Matt.

"When did we say that?" James laughed. "We're just messing with you."

Matt glared at him. *Of course.*

"You were there when Damien Surtair took it," Matt said.

"And he was stealing it for someone else," noted James.

Matt scowled. "Yeah. The Tyrant."

"You heard about the Tyrant?" Kylie tilted her head.

"Yes," Matt said, then peered down at James. "I think certain people want to be associated with the Core Stone. That attraction to power is like a draw to fame."

"You know, there was research done some time ago regarding Rare Souls and the Core Stones," James started and returned his gaze to Matt "Everyone is going to be drawn to those stones, regardless. But I believe that Rare Souls have a special kind of attraction. They can just...feel the connection from afar." He stared off into the distance. "And they want to satisfy the feeling."

Matt turned his attention to the window, to the world outside. "What was this research?"

"Optyman research," replied James. "Optyma was the home of the Core Stones. Its people knew those stones and their creator better than anyone else. They always will."

"But not all Optymans are *Rare*..."

James shook his head. "You don't have to be *Rare* to have power over the stone. Look at Streak," he pointed out with a smirk. "But the *Rare* were divine on Optyma. To the Lapaists, the Rare Souls were seen as saints."

"I want to say something about that, too," Matt said. Kylie and James returned their gazes to him. "I believe there are two stones in New Harbor right now."

Jason Streak and the Rare Sniper.

James walked over to Matt, then put his hand on his shoulder. "Matthew, there may be even more than *two* in this city as we speak. Be patient. Those stones want to be found."

Matt lay in bed with his eyes closed tightly. He could hardly focus with the stones crossing his mind.

When he opened his eyes, he found himself in the chrysanthemum field.

"I want answers," he demanded as he stepped toward the lady in blue on the hill. "For the Core Stones."

She turned to face him. Her dirty blond hair drifted with the breeze. "*The wind feels like home,*" she whispered.

"Answers. Now."

"*You want me to interfere with your research?*" she asked.

"Haven't you already?"

Her smile faded. "*Perhaps. But I don't have all the answers you seek. Just advice.*"

"Okay, then give me advice," Matt said. "Scandals are taking over every corner of this damn city, whether it deals with those stones or not. A man is missing because he tried to steal one of them."

"*I understand…*"

"Then tell me," he choked out. "What do I need to do next? There are people I love who might be in danger. I *almost* lost someone already."

The lady in blue stepped forward with a sigh. "*Matt, take this advice. Be wary of the mask.*"

He shuddered. "What mask?" he demanded. "The sniper's mask? My mask?"

"*Everyone wears a mask. It can be one's greatest strength and weakness.*"

"But what does that have to do with the Core Stones?" he begged. "Please…tell me. Are there three stones in New Harbor?"

The lady in blue returned her gaze to the distant sky. "*You want nothing to do with those stones.*"

"I do. You know what I want."

"*You don't know,*" she whispered. Her gaze dropped to the yellow chrysanthemums. "*Those stones should never fall into the wrong hands.*"

"That's what I'm trying to prevent," he urged. "The Rare Sniper has a stone, and this 'Tyrant' wants Streak's stone. I feel like New Harbor is in danger."

"*And it is,*" she told him softly. "*You should still avoid the stones.*"

Matt shook his head. "It's hard to."

"*I despise the stones,*" she warned him. They locked eyes. "*And if you risk too much…you will hate them, too.*"

Matt furrowed his brows. "How could I hate them?"

"*The stones corrupt people—even people who aren't* Rare," she confessed. "*To put it simply, the stones inspire greed.*"

The lady in blue paused as Matt listened intently. He noticed a tear in the corner of her eye, and his stomach twisted. This dream was nothing like any of their other conversations. He took in Christine's words.

Perhaps he was meeting a ghost.

"*I've witnessed someone's power turn against them,*" she lamented.

"How?" he asked cautiously.

The lady in blue stared ahead at the dwindling sunset. She remained silent.

Matt felt a chill in the air. He held his breath as she turned to face him again. Her gaze was a warning.

"*Beware the mask. Look beyond it,*" she whispered.

Before he could say another word, he opened his eyes. His gaze wandered to his fire dagger in the closet.

Matt started his night with a stroll through inner Canton. A walk while on the lookout for crime should clear his mind. He passed by the same club Katelyn was camping out in when he helped her weeks ago. A party of people were outside, drinking and cheering alongside the neon lights.

"You don't deserve to be here!" a man yelled from an alley nearby. Matt perked, then crept closer to the backstreet. "I'll turn you in myself if you don't scram!"

A drunk man threw his empty beer bottle at a pair of girls hiding in the alley. He slurred his words, stepping forward sluggishly. Before the man could reach them, Matt bolted forward, putting himself in between the drunkard and the girls.

"Holy shit." The man scrambled back. "Speedfire—"

"Go the other way." Matt raised his fist. "If you know what's good for you."

The drunkard swallowed, shaking. "You need to stop them." He pointed at the girls behind Matt, who were huddled in their capes. "They're Optymans."

Matt glared at him. "And?"

"They're like *her*. The bitch you fight," the man hissed. "I bet they even work with the sniper. They're probably Easterners. *Island rats.*"

Matt peered over his shoulder. The girls were identical, with tan skin, dark hair, and youthful faces. They looked no older than him.

"Even if they were Eastern Optymans," he said, facing the drunkard again, "they're *kids.*"

The man trembled as he backed away. He was making no progress confronting the Optymans with Speedfire in the way. Without another word, he raised his middle finger, then staggered out of the alley.

The Optyman girls were silent as they cuddled against each other for warmth. Matt approached them carefully, then kneeled beside them.

"Sorry about that…" he said. "I can escort you to a shelter if you'd like."

The closest twin shook her head. "The shelters won't take Optymans."

He blinked. "*Really?*"

"Speedfire…?" The younger twin peeked her head out. "I thought you hated us."

Matt's heart sank. "And where did you hear that?"

The twins shared a glance. "That's what people say," the older girl said. "You fight Optymans…"

Matt grimaced. "Well, 'hate' is a strong word. And I fight *one* Optyman," he replied. "I don't hold anything against your people."

Just your president, he thought.

"What are your names?" he asked.

"Harper," the older twin answered

"Ivy," the younger one said.

"Well, Harper and Ivy," Matt offered his hand to the girls as he stood up, "let's see if I can get you into a shelter. Someone in this city has to have a heart."

The night neared its end with the coming of twilight. Matt sat on the edge of a building, staring out at the harbor with his hands in his lap. He kept his mask on.

Everyone wears a mask.

The blue lady's words rang through his head. Perhaps Streak put on a public mask, and so did Salus.

A mask was another way of telling a lie, after all. And Matt was one of the world's greatest liars.

Footsteps approached him from behind. Before he could react, the Rare Sniper lowered herself beside him, letting her legs hang over the edge of the roof.

Matt stared ahead, frozen. "What are you doing?"

"I had a feeling you would be here," she whispered. "Your head looks better."

Matt shifted his gaze to her mask with a temptation to rip it off. If he tried, however, there was no saying she wouldn't do the same to him.

"You came out to see me?" he asked.

"No. I wanted to watch the waves." She glanced at him before she returned her gaze to the bay. "I love how the wind carries the water."

The wind feels like home. He recalled what the lady in blue had said.

The wind feels like Hell, he thought instead.

"You missed me," he said.

The sniper tensed. "No...?" she replied, confused. "I'd rather not see you again, honestly."

Matt guffawed. "*What?* No," he stammered. "I mean...you *missed* the shot. You only grazed my arm that night."

"Ohh..." she murmured. "Right." Her eyes lingered on him for a moment. "What a pity. You survived."

"No thanks to you," he muttered. "The Reapers would have taken me. You messed up their mission."

The sniper nodded slowly. "The Reapers were still in the area. All they had to hear was the gunshot followed by your scream." Her gaze followed the wafting waves below. "And just for a night, you were dead to them."

Matt's heart dropped. These words were the last thing he wanted to hear, and he hated what she was implying.

"You shot me..." he said quietly. "And you missed—"

"They don't call me a 'bad shot' for nothing."

His mind flashed back to the night she had pulled him out of the river, and then to the moment she stood in between him and The Reapers. He didn't want to admit that she had been saving him.

"Did The Reapers ever find out?" he asked, trying to hide his concern. "That you failed?"

"You're still in the news." Her eyes moved to the moon.

"I wish I could figure you out." He tightened his hood. "I want to get to the bottom of this. You have all the answers I need."

"Just because one has an answer doesn't mean they have a solution," she argued.

"They're the same thing."

"They're not."

He glared at her. "Then what do you mean?"

"An answer just tells you something. A solution fixes the problem." Her shadowed eyes rested on him. "If I told you everything right now, you still wouldn't know how to handle it. Any answer I give you would only create a bigger problem." The wind carried her husky voice, ruffling the feathers on her cape. "You want to know why?"

"Tell me."

"You would be stuck," she hissed. "You wouldn't know how to save the day. What would you do if I told you *everything?*"

"Why would I tell you?" he shot back.

"I'm trying to make a point," she snapped. "How would my words be enough proof to end this whole conspiracy?"

"I think I'd report you to Jason Streak first," he told her. "Since he's your primary target."

The sniper looked away. "The city loves you right now, Fire. But they love certain people more," she stated quietly. "You mess up, and they're going to hate you. Congratulations, you got your answer, but you didn't resolve anything."

Matt grimaced. "I'm surprised you're even talking to me."

She rested her hands on her lap. "Then do my words hold any meaning to you?"

Matt stared at her desperately. *Yes.*

"You did something no one else had the nerve to do," she added. "You gave me this name."

"The *Rare* Sniper?"

Matt recalled when he had suggested the title to Harry, and Harry was the one who shared it with the public. Harry credited Speedfire for the name, however.

"You're *Rare*, and you're a sniper," he said blankly.

"It's an identity. I think you're smart," she shared with him, "but also reckless."

"Do you like the name? Is that what you're trying to say?" he exhaled.

She shook her head, which made him frown. "It's what I am. The title of a false assassin," she said, her voice low.

Matt stiffened. "*False*...assassin?" He glanced her way. "What does that mean?"

"The Reapers." Her shoulders sank. "They finish all my victims in the hospital."

"*What?*" He shuddered. "You just shoot them?"

"I put them all in a vulnerable place. Their blood is still on my hands." Her dark gaze met his. "As your blood may be one day."

The wind chilled his spine. He held her attention, finding himself too attached to her violet eyes. "And you'd let it be," he murmured. "Right?"

The sniper turned to the harbor. Matt figured he would keep the conversation going if it meant he could get something out of her.

"So...what should I call you? What name would you prefer?" he asked.

"Names are only chains," she lamented. "The public gave you your name because you're a hero. They wanted to commemorate you. But do you *feel* like a hero? Or does the pressure eat you alive each night?"

"I didn't want my name."

"I didn't want mine, either. I would have wanted something different. An alias this world affiliates with something beautiful and heroic. Like *Speedfire*."

"So, you *do* prefer something," he remarked, tilting his head. She stared ahead.

The Rare Sniper brought her knees up to her chest, then fixed her eyes on the rushing waves of the harbor. "Night-Raven would have been cool."

Matt was at a loss for words. *Night-Raven.*

The black feathers fluttered against her cloak. Something about her statement made his heart ache, and he tried to shake the feeling off. All he knew about the Rare Sniper was that she was his nemesis—and she was supposed to stay that way.

He *wanted* her to stay that way.

Matt turned his head, bitter toward his own thoughts.

"Night-Raven?" he spoke up finally.

Matt looked at her again as she let go of her legs. He had his own distant dreams, as did everyone else. Of course, the Rare Sniper would have one. She was still human.

"You mentioned chains," he added quietly. "Are you being forced to do this?"

Her eyes shifted back to him. "If I am, what would you do about it?"

Matt frowned. "I..." His voice faltered. "I don't know."

"Everyone looks for answers," she said. "And maybe you're just another one of those stuck-up vigilantes who will do nothing in the end. But you're not. I *know* you're not. You're just...*here*. You're someone important."

"I'm not—"

"You are. And you're concerned about this neighborhood for a reason. No matter how many times I try scaring you off, you're still here. You keep coming back for *me*."

"If you believe that, then why do you keep coming out here? You're hurting innocent people."

She exhaled. "I can't control *it*."

"Control what?"

"Death," she admitted. "We live in a world where our fates are in the hands of those more powerful than us." He watched her intently. "So, I'll keep coming back."

He thought of Christine, Maddie, Harry, and even James—all tied to the scandals between Streak Corp and Sal-Tech. He worried for them, and his choices somewhat determined their fates.

"I'm worried about a friend," he mentioned. "He might be a target."

"I don't have a target tonight."

"I didn't mean tonight. I'm worried about the future."

She breathed out softly. "Me too."

Matt knew he wouldn't be getting any answers from her. She had given him advice, though. Clues. He had something to use. But she had given him even more than that. A glimpse into her mind.

She shared what may very well be the most common fear of all.

She's afraid of death, he pondered.

"Those men...*The Reapers*," Matt mentioned. "Would they do something to you if...you failed?" He waited for her response, but she kept quiet, watching the horizon. "*Did* they do anything to you?"

She shuffled slightly. "I'm still here," she answered sharply. "So, if they did do anything, why should it matter? I'm not dead."

"But are you afraid of dying?" Matt asked, eyeing her feathers.

The Rare Sniper closed her eyes. "Death is natural," she sighed, "yet that fact alone doesn't make it any less terrifying."

"But you are..." he said quietly. The sniper closed her fists. "You wouldn't be the first to feel that way."

"Or the last," she said. "But you would know, right? Can you show me?"

Matt blinked, shuffling back. "What—"

"Come on, Speedfire. *Tell me*," the sniper demanded. "Make me believe how wrong I am. Tell me that I *deserve* it. Yet these fated chains are inevitable. Disasters can never learn to fix themselves. And we're just a part of the paradox's parade. What does it mean to be suicidal yet afraid of dying? To be self-sacrificing while yearning to live?"

Matt held his breath. "You really feel that way?" he choked out.

The sniper released her tension. "This changes nothing, Fire. Keep moving on. Speak your truth, and let's be done with it."

Matt held her darkened gaze. He couldn't tell whether this passing wind was hers or something natural. Yet he knew how it made him feel—cold and in denial.

How else was he supposed to react to *Night-Raven*? He had to say something—*anything*.

"I'll find you," he whispered, then stood up. She watched him. Her whole demeanor remained calm. She trusted he wouldn't attack her, which he noted. "Can I promise you that?"

"I think that's destiny," she replied. "*Darkness there and nothing more.*"

Matt held her violet gaze for a moment too long. The raven's eyes showed nothing but grief.

'Tis the wind and nothing more...

As he left the area, a hint of petrichor lingered in the air. The sniper continued to fog his mind.

He was not looking for answers. He needed the solution, and the key remained tied to his choices.

Chess is just another game of choices, he pondered.

Perhaps he and the sniper believed they were just pawns. But even a pawn could corner the king.

Chapter 30

Food for Thought

Matt lay on his back and stared up at the starless sky, ignoring the sounds of the city. The Rare Sniper was the only person on his mind.

He spent the rest of the week pondering his conversation with her, *the false assassin*. Although he could never trust her, he found her words and actions believable. None of her victims had died on the street, having been rushed to the hospital after the shootings instead.

So, what are her intentions? he questioned restlessly. *Most of them end up dead still.*

Perhaps she was truly a "bad shot" and botched every assassination attempt. Too many failures would bring about her greatest fear. Yet her feelings told another story.

Matt rested on the same rooftop he had met with the sniper on—the same place she had blown him away from, where she had returned his fire dagger, and where she had shared "Night-Raven" with him two nights ago.

He waited for her to appear. He wanted to see her familiar dark guise approach him from the depths of the city, all so he could pester her with more pointless questions. But she never came.

Matt's stomach grumbled, and he closed his eyes bitterly. He was wasting his time. He could be patrolling the streets elsewhere, spending his hours helping those in need. But here he was instead, waiting for his nemesis to make yet another inevitable appearance.

"Come on," he groaned. He sat up and stared at the flickering lights against the water. One thing caused these waves.

Wind.

Everywhere he went, everywhere he looked, all he could feel was the Rare Sniper.

His stomach growled again, and he stood up. He wasn't ready to return home yet, so he considered searching for food elsewhere. He wandered down the road and strolled along the streets of Canton. Most stores were closed at this hour, but he figured he could find somewhere to rest for a quick meal.

Matt stopped. *The Jasmine Garden.*

The small restaurant was usually open until midnight. He turned down the road and found the diner a few blocks down.

Katelyn did promise me free food, he thought eagerly. He knew better than to use his guise to get a free meal, but he was desperate. He deserved a reward, even if it was a small bowl of soup to get him through the night.

The bells above the door chimed at his entrance. Matt shoved his hands into his pockets and strode toward the counter, humming as he waited for service. He spotted three workers in the kitchen and caught Katelyn Crae-Zhao hanging her apron on the wall.

"Just a minute!" she hollered as her eyes glimpsed him. She stopped, then turned around again. "Holy sh—"

Matt waved to her.

"Speedy!" Katelyn squealed. She rushed out of the kitchen. "What are you doing here?"

"I'm starving," he said. He peered up at the menu. "So—"

"I got you covered," she promised. "Hold on. Let me get my notepad."

Katelyn scrambled for a sheet of paper and a pencil. Matt stared at the soups and salads on the menu.

"That's Speedfire," a familiar voice spoke up nearby.

Matt tensed. He hardly noticed any other customers in the diner until he turned around. Sat at a table for two, James and Kylie watched him. Matt gasped, then faced Katelyn.

"Hello!" James called over. "Speedfire!"

Matt gripped the counter. He turned around to see James waving to him with a wide grin. His hair was down, and he was missing his glasses. James wore a casual red shirt and black jeans, while Kylie sported a blue tank top and dark leggings.

"Alright, what do you want?" Katelyn asked. Matt breathed in and faced her again. "I still need to ask my manager if it's okay to give you something."

"Yeah, uh, dumpling soup," Matt answered. Katelyn jotted down his order. He winced as footsteps approached him from behind. "Small bowl is fine."

"What brings you here, Speedfire?" James spoke up. Kylie snickered beside him.

Matt inhaled sharply and turned around to face his coworkers. "Food."

James laughed, "This is a nice place. It's hard finding a restaurant that's open past eleven."

Matt nodded nervously. "Yeah."

Keep it together. He took a deep breath. *No one knows your identity*.

The smug smirk James wore and the mischievous look in his eyes made Matt question otherwise.

"Open until one in the morning," Katelyn mentioned proudly. "Those night owls need somewhere to eat, right?"

"And this city never sleeps at night." James winked at Matt. "You'd think more places would be open."

"So, uh, do you two need anything?" Matt asked.

"It's not every day you see a vigilante walk into a restaurant," James pointed out. "I hear about you on the news a lot."

"You do?" Matt fought the urge to kick himself in the shin.

"A part of my job is browsing through the news," said James. "There's always an article about you."

Matt was thankful for his mask. James could not see his worried frown underneath.

"As there should be," Katelyn added. "He's saved my life a couple of times now."

"Has he?" James raised a brow. "Are you his little sidekick?"

Matt coughed, and Katelyn giggled. "No, no," she shook her head, "I can't do what he does. I mean, I'd love to. But I'm not cut out for that kind of thing."

James crossed his arms. "Really?"

Katelyn put her pencil down. "Well, I don't know how to fight." She gestured to Speedfire. "But I sometimes help him find crime. If I see something sketchy down the block, I always give him a call."

James smiled. "Cute." He eyed her nametag as she turned red. "And you're...Katelyn?" She nodded quickly. "Where are you from?"

"Seattle," Katelyn answered, clearing her throat. "I moved here back in June to study investigative journalism."

"Journalism. Nice," James commented. "Kylie studied that, too."

Kylie groaned, "*Communications*."

"Same thing."

Kylie rolled her eyes. "At least I got a job associated with my major."

"And I still got a job, even with my major," James argued playfully. Matt leaned against the counter and stared at his written order. "Anyway, Katelyn, what school do you go to?"

"Towson University," Katelyn replied with a smile. "My dad went to school there, too, before he moved to Seattle. He's from Scotland."

Matt listened quietly, yet this conversation sparked a yearning to hang out with Katelyn more casually. He wanted to learn more about her.

"What about your mother?" asked James.

"She's from China. Stayed on the West Coast all her life. And I know I got my looks from her and *not* my dad. He's one of those crazy redheads." Katelyn laughed, playing with a loose strand of her brown hair. "I've got some wild ancestry. My father was rumored to be a descendant of the *real* King Macbeth."

"*Macbeth?*" Matt gasped.

"That's random," Kylie muttered with a yawn.

"Yeah, my father's parents believe they're descendants of Macbeth. I just go along with it," Katelyn said.

"Sounds fascinating," James replied. "You should do more research on that."

Katelyn snickered, turning her head to hide her growing blush. "Thank you," she said with a grin. "Uh, don't mind me asking, but where are you from? You have an accent."

"London," James answered. "I, uh...don't have any English blood in me, though. My ancestors were avid travelers."

"Your parents are immigrants, too?" Katelyn gasped.

"Yes, my mum was born in Egypt. She traveled a lot, studied in Amsterdam, and visited different nations," James explained. "She met my dad in Greece, and they moved to her England home a few years later to start a family. Then my sister and I moved to London after..." His voice trailed off. "Our parents left."

"And now you're here!" added Katelyn.

"*Yes*. I'm here," he repeated with a grin. "One day, I'll be out at sea again. I take after my folks. Traveling is my passion."

Matt tilted his head. "Out at sea?"

"He has a boat," Kylie mentioned.

"Are you a sailor?" Katelyn gasped.

James crossed his arms, smirking. "Pirate."

"Sounds about right," Matt muttered under his breath.

Katelyn clutched her notepad. "I haven't been on a boat in ages. You should take me for a ride in the bay, Mr. Pirate Man."

"I'd love to if a certain someone here would stop making me work overtime," James replied as he nudged Kylie.

Katelyn turned to Matt. "Well, Speedy, what about you?"

"What? Me?" Matt stuttered. "I don't really do boat rides—"

"No, not that, silly!" she laughed. "Where are your parents from?"

"Oh."

Matt felt James' eyes on him. His gaze shifted to Kylie, who seemed bored of the conversation.

"My dad had Irish and Welsh in him," Matt counted off. "And my mom was...Irish. And Sioux. But that's all I know."

"Roots are intriguing," James uttered.

Matt gulped. "Sure." He glanced at Kylie. "Uh, what are you two doing here so late?"

"Just having a late-night dinner," Kylie muttered. She gazed back at Matt with a scowl. "It's what happens when your day gets occupied by every little problem out there."

"I didn't think today was all that bad," James told her. "Despite the overtime."

"It wasn't. It's just been busy," she sighed.

"Oh. So, you're not on a date?" Matt teased them. He felt fearless as Speedfire. He could get away with saying just about anything to them right now.

Kylie tensed. "What? No, we're just getting something quick to eat."

James laughed, then leaned into Kylie. "A midnight date does sound fun—"

"It was a long day," Kylie continued, pushing James away while she kept her gaze locked on Matt, "as I'm sure it's been a long night for you, Speedfire."

"So far." Matt shrugged. "The nights are longer here in New Harbor."

"Oh, shit," Katelyn hissed as she stared at her notepad. "Speedy, your order! I almost forgot."

"It's fine—"

"Mr. Wan!" Katelyn yelled. She ran back into the manager's office. "Wan! Speedfire is here!"

"Speedfire?" an old man wheezed back.

"He's the vigilante that saved me back in August. Remember?"

"Ah, that one. What is he doing here?" her manager asked.

"I promised him a free meal. He wants a small bowl of dumpling soup tonight."

"What?" Mr. Wan gasped. "I never said he could get a free meal."

Katelyn winced. "But—"

"No! No free food!"

"Mr. Wan, please!" Katelyn begged. "I thought you said we could!"

"When did I say that?" her boss snapped back. "I said that would be a funny idea. I never said we should."

"Aw, come on—"

"You offer another customer free food again, you're fired!"

Katelyn slumped out of the office and looked up at Matt. "Sorry."

Matt grimaced. "Damn it."

"Do you still want the dumpling soup?"

His stomach grumbled louder. "No, it's fine. I didn't bring any money." He turned toward the door, then felt a hand on his shoulder.

"Wait," James said, pulling out two twenty-dollar bills. He handed Katelyn the cash. "That should cover both of our meals. And a tip for you."

Matt's mouth fell open. James pulled his hand back and smiled at him.

"Aw, that's so sweet," Katelyn said. "One dumpling soup, coming right up." She retreated to the kitchen and left Matt alone with his coworkers.

Matt's shoulders sagged. "You didn't have to do that."

"Why not? You've done a lot for this city, haven't you?" James replied. "I can't just let you starve."

"But...I..." Matt exhaled deeply. "Thank you."

"Well, it's late. Obviously." James beckoned Kylie and nodded toward the door. "We'll see ourselves out."

"Finally," Kylie murmured as she passed Matt. "Strange. I thought you didn't like vigilantes much."

"Shh, Kylie. Speedfire is *different*." James paused next to Matt, then leaned closer. "Do me a small favor?" he whispered.

Matt glanced at James. "What?"

James dropped his smile. "Remember to take care of yourself, too." He patted Matt's back, then continued on his way.

Matt tensed as James left the building with Kylie.

"So, who was that?" Katelyn spoke up as she returned to the counter.

"Oh, uh." Matt sat on a stool in front of her. "James and Kylie. They're coworkers of mine."

"Wow. Do they know who you are?" Katelyn asked.

"No, no. I haven't told anyone." He hoped they didn't put the pieces together. "But it wouldn't surprise me, to be honest. James is very perceptive."

"He seems nice. Pretty cute, too," Katelyn added, then coughed. "I mean, 'cute' as in...ah..." She lost her voice as her face turned red again. "He was *pleasant*."

"Yeah, sure." He rested his arms against the counter. "He's odd."

"You would say that, Speedy," Katelyn teased.

"Okay, but odd in a good way," Matt added. "I really like him."

"You should tell him who you are. He just paid for your soup."

Matt frowned. "Kate, I'm still wondering if I should tell *you*," he confessed. "And I want to. But the thing is, James knows me personally. I'd tell him, but...I don't know. How would he react?"

"He'd probably buy you another bowl of soup," Katelyn snickered. "I wish I had a coworker like him. Instead, I'm stuck with grouchy Mr. Wan."

Matt smiled slightly. He was happy to have someone like James beside him for five days a week, even if his coworker had a suspicious eye for Streak's Core Stone. Perhaps working alongside James was what made spending every day at Streak Corporation worth it.

Chapter 31

Love Within a Daydream

Jason Streak left New Harbor in mid-October to visit the other locations of the company. He announced to the staff that he would return in early November, leaving the headquarters in the hands of Lorelei Modisette.

With Lorelei in charge, Matt was unsure how to feel. He hardly talked to the woman, and when he did, she always wore a stone-cold expression. Madame Modisette was a productive leader, however, and she had already found a new manager to fulfill the industrial area warehouse duties.

As Matt analyzed a recent article detailing Jason Streak's business trip, someone tapped his shoulder, and he turned around to face Kylie. He noticed James was away from his desk.

"Yes?" he asked, confused.

Kylie handed him a stack of papers, chewing a piece of gum. "Can you deliver these to Madame Modisette?"

Matt sighed and took the papers. "Anything else you need?"

Kylie glimpsed James' empty seat. "Do you know where he went?"

Matt shook his head. "He tends to wander off."

"He does," she murmured, then rolled her eyes. "I bet he's talking to Elaine."

"Is he? I always assume he's with you," he told her. She turned back to him. "I see him go into your office a lot." He refrained from mentioning the night he saw them at the Jasmine Garden.

"Maybe." She smirked. "I think he gets bored."

Matt stood up as he held the papers close to his chest. "Yeah, but I swear, he gets more done than me."

Kylie crushed the gum with her back teeth. "He's a fast reader." She peered around the rest of the department. The social media workers scrolled through their phones and laptops, concentrating. "He likes you a lot."

Matt cocked his head. "Okay?"

"He talks about you sometimes." She smiled. "Quite a lot, actually."

Matt frowned.

She patted him on the back. "Get those papers to Lorelei," she told him, then returned to her office. "And if you see James, tell him to get his ass back to his desk."

Matt took a deep breath and rode the elevator to the ninth floor. He passed by Madeline's office, then Harry's empty room. Matt missed his presence around the headquarters.

He opened the door to Lorelei's office and stopped when he saw Christine talking to her. Lorelei and Christine shifted their attention to him instantly.

Lorelei stared at him coldly. He gulped.

"Uh, Kylie needed me to deliver these," he said, holding the papers out.

"Put them on the desk," Lorelei ordered. She turned back to Christine and sighed. "You know I don't have any say about the situation."

Christine grimaced. "I just figured..."

"I refuse to get involved with your uncle's personal affairs. You know that," Lorelei stated as Matt set the files on her desk. She turned to him and nodded. "*Merci.*"

Matt stepped back. He walked toward the door, paying close attention to every word.

"I don't know what he wants from me," Christine mentioned. "Madame, please. You and Uncle Jason are close—"

"Whatever deal he's made with Edinburgh, as well as your situation, is none of my concern," Lorelei said. "I refuse to talk your uncle out of anything."

Matt was ready to close the door until he noticed Christine waving to him.

"Wait!" she called out. She glanced at Lorelei. "Thank you, Madame." She jogged to the door, stepped beside Matt, then closed it. "Want to go out?"

"Right now?" he asked, surprised. "What was that all about?"

Christine shook her head. "Nothing. I don't want to think about it."

Matt tilted his head. If she needed to clear her mind, he would gladly help her. He offered his hand to her with a smile.

Christine glanced down at his gesture, took his hand, then guided him down the hall.

Christine had chosen the Inner Harbor mall as their destination. Crowds of people bustled around, but even with all the distractions around him, Matt's mind lingered on the conversation between Christine and Lorelei.

"Want me to get you anything?" she asked.

"What?" He glanced at her and frowned. "Why?"

"We're at *the mall*. Who goes to the mall without buying anything?"

"Shouldn't I get you something instead?" he remarked. "Besides, *you* wanted to go out somewhere."

"Matt," she asserted. "I want to buy something for you."

He sighed, "There's nothing I want."

"But I insist." She peered over at a flower stand in the center of the mall. "Please."

"You're the one who's not feeling good," he exhaled.

"I'm fine," she assured him.

"Emotionally?"

"Physically..."

He rolled his eyes to the glass ceiling. "Will buying me something make you feel better?"

"*Please?*"

Matt huffed. "Okay."

They stopped in front of the floral stand, and he examined the variety of flowers for sale. Roses, tulips, sunflowers, daffodils, carnations, dahlias...chrysanthemums. Arrangements embellished the shelves, and a couple in line ordered a custom bouquet.

He could get a vase for Madeline or set it on his bedside table. If he got an arrangement of yellow mums, he would never escape the dreams with the blue lady—even in reality.

"Maybe a flower bouquet?" Matt suggested.

Christine gasped, "Really? You like flowers?"

"My room could use more life," he joked.

Christine dragged him closer to the stand. They peered down at the bouquets as the florist helped an elderly couple on the other side of the display.

"What do you want?" she asked.

Matt contemplated for a good minute. His eyes regrettably fell on the yellow mums.

"What is your favorite flower?" he replied.

Christine gaped. "Um." She pressed her lips together and returned her gaze to the flower display. "I always liked roses."

Matt smiled and stepped closer to the roses. "Any specific kind?"

"Hey, I'm buying this for *you*," she reminded him.

"I know."

Christine blushed slightly, then followed him over. "I love red roses. But these always stood out to me." She reached over and caressed the yellow roses with red-tipped petals. "They remind me of fire."

Matt tensed. *Oh.* His brows knitted as he hid the sudden flush in his cheeks.

"Fire...?" he echoed.

She nodded quietly as the florist approached them.

Matt cleared his throat. "Can I get a bouquet of those, then?"

Christine crossed her arms. "Sure."

"How may I help you two?" the florist offered. He was elderly with tan skin and white hair. He wore a pair of glasses and welcomed them with a warm smile.

"Can I get twelve of the red-tipped roses?" Christine mentioned as she pulled out her wallet. "And that should be it."

"The circus roses? They're always so wonderful," the florist exclaimed. He pulled out the wrapping and began to gather a dozen yellow flowers. "So, how long have you two been together?"

"Huh?" Matt coughed.

"We're just friends," Christine corrected him. She pulled out a credit card and exchanged it for the bouquet. "Or, uh, coworkers."

"No, we're friends," Matt said. Christine turned her head to hide the redness in her cheeks.

The florist chuckled and swiped her card. "Flowers make great gifts for anyone. You two enjoy the rest of your day."

"Thank you," Christine replied as she handed Matt the flowers.

They walked away from the stand as the florist turned to help a young couple nearby. Matt glanced down at the roses, then caught Christine watching him.

"That was funny," she spoke up.

"What? That old man?"

"I've never seen you look so stumped."

"Okay, to be fair, I wasn't expecting him to assume *that*," Matt argued. "Not that it was a bad thing. It's just..." He glanced her way, and she kept smiling. "You know what I mean."

"Matt, it's okay. You're getting yourself all flustered," she teased.

"I'm not trying to," he groaned.

Christine stopped, and her face dropped immediately. She spotted a few people across the mall, watching her and whispering amongst themselves.

"Uh, we can start heading out," she suggested, leading the way toward the exit. Matt followed close behind her, then peeked over his shoulder at the group of people.

"Wait, Christine—" Matt caught up to her as she swung the mall doors open. "What was that about?"

"Nothing. I sometimes get recognized in public," she said. They joined each other on the sidewalk, keeping close to the docks. "That's it."

"Oh." Matt's eyes moved to the bouquet of roses. "*Shit.* I'm sorry."

"The florist probably didn't know who I was," she said. "Those other people, though..."

Matt glimpsed the surrounding area. Advertisements from Sal-Tech plastered the screens on the buildings. He shuffled closer to Christine's side. "Is everything going to be okay? I don't want people to assume anything or...*gossip.*"

"Eh, I didn't want you feeling uncomfortable in there." She shrugged. "It wouldn't surprise me if people think we are a couple. Especially when we go out."

"Like at the Jasmine Garden?" he added. "I don't think people have taken pictures of us."

She rolled her eyes. "I only worry if they post it on social media. I'd rather have nothing to do with Oracle. People sometimes post whole conspiracy threads on VisionHive, too."

"Conspiracies?" he said with a frown. "About you?"

"Well, yeah. Every New Harbor citizen recognizes the face of Christine Lenore Elerare," she scoffed. Her fake smile dropped. "Ah...that was a joke, by the way. My actual name is 'Jason Streak's niece,' or sometimes 'Marissa Oleander's granddaughter,' in case you didn't know."

Matt's frown deepened.

"My uncle tells me to always be careful in public, mostly for his reputation. I shouldn't go hanging out with a guy my age. Especially with Edward in the picture now."

"You've been going on dates with him, right?" Matt asked.

"*Yes*," she groaned. "Well...he calls them dates. I call them *business meetings*."

"Of course you do," he said as she closed her eyes proudly. "Is he tolerable?"

"Good question. Tell me what you think of this," she said, and he raised a brow. "During our last meeting, he said I should try looking 'less Optyman.'"

Matt blinked. "What the hell does that even mean?"

"I asked him the same thing. He suggested I dye my hair. Told me he likes brunettes," she continued. "I guess I look too much like my father. But why not? I could be a whole new person. Anything for the esteemed Edward Edinburgh." She glanced his way. "Except, there's one thing I won't do for him."

He bit his lip. "And what would that be?"

"Give up my time with you." Christine shared a smile with him. "But aside from the Edward shenanigans, it's fun messing with reporters. Trick them into writing fake articles," she said. "Fake dating would be fun."

"Oh no. Not fake dating," Matt laughed.

"But so would real dating," she continued, lowering her gaze to the water.

Matt slowed with her as she stopped to admire the harbor. Her eyes rested on the Streak Corporation headquarters in Fells Point. The voice of Kiera Salus and her campy advertisements echoed in the vicinity as Matt watched Christine. He wanted to find the best response without getting distracted by the repetitive Sal-Tech commercials.

"Christine?" he spoke up, catching her attention. "Just out of curiosity..."

"Yes?" She tilted her head.

"Have you dated before?"

Christine glowered. "No," she answered quietly. "Not that I really want to. Maybe it would have been nice to experiment. Try something new, you know."

"Yeah..."

"It didn't really occur to me until now. Just...maybe I would have liked to have a choice in that," she sighed. "See if I could make my own connections rather than go with what my uncle has planned."

"Until now?" Matt repeated, and Christine's face paled.

"I mean *recently*," she corrected, looking away. "The idea is nice. But reality is always mean to me. So, it's whatever."

"Hey, come on. Don't say that," he said, nudging her. She frowned. "Just tell your uncle that you aren't ready. And Edward is a lot older than you, too. That should be a good excuse."

Christine's cheeks turned red. "Okay," she stammered.

"But is there something else on your mind?" Matt continued. "I don't want you to feel like you can't talk about it—"

"I don't know," she coughed out. "I said the idea was nice. It doesn't mean I'd ever actually want to date anyone. Just a little daydream, is all." She glanced at a nearby holo-sign. He followed her gaze to an advertisement for *The New Harbor Sun* that showcased a headline dedicated to the city's vigilantes.

Matt held his focus on the holographic ad for the local heroes. He realized she had never mentioned her second encounter with Speedfire to him. Not that he wanted to pressure anything out of her, but he was curious.

Perhaps a little *too* curious.

After all, Christine was hinting at *something* with these sudden feelings. And as much as he would hate to pry, she seemed desperate to talk about relationships. He just needed to let the conversation flow, show her that he's fine with hearing whatever she wanted to say. Still, his curiosity consumed him.

His eyes rested on those roses that reminded her of "fire."

"So, it's been a while since we talked about vigilantes," Matt mentioned.

"Oh." She rubbed her arm. "I suppose."

"And I was wondering if anything *recent* happened," he emphasized. She tensed. "You don't say anything bad about them anymore."

"Okay, if you're trying to get me to admit that I have a stupid crush on one of them, it's not happening," Christine countered, crossing her arms.

Matt gasped, "That's not—"

"Speedfire is really the only one we talk about. And, *no*," she asserted, closing her eyes. "He's..."

Matt furrowed his brows. "He's...?"

Christine nibbled on her bottom lip. "I don't want to talk about it."

Matt leaned into the railing. He was expecting to get a much different answer out of her.

"Hey, Christine..."

"I can't talk about this."

Matt dropped his shoulders. She shivered as she tightened her arms around herself. The deeper they dove into this conversation, the worse it would get.

"I'm sorry. I didn't mean to sound rude," Christine sighed, then released her arms. "Love is tricky. I just know it's something I couldn't commit to."

"You think so?" he asked.

"I wouldn't try."

Matt looked away for a moment. He wondered if she was willing to stay in her daydream.

"Me neither," he admitted quietly.

Christine glanced over at him, confused. "Why not?"

Matt inhaled anxiously. "I think I have a problem with making attachments in general."

"Really?"

Matt nodded. His eyes flickered to the black ring on his right hand, then to Christine. He had several different answers he could give her, but she was right about one thing.

Love is tricky.

He had never tried to find love before. While he watched his peers in school moving on from one relationship to another, he stayed in his own corner, held down by his self-disposition. He lacked what others would call a "normal" kind of attraction, as he never actually *cared* about finding a partner. He had his fair share of moments when he wondered what it would be like to date someone. He found some of the boys and girls in his school attractive in a personal way—peers who were quiet and closed-off, yet nice to him regardless. But he never bothered pursuing any relationships for a few reasons, and one being that he knew he would never be a fulfilling partner.

"I've never been in a relationship. I don't really have any feelings like that. So, I try to avoid it," Matt confessed. "And I really doubt I could make anything work."

"What do you mean?" she asked, concerned. "Did someone make you feel that way?"

Matt shook his head. He knew his main reasons for avoiding romantic relationships. And unlike Christine, he never *daydreamed* of being in one. He only had mere thoughts of the concept. However, he could give her a few excuses. He had witnessed the toxic boys his sister would bring home over the years. But even then, using trauma as a reason for evading relationships was simpler than explaining asexuality.

Simpler, but not better.

"If I were to date someone, I couldn't give them what they want," he said. "Let's just stick with that."

Her brows knitted. "You're not the only one with attachment issues," she admitted. "If that's what we're calling it."

Matt winced. "I don't want to sound like I'm calling it an issue. It's not."

Christine nodded, then brushed her hand through her hair. "People have legitimate *issues* out there. You're just...you." She smiled. "In the best way you can possibly be." Matt felt the heat rising to his cheeks. "And if you want something, take it. Take a risk. But I can't see you letting anyone down. Hell, if it makes you feel better, I know someone who has had three failed marriages."

"Who?" Matt was glad to shift the subject away from himself.

"Lorelei is divorced," Christine replied. "Twice."

"*Twice?*"

She nodded grimly. "And widowed once."

His curiosity piqued even more. "What about your uncle?"

Christine laughed. "No way. I could never see him in a long-term relationship."

"Okay, now you've got me hooked."

She raised her shoulders. "He's dated before," she said. "Never worked out. When he was my age, according to my grandmother, he used to date someone new every other month."

"Oh, wow." He smiled slightly. "I would have never guessed that about him."

"Yeah, me neither. He's more focused on business now. He has no time for relationships." She crossed her arms as they continued to walk along the pier. "It's fun to think about, though."

"What is? Your uncle's past?" he teased. "Or making a history of messed-up relationships for yourself?"

"Both." Christine nudged him playfully. "You shouldn't have anything holding you back."

"Okay, but that's if I even want to. Unlike you, I'm not *experimenting*," Matt remarked. He looked her way as she narrowed her eyes, smiling. "But if I did try, it'd have to be with the right person."

"If that's even possible," she uttered, then paused before him. She lifted her hand, then slowly wrapped her fingers around the bouquet. Matt loosened his grip, letting her slip the flowers from his grasp. His face reddened when she took his hand, then raised it to her cheek. His black ring rested against her face as she stared up at him, her emerald gaze striking through his racing heart. "I really like your ring."

He swallowed hard as his heart hammered. "Okay..."

Several people passed the docks, distracted by their own conversations. Matt doubted Christine even cared about anyone snapping pictures anymore. Her eyes were on him, and only him.

With a gentle sigh, she lowered his hand. "As fun as it sounds, I don't think I'll ever be ready for love," she confessed. Her smile fell slowly, and she returned the bouquet to his hand. "It hits people unexpectedly, right?"

Matt blinked, then nodded shakily. "Right..."

Christine returned the nod and strolled ahead. He stood there for an extra few seconds, watching as her auburn hair drifted against the back of her dress.

She looked back over her left shoulder, and her smile met his eyes. His posture dropped.

Matt gazed down at the bouquet of circus roses in his hand—her favorite flower. Quietly, he held them closer and followed her pace, leaving his ill feelings behind.

ACT III

BLOOD ON
THE HORIZON

Chapter 32

RECKLESS PRIDE

Streak returned from his international trip within the first week of November. Articles from every news site recorded all his visits, which meant only more work for Matt and James.

Over the past week, Kylie had sent James to visit the warehouses, where he would take pictures for his colleagues to post on Oracle. Despite being left to work alone, Matt knew the warehouses were the main draw to these scandals.

Optyman-inspired blueprints and weapons...

The warehouses held everything. And Matt wondered what James was really getting access to in the industrial center. Regardless, he still feared James would do something reckless enough to catch the sniper's attention.

While James returned for his break to visit Kylie, Matt pushed himself away from his desk and hopped onto the elevator. On the ride up to the tenth floor, Matt planned the conversation in his mind. He wanted to warn Streak about James' possible betrayal, but at the same time, he didn't want James to lose his job.

Just save James, he reminded himself. *Save him from his own mistakes.*

Matt opened the office door and stood there, shocked. Billy Flyes turned around in his seat at the desk, and Streak's stern gaze shifted to Matt.

"I...I'm sorry," Matt stuttered. "I didn't mean to interrupt."

"You could knock first," said Streak.

"Ah...it's not a problem," Billy assured them.

The heat rose in Matt's cheeks even more when his eyes fell to the desk. The Core Stone sat there, inches away from Streak.

"No, Mr. Streak is right. I should have knocked," Matt said. "I'll wait outside."

"Good." Streak waited for Matt to step out of the room before he continued the conversation.

Matt shut the door, then slid down to the floor and waited. He could faintly hear the conversation on the other side, and his heart raced.

"Trust me. I know all about the news surrounding the Tyrant. Nothing will happen to my stone," Streak's muffled voice stated.

"My father was just worried," replied Billy. "He doesn't want to become a target, either. We need to keep it a secret."

"I get the secrets, but the public already knows I own this stone. I'm not giving it up, and your father won't convince me otherwise," Streak lectured.

Billy sighed, "Mr. Streak, I know it means a lot to you. But it's not safe."

"Then someone needs to handle whoever is after it," Streak snapped. "Go on. Get your troops together and find those scoundrels. And catch Surtair while you're at it."

"The police have been on the case. I can't start an investigation," Billy pleaded with him. "I'm just here to deliver a message. My father wants you to think about it."

"And my answer is final. The stone stays with me," Streak concluded. "I've already had Kendric Bazyl on me about using it for his science projects. Since Bazyl no longer has Fren to go to for his stone, he's resorted to asking me. He's the only person I'll trust with it, but even then, I'm not giving it away."

"But if you can just consider—"

"That's enough!" Streak raised his voice. "No one is taking my stone. I'm its judge. Nobody else."

"But you're willing to negotiate with Bazyl?" Billy said. "You're going to make me bring this up with Mayor Fare. And I don't want to do that."

"Go ahead. See how the mayor will react," Streak countered. "And Dr. Bazyl will only borrow my stone. Unlike your father, he isn't asking to *keep* it."

Matt leaned closer to the door as Billy cleared his throat. "Mr. Streak, you can trust my father far more than Bazyl. Whatever that man intends to do—"

"Will benefit me greatly. He's dehumanizing the *Rare*," Streak uttered, lowering his voice. "The Rare Sniper is a monster. And so was Jake Agnes. It's just a matter of time until we prove they are biological abominations. And the same goes for those Rare Mutations."

Matt perked, intrigued. *Rare Mutations?* He had never heard of the term before, but as much as he would like to push Streak for explanations, he would hate to admit he had been eavesdropping.

"Dehumanizing the *Rare* isn't the solution to anything," Billy argued. "You and Bazyl are targeting a demographic that doesn't exist. If anything, this 'project' in the long run only aims to eradicate the Optyman population, and you know it."

"An Optyman Rare Soul is attacking *my* employees," Streak seethed. "You have no right to argue with me, Sergeant Flyes."

"If we hide those stones, we won't have to worry about the *Rare* anymore," Billy mentioned. "There isn't any need for scientific research. I promise you—"

"Sergeant Flyes, I don't want to hear it," Streak interrupted. "Leave. *Now.*"

Matt scrambled back from the office. He slid to the wall as Billy opened the door. The sergeant exhaled deeply, then spotted Matt at his side.

"Hey," Billy sighed. "Sorry about that."

"Oh, what? No, I'm sorry," Matt blurted out. "I kind of interrupted you guys."

Billy shook his head. "That meeting had nothing to do with business. It wasn't really...important?"

Matt didn't want to mention the eavesdropping, yet he saw the Core Stone. "I, uh, saw the stone on his desk."

Billy stepped closer to Matt. He peered around the corner. "Yeah," he whispered. "Do you already know?"

"Know what?"

"My father has one of the stones."

"Oh..." Matt fell silent.

"Um. I don't want to ask much, but I was trying to get Mr. Streak to hand the stone to someone else," Billy mentioned. "Perhaps someone that's not a public figure. We've been worrying about Jason and the stone's safety."

"Yeah, I get it." Matt held his tongue, fighting the urge to ask about the Rare Mutations.

"Okay, so would you possibly want to convince Mr. Streak otherwise?" Billy continued. "My father and I are getting nowhere. We aren't going to take it from him, y'know?"

Matt grimaced. He knew he would get nowhere with Streak.

"Who would you give it to?" asked Matt.

Billy shrugged, "Maybe Madame Modisette could take it? Or your sister?" Matt coughed at the mention of Madeline. "That way it's still close to Mr. Streak, but it's not with *him*."

"You think Maddie would take it?" Matt didn't want his sister anywhere near the stone, especially with everyone's eyes on it.

"You and your sister have a history with Optyma. My dad fought alongside your parents. I would trust you two over Mr. Streak, and I hardly even know you," Billy told him. "It's safer than having Mr. Streak carry its burdens. No one would even know you have it."

Matt shrunk back. As much as he would like to hold the stone—

"I don't know..."

"Please," Billy begged. "I—okay, I'm sorry. I doubt anyone will convince him. But if you can try, I'd appreciate it." He checked his watch, and his frown dropped even more. "I should get going. My father needs me. Keep in touch, maybe?"

Matt nodded. "Need my number?"

Billy smiled. "Hang on." He pulled out a business card, then handed it to Matt. "If you get anywhere, send me a text."

"I will," Matt promised.

Billy patted his shoulder, then continued toward the elevator. Matt took a deep breath and stepped into the room.

Streak typed on his computer with a stern expression. He glanced Matt's way and raised an eyebrow.

"You're back."

"I need to speak with you, sir."

"Sit." Streak gestured to the seat Billy had occupied moments ago. Matt situated himself and held his hands together. "Go on."

"Um," Matt cleared his throat, "I'm worried about a few things."

"If it's about social affairs, you need to speak with Kylie," Streak mentioned as his eyes glossed over his screen.

"It's about James."

Streak turned his gaze to Matt. "James Salamar?"

Matt felt himself sweating. His eyes fell to the Core Stone, but he controlled the urge to stare at it for too long.

"Remember the argument you two had at the anniversary gala last month?" Matt mentioned to him.

"I recall it clearly," stated Streak.

"Okay. So, well, James has been dropping hints of wanting to work with Sal-Tech," Matt continued.

"And?"

"I'm just worried," Matt admitted. "He might do something. I know what happened to Jack and Harry. And even Noah Mallory. They got in trouble for stealing confidential items for Sal-Tech."

"They did," Streak muttered as his eyes glanced down at his desk.

"I...I don't want anything to happen to James, either. But I feel like he'd try something," Matt stammered. "It seems the sniper is targeting anyone who has access to intel related to Optyma here.

"Are you certain?" asked Streak.

Matt lifted his shoulders. "I'm just speculating."

"I know. So much trouble has corrupted these streets," Streak mumbled, then rubbed his temple. "Alright, Matthew, I understand your concern. Quite a few employees seem to be a bit *devious*."

"Uh...yeah, that's one way to put it."

"There's always a...hmm, what do you call it? A motivator?" Streak pointed out. "Somebody that gets people fired up."

"Do you think it's James?"

"Could be, considering what you just told me. I'll look into it more. Thank you," Streak told him. "He'll be dealt with."

Matt stood up with a tremble. As he walked toward the doors, Streak called out for him.

"Matthew, just another moment."

Matt turned around and bit the bottom of his lip. "Yes?"

"Don't discuss this with anyone else. Let's keep it between us."

"I—uh, of course."

Streak smirked. "Good." He returned to his computer and typed away at the keyboard.

Matt could feel his heart beating faster as he left the room. Regret struck him as he didn't even get a chance to ask about the Core Stone for Billy. Instead, his anxiety focused on what lay ahead. He wanted to return to James and tell him not to do anything reckless; to turn away anyone called the Whip-Master. But his fear kept him silent.

With his gaze on the floor, he turned down the hall toward his desk. He looked up, and James stood across from him with a smug smile.

"I was wondering where you went," James mentioned.

"You get to wander off all the time," muttered Matt. "So, what?"

The smile on James' face dropped. "Is everything okay?"

Matt glanced at him before he turned his attention to the computer screen. He faced the homepage of *The New Harbor Sun* and sighed.

"No."

He'll be dealt with.

Matt's stomach twisted itself into knots. He wanted to go home.

Chapter 33

Matt took off work early to spend the afternoon plotting an encounter with James. He put his Speedfire gear on and headed out of the apartment before sundown.

Why does Streak need this to be a secret?

His heart felt heavy toward the dark possibilities in his head.

He waited on a rooftop near the headquarters. James usually left work around this time, and Matt hoped to meet with him alone. He saw no signs of the sniper nearby, nor The Reapers, so he assumed the coast was clear.

Matt perked his head up when he saw a figure departing the office. James wore a black jacket, huddling himself against the wind as he walked down the sidewalk. Matt slid down a pole attached to the side of the building and stepped out from the alley.

James stopped, catching a glimpse of Speedfire from the corner of his eye.

Matt held his hands up. "Don't freak out. I'm just here to help."

"Speedfire?" James smiled. "What's the issue?"

"You might be in danger," Matt explained from across the street. Fortunately, no one else lingered nearby.

"That's not news to me. I'm always in danger," James remarked.

"No, it's serious," Matt groaned. "The Rare Sniper might be after you. I'm just watching over you for now. At least until you get home safe."

James burst out laughing, throwing Matt off guard. "I mean, that's not a surprise. But why would the sniper target me?"

Matt frowned. "Anyone at Streak Corp could be a target."

"And you don't think I know that?" said James.

"I don't know what you know."

"You don't." James smirked. "Matthew."

Matt's eyes widened. He drew his breath in against the mask on his face.

He knows.

James stared at him across the road, waiting for a response.

"Matthew, I know you're Speedfire. You don't have to hide it," James said.

"How...how do you—" Matt lost his voice.

James huffed as he crossed the street. "I had my suspicions." He lifted his hand slowly, then flipped the hood off Matt's head. "So, why are you watching me?"

Matt shook his head. "I...I don't understand. Why—"

"You're the only one investigating anything. But if you insist, you may cover me as I walk home," added James. "Just in case a certain sniper comes out to play."

"I didn't want to scare you."

"Do I look scared?"

Matt followed James. "No..."

"You don't have to worry about me," James sighed. "Besides, I haven't exactly done anything to catch the sniper's eye."

"No, but..." Matt sucked in his breath. "I told Streak something."

"What? That I'm stealing Optyman intel from his warehouses?" James deadpanned.

Matt stared at him, dumbfounded. James stopped, then took his arm to guide him forward.

"I haven't told anyone else about this," Matt stuttered. "James, I'm sorry—"

"Let's get back to my apartment, and then we can talk," James replied. He steered him toward the parking lot. "I can't take you seriously while you're wearing that mask."

Matt felt out of breath. He didn't know what James knew, after all.

His heart raced as James drove down the harbor silently, about a ten-minute drive to his apartment. Matt's eyes followed the glistening water the whole ride.

"Come," James said and opened the door for him. "Before the sniper gets us. Right?"

Matt didn't know how to feel about the joke. He followed James inside the building, a far smaller apartment complex than Leo Towers. James pulled his keys out from his pocket, opened the door to Room 11, and beckoned Matt inside.

"Alright," James exhaled as he closed the door and removed his jacket. He gestured to the couch. "I think we're safe to talk now."

"If I'm honest," Matt said as he pulled his mask down, "I don't know what's happening."

"You're Speedfire," James noted. "And you're the first person in this city to cross the Rare Sniper. I'm certain you understand what's going on."

Matt sunk into the sofa. "I mean by how you're involved. I'm confused."

"Don't overthink it." James sat on the chair across from Matt, untied his hair, and let it fall just above his shoulders. "Just breathe. We can talk."

"About the situation?"

James shrugged and leaned back. "Several things, I suppose. Your fears, for one," he alluded. "So, as Speedfire, I'm guessing you've been looking into the conspiracy behind the Rare Sniper."

Matt nodded slowly. "I have. My sister and another friend know about everything, too."

"Madeline is in on it?"

"Yes. And Harry Faresoul."

"Ah, the former department manager. That's right," James sighed. "You saved him."

Matt peered around the rest of James' room. A few paintings of castles hung from the wooden walls, and a sword rested on a mantle across from him.

"I just want to get to the bottom of this," Matt told him. "So far, the only people behind the shootings are the Rare Sniper, a group of mercs called The Reapers, and their boss."

"How did you find out about The Reapers?" James arched his brow.

"I had an encounter with them," Matt mumbled, reluctant to remind James of his concussion. "I've learned a lot. Every victim has a connection to Streak Corp and Sal-Tech."

"So, you believe I could be next on the hitlist?" James inquired. Matt nodded silently. "Fascinating."

"*Fascinating?*" Matt repeated.

"Just this whole ordeal. You're special, Matthew. I doubt anyone else could be pulling all these strings together."

"I don't know. I'm sure someone will figure it out sooner or later," Matt exhaled. "Maybe you?"

James laughed, "Me? What makes you think I would have an interest in all this? You're practically setting yourself up for danger."

Matt grimaced. "That's not my intention. I want to save people."

"A noble cause." James stood up and strode toward his kitchen. He opened the fridge and grabbed two water bottles. "Sadly, not everyone can be saved."

"I'll save as many as I can," Matt added. James handed him the water and took a step back. "I've been a vigilante for two years. It's what I do."

"What inspired you to become one?" James questioned.

Mom...

"History, I guess," Matt said instead. "It always felt like a calling to me."

James sipped his water. "What part of history?"

"Sky," Matt added. "She's the best vigilante in history."

James pressed his lips together. "She changed the world. Even had an influence in Optyma."

Matt sighed, "Always Optyma." He stared at the bottle in his hand, admiring the space between the cap and the water.

James continued, "I did research on the fallen nation years ago. Quite tragic. Some say it was a country that should have never existed."

Matt faced James. "That feels wrong to say."

"I never believed that. However, I do know certain people who do. Take Jason Streak, for example. He despises anything that deals with Optyma. Yet, he possesses one of its stones. And what are the odds that an *Optyman* assassin is targeting him?" James emphasized. "Fascinating how that works. He's obsessed with a piece of the nation, yet he loathes it."

"That's the second time you've used 'fascinating' now."

"Don't mind me. I think a lot of things in this beautiful world are fascinating. Like you." James smiled, and the heat rose to Matt's cheeks. "Anyway, Optyma is a secluded mess today. Sightseers and explorers have gone missing on the dead island, and that's if the underground agencies watching the surrounding area don't catch them first," James explained. Matt tensed. The aftermath of the war claimed even more lives. *Missing persons*—several every year, all due to Optyma. "But why do people like Jason Streak despise Optyma when it's no longer a threat? They act as if President Jake Agnes is still alive."

Matt found himself despising that name further each day. His life had changed forever because of the president's actions.

James continued, "The president's main motives remain a mystery still. Maybe *that* is the threat. What made the president bomb Baltimore during what had been a *civil* war?"

"I don't know," Matt muttered. He distanced the thought of his parents. His mother's face. Her comforting smile. His father's obnoxious laughter. His tight hugs. *Everything*. Matt closed his eyes, biting his lip.

"He wanted to change the world." James put his water down on the table beside him. "Not in the best way possible, but I like to believe there was reason behind his motives."

"How could you say that?" Matt shot a glare at him. "He was evil. He killed millions of innocent people. His own *sister* waged a war against him—"

"I didn't mean it like that," James retracted. "A part of the war remains hidden from the world. But I promise I won't bring it up with you anymore. If it disturbs you that much—"

"Sorry," Matt stammered. "I didn't mean to snap. It's just...hard."

James took a breath. "It's...a touchy subject. Jake Agnes caused devastation that will last centuries. He was the harbinger of an apocalypse, as crazy as it sounds."

"Over two million lives were lost. It sure sounded like one." Survivors only ever described the landscape of Optyma as apocalyptic after the catastrophe.

"Did he think about that, though?" James pondered. "Did he question his morality at that very moment? That slaughtering millions would have resulted in the rebirth of New Harbor?"

Matt rested his gaze on James and laid his head against the cushion. He breathed in and out slowly, and he just listened. He had no idea where this topic would go, but he agreed with James about one thing—it was fascinating. Cold yet riveting.

"Now, I don't want to be like Jake Agnes, but I have a dream, just like anyone else. I'd love to see the world bloom into something different," James explained softly. "Into a world that accepts all of mankind's imperfections. To accept what makes us whole."

Matt opened his mouth slightly. "It's a hard thing to do by yourself."

"I know. President Agnes may have caused an apocalypse, but he had a following. He was never alone," James mentioned. "A single person can manifest the perfect solution to the world's problems. They just need the resources."

Matt met his gaze quietly.

"And you're already making your mark, Matthew," James told him. "*Speedfire.*"

Matt smiled slightly. "I guess you are, too."

"In what way? I wouldn't call myself a vigilante like you."

"You're at least thinking about changing the world." He thought of all the people who could shape reality. People like Jason Streak—who had those resources at his fingertips—yet he chose to mass-produce weapons of war instead.

James stared at him through the silence. "Thinking is one thing, but taking action is another," he said. "And you're thinking about Jason Streak."

The smile dropped from Matt's face.

"You want Streak to change the world, right?" James chuckled. "I think he already is, but not in a good way."

"I never implied that."

"But it's the truth." James frowned. "I don't have all the answers, but Jason Streak knows everything about the Optyman War."

"What does he know?" Matt asked skeptically.

James raised his shoulders. "More than me. I'm sure he knows what truly sparked the war between Jake and Kayla Agnes." He grinned. "If you're friends with Streak, maybe he will tell you."

"Okay, I'm not friends with him."

"But you're friends with *a* Streak."

Matt blinked. "You...think Christine knows more about the war?"

"It wouldn't hurt to ask her," James advised. "Only if you're curious, of course."

"Maybe I can try asking Streak, too..." He wondered if Madeline was learning more about the Optyman War as she worked right under Jason Streak. She never shared anything new with him, but he needed to find someone to quell his curiosity.

"Matthew, I'm going to be honest. I don't trust Streak."

Matt stiffened and lifted his head. "What don't you trust about him?"

James shrugged. "Everything. Billionaire, stone-keeper, tycoon."

Tycoon. Sal-Tech.

"He's jealous of Kiera Salus," Matt mentioned quietly. "I think."

"Oh, he definitely is," James sighed and looked at the ceiling.

"He wants to control the whole weapons industry," Matt muttered.

"He does."

Matt frowned and looked over at James. "He told me that you will be dealt with."

James smiled. "He did."

"Then what are you thinking?" Matt exhaled, frustrated.

James parted his lips. "Don't trust anyone."

Matt gathered a quick breath. "What about you?"

James held his gaze. "Put yourself first, Speedfire."

Speedfire.

"But I must say, secrets are the true killer," James continued.

Matt glowered. "I know."

"Hiding things isn't any way to gain someone's trust."

Matt gripped the neck gaiter under his chin. The mask was a lie. A secret. Something he kept from almost everyone he knew.

"Don't trust Streak," he mumbled, then faced James again. "Why?"

"You already know why." He smirked again. "Jason Streak practically owns the whole industry."

"I don't think he would be the boss behind the sniper. She's attacking him."

"Are you sure about that?"

Matt had his suspicions regarding the sniper's superior. Between Jason Streak, the Tyrant, and The Reapers, he still couldn't jump to conclusions.

"I'll keep it in mind," Matt said. "No more secrets."

"Matthew," James expressed, leaning back, "you're a saint."

His face dropped. "I'm not."

"Saint *Matthew*. Perform a miracle. Solve this scandal."

Matt fought the urge to make a comeback. "Okay, King James."

James gaped at him, then looked away. Matt smiled faintly.

"Okay," James laughed. He exhaled and stood up. "I should tell you something."

Matt tilted his head. "What is it?"

"James is not my real name," he confessed.

Matt's jaw dropped. "*What?*"

The faint smirk fell from James' face. "It's my middle name."

"Oh." Matt waited as James stood there in contemplation. "Why do you use your middle name?"

"For the professional setting," sighed James. "I don't normally use it."

"So, what's your real name?"

The smile rose on his lips once again. "Alexander."

"Alexander James..."

James crossed his arms. "I usually go by 'Xander.'"

"Xander?" Matt stared up at "James" with uncertainty. "Why don't you use your preferred name at work?"

"Why do you go by *Speedfire*?"

Matt scowled. "That's different."

"Is it?" he teased with a smile. "If I can ask for a favor, though, please continue to use 'James' in the workplace."

Matt never expected to get this sudden yet casual truth from his coworker. He intended to dedicate this night to protecting "James" when the name itself was a lie.

"I should go," Matt said, standing up.

He met Xander's eyes as he straightened himself. Without the glasses and his hair down, he looked like a completely different person.

Matt pulled the mask over the lower half of his face. "Xander."

"Matthew."

"I'll solve the scandal. Whatever it takes."

"I trust you will. But be careful. There are powers at play here," Xander said as he strolled toward the kitchen. He took a napkin from the counter. "And they could shatter anything."

Matt stood in the doorway as Xander dabbed his nose. He left quietly, sneaking one last glance into his coworker's apartment. He noticed a few drops of blood on the napkin in Xander's hand.

Chapter 34

"Mom!"

Matt called out for Eveline as she left through the doorway. He reached for her, but her shadowed form disappeared into the fog of the hallway.

"Promise you'll come back!" he begged. "Please!"

Matt lay in bed and stared at the ceiling in darkened silence. Dried tears stained his cheeks, but he did nothing to wipe them away. He breathed in and out again. And again. And again.

He dragged himself out of bed, even if the sun had yet to rise. He undressed and got into the shower, letting the hot water wash away his sweat and tears. With his eyes closed, he tried to shift his mind elsewhere, to think of something other than the conflict at hand.

After Matt washed up, he dried himself and threw a black shirt on. He sat on his bed with his laptop and searched for any updates on Damien Surtair or the Tyrant. Nothing new. Nothing worthwhile to use for research.

How could someone try to steal a Core Stone and get away with it? Matt gritted his teeth.

The incident happened over two months ago, and all people could say about Damien was that he vanished from the face of the earth.

He typed "tyrant" into the search engine. The definition and lists of tyrants across history popped up in his feed.

President Jake Agnes.

His door opened, and Madeline's figure stood in the corridor.

"Matt?" She flicked the lights on. "What's going on? I thought I heard the shower running."

"Sorry," he mumbled and tossed the laptop aside. "Just stressed."

She sat beside him on the bed. "What's up?"

Matt cried quietly, "I don't know what I'm doing anymore."

"Hey…" She placed her hand on his back, pulling him into a hug. "It's okay, don't cry. It'll be alright."

"Maddie, you don't even know," he exhaled, choking back his tears.

He had his worries and concerns. But until recently, it dawned on him that his anxiety was Streak's doing.

Jason Streak was at the center of it all for a reason.

"Do you need to get anything off your chest?" Madeline asked. "Did the sniper hurt you again?"

"It's not just that. It's this whole case, and I'm worried," Matt admitted. "I've got too much to say."

"Then let it out." She backed up on the bed and patted the spot beside her. "Tell me everything."

If he told her everything, she would be mad at him. Not that Madeline was the sole reason for how depressed he felt, but the position she put him in was. He hated working for Streak Corporation. He wished he could go home to Miami.

"Okay." He wondered where he should begin and how Madeline would react. At this point, it didn't matter. She was here to listen.

Madeline nodded. "Okay?"

"Christine has an issue right now," he started, peering back at his sister. "She doesn't want anyone to know, so keep it between us." The mention of Christine brought more tears to his eyes. "Streak is trapping her in the company. He wants Christine and Richard Edinburgh's son to take over the business one day. *Together*. And he wants Edward to inherit the company through her."

"I did hear about Edward taking her out…" Madeline said quietly.

"Yes." Matt wiped away a tear with the palm of his hand. "And I don't know how to help her," he cried. "She deserves better than that. It's been on my mind for weeks, and I feel like time is just…ticking.

"But Streak is a hard bargain. I've seen it. It's like you can't change his mind about anything. And there's a reason Christine never adopted the Streak name. Why does she love her missing father more than her uncle?"

"We don't know the whole story here, Matt."

"And then there's the Rare Sniper, who I don't even want to think about right now," he continued, rubbing his eyes. "Because there's also the Tyrant out there stealing Core Stones. Damien Surtair is just gone. But the sniper is an assassin. She has a boss, and I have a hunch."

"Who?" Madeline breathed.

Matt focused his attention on her. "Jason Streak."

Madeline's jaw dropped. "*Matt!*" She backed away. "You can't just accuse him!"

Matt scoffed, "Why not? He's completely innocent, right? Look at what he's putting his niece through, what he's putting the *Optymans* through. Also, all of the sniper's victims have *wronged* Streak. Maybe we should ask Harry this, too. Why did he never go back to Streak Corp?"

Madeline stammered, "Harry has his reasons. Don't blame him."

"I'm not. I'm just saying. It's hard to stand up to Streak, unless you're James Salamar. But there's something new I learned about James, too."

"Is that who's putting all this in your head? Matt—"

"His real name is Xander. And I was just with him a few hours ago. He was bringing up Streak's vendetta against the Optymans and Jake Agnes," Matt said. "I don't want to hear anything about Agnes ever again. *I hate him.*"

"Hey, calm down, it's okay," Madeline reached over and patted his back again. "Let's just think about it. Are you sure Streak is hiring the Rare Sniper to kill people?"

Matt sucked in a sharp breath. "I could be wrong, but I believe he is. He's using Sal-Tech and the Optymans as red herrings."

"Okay, but Jason has done so many incredible things for this city. For this *world*," Madeline said as she stretched her arm out. "I doubt he'd do something as risky as hiring...hit people."

"Maddie, he is protecting his business. He wants to *keep* owning the whole industry."

"And what happened to the sniper being an Optyman?" She crossed her arms. "You and Harry were very set on that being true."

Matt closed his eyes, imagining the sniper's feathered cape drifting in the wind. Her violet irises haunted him from afar—the raven in the shadows.

"She's still Optyman. The Optymans have a long history of assassins," he mentioned quietly. "But...I think she's being forced to target Streak's employees. To protect *his* assets. Any of that intel her victims stole could be used to blackmail Streak Corp."

"Like what?" she demanded.

"Optyman-related designs." Matt shuddered. "Illegal weapons that could have ended the war. But no one's allowed to know about them." He stared at his sister desperately. "We don't know how the war ended. We don't even know how it *started*."

Madeline frowned and looked away. "Matt, this man gave me my whole career."

"Maddie, no, wait." He paused for another breath. "Please. Trust me. I could find proof—"

"Matt, he *gave me my whole career*," she repeated with a glare. "I would have nothing if it weren't for Jason Streak. And you're just accusing him of murder!"

Her words echoed in his head.

Trust me—

I don't.

Matt scowled. "Okay." He cocked his head back. "Fine."

Madeline raised an eyebrow. "Fine?"

"Yeah." He curled his lips. "He took everything from me, though."

She rolled her eyes. "Oh, come on," she muttered.

"No, I mean it. I don't want this shit," he spat. "I don't want to work for his dense company. I never wanted to move to New Harbor. Maddie, because of *him*, he took us away from home."

"I actually wanted this," she said and pointed to herself. "This is my dream job."

"Well, it's not mine. Being some stupid apprentice for a gunmaker is *not* my dream. I wanted to go to art school!"

"To hell with art school!" she screamed back at him. "You can't make a career out of art!"

"I would have found something out of it!"

"Like what? Spraying the city with paint?"

"Why the hell would I do that?" he shot back. "That's vandalism!"

"You basically vandalize shit every night, Matt!"

"That's vigilantism."

"I don't care. You're too talented for that," she brushed him off.

"Wow. What happened to 'Oh, I'll listen to you, Matt! Tell me everything!' Where did that go?" he said. "You're willing to believe Streak over me. Is that it?"

"I'm not letting you accuse *my boss* of being a murderer!"

"He is the sniper's boss!" Matt screamed.

"Matt, stop!"

"I will if you let me live my life! I'm going to leave!"

"You're not leaving!" She followed him as he stood up. "Stop!"

Matt walked toward the door, but she stepped in his way. "Maddie, I have to get out of here."

"I need you. Don't," Madeline begged. "Just...sit down. We can talk."

"You won't listen."

"I will," she promised. "Don't walk out there, okay? It's still dark."

"Wow, as if I haven't gone out at night before."

Madeline frowned. "Matt...just listen to me."

"Forget it," he murmured and turned from her. "I'll figure something out."

"I don't want you accusing Jason Streak. That's all," she begged him. "Don't do that to yourself."

"Do what?" he snapped back. "I'm trying to save people, Maddie. People are getting killed because of him!"

"It's not his fault someone is targeting his business!"

"He's the one targeting it," Matt stated. "Xander's right."

"You mean James?"

"Xander."

Madeline huffed. "I'm starting to think 'James' wants to blackmail Streak Corp. I don't understand why you would trust him after what he said at the gala."

"I don't know. Maybe it's the fact that he saved me from a concussion, and he figured out I'm Speedfire," he remarked. "He helps me every day—"

"Okay. But what will Christine think if you start accusing her uncle?" Madeline said.

"I think she'll have my back."

"He is her *uncle*."

"Who's tying her down to his manipulative business," Matt finished for her.

"She's still sticking by her uncle's side. The fact that she would go through with it for him speaks volumes," Madeline said.

"I don't know," Matt muttered, peeking at the blinded window. "It speaks volumes about Streak. Not in the way you think, though."

Before Madeline could reply, a loud chirp cut through their tension, and Kiwi pounced onto the bed.

"Okay," sighed Madeline. "If you hate it, then quit."

Matt lowered his shoulders. "I'm working there for you."

"*Then quit,*" she hissed. She turned around and stormed out of his room.

Matt's lips quivered as Kiwi pawed at his hand. His fingers brushed against her head as he moved to his bedside table. He ignored the vase of wilting roses and grabbed his prescription bottle. He popped two tablets into his mouth, then stared at the sky outside.

Twilight.

He couldn't stand to be in the same building as his sister right now.

Matt didn't know where he was going. All he knew was that he needed to leave.

The cries of thunder echoed across the city before the rain fell. Matt was soaked in no time as he walked the slippery streets into Fells Point, keeping close to the piers. The chilling wind gnawed at his skin. He forgot to bring a sweatshirt with him. Even his Speedfire jacket would have sufficed. But he didn't care.

He was going anywhere but home.

Lightning struck the bay, and his gaze turned to the distant flashes. The sparks reflected against his eyes, distracting him for just a moment too long. Fatigue hit him as he fixed his attention on the raging river. A silhouette watched him from the water; its figure wisping with smoke and shadow, its beady white eyes staring at him. The same figure who haunted his dreams earlier tonight.

Mom...

Maybe he still couldn't live with the fact that the bodies of his parents were halfway across the Atlantic Ocean. They were never brought home, given a fake funeral instead, and leaving Madeline and Matt to fend for themselves.

The war took away his chances of ever having a normal life, and as always, he had no say in anything.

What if she's right? Matt sauntered down to the pier, the clanking of stone following his steps. *I'm losing my mind.*

Despite working for Streak Corporation, "James Salamar" had never showed any appreciation for Jason Streak. And if Xander despised the man, why wouldn't he try to frame him?

And he wants Speedfire *to do it*, Matt reminded himself.

Perhaps Madeline had a point, but Matt didn't want to hear it. Even if Jason Streak was innocent, he still possessed dark secrets from the Optyman War.

Matt paused at the edge and stared down at the water. The odds of lightning striking him were low, but not impossible.

A set of footsteps stopped halfway across the pier behind him. Matt faced the bay, trying to find his mother's shadow again, yet his efforts were in vain. He turned around slowly, and to his regret, he came face-to-face with New Harbor's Reaper.

What does it mean to be suicidal yet afraid of dying? He shuddered against the wind as her words haunted him. *To be self-sacrificing while yearning to live?*

The sniper could be another figment of his imagination tonight. Maybe he shouldn't have taken his pills and stormed off, but still, he was in no mood to care.

He wasn't even Speedfire tonight. He was nothing at this moment, and he could easily act like it.

"Are you a vigilante?" Matt spoke up, his teeth chattering. The Rare Sniper tensed, her gaze already questioning his sanity. "Vigilantes are people who take justice into their own hands." He swallowed, shaking. "Doesn't exactly make them good...since *justice* itself is subjective."

She loosened her posture. "No." Her voice sounded softer, yet still husky.

The rain mixed with his tears as he focused on her. "I would have assumed you were Speedfire."

The sniper sighed as she looked to the left. Her head shook slightly. "Speedfire and his tired blue eyes," she said, returning her gaze to him as he turned his head. "No...he seems to be missing tonight."

Matt closed his eyes and inhaled deeply. *Just get it over with.*

"Are you here to kill me?" he asked. The sniper raised her brow. "I work for Streak Corp. And you found me all alone."

She tilted her head, remaining silent.

"It might be for the better," he continued, trembling. His eyes found the pistols attached to her holsters. "All I do is ruin everything. I mean, what's the point in keeping your burdens alive? They let you down. So, let them go."

The wind brushed through her feathers as she listened quietly. Her arms remained at her sides, just inches from her weapons, from the Core Stone in her pouch.

"Please..." he whispered. "Why else are you here if you're not going to do it?"

"I heard a bird crying in the rain," she said. He pressed his lips together, tightening his arms around himself. "I know who you are."

Not Speedfire. His gaze dropped to the dock, his sodden face staring back at him. *Just nobody.*

"I know who I am, too," Matt said. "My parents were war heroes. But I don't get the privilege of knowing what they did overseas. I don't even get to know *why* they're heroes. My sister manages the largest defense contractor in the world. And then there's me." His shoulders sank. "I'm just...nothing. Nobody. I'll never be them. I'll never be my aunt. No matter what I do, it's never going to be good enough."

All Matt wanted to do was save his sister and this godforsaken city he was pressured to move to. Instead, he made matters worse with every step he took.

"I'm her greatest burden," he choked out. "She gave up her life just to take care of me. And *why?*" He gripped his arms, pinching himself as lightning flashed across the sky. "All I've ever done is hold her back. Why didn't she just give me away? Why did she ruin her life for me? I wish I could give everything back to her, but I just *can't.* Instead, we fight, and we make up. Then we fight again, and it keeps getting worse, and worse...until there's nothing left."

Matt held his breath, his tears warming his cheeks for just a second as he faced the sniper. Between her violet eyes, the long hood, her vague voice, and smeared makeup, he could still never figure out her emotions. But he had this moment to notice the smudged lines of eyeshadow running down her cheeks, barely hidden by her mask.

The Rare Sniper stepped forward, and Matt held his ground. Her gaze wandered to his shivering arms, then to his lack of warm clothes.

"Love is a choice," she said, her voice softening. He curled his lips as his eyes welled with more tears. "Your family could choose to love you, or they could choose to abandon you." Her head tilted again as she sighed. "Even the loveless know that."

Matt breathed quietly. "Do you love someone?"

She kept her gaze locked on his eyes, then nodded slowly.

His body ached, his mind was drowsy, but his heart raced repeatedly. He turned away from her, sinking to the ground.

And you would do anything to save the ones you love. He leaned against the guardrail, closing his eyes. *Anything.*

The rain grew heavier, and his breath slowed. He shivered relentlessly, and he drew his knees close to his chest.

"All I do is hurt everyone I love," he said, keeping his eyes closed. "Even when I'm away from her, I hurt her."

He pictured the ghost on the water, and he felt himself slipping away.

The sniper could do what she wanted with him tonight. But he knew her well enough to predict that she would walk away, and he could finally be alone.

Even with a clouded mind, all he could do was dream about her.

Chapter 35

A Legend and Her Shadow

The sun cast a glare on Matt as he stretched across a metallic surface. His eyes fluttered open, and he stared up at a blue sky. He moved his hand, finding himself on a bayside bench with a black blanket over his body.

"Shit..." he murmured. He sat up, rubbing his eyes, then found his apartment a block ahead.

He lifted the heavy cover and glanced at the bench.

What did I do last night...?

Matt pulled the blanket around him, then walked back to his apartment. His eyes were tired, he still felt groggy. He recalled Madeline's words last night.

Then quit.

He wasn't quitting. *Yet.* But he could call out. *Again.*

Without a word, he slipped into the apartment, where he passed Madeline in the kitchen making coffee.

"Where the hell did you go?" she asked.

Matt glared at her as he wore the blanket like a cape. After a silent stance, he turned to his room and collapsed into his bed.

Matt was tempted to walk out of Streak Corporation. As he grew up with Madeline, he learned that most of what she spewed in a heated argument was indefinite. She never meant most of the hurtful things she said.

But two days later, she was still not talking to him.

Matt sat alone in the cafeteria as Xander mingled with the other employees by the door.

"I heard Streak's holding a conference because of some issues with the Core Stone," a woman mentioned. Her black hair was rolled up into a neat bun. "Apparently, the mayor of New Harbor will be there. He's letting a few employees attend the meeting as well."

"Are you attending it, James?" a man with short dreadlocks asked.

Matt frowned. He wondered if anyone else in the building knew "James" was an alias.

"Kylie is reserving me a spot," Xander replied. "It'll be fun to watch."

Fun to watch, Matt repeated in his mind. He never recalled a conference ever being *fun*.

"If you want to attend any conferences in the future, I suggest you get back to work."

Matt glanced over as Christine stood before the workers with her hands on her hips.

Xander turned and smiled. "Of course," he said. "As if we haven't been working all morning. We're taking a small break."

Christine raised an eyebrow. "My uncle wouldn't appreciate you all spreading gossip about his upcoming conference with the mayor."

"You're talking as if you'll be taking over his position one day," Xander said. Christine's expression dropped into a bitter glare. "I respect that, of course. Must be a heavy burden."

She scowled. "Keep talking. I dare you."

"I could talk all day," he said smugly.

She huffed. "Finish your break, then get back to work," she muttered. She stepped away from the group and turned toward Matt. He shifted his attention to the floor.

"Hey," Christine spoke up behind him. He glanced up at her as he caught her floral scent.

"Hey," replied Matt. They both wore solemn expressions.

"Are you okay?" she asked.

"Yeah, why?"

"I don't know," she mumbled. Her eyes dropped to the table. "I just feel like something's wrong."

Matt picked at his nails as she slid into the seat beside him. "What do you mean?"

"You didn't answer my texts yesterday..." She slumped her shoulders.

He froze. "What?" He scrambled for his phone, then opened his text messages.

Christine:

> Hey! Can we hang out today? :)

> Please!!!

> There's a new spot I want to show you!

> Matt? Are you ok?

> :(

"Shit. I'm sorry..." he winced. His eyes teared up as he held his breath. "I slept all day, and my phone was dead."

Her shoulder brushed against his. "It's fine. I hope you're okay." She glanced at Xander. "Everyone seems to be in a mood."

He followed her gaze. "Don't mind him. A lot of weird shit comes out of his mouth."

"No, it's not James," she sighed. "Something's off with your sister, too."

"Oh." Matt looked away. "She'll be fine."

"And what about you?"

He met her concerned gaze, and his head still spun with fatigue. "I could be better. But I'll survive."

Christine raised her hand, smiling faintly as she pushed his bangs to the side. She stared into his eyes deeply, and his heart lurched at her touch.

*Please do that again...*he begged as she lowered her hand, scooting closer to him. *Please...*

"Can I still take you out?" she offered.

Matt stopped his slight shaking. "Right now?"

She nodded. "If that's okay. I think you could use a break."

"You just told James and his brigade over there to stop taking one," he laughed.

"I don't like what he's talking about," she said. "You know what I mean."

Christine intended to halt their topic of conversation. She didn't care if they worked or not. Matt understood completely.

"Well, if you insist. A 'business meeting,' right?" he teased.

"Shut up." She blushed and rolled her eyes. "There's an Optyman museum in Riverside that opened recently. I've been waiting to go with someone."

"An *Optyman* museum?" Matt smiled. "I'll go on one condition."

Christine bit her lip, hesitant. "What is it?"

"Wear your cape."

The large museum had a silver-colored structure, and its wide lawn was filled with autumn oaks, bushes, and pines. Christine rolled the motorcycle into a parking space and helped Matt off the bike. She then pulled her white cape out from under the seat, wrapping it across her jean jacket.

Welcome to The Heartwell Museum!

Matt passed the sign, noting the logo of the silver wings.

They walked inside and checked in, where the clerk directed them to the different sections of the museum. Three exhibits were dedicated to Optyma, while another segment was devoted to Líthos, Greece—the hometown of Sky. Matt tugged on Christine's jacket and pointed toward Sky's zone.

"Please," he whispered. "I'm a huge Sky fan."

"I know," she replied with a smile. "We can go through there first."

Matt and Christine walked through the Líthos gallery. The town of stone was what the citizens had called it back in the day. Nowadays, the place has become a tourist attraction for avid fans of Sky and the Stathis family. While it used to be a town for trade, its income centered around tourism as the legend of Sky grew over the years.

"Are you two familiar with the legendary vigilante?" a tour guide cleared his throat behind them. They turned around and came face-to-face with a friendly Greek man. He had dark hair, round glasses, and a warm smile.

"He's one of her biggest fans," Christine mentioned as she gestured to Matt.

"Well, then! Allow me to show you what we have. I'm Preston, and I can be your guide for today." He beckoned them as he walked toward a few tapestries. "Sky's tale is also tied to Optyma. She set foot in the nation before."

Matt gazed up at the intricate designs. He recognized some of them from the history books he used to read. The Stathis family had a lot of love for silver and gold colors. Jade Stathis, on the other hand, preferred the various blues. He could tell her custom-made tapestries were blue with silver stars that aligned the fabric.

"The Optyman people loved her. As did the people of Hasa in Egypt," Preston continued. "They say their lives changed for the better when she made her stay there."

"She made quite an impact on the world," Christine mumbled. She followed the guide but fixed her gaze on the Stathis draperies.

"She certainly did, even with all her flaws," Preston commented. "May I share an interesting discovery made about her? There were signs that our heroine was schizophrenic, though these accusations didn't come up until after she had passed away."

Matt glanced at the guide. He had recalled reading a few essays on Jade Stathis' schizophrenia, but he never thought of her differently. He still loved and admired her actions. She was proof that even the most broken people could shape the world.

Jade Stathis died of pneumonia while crossing the Mediterranean Sea in 1936. During the last of her adventures, she ultimately succumbed to something many of her loved ones had warned her about. Yet Jade was fearless, even in the face of death. She provided strength against criminals and gave financial aid to the poor. Even the tides of World War I could not hinder her morale. After Matt had read about her passing, he often wondered how she would have fared during World War II, but she never had to bear witness to those tragedies. Instead, her children had taken her ashes and let her rest in the sea that claimed her.

"Do you two know about the Jade Stathis Museum in Dover?" Preston spoke up. Matt shook his head, and the guide grinned. "If you ever find yourself in England, you should check it out."

"Why in Dover?" Matt asked, curious.

"She had a small manor near the cliffs. Her old home is the museum," Preston mentioned. "The government turned it into a national museum about ten years ago. It has a lot of memorabilia. That's where her empty urn is."

"Wait...I thought her home would have gone to her descendants," Christine added, confused. "Was it sold?"

"Oh. No." Preston's cheerful attitude dropped. "So, the descendant who lived in the house passed seventeen years ago. She and her husband were gunned down. I think they were targets of a lunatic."

Matt's jaw dropped. "*What?*" Over all his years of researching Sky, he never recalled hearing about her descendant's assassination.

"Doesn't Sky have more descendants?" Christine questioned. "Why turn it into a museum if someone else could have inherited her property?"

The guide shook his head with a sigh. "I heard the kids survived, but there aren't any records of what happened to them." He leaned closer, lowering his voice. "There's a wild conspiracy about it being an inside job. Vigilantes cause a lot of controversy, after all."

Matt looked away, shivering. The last thing he would want is for anyone to come after Madeline because of Speedfire.

But Jade wanted her identity to be a secret. She had no control over her alias after her death.

On a shelf nearby sat a few wood carvings of animals—a bunny, a fox, and a dove. Matt tilted his head as he peered over at them.

"What are these?" he asked, wishing to change the topic.

"A few statuettes found in Lady Jade's quarters," explained Preston. "Historians say they were a gift to her excellency. One of the poorer folks in Hasa gave them to her." He pointed to another figure on a shelf—a wooden griffin. "This one was found in Hasa."

Christine leaned closer to examine a word carved along the chest of the griffin. The figure stood on its hind legs, spreading its wings. "*Anzú?*"

"We believe this figure is supposed to represent the ancient Sumerian deity," the guide explained. "But how it relates to Sky, we're still unsure."

Christine stared in awe at the griffin, then moved along with the guide. Matt, meanwhile, felt a deep temptation to hold the dove. Despite the sudden desire to take the wooden bird, he shoved the feeling aside. He pushed on, following the other two closely.

The guide stopped in front of a painting depicting Sky in a dance amongst the fluorescent clouds. Ribbons swirled around her as she flew in the air with grace.

"She's so beautiful," Christine uttered as she stared at the painting.

"I agree," the guide said, then walked onward. "I'd like to show you a new painting we just got. A pair of anthropologists found this one in Hasa a few years ago. Carefully crafted by an artist named Shakir Zahir from the nineteenth century."

Matt gaped as he stared at the large-scale painting. Sky stood steadfast as the ribbons attached to her attire blew in the wind. Beside Sky, a different figure knelt on the ground. Cloaked in a black guise, with a hood over his head and a dagger clenched in his hand, was someone Matt had never seen before. As he had felt toward the wooden figurines, he could not take his eyes off him.

"Who is that?" Matt asked. He stared into the black eyes of the dark figure.

The painting displayed them as polar opposites. While Sky wore soft blue colors and stood in the sunlight, the boy beside her was drenched in dark clothes and bowed in the shade.

"Not many remember him, but that is the thief known as *Shadow*," Preston informed them. "He was a partner of Sky's in Hasa. We don't know much about him, but we occasionally find something new."

"How come he's not recognized by many Sky historians?" Christine questioned.

Preston glowered. "I don't know. But Sky was not known for having partners. Some historians say he was her greatest companion. Others say they may have been enemies," he explained. "If I am to make a guess, he preferred to be in her shadow."

Matt never knew Sky had a partner-in-crime, ironically. The dark-clad boy seemed forgotten by many enthusiasts and historians. Instead of moving along with Christine and the guide, he wanted to stay with Shadow.

His gaze glossed over the painting again, but he caught his breath when he stared at the flowers beside Shadow. A flash of yellow was all he needed to see—small petals and florets with tooth-like edges.

Sky and Shadow stood upon a field of yellow chrysanthemums.

Matt and Christine finished their trip through the museum earlier than expected. Christine had been right when she said it was smaller. So far, it was only one of two museums dedicated to Optyma.

While this time with Christine gave his mind a break from the case of the Rare Sniper, his attention was fixed on something else—the yellow flowers and the shadowed partner.

He lay in bed early, attempting to put his mind to rest. He glanced at the vase of circus roses on his bedside table, then his eyes found the zolpidem bottle.

He took two pills, then shut his eyes.

Time passed, and his sister came home. Still, she said nothing to him.

A breeze drifted through the open window, and he opened his eyes. He stood in the field of yellow mums once again. The wisps of leaves and flower petals swirled around his head. He followed the wind's direction to where the lady in blue sat on the hill.

Matt walked up to her slowly. The sunset was the same as always, as were the swirling clouds and their endless patterns. He sat down beside her. Her eyes were closed, and she held a wooden figure of a dove.

Matt picked one of the flowers from the ground. He twirled it between his fingers.

"Is this actually your favorite flower?" he spoke up.

She opened her eyes, staring ahead at the setting sun. "*They were my partner's favorite.*" She smiled. "*I never really had a favorite flower before.*"

Matt felt his chest tighten, so he exhaled slowly. He peered over at her as she rested her gaze on the sun again. She looked different from how all the paintings had depicted her. She wore a blue dress with her hair tied back in ribbons. She didn't look like a perfect model, as her olive-toned complexion had a few blemishes and rosy cheeks. Her eyes were still a reflection of the sky.

What stuck out to him the most was that she was his age—a late teenager. All those paintings and pictures depicted her as a woman in her twenties.

"Jade?"

Blue Jay.

She faced him with an expression so calm yet vain. "*Matt.*"

Perhaps his head had been playing tricks on him all along.

Perhaps this was all just a fantasy of him meeting his childhood hero.

Perhaps he was lost.

If he was, these moments in his mind still meant everything to him, even when he was just a child who ran around with an imaginary heroine. No one compared to that young friend dressed in blue—a girl full of radical energy and dignity.

Jade grabbed his hand. "*Welcome back.*"

Chapter 36

The Raven and the Demon

Work became a drag for Matt. He couldn't stand the silent treatment from his sister, but he needed to be there. He had a scandal to uncover. He had mysteries to solve. And he would be no closer to unveiling the truth if he did quit because of Madeline.

Matt stared at his notes on the computer screen, exhausted out of his mind. Xander left the cubicle and disappeared over the last thirty minutes—*go figure*—but Matt had nothing to complain about. His coworker had packed the document with notes and links. Even though Matt had been stuck at the desk the whole morning, Xander *still* got more done than him.

How?

Matt threw his head into his hands. He was frustrated with *everything*. Madeline, Xander, Streak, even Speedfire—

"Hey!" Christine hopped into the empty seat beside him.

Matt jolted. Christine leaned back in Xander's chair, crossing her legs.

"What's up?" Matt asked, rubbing his eyes.

"I want to ask you about something," she said. "Something you might be interested in."

"Oh." Matt sat up, then turned his seat to face her. "Okay?"

"So, it's about Speedfire."

Matt curled his lips to hide his frown. *Oh no.*

"After that trip to the museum, Sky has me thinking about vigilantes again," Christine continued. She leaned closer, lowering her voice. "You also know about...that *one* time."

"When *he* saved you?" he whispered back.

Christine nodded quickly. "I spoke to him again after that," she confessed.

He exhaled. *That took quite a while for you to finally tell me.*

Matt raised a brow. "You did?" he replied, sounding surprised. He recalled the night they shared on the pier. That was over a month ago. He realized Christine hadn't been walking home so late at night, and other troubles in the neighborhood occupied him. He still kept an eye out for her, however.

"It was a nice talk," Christine mentioned, glancing at the black screen across from her. "He admitted to watching over me."

"Okay..."

"But it's usually when I'm working a late shift. That's when he shows up. And I'm working late tonight," she said. Matt nodded again, keeping this in mind. "I was wondering..." Christine paused, blushing. "Do you want to walk with me later? If you're still up by then. I'll be off around eleven tonight."

"Wait, what?" Matt replied, blinking.

"We can find Speedfire together." Christine smiled at him and narrowed her eyes.

Matt stared at her as blankly as he could.

"Well?" She tilted her head.

"Uh..."

Matt's eyes dropped to his knees. *What the hell am I doing?*

"I thought you didn't like vigilantes," he spoke up.

Christine's expression fell. "That's changed. For Speedfire, at least..." she said quietly. "You know that. And you like vigilantes."

Matt shook his head, turning his chair to face his desk. "I've got plans later," he told her, avoiding the disappointment in her eyes. "And vigilantes *interest* me. That doesn't mean I see them as my heroes."

"I didn't say they were," Christine replied.

"Yeah, well," he glanced at her before returning his attention to his note sheet, "you seem to think otherwise for some reason."

Christine exhaled, and Matt stared down at his keyboard. He closed his eyes, breathing in sharply.

"Okay." She wrapped her arms around herself. "It would have been really late, anyway. I'm sorry."

Damn it. Matt huffed, then turned back to her. "Is there a reason you want to find him?"

"He's interesting," she said with a sour look.

"Sure." He grimaced. "Any other reason?"

"Maybe I just like him."

"And...?"

"I thought you might like him, too..."

Matt knitted his brows. As much as he enjoyed being a vigilante, he struggled to even like himself. There were so many things he could improve on.

Perhaps he was being too harsh. Christine was only thinking about his interests.

"You can't yell at me the other day for lazing around when you're just sitting in my seat," Xander lectured, walking over with a scowl. "Get up."

Christine swiveled the chair to face him. "And what were you doing for the past hour?" she remarked. "I doubt you were working."

"I was on break," Xander argued.

"And you spent your break in Kylie's room?"

"No," Xander scoffed, crossing his arms. "I was stopping by to give her an update."

"An update on what? Your affair?" Christine deadpanned. Matt covered his mouth.

Xander cocked his head to the side. "And what affair would that be?" he replied, unfazed.

"I'm pretty sure Kylie is engaged, but hey," she said with a shrug, "don't let me be the judge."

"And here you are, flirting with our antisocial coworker in my chair. Do you mind?"

"I'm not flirting. He's my friend," Christine snapped. Matt turned, hiding his grin. "I was just inviting him out somewhere."

"She's right," Matt said, looking up at Xander. "She was keeping your seat warm for you."

"Ew. No. Get up," Xander exhaled roughly. "Go sit and talk about Speedfire somewhere else."

Christine tensed. "Eavesdropping now?"

Xander narrowed his gaze at her. "Act like you never eavesdrop. I can hear you from a mile away."

Matt winced, "Guys, stop—"

"Well, I'm not spreading gossip about my uncle's business," Christine hissed at Xander.

"Sure, but you're talking about such a central figure in this whole scandal," Xander expressed. "Someone your uncle *clearly* despises. I'm certain everyone in this building overhears his vents to Madame Modisette at some point."

Matt smacked his forehead. Christine huffed as she turned away from Xander. "I don't share my uncle's opinions," she mentioned.

"Are you sure?" Xander mocked.

"It's none of your business," Christine said.

"Hm. Maybe," he mentioned with a smirk. "I had the honor of meeting Speedfire, too. Like you."

"You didn't hear anything about that," she countered.

"And I bought him soup at a restaurant," Xander continued proudly. Matt turned away, hiding his reddening face. "So, what have you done for your local hero?"

Christine dropped her gaze to the floor. Matt peeked over at her, uncertain. He never expected anything from anyone, but that would be impossible to tell her without revealing himself.

"Fascinating," Xander uttered, "how you're suddenly interested in finding Speedfire. You just *need* to know more about him. And why?"

"Mind your own business," Christine hissed.

"Mind yours, too. What are you planning? Are you trying to lure Speedfire out now?" Xander continued.

"Can we stop?" Matt spoke up, yet his attempts were futile.

"I'm not planning anything," Christine muttered.

"Really?" Xander grinned slyly. "So, you're not trying to uncover his identity for your uncle?"

"No!" Christine snapped, standing up. Xander remained still while Matt leaned back in his seat, shocked. "My uncle would flip out if he knew I was trying to see Speedfire. But I know what I could tell him." She sharpened her glare at him. "He wouldn't be distraught over firing your ass."

"Well," Xander pushed past her, "at least you're finally out of my seat." He sank back into the computer chair. "But have fun tonight. If that's what you plan on doing."

Christine stepped aside with a quiet frown.

Xander shifted his seat around. "And be careful, too. With Speedfire." He winked at Matt. "Unlike certain people, at least *I* have no intentions of hurting him."

"*James!*" Matt scolded him. Xander glanced at him, dropping his grin.

Christine wrapped her arms around herself again, then turned away. Matt watched her disappear around the corner of his cubicle.

"What the hell?" Matt groaned, glaring at Xander. "Do you want to get fired?"

Xander laughed as he grabbed a tissue from his desk. "No, but it would be funny if I did."

"Christine didn't deserve that."

Xander rolled his eyes, then wiped his nose. "Please, Matthew, she's Streak's niece—"

"I don't care what you think of Jason Streak," Matt lectured him. "She's not *him*."

He stood up as Xander sat back silently, then followed Christine down the hall, where she waited for the elevator doors to open. As soon as she stepped onto the lift, Matt squeezed in with her, dodging the doors.

Christine inched against the wall, stunned. "Matt—"

"Hey, wait," he breathed out. "I'm sorry. Please don't listen to James. He's—"

"An ass. Whatever," Christine sighed. "I can't stand him."

Matt frowned. "I'm still sorry..."

"You don't have to apologize on his behalf."

"No, I mean about tonight," he said. "We can always hang out another time."

She looked away. Matt didn't want to know what was going through her mind. He would still be there for her tonight; not in the way she wanted him to be, but he wouldn't keep her waiting.

However, he contemplated Xander's perspective, which ironically was the same as Madeline's.

What will you do if you learn my identity?

Christine leaned her head against his shoulder, snapping him out of his thoughts. The gesture was brief and silent.

The elevator doors opened, and Christine walked through without another word. She left Matt alone on the lift, and he watched her until the doors closed him in.

Matt kept tabs on anything suspicious around the office. Xander gave him more news on the suspected conference, along with rumors of a small holiday party near the start of December. Matt also managed to get an apology from Xander regarding the outburst at Christine, though Christine remained distant for the rest of the day. She avoided the marketing department, leaving Matt with the awkward tension left behind.

"She's working late tonight," Matt sighed, shutting his computer down. "Just apologize to her at some point."

"I will," Xander groaned, rubbing his temple. "She probably won't let me, though."

"Tough shit. Just because you know my secret doesn't mean you get to make it your business," Matt remarked, shoving his chair into his desk. "And what you said was uncalled for."

Xander flashed a grin at him. "Anything I say is uncalled for. Now, run along. Be careful," he said with a wave.

Matt left the office at sunset to avoid walking home with Madeline. He still didn't know what to say to her, so he kept his distance. Instead, he put his worries aside and thought of Speedfire.

He needed to escape tonight.

Matt found himself on the rooftops of the harbor once again. His mind drifted all over the place, to the painting of Sky and Shadow, to the concept of Jade Stathis visiting his dreams. He feared her presence may be a sign that he was going insane.

What is 'real' anymore? Matt thought with a sigh.

"I see you up there," a silvery voice called out from below.

Matt peered down at the sidewalk and met eyes with Christine. She held a book in her hand, tilting her head.

"You have a sharp eye," he replied and stood up.

"It's not every day you see someone sitting on a rooftop," she remarked.

With that, Matt found a pole attached to the corner of the building and slid down. He took a step toward her, and she stepped back quickly.

"Were you looking for me this time?" he said, even though he already knew the answer.

"Maybe. What are you up to tonight?" Christine asked. He expected her to have more excitement in her eyes. Her face remained impassive, however.

"Patrolling." He glanced around the harbor. "Keeping an eye out for...certain people."

"So, you're still stalking Jason Streak's company?" she pointed out, shoving her book into a pocket bag.

"I have a hunch," he noted. "I think some people may be in danger."

"Like who?"

He felt tempted to say her. In a way, she was a target. "James Salamar" could be a good enough answer, though he didn't want to make himself look too obvious.

"Targets of the Rare Sniper. Could be anyone affiliated with Streak. Even you."

Christine frowned and stepped away. "Well, good luck. I'll be on my way."

Matt's eyes widened. "Wait," he breathed out. She turned around. "Did you...uh, want anything?"

"No..."

His shoulders sagged. "Then why bother getting my attention?"

"I don't know," she said.

"Really?"

She was still bitter from earlier. He mentally cursed Xander in the back of his head.

"I'm not in the mood," she mentioned, glancing to the side.

"Well...do you want me to walk you home?" Matt offered.

"Nope."

"Even with everything going on?" He thought about the consequences of letting her go alone. By chance, the sniper could be around the area. Even The Reapers could be lurking nearby. On the other hand, if Streak was secretly their boss, he doubted he would target his own niece.

"Nothing has stopped me from walking back any other night," she said.

"Except, I did stop someone from jumping you before."

"Sure." Christine scowled, keeping her eyes on the pavement.

"It's been a while since the Rare Sniper has targeted someone, though," he pointed out. "Like Harry Faresoul. I was there when it happened. I know how she does it."

Christine huffed and pulled her arms around herself. "I don't want you anywhere near me."

Her comment stung him. He stood there in disbelief, wondering what he had done wrong—*if* he did anything to hurt her.

"And don't follow me, either," she scolded him.

"I won't," he said, then backed away. "Stay safe."

Christine turned around slowly. Matt watched her for a moment, and before he left to return to the rooftops, she stopped. The wind brushed through her hair as she kept her arms huddled around herself. She exhaled sharply, staring at the ground, yet she caught his attention. He stood still, waiting for her.

With a sigh, Christine turned around. She gazed at him solemnly, and her eyes dropped to the ground again.

"I did want to see you..." she admitted.

She returned to him, giving herself enough space between them.

"What do you need?" he asked as she met his eyes.

"Can we talk?" Christine asked. "Just for a few minutes."

Matt lowered his shoulders. He held his hand out to her. "Want to join me up there?" he offered, nodding to the rooftops.

Christine's lips parted as she gazed at the buildings. She nodded, then took his hand.

Their trip to the roofs remained quiet, yet Matt was at ease. He guided her up the fire escape, seeing she was careful with each step she took. They reached the top of the building, and he helped her up the ledge. Christine released his hand as she overlooked the harbor from above. The view was remarkable, from the headquarters to Fort McHenry across the Patapsco River.

"Here," Matt said, sitting down on the edge. He patted the spot beside him, and Christine followed. "I like to start and end my nights doing this."

He brought a smile out of her. She sat along the ridge and stared at the streets below. "Must feel great," she exhaled.

"It's the little things that make the nightlife," he mentioned, leaning his hands back against the rooftop.

Christine gazed out at the horizon. "Even when you have to deal with..." Her voice drifted off as she found the right words. "What you were saying earlier."

"The certain people?"

She glowered. "The sniper..." she mumbled, shifting her gaze to the water. "So...if you're fine with me asking, what is it like for you to fight the Rare Sniper?"

Matt frowned beneath the mask. "It's terrifying," he answered. Christine gaped at him, concerned. "And I mean it. I've never fought anyone like her before."

"Even when you've handled a lot of other criminals?" she added.

"She's *Rare*. She's dressed like this demonic raven. I've never been blasted off a roof before," Matt continued. "And she just shows up out of the blue. I never know what she's going to do next. Whereas with other criminals, I know their motives. It's how I can take them down. But the sniper? She's just...too unknown to me." He watched the wind push the water, as haunting as it was for him. "And that's not even the most terrifying part about her."

Christine swallowed, breathing out faintly. "Then what is?"

"She's threatening people I care about. And it seems like she's being *forced* to do it." Matt closed his eyes, clenching his fists. "It's all fear. Whatever is going on between us, we're both afraid. And fear can make some people unstoppable."

The wind drifted around them. Matt felt sick to his stomach whenever he felt the softest breezes. He feared the Rare Sniper would one day come across him like this—sitting unarmed and unaware with Christine. She had already attacked Harry in front of him.

"A demonic raven," Christine echoed, opening her eyes to the empty night sky, "who fights a speed-demon." She gazed at him, smiling faintly.

His cheeks burned red. "That's how you see me?"

"It's a joke," she said with a shrug. "I overhear some people on the news calling you that."

"It wouldn't surprise me if your uncle did, too," he told her. "But I...I didn't really mean to call her a raven. That just slipped out."

The sniper's desired alias should remain a secret. That was something he was intent on keeping.

"What else is she supposed to be?" Christine sighed, fixing her gaze on the horizon. "Other than a monster born at night..."

Matt frowned, following her gaze to the bayside.

"I wanted to say something else, too," she added.

"What?"

"I have a friend," she mentioned. His heart thudded. "He likes vigilantes. He's into what they do."

Matt swallowed hard, keeping himself from shaking.

"I was trying to get him out here," Christine continued, and her gaze flickered back to him. "He didn't want to, though. He was too busy."

"Oh. I'm sorry..." he mumbled back. "Maybe another time, I don't know. I'll be around—"

"No, no," she brushed him off, shaking her head. "I'm done after tonight."

Matt raised a brow. "Huh?"

"My uncle's been pushing these late-night hours on me, and honestly, I've had it," she exhaled. "It's safer for me to walk home before sunset, anyway. You would know."

Matt's heartbeat relaxed, yet he was still shocked to hear this. "Yeah..."

"And if my friend wants to see you, he's more than welcome to come out here and find you," Christine continued.

"I wouldn't really recommend it," he said. "But—"

"But people do whatever they want," she said, facing him as she faked a smile. "Don't give up on what you do. Keep fighting your demons. They'll eventually stop coming back."

Matt stared at her, meeting the pain behind her emerald eyes. "Never stop fighting yours, either," he said quietly.

Christine took a small breath. Her gaze dropped to the harbor, and slowly, she slipped her hand through his fingers. He tensed slightly, then glanced down at her hand entwined with his hand. His heart beat rapidly again.

"My friend has a big heart," she mentioned, closing her eyes. "He's a lot like you."

Matt pressed his lips, keeping quiet. Her grip in his hand shifted.

A bead of sweat trickled down his head. *Is she trying to feel for my ring?*

"You remind me of him, actually," she continued. He glanced at her as she continued to face the harbor. "Maybe you know him...or..."

Matt pulled his hand from hers. He leaned away as she looked taken aback.

"What?" she breathed out, confused.

"You're not getting anything from my personal life," he said bitterly. All he could think of was Xander's warning. He thought of Madeline's worries and Streak's hatred for Speedfire. He was being too careless. "I have nothing to do with your friend. Or you. I'm just here because I need to be here. You don't know me."

Christine sagged her shoulders. "I kind of do."

Matt scowled, then shuffled himself away from her. As he did, his phone vibrated in his pocket. "You should be getting home now. It's late."

She watched as he reached for his phone. "You don't say?" she remarked. His heart felt heavy.

Katelyn:

> Spotted some creeps robbing a flower shop. Want to help?

Katelyn's confidence was like a light in the dark for him.

Matt turned his phone away from Christine as she frowned at the message. "I have to go," he said, standing up. "Need help down?"

Christine stared at the empty road. She shook her head. Matt typed a quick reply.

Matt:

> Hang tight. Just text me the address.

Matt shoved the phone in his pocket, then glanced down at Christine. She wrapped her arms around herself, shielding herself from the chilling breeze. Guilt was eating him. After how he treated her earlier—even before Xander came back from his break—and now, it was clear to him she was having a bad day. And he was the reason why.

Both reasons why.

He cleared his throat. "Miss Elerare…"

"No, I can climb down," she said, swallowing.

Matt exhaled, loosening his posture. He held his hand out to her. "*May I help you down?*"

She glanced at his gloved hand, shivering. "You have better things to do."

"Something better than helping you?" Matt smirked, then slipped his fingers through hers. "Never."

Chapter 37

THE TELL-TALE HEART

Matt saw the broken windows of the flower shop the second he turned the corner. Three men in masks pillaged the store inside. Before he could step forward, Katelyn joined his side, beaming with determination.

"Kate," he hissed. He stepped ahead and turned around to face her.

"Oh, they're going down." She attempted to crack her knuckles.

"Stay back. I can handle it." He pulled the knife out from his belt, and she tugged on his jacket. "What?"

"I can help!" she insisted.

"Call the police," Matt said. "That's how you can help."

"I helped you take out that stalker before," she pointed out. "I've been practicing my punches."

"Have you really—"

She punched his arm lightly and laughed. "Now imagine that but with full force."

"Kate..." he sighed, rolling his eyes. "Stay behind me."

She saluted him and followed his trail as he crept toward the flower shop. Matt peered beyond the window, spotting the three robbers around the cash register.

"There's hardly anything in here. Find the safe," one of them barked.

"It's in the back, but we need an electronic key," a bulky robber mentioned.

Matt launched himself over the glass and felt the shards break beneath him. He glanced down at the floor, then up at the men who stared at him in shock.

"Shit, it's Speedfire!" the shortest of the men screamed out.

He ran for the door, and Matt intercepted his path. He sprinted forward, then kicked the robber to the ground.

The bulky man picked up a bat, swinging toward Speedfire. Matt dodged the blow, then kicked the thief's shins. The thug tripped and fell to the glass. He screamed horrifically as the shards pierced his right eye.

Matt stood up, caught his breath, and turned around—*THWACK!*

The leader shoved Matt against the shelf, and the surrounding clay pots shattered as they hit the floor. Matt's heart raced. He lifted his arms to block the man's attacks.

THUD!

Matt lowered his arms after hearing the blow. The robber's eyes rolled to the back of his head, and he tumbled to the ground. Katelyn stood before him with the baseball bat. A look of terror clouded her face as she trembled.

"You okay?" Matt asked, scrambling to stand up. He put his hand on her shoulder.

Katelyn nodded, then gulped. "Yeah. You?"

"Yeah." He stared down at the men. One robber was unconscious, the other held onto his bleeding eye, and the last looked half-asleep.

"I did call them, by the way," Katelyn mentioned. "The police."

"Good."

"Did I do alright?" she asked.

Matt took the baseball bat from her. He threw it to the ground near the register. "Yes."

She smiled. "I still think we'd make a great team."

"I thought we already did," he joked.

Katelyn's face flushed red, and she glanced away. "Really?"

Matt was still unsure how he felt about letting her be a vigilante with him. The role and duties could be too much for her to handle. But if Matt was honest with himself, it was sometimes too much for him to handle.

"I have some ideas," she added as she gestured to his jacket. "Maybe some redesigning."

"What? No, wait..." He shook his head. "That's not necessary."

"Oh." She stared at his whole outfit, from head to toe. "I wasn't thinking of redesigning your whole suit. More like..." She grabbed his elbow and felt the firmness of the material. "Giving you some extra protection. You could use some padding there."

Matt followed her gaze and lifted his elbow. "Actually, that might work."

"I've been crafting with friends. I think we can put something together," she offered. "If there are any other designs you want me to try, let me know."

Matt least expected Katelyn to admire his whole aesthetic out of the blue. He glanced down at his apparel. If he could change one thing, it would be his belt. Whenever he met with the Rare Sniper, his eyes often fell on the logo she wore—the open semicircle with the arrows pointing out from each end.

"Well, since you're so insistent," he mocked her lightly, and she returned a bright smile, "there is something I have in mind."

"Okay?" she squealed.

"Can you design an insignia?" he asked. Her eyes widened. "Let's start with that."

The sirens neared the area. This whole routine with Katelyn felt all too familiar now.

Matt faced her again before stepping aside. "I need a symbol."

The night remained long and tiresome for Matt, yet even after lending his company to Christine and battling a trio of vandalizers with Katelyn, he was still reluctant to go home. His battle with insomnia was never-ending, and with his adrenaline rush persisting, he chose to settle on a rooftop along the harbor. The crisp breeze of the bayside could calm him for the time being, and after he was done relaxing, he could return to his bed. By then, Kiwi's purrs would soothe him until morning.

And morning could be forever from now.

An abrupt breeze shook Matt off from his late-night thoughts. He shuddered, huddling himself together.

The wind brushed against him again, and this time, he heard the faint echo of a feminine voice.

"*Fire.*"

Matt tensed. His focus was fixed on the horizon as he listened to the wind.

"*Fire...Speedfire...*" the wind whispered again.

Matt brought his palm to his temple. He was hearing things again. The wind repeating his alias was just his imagination, and maybe it was time for him to go home.

"*You...hear me...*" the voice persisted, hoarse yet melodic.

Her voice.

Matt recalled the many evenings he would stroll the beaches outside of Miami. Despite the distance, he could hear voices carried by the wind. Laughter and stories would travel along the water, drifting among the sand. Sounds from minutes ago swept beyond the dunes. He was always fascinated by this strange science of wind and sound.

But nothing fascinated him now. He felt terrified.

"*After a long night...you finally sit alone,*" the sniper's voice echoed.

Matt swallowed hard as he stared ahead. He glanced to his right, then to his left. The sniper was nowhere to be found. As the wind blew against him again, he found the breeze was coming from the north. He turned his head to face the direction for a moment, yet the night kept her silhouette veiled. But just by turning his head, he had given her a sure sign that he was listening.

"*I think...it has been some time,*" she continued. "*At least since you...saw me...*" Her voice stretched across the wind, and Matt was unsure if he could hear everything she was saying. "*But I have seen you. Night...after night. And you...,*" Matt winced as a sudden gale whistled against his ear, "*are everywhere.*"

Her cursed words never left his mind after they had spoken on this rooftop. She haunted him through the wind, whether as the Rare Sniper or *Night-Raven*. And even for a moment, he had pitied her.

Now, all he could do was dread her return.

"*You were with Jason Streak's niece. You're getting closer to her. Even risking something...taking her up here,*" the wind whispered. "*But you've met with her more than once, twice.*" Matt clenched his fists as his eyes fixated on the ground, listening carefully. "*Why is that...?*" His hood fluttered in the breeze, but he ignored it. "*Then you persisted. I saw you fighting with...that other girl. You stopped those felons.*"

Matt wanted to speak up, but was the sniper even close enough to hear him?

But I have seen you. Night...after night. He reflected on her words. The Rare Sniper has been watching him, stalking him all this time.

A twisted feeling crept into his stomach. Just a few days ago, he recalled waking up on a bench with a black blanket, his memories still fuzzy from that night. He remembered the fight with his sister, remembered leaving the apartment taking more pills than he should have. And then he blacked out.

"*I do see you,*" the sniper hummed. Matt shuffled slightly. "*What...? Do you not enjoy being stalked? I see how you take down criminals every night...decimating the crime rates of Canton. You know...how to hold yourself up, Fire.*"

Matt closed his eyes, irritated.

"*But why shouldn't I stalk you? Perhaps I just want to see that The Reapers are not after you...even if they still have their eyes...on you,*" the Rare Sniper lamented with the passing chill. "*It's just as you...watch over Jason Streak's niece on those late nights...like tonight. How you watch her...and for what reason? Why?*"

The waves splashed against the walls of the harbor, causing Matt to open his eyes. He cast his darkened gaze to the streets below, staying in silence.

"*Can you share with me your feelings in those moments?*" the wind mocked him. "*Can you give me a* sign, *Speedfire?*" His arms felt numb as the gust chilled him. He had no way of answering her. "*No. You won't. Go on and justify your own watchful gaze. We are stalkers at nightfall...but we do it for the greater good. Am I...right? Is there ever a case where stalking is moral? Tell me, Fire...Confess your sins, and I will share mine.*"

Matt had enough, yet he wanted to see her. He wanted to hear everything from her. The gravel scratched against his shoes as he stood.

"I know what it is," he spoke up, tilting his head to the left. "You're afraid of confrontation. You can't handle it."

Matt waited a few seconds. That was all it took for the wind to finally die. He turned to face the other end of the roof, and the Rare Sniper stood opposite him, holding the wind back.

"But I'll admit," he continued, "that it's nice how I'm not alone. You can join me in death for stalking, I guess. But who *isn't* afraid of dying? After all, death itself is a form of confrontation."

The sniper's violet gaze cut through him. "I just want to know why."

He glared at her, breathing steadily. "*Why* what?"

"Why you stay here, watching over Canton," the sniper said. "Maybe it's been on my mind, how *you* got involved. How...and why...and *what* it is that draws you in. You defended Harold Faresoul months ago, and now you watch over *her.* What you do means more to you than just some goddamn *greater good.*" She stepped forward, shaking.

Matt lowered his hand to his fire dagger. "*You* have a lot of nerve questioning *me* why I do the things I do," he seethed.

She narrowed her eyes. "We're two sides of the same coin."

"Don't even go there."

"You care about them. That's why," she uttered scornfully. "All those people working under Jason Streak...they mean something to you. You're not some random vigilante who came across me. You patrol this area for a *reason*."

Matt swiped the fire dagger from his belt, lighting it in seconds. "And my reason is *you*," he hissed, even if she already spoke the truth. "You want to end this tonight? We can end it. Right here, right now."

A quiet whistle echoed from the gentle gale. The sniper reached for her mask, hovering her hand over the dark cloth covering her lower face. Matt's breath faltered, his eyes widening. Before she could pull the mask down, she released her grip, then lowered her arm. Matt's shoulders sank with disappointment.

"I'll have to refuse," she sighed, crossing her arms. "You said it yourself, Fire. I don't know how to handle confrontation." She tilted her head slyly. "But it's okay. Maybe I won't hurt the ones you...," she paused, contemplating, "*love...?*"

He pointed the dagger toward her. "*Stop*."

"You can let them hurt you first," she whispered. "Like *her*."

Matt kept his dagger raised as he eyed her intently.

"Jason Streak's niece," the sniper murmured. "It would be poetic if she was my final victim."

Matt snapped, "If you touch her, you're going to find out how merciless I can really be."

The Rare Sniper fell quiet as the flames flickered in the air between them, her gaze devoid of any clear emotions. Matt gripped his dagger, desperately meeting her eyes. His heart raced rapidly, and the tremor in the sniper's wrists returned. Even through this silence, he could tell they were calling each other's bluffs.

The sniper never "mocked" her potential victims, and Matt could barely believe the threat he had just made to her. But even he wasn't sure what he would do if anything happened to Madeline or Christine.

"Then show no mercy," she demanded. "My midnight sins can die with the dawn, for I will never quell your tell-tale heart."

Matt had no time to react as the Rare Sniper leapt backwards off the rooftop. The wind blistered around him as he inhaled, and he launched himself ahead to catch her. As he reached the end of the roof, the sniper landed on the building below. He didn't think twice before jumping after her, his dagger leaving a trail of fire in the air behind him. His eyes were set on her as she escaped from him. The sniper glanced over her shoulder, finding that he was following her.

But not for long...

He knew what would happen next. Time and time again, she would summon the wind to guide her into another hidden corner of the city. But this chase felt different. *Déjà vu?* Matt had pursued her before—or at least he *tried* to. He kept his sights on her this time, balancing and sprinting against the ridge. As the moon hid behind a passing cloud, the sniper summoned a gale to boost her to a distant structure. The jump was too far for Matt to make, but he was determined.

The Rare Sniper turned around after sticking the landing. She stood before the edge, glaring at him from the distance—taunting him. Matt wasn't ready to halt, however. He could push himself farther than before. With one last step, he leaped, flying across the wide alley. His heart thudded upon the quick realization that he wasn't going to make it; not because he was too far, but since the sniper had already swept the storm toward him. The wind struck him mid-air, and he went flying back. His body slammed into the concrete roof, and he lay there, thunderstruck. He lifted his head, catching one last glimpse of the Rare Sniper before she dived into the neo city.

Chapter 38

Nothing Stays Unspoken

Tell-tale heart...Rare Sniper...Confrontation...

With his eyes closed, all Matt could picture was Christine held at gunpoint.

Xander's phone started buzzing on his desk, causing Matt to jolt out of his daze. And just like that, he was back in the office.

He glimpsed the contact—Aspen Law—then eyed his coworker as he answered the phone.

"Hey, what's up?" Xander exhaled, leaning back with the phone to his ear.

Matt focused his gaze on the screen in front of him. He urged himself to stay awake.

"You passed?" Xander gasped with a smile. "I knew you had it in you." He paused, then glanced at his desk. "Look, I'm at work right now. Maybe later. But—no, I'm not taking you out for ice cream. It's the middle of November."

Matt couldn't focus on anything with Xander talking on the phone beside him. Instead, he laid his head down on his desk and huffed.

"Here. I'll treat you to dinner tonight," Xander continued. "You can drag Carly along, too. Okay?" He grinned. "Alright...I have to go now. Tell me all about it later...Uh-huh. Okay, bye."

Xander tossed the phone onto his desk. "You get a pick of *any* restaurant, and you want fast food," he sighed.

"Who was that?" Matt asked, tilting his head to face him.

"Aspen. My ward. They passed a test, so I'm obligated to treat them," Xander explained. "But keep in mind that they *passed*. Never said a word about acing it."

Matt lifted his head, then rubbed his eyes. "You're someone's guardian?"

"Yes."

"You never mentioned that before."

Xander shrugged. "They don't like it when others talk about them," he said. "Otherwise, I would've bragged about them sooner."

Matt had a dozen questions swarming through his head now. He didn't want to bombard Xander, but his curiosity beated him.

"How come I haven't met Aspen?" Matt asked. "When I stopped by your place—"

"They were spending the night somewhere else." Xander flicked his hand through his bangs. "I think you two would get along, though. I should introduce you one day."

Matt frowned, and his gaze drifted down to his desk again.

"Is everything okay?" Xander asked.

Matt tensed. "Not really—"

"Matthew," Xander sighed, turning his chair to face him, "you don't have to lie. I know your sister has been bothering you." He smirked slightly. "And Christine."

"Okay, not Christine," Matt argued.

"Mostly your sister," Xander said. "You leave at different times. And you're not talking."

Matt breathed out roughly. "I can't talk to her about anything."

"Okay. Why?"

Matt clenched his fists. "I told her what *you* believe about Streak. And now she thinks I'm losing my mind."

"Ah..." Xander's postured sagged. "You didn't have to tell her."

Matt scowled. "I tell her everything," he said. "Eventually." He faced Xander, and all he saw was guilt in his eyes. "Look, it's not your fault. You're trying to help me figure out the scandal."

"Does she think I'm looney, too?" Xander asked.

"Probably. But this feels different. I'm losing her."

Xander shook his head. "Don't say that. It'll work itself out—"

"No, you don't get it. I don't know if she even likes me anymore," Matt cried. Xander sat back, frowning. "We clash. And...I think you know what we clash about. She's worried about me, but she doesn't really understand me. It's this constant swinging with her. And we try to hold on. But as soon as I say the wrong thing...we fall apart."

Xander nodded solemnly. "But she loves you."

Matt slumped back. "I doubt it sometimes..."

"And she has sacrificed whatever was left of her childhood for you. She wants to see you succeed, but she also wants to keep you safe," Xander continued, lowering his voice. "She sees the one person who means the world to her going out there, risking his life almost every night. And she lets you. But she's concerned about the future. Her future, your future..."

Matt stared at him desperately. "I don't want to make her feel bad."

"And she doesn't feel bad about you. She just wants to protect you." Xander glanced away. "But at least you and Madeline talk. You try to."

Matt caught the hint of uneasiness in his eyes. Something else was on Xander's mind, and Matt didn't need much time at all to figure it out.

"What happened...?" Matt asked quietly. "Between you and your sister?"

Xander exhaled as his gaze dropped. "Nothing that you should worry about. My sister and I still talk," he assured him. "It'd take the end of the world to get us back together. But focus on yourself. Take that first step."

"So, should I talk to her? Right now?" Matt replied anxiously. "She's busy with everything else—"

"But you're more important," Xander said, putting his hand on his shoulder. "You will *always* be more important."

Matt swallowed. "Okay..."

"Now," Xander pulled away, "what about Christine?"

"That kind of goes back to when you two had that argument the other day," Matt countered. "But also..." He leaned closer to Xander. "About the whole 'Speedfire' thing. I think I bummed her out."

And then we did meet. Matt felt sick just thinking about the heartbreak in her eyes. *Then she saw that text from Kate...And the Rare Sniper just—*

"Matthew," Xander interrupted his thoughts. "She's fine."

"No, I was hurting her," Matt confessed. "And now she's avoiding me."

"Hardly," Xander scoffed. "She comes down here a lot."

"Yeah, to drop paperwork off to Kylie."

"But she's always looking at you," Xander mentioned.

Matt pressed his lips together and fell silent.

"All the damn time," Xander continued. "She can't take her eyes off you."

"*James,* she doesn't look at me," Matt hissed.

Xander curled his lips into a smile. His eyes darted toward Kylie's office door. Matt peeked over his shoulder, then caught Christine standing there just as she turned away. He gasped.

"Go." Xander prodded him, and Matt stood up. "She's headed for the elevator."

"Damn it." Matt turned and watched as the elevator doors closed behind Christine. "I might be back."

"Might?" Xander laughed.

"I don't want to work," Matt groaned as he stepped away. All he had to do was talk to them. Break the ice. He had no idea where Christine was going, but he knew where his sister would always be.

Matt climbed the stairs slowly, preparing himself for the confrontation. *Just...let it out. Xander is right. She loves me. She won't just stop loving me. And unlike a certain sniper, I know how to handle confrontation.*

As soon as he reached the ninth floor, he spotted Christine stepping into his sister's office and closing the door behind her.

Matt froze. *Oh.*

He breathed out quietly, then walked across the hallway. He stood in front of Madeline's room and reached for the doorknob. As soon as he heard Christine speaking up inside, he halted.

"I just need to know what's wrong," she demanded. "If you're okay, or if—"

"I'm fine," Madeline replied, frustrated. "There's nothing to worry about."

"But it's been over a week," Christine said. Matt peeked into the slanted window of his sister's door. Christine stood before Madeline's desk, keeping space between them. "What happened?"

"Has Matt said anything to you?" Madeline asked.

"No. Not really," Christine replied. "But even my uncle has noticed you've been down."

"Maybe I just need some space from...certain things," Madeline emphasized as she glared at her desk. "A lot has been on my mind. I'm stressed, and there are too many projects I'm getting ready for next year."

"Can I help?" Christine offered, stepping forward. "I know it's—"

"Christine, please..." Madeline cut her off, rubbing her head. "Do you need something from me? Or did Matt send you up here?"

"He didn't. I just want to make sure you're okay," Christine remarked. Matt leaned against the door, listening carefully. Maybe she overheard Xander telling Matt to speak with his sister and beat him to it.

Madeline frowned. "Why?"

"I hate seeing you like this." Christine gestured to Madeline's sagging posture. "And Matt's been so depressed this past week."

"Matt and I need to talk it out ourselves," Madeline exhaled. "And I'm not exactly ready for that yet."

Matt rested his forehead against the door. He wasn't expecting to hear that. Or maybe he did. He just didn't *want* to hear that.

"Well...if you do need to talk about anything." Christine glanced at the window. "There's so much going on...and..."

"Since we're here, do *you* need anything?" Madeline pointed out. "I mean, you can't be feeling any better about what's going on inside and outside the company."

"Like what?" Christine replied sheepishly.

"You know what I mean. The shootings. The scandals," Madeline continued. "Whoever is targeting your uncle. Or anything else that I don't know about. Let it out."

"I just want you and Matt to be safe...and happy," Christine admitted. She fidgeted with her hands. "I care about you both."

"I care about you, too. Just don't get yourself worked up over anything," Madeline said, leaning back. "I'm sure your uncle can find a way to make you feel better about the—"

"I can't talk to him like I can talk to you," Christine interrupted. Madeline blinked, then straightened herself.

"Okay." Madeline cleared her throat, and Matt watched as a concerned look came over her. "So, 'talk' in what way?"

Christine bit her lip. "Just...problems. Feelings. I don't know," she stammered. "Like...Matt listens to me. I can say anything. And he gets it. He understands."

"What exactly do you talk about?" Madeline asked.

Christine's eyes flickered to the wall as she rubbed her arm. "I mean...not *everything*," she corrected herself. "But I feel comfortable telling you, too. Because you...you practically raised him. And you'd understand. At least, I hope you would."

"Oh." Madeline nodded slightly. "Okay?"

"Like, other people just don't get me. They won't listen, or they assume everything about me," Christine huffed. "And I think you know that I'm part-Optyman. The Optymans don't even want anything to do with me. My uncle didn't even want—I mean—he knows my worth. Or he made up my worth."

"Made up your worth?" Madeline repeated, confused. "Oh...wait a second..."

"And I can't say anything," Christine continued, glancing at the ceiling. "You know, people will just *stare*. It's like they want something from me, and maybe it's anxiety speaking, but that's all I feel. I can't trust people. I know they want to do something to me, but I don't know *what*."

"Christine, hey," Madeline spoke up, "take a deep breath—"

"And my uncle would never let anything happen. But he's protective of me for himself. Because, you know, reputation matters," Christine stuttered, then forced herself to shrug. "But I don't know what to think of everyone I meet. Maybe all they see is some gateway to my uncle's success. I'm just some extension of the Streak name." She picked at her nails, her eyes darting to the corner of the room. "And some people here freak me out. Maybe you know what that feels like? You can meet someone, and they seem so pleasant and nice on the outside. But then...you're alone with them, and it's not the same. Suddenly, something's wrong."

"I know. I've met some strange people in this business. And...it doesn't seem to get any better."

Christine wiped her eye. "But why does it feel like *everyone* is that way?"

Madeline furrowed her brows. "Everyone...?"

"But not you," Christine said. "And...not Matt..." She paused, and Matt moved away from the window. "I know I can be alone with him. And I don't have to worry about anything." She rubbed her eyes again. "But then he's gone, or you're gone, and I'm back on high alert."

"Christine, you should never have to feel that way," Madeline mentioned. She stood up and walked around her desk. "If you need to talk or just hide somewhere for a bit, you come here. Okay? You can come here, and you don't even have to explain anything."

"No, no," Christine trembled again, "I can watch my back. But I don't want to feel like I need to." She closed her eyes, tensing. "I'm just trying to be okay."

Madeline smirked as she looked down. "And Matt makes you feel okay."

"He does," Christine choked out. "And you do, too."

Matt rested his hand against the door. His heart hammered as he listened to every word. He didn't want to make any noise outside, even if he felt guilty for eavesdropping.

"Well, not to rat him out, but he did tell me about your situation," Madeline mentioned. "With Edinburgh's son. Your uncle's setting you up."

"That doesn't matter. Really," Christine sighed.

"Sure," Madeline breathed out quietly. "You definitely don't feel the same way about Edward Edinburgh. That's all I can say."

Christine stared at Madeline with concern. "No, but—"

"My brother makes you happy. That's what should matter," Madeline asserted. "I can't tell you what's going on between us. But it doesn't change anything with you. So, keep each other company. And as I said, you are always welcome here." She reached her arms around Christine, pulling her into a gentle hug. "Stop by my office in the mornings, okay? We can chat about whatever you want."

Christine trembled as she held onto Madeline. "Thank you…"

Matt backed away from the door, bumping into the wall across from the office. He was at a loss for words. Deep down, he wanted to burst into the room and fall onto his knees, begging his sister to forgive him. He wanted to spill everything to Christine. But he knew why he and Madeline were fighting.

Jason Streak…and Speedfire…

It all came down to his safety in the end. But he was willing to take any necessary risks to stop these scandals.

Before he could move, Christine stepped out of the room. She shut the door behind her, then turned to face him. She froze.

"Uh…" Christine brushed a lock of hair behind her ear as he stood up. "Do you want to talk to your sister? I was just…"

Her eyes drifted to the floor, her expression still sullen. No one here was in the right state of mind, but all they could do was help each other and hope for the best. Matt kept his theories to himself, and with the way the sniper had threatened to target Christine, he wondered if he was running himself ragged into a dead-end.

Would Streak do anything to hurt her? he thought. *Would he even do anything to protect her?*

Regardless, Matt was prepared to stay by her side. He could sacrifice a night of being Speedfire for her.

"Actually," Matt crossed his arms with a smile as he caught her gaze again, "I wanted you."

Chapter 39

<u>With Power Comes Convenience</u>

The rest of November was a blur to Matt, but he needed to distance himself from the scandal. He couldn't lose his mind completely when he was this close to solving the case. Instead, he spent some nights as Speedfire, but most of his days with Christine. They had too many items to check off on her never-ending itinerary.

Strolls through Scintilla Park in the snow.

Lunch and dinner at different restaurants.

Movies with dinner at home—must be Matt's place.

More tours and rides through the city.

By early December, Matt and Christine tallied off most of her list—until she added more to it. And the Streak Corp holiday party was on the itinerary, to Matt's reluctance.

Matt dressed himself in a red sweater and a pair of jeans for the party. He opened his door to see Madeline give Harry a quick kiss on the lips, and after a moment, they pulled apart.

"Matt! You're coming too!" Harry waved him over. "Did Maddie tell you I started a new job? I got hired last week."

Matt deflated. Madeline hadn't talked to him about anything other than dinner or work. But they were at least talking again, albeit briefly. Harry, however, knew nothing of their ongoing dispute.

"Yeah, I heard something about it," Matt lied. "How is it?"

"It's great! I'm fixing ships in the harbor." Harry grabbed a cookie from the counter. "The U.S.S. Callisto is coming into port soon, so I'll be able to check her out."

"The Callisto?" Matt asked, confused. "Which one is that?"

"It's the ship that saved the Optyman refugees," Madeline added. "Marissa Streak designed it over twelve years ago."

Matt faked a smile. "That sounds great."

Harry beamed. "I can't wait to start."

Matt turned his attention to their attire. Harry wore a Santa Claus sweater, and Madeline donned a blue gown with golden glitter. He wondered if now would be a good time to ask Harry about his feelings toward Streak. The temptation lingered as they headed outside, but he could feel his sister's gaze on him. She knew what was on his mind.

This feud was far from over.

As soon as they entered the headquarters, the smell of gingerbread and warm eggnog overwhelmed them. A smaller crowd stood in the foyer, their chatter filling the air.

"This is dangerous," Harry said as he eyed the dessert table. "My stomach is going to kill me tonight."

"You know what I say," Madeline mentioned, patting his shoulder. "Calories don't count during the holidays."

Harry facepalmed. "My ma says the same thing."

"I still need to meet her," Madeline laughed. "I was thinking we can—oh. Hey!" She paused as she caught Xander passing her toward the doors. "What are you doing?"

Xander froze as she caught his attention. He wore a crimson sweater and black jeans, but his hair was down, and his glasses were missing. "Excuse me?"

"I'm surprised you're here after the stunt you pulled at the last party," she mentioned with her hand on her hip.

"Ah, well, I was actually getting ready to leave," Xander replied.

Matt frowned. "But we just got here..."

"Oh." Xander blinked. "I mean, I can stay for another few minutes—"

"Sure. But we need to talk," Madeline said. She glanced back at Matt with a glare. Matt inhaled quietly as Harry watched, confused. "I don't know what your whole deal is with Streak Corp, but you need to leave my brother out of it."

Xander scoffed, "I'm hardly doing anything."

Madeline narrowed her eyes at him. "Don't play dumb with me. I know everything."

"What's going on?" Harry whispered to Matt. "Are they okay?"

"Uh..." Matt winced. "Sort of—"

"No," Madeline cut him off. "We're putting this behind us. Stop messing with my brother."

Xander frowned. "I'm not."

"Bullshit," Madeline hissed, then lowered her voice. "You've been getting him all worked up. And your damn 'ideas' are going to get him in trouble."

Xander leaned closer to her. "Sounds like you're afraid. Eye-opening, isn't it?" He tilted his head. "Someone's going to catch the culprit one day, Madeline. And I doubt this city will handle the truth kindly."

Madeline exhaled sharply. "Well...whatever the *truth* is," she snapped, "leave my brother out of it."

Xander nodded as he stepped back. "Say no more," he said, raising his hands in defeat. "I don't want to be enemies."

"Good." Madeline turned to Harry, then beckoned him to her side. "Let's go treat ourselves."

"Matt!" Christine called for him. She rushed through the crowd, then pulled him in for a tight hug. Madeline and Harry stepped aside. "You made it!"

Matt held her, relieved that the tension between his sister and Xander was dying. "Only for you," he teased.

"No, I'm pretty sure your sister dragged you here," she remarked.

Madeline shrugged. "He didn't have to come if he didn't want to."

"You would have guilted me into it," Matt said.

Madeline rolled her eyes playfully and smirked. "Anyway, Christine, how are you doing?"

"I'm fine," Christine replied. "I had to set a lot of this up."

"It looks beautiful," Madeline mentioned. Her gaze moved to the evergreen tree garnished with silver ornaments. "You did great."

"I'm slowly getting better at decorating," Christine laughed shyly, running her hand through her wavy hair.

"It's way better than how I decorate. I throw the tree up, a few lights here and there, then that's it," Madeline said.

"I don't even bother decorating," Harry sighed. "I visit my ma in New York for the holidays. And this time, my family is *not* going to Alaska. At least, not without me."

"I'm going to miss you so much," Madeline told him, then wrapped her arm around his.

"You're welcome to come with me," he offered. "You did just say you need to meet her."

Madeline's face flushed red. "Really?"

"Yeah, we can spend the night in my old bedroom or rent a hotel. There's limited space, but it's still nice."

Matt backed away. The isolation was worse than being a third wheel. He tried fixing his attention on the decorations near the floor, how the pastel yellow lights illuminated the room. His attention shifted when he felt a light hand on his shoulder.

"It'll be okay," Christine whispered.

"What?" Matt tried to hide it, but she must have read his face too well. "I don't want to join them. I intrude on them enough as it is."

"Oh." Christine paused as Madeline and Harry left to dig into the desserts. "I doubt they feel that way about you..."

"They adore you. Stop doubting yourself, Matthew," Xander sighed. "Don't let one argument ruin your relationship."

"I'm sorry." Matt rubbed his arm. "Maddie doesn't even like you right now."

Xander rolled his eyes. "I did that to myself. Why are you apologizing?"

"Because I—"

"You heard her. She's more mad at me than you, it seems," Xander said. "I need to get going, though. Have fun—"

"Why are you leaving so soon?" Christine remarked. "I would have loved to see you make a fool of yourself on the dance floor."

Xander cocked his head with a fake smirk. "By all means, why didn't you just ask me to dance earlier?"

Christine straightened herself. "Okay," she said. "Lead the way. Let's dance."

Xander gaped. Matt tried to hold back his laughter. For once, Xander was stumped.

"Well...*no*," Xander emphasized. "I need to leave. I told Kylie I'll be waiting for her outside."

Matt glanced at the tables as Christine gave Xander a smug look. Through the crowd, he spotted Kylie with a glass of red wine, and Edward Edinburgh talking to her.

"It looks like she's getting herself tipsy again," Matt mentioned. "And she's with Edward..."

"What? Really?" Christine gasped. She peered over at the wine station. "He's drinking with her, too."

"What a guy," Matt sighed.

"She keeps drawing all these imbeciles to her," Xander commented as he looked back. "Like Noah Mallory. He was hitting her up right before he got shot by the sniper."

Christine raised a brow. "You know about Noah?"

Xander yawned, "Kylie told me everything." He glanced at Edward with a scowl. "Perhaps this 'Edward' can give her a ride home instead, and the sniper will shoot him, too."

Matt and Christine's jaws dropped. Xander turned to them, confused.

"What's wrong?" he said.

Matt stammered, "You can't just say something like that." He figured he would get used to Xander's unhinged commentary by now, but he was wrong.

"But...that's what happened to Noah," Xander replied. "Right? The sniper shot the car tire while Kylie was in the passenger seat." He crossed his arms, his fists clenching as his voice dropped. "At least the car didn't swerve into the water. And Kylie didn't get a scratch." His gaze flickered to Matt and Christine. "The sniper's lucky she deals with someone as *passive* as Speedfire."

Matt breathed deeply as Christine looked away. "Yeah..." he said.

He recalled his words to the sniper the last time they met. They were both making threats that wouldn't go anywhere. At least, he hoped those threats would never come to fruition.

"Wow. Why the long faces over here?" Kylie spoke up as she leaned against Xander. "You ready to leave?"

"Just waiting for you," Xander huffed. "What did *that* guy want?"

"Pfft. He liked my hair," Kylie said, throwing her sparkled braid across her shoulder. "He knows about me, too. I guess I have a reputation around this place."

"Did he want to get to know you better?" Xander teased.

"*Maybe*," Kylie laughed. "I'm not interested, sorry. I've been wearing my ring, too. The men here can't take a hint."

"They wouldn't even know how to read a picture book," Xander said as Kylie's engagement ring twinkled under the lights. "Egotistical and undesirable."

"You can say that again," Christine muttered as she shuffled closer to Matt.

Xander smiled slightly. "Sounds like you don't like him, either."

"Edward? Oh...yeah." Christine bit her lip. "The worst he's said to me was that I should try looking 'less Optyman.'"

Xander's face twisted with disgust. "Well, you may be a bitch, Christine Flerare, but you're not an object."

She beamed lightly. "I'm only a bitch to you, James."

Xander held his hand over his heart. "I'm so honored." He stepped aside with Kylie. "Perhaps we can dance another time. Maybe to something a little less *holly jolly*."

Matt prayed under his breath as Christine and Xander shared another look. *Please just get along.*

"As fun as it sounds, I don't think I'd dance with someone who doesn't like me," Christine said.

Xander stepped beside her and sighed. "It's not that I dislike *you*, Christine. You just remind me of someone I despise."

Christine scowled. "Well...don't expect me to apologize for that."

"Oh, no. If anything, I should be the one apologizing," he insisted. "But don't expect my apology to last."

Christine knitted her brows, her face dropping with confusion, as Xander and Kylie left the building. She kept her eyes on him until he was out of sight completely.

"This must be a fun party for you already," she commented.

Matt glanced at the decorations. "Is it bad that I want to leave?"

"And follow James? You'd miss the charity auction," she teased. "My uncle hosts them every year."

"Where is he, actually?" Matt asked.

Christine pointed toward the tables, where Streak stood with a few men in fancy suits, and among them was Richard Edinburgh. Streak himself wore a black suit with a gold snowflake-patterned tie.

"He's looking extra pompous today," Matt whispered to her.

"*Stop*," she snickered. "Someone might hear—"

"Hey, Christine," a familiar voice spoke up. Their laughter halted. She turned around to Edward Edinburgh.

"Oh. Hi, Edward," she replied.

Edward smiled as he held a glass of eggnog. "Your uncle knows how to host the best parties."

She faked a grin. "Glad you're enjoying it."

Matt shuffled back to give them space. He felt invisible to Edward, which was probably for the better. He was already dealing with too much awkward tension tonight.

"So, it's been some time," Edward mentioned. "I made reservations next week. There's this high-end restaurant in the Inner Harbor, right on the water."

"I might have plans already," Christine said, glancing at Matt.

Edward lifted a brow. "It would be after work. And your uncle told me that work shouldn't interfere. I could make reservations any time—"

"But I made some plans on my own," she cut him off. "Sorry."

Edward shook his head, then caught Matt watching. "Don't mind me. We've been planning some dates."

Matt bit his tongue. "Yeah."

"And they've been going well," Edward continued. "We know so much about each other already."

Christine coughed. "Uh-huh."

"Christine, what's my favorite sport?" Edward asked.

She pursed her lips. "Baseball," she answered blankly. "Your favorite city is Los Angeles. You love skiing. And you hate crabs."

Edward sipped his eggnog. "Spot on."

Christine nodded slightly. "Okay," she said. "So, what about me?"

Edward lowered his glass. "Hm?"

"Like...what's my favorite flower?"

"Let me think." Edward stared at the ceiling, his lips twisting with contemplation.

Her face dropped to a frown. "It was in the vase during our first dinner."

Matt watched them uncomfortably as Edward laughed. Her shoulders sagged with disappointment.

"That's a trick question," Edward replied. "You don't have a favorite flower. There was nothing in the vase."

Matt turned away and rubbed his eyes. He would rather be anywhere than here.

Christine breathed deeply as her gaze moved to the floor. Edward, meanwhile, beamed with confidence. And Matt was tired.

"Red roses," Matt spoke up softly. Christine and Edward faced him instantly. "But you also love the variegated ones. You say they remind you of fire." Christine's lips parted as Edward's gaze turned sour. "Your birthday is on the summer solstice. You're not vegetarian, but you enjoy trying the vegan dishes whenever you go out to eat. So many *easy* things to remember, and yet...you're still unique."

Christine smiled faintly as Edward glared at them both.

"You know what..." Edward stepped back, then finished his eggnog. "I'm going to go."

Christine watched as Edward left through the crowd, then took a deep breath. She faced Matt again with a smirk.

"You're a madman, Matthew Ellis."

"For what?" he remarked. "Roses are easy. He's the crazy one."

She swatted his arm lightly. "Because he doesn't care. He's probably getting a refill on the eggnog." Her eyes glossed over the crowd, and she tensed. "Shit."

"What?" Matt tried following her gaze before she pushed ahead. "Christine, wait!"

"He's talking to my uncle," she cried back. "Just stay there. Oh, my God..."

Matt gasped. He pushed through the crowd to reach Streak and Christine. A few people blocked him off, but he squeezed through in time to hear the livid tone in Streak's voice.

Streak stood in a corner with Richard and Edward, far from the other partygoers. Matt snuck closer, hiding behind the decorated tree nearby.

"What are you doing?" Streak lectured. "You told Edward you're calling off the deal?"

"No," Christine muttered, turning her head away.

"*Look at me*," Streak ordered. Christine fixed a bitter gaze on her uncle. "What is with you tonight?"

"Nothing—"

"We can't push this aside," Streak interrupted as Edward shared an awkward glance with Richard. "Didn't you want a ticket out of the business? This is it."

"Well, screw it," Christine snapped. "I'm not doing this anymore."

"We've been planning this for over a year. I already have someone lined up to take over your position," Streak added. "You're not walking away. You can't."

Christine caught a glimpse of Matt behind the tree. She frowned, then looked back at her uncle. Streak pinched the bridge of his nose, feigning a headache.

"Jason," Richard stepped in, "this was all planned."

"It was," Streak murmured.

"I made a change of plans," she said coldly.

Streak's dark gaze met with hers. "We'll talk later. You're not getting out of this."

Christine stepped away and pushed herself through the crowd. Matt had no words as she left him hiding close to Streak and his acquaintances.

"*Ignorant*," Streak muttered as he faced Richard and Edward again. "I apologize. She's been acting this way for months now. I can't understand why."

"Does this have anything to do with that boy? Madeline's brother?" Richard asked. Matt held his breath as Edward crossed his arms.

Streak groaned, "No. He's honestly the least of my worries. Christine is just being difficult. And she should know better."

"Ah, but she's still young. You know how children are," Richard added.

"But she's not a child anymore," Streak said with a scowl. "I tried to raise her the best I could, Richard. But she's got too much of her damn father in her."

"Yes, I've seen," Richard sighed. "She doesn't quite look like a Streak, or anything like her mother."

Streak muttered, "Looks nothing like her mother, and acts nothing like the rest of her family. If Amelia never met Issac in the first place, none of this would be happening."

"Their marriage was fast, wasn't it?" Richard mentioned. "They only knew each other for a few months before tying the knot."

"Yes," Streak answered bitterly. "Christine was an accident. Amelia told us she was pregnant just a week after the marriage."

"A shame," agreed Richard. "Why, Jason, you never had an heir for yourself."

Streak scoffed, "Amelia had the heir. I never wanted kids."

"Eh, that girl is just...not all the way there," Edward sighed. "Too bad she doesn't have a prettier twin."

Matt tilted his head, urging himself to stay behind the tree.

"The 'twin gene' seems to run strong in the Streak family," Richard joked. "Such a pity."

Streak rolled his eyes. "Trust me, I don't intend on leaving Christine any of the family inheritance. You're getting everything, Edward."

"She sounds like she wants nothing to do with it," Edward yawned. "She's just a mediocre asset in the end. Maybe she'll be decent in bed."

Matt clenched his fists as the Edinburgh men chuckled at their own jokes. It took every ounce of control in him not to go over and sock Edward. Instead, he turned away. His eyes were set on the doors to the lobby, where Christine had left moments ago. Matt stepped forward—

"Hey!"

Matt looked over his shoulder as Edward approached him. He stopped, keeping his fist clamped.

"Madeline's brother. I need to ask you something," Edward spoke up.

Matt scowled. Streak and Richard continued chatting in the corner. Edward must have caught Matt eavesdropping.

"What?" Matt replied dully.

"I have some concerns about Christine. You and her, particularly," Edward mentioned. Matt glared at him. "You see, Christine and I have plans—"

"Oh, yeah. I know."

Edward nodded slightly. "Okay. Well, I'm going to ask if you could—"

"What?" Matt cut him off. "Stop hanging out with her?"

Edward furrowed his brows. "Don't act oblivious. You two are doing more than just *hanging out*, and I want you to stop."

Matt scowled. "She's my friend."

"Don't give me that crap," Edward murmured. "I see the way she looks at you. You're more than that."

"And?" Matt stepped closer to him. "What are you going to do about it?"

Edward tensed. "She's supposed to be—"

"If you say anything like that about her again, I'll knock your teeth out," Matt seethed. Edward leaned back, sneaking an anxious glance at the nearby partygoers. "So, if you'll excuse me, I have somewhere to be."

Chapter 40

TAINTED HISTORY

Christine was an accident. Streak's words echoed through Matt's mind as he escaped the party.

He pushed the doors open, stepping into the icy breeze. He heard her sobs first, then he spotted Christine leaning against the building, her knees huddled to her chest.

Déjà vu struck him as he found her crying alone.

"Christine?"

She wiped her eyes. "Matt..."

"Are you going to be okay?"

"No...I don't want you to worry about me. I'm sorry."

"Don't be sorry," he said as she stood up. "What do you need right now?" He took his sweater off and handed it to her.

"Can we walk?" She slipped the sweater on over her sparkly white dress.

Matt offered his hand, and they strolled close to the edge of the pier, keeping enough distance from the corporate headquarters.

"I feel like I'm too much sometimes," Christine sighed as her gaze drifted to the metal railing. "I don't know if you feel that way."

"Too much of what?" he asked.

"Too much to handle."

"For your uncle?"

"For anyone." Christine frowned as she watched the snow flurries.

As much as he felt like a burden to his sister, he knew better than to agree with Christine. "You shouldn't say that about yourself," he said.

"I can't help it." She bit her lip and wiped a tear from her eye. "I was always too much, even for my mother. And maybe that's why my father left without me, too. Just dump me off with the incredible Jason Streak. He can handle anything, right?

"But no. He hates me," Christine whimpered. "Just like my mother hated me."

Matt wanted to tell her that perhaps Streak did not hate her; her uncle hated only a part of her ancestry. But he heard Streak's words loud and clear. Streak always believed she was an accident, and he blamed her existence on any setbacks he faced.

"People always praise him for raising his sister's daughter like it was nothing," she continued. "But I spent more time with the nannies, and they were never the same each year."

"You can't blame yourself for their issues," Matt told her. "You're loved, Christine. Everyone would say you—"

Christine scowled. "You're wrong."

Matt gaped. "What?"

"You're wrong," she repeated. She stared ahead as they made it to the backside of the headquarters. They rested at the end of the pier, and she grabbed the railing. "I'm not loved. No one gives a damn about me." She glanced at Matt again. "Don't you know? I'm just an asset. A hopeless asset with a trail of bad luck following me to my grave. So...no, Matt. I'm not loved."

Matt leaned against the cold guardrail. "Are you sure?"

She huffed. "The last time I felt loved was when my father swung me in the air and let me ride on his shoulders. When he'd read my favorite books to comfort me in the hotel room." She folded her arms around herself. "Love felt like it was just the two of us against the world. But maybe it was only him all along. And I'm just...here."

"Stuck in whatever Limbo your uncle is putting you through," Matt finished for her.

"Exactly," she exhaled. "So, you know...that's just it. Whatever love there was, whatever love there is, or ever will be...I've lost it."

Matt tilted his head. "So, you're still unloved?"

She forced herself to nod. "Yes."

"You can't think of one person who could possibly love you?" he asked.

Christine blinked. She looked over at him as he smiled slightly. "*No.*"

"Okay."

She blushed and looked away. "Nope." Her eyes fluttered to the sky. "Yeah, wow, speaking of that." She faced him again. "What about you?"

Matt coughed. "Huh?"

"I know you and Maddie are still not talking," she countered.

"Wait, we're fine," he stuttered. "We just had a small argument."

"A *small* argument," she echoed. "That's been going on for a month now?"

His shoulders sagged.

"Matt," she sighed and turned away. "Don't hurt yourself over it. That's all I was going to say."

He had no idea how to respond, so they both stared at the gentle waves of the bay. His mind drifted back to that night in September when they watched the harbor together. He would bring it up, but he was "Speedfire" then. Even if she wanted to know his secret—and she almost had it—he didn't know how to tell her now.

"It's hard not to," he confessed.

She laid her hand over his. "Don't hurt yourself over things you can't control."

"But I could have prevented it..."

He clutched the railing, closing his eyes as she breathed deeply beside him.

"Every time I screwed up, I would tell myself the same thing." Christine pulled her hand away. "But the remedy of those words became less and less effective over time." She stepped onto the railing and climbed over. Matt watched, stunned. His heart raced as Christine balanced herself on the other side of the guardrail, just inches from falling into the water. "The real pain was knowing how helpless I was all along. I just pray that you never have to know that feeling. That all your problems can be fixed with time and care."

"Hey..." Matt stammered, grabbing the metal. "What are you doing?"

Christine remained silent as she stared down at the freezing water.

"Christine?"

Matt trembled, tempted to climb over with her. *She wouldn't jump in. No*...he told himself anxiously.

He reached over and touched her arm. She jolted, then glanced back at him.

"Can you climb back over?" he begged. "Please."

Christine looked back at the water. "This bay used to be so filthy back in the day; before the war, back when it was Baltimore. Then New Harbor came to be." She huffed, then feigned a smile. "Kiera Salus organized a major cleaning for the bay a couple years ago. I can't publicly show support for Sal-Tech, but I can tell you, at least. That's one thing I like that she did."

"My lips are sealed," he said, trying to keep calm. "The history is incredible."

"It is." She shifted her gaze to the horizon. "But I think someone is trying to hide history. Or rewrite it."

Matt wanted to admit this was the strangest conversation to have while she was hanging on the edge of the pier, but he listened. He stayed put so he wouldn't startle her.

"Rewrite it? How?" he asked.

Christine furrowed her brows. "Baltimore was known for its history. All the wars it's been through, and all its culture." She released a cool breath as the wind chilled the area. "Now it's...New Harbor. And everything from before the Optyman War is gone. You don't hear about the Revolutionary War or the War of 1812 here. There's only the War of Optyma. It's not Patterson Park, it's Scintilla Park. And it's impressive if anyone remembers the Constellation when the Callisto gets all the focus nowadays." She gripped the metal even tighter as she slid closer to the edge. Matt stayed frozen, listening as carefully as he could. "I just think whoever oversaw the rebuilding of New Harbor wanted its prior history to be forgotten. I don't understand why we're not allowed to remember everything. But I can't say too much...The walls have ears." Her gaze flickered all around the area.

Matt swallowed hard, shaking from the cold and his rising anxiety. "That's an...interesting theory," he coughed.

"*Theory*," she echoed. "This is just the tip of the iceberg. And we are its *helpless* victims."

Ice. Matt's worried gaze fell to the freezing bay. *Okay...*

He noted her emphasis on helplessness again. Her stranded feelings dealt with more than whatever future her uncle had in mind for her. She was bothered by her knowledge of the past.

"The Optyman War was a *civil war*, mind you," Christine commented. The snow coated her hair, and she stared ahead with a solemn look in her eyes. "So, how come a foreign war shaped Baltimore as we know it today?"

"President Agnes targeted the city..." Matt's mind wandered to the conversation he had with Xander many nights ago. Xander had advised Matt to potentially question Christine about Streak Corp's involvement in the war. And she seemed ready to talk about this city's tainted history.

"New Harbor is an Optyman city," Christine said. Matt frowned deeply. "Just like Hasa in Egypt was. But Optyma doesn't exist anymore. And still...this place is Optyman." She glanced over her shoulder, faking a smile at him. "You've seen the discrimination. No one treats the Optymans kindly here."

"Or anywhere," he added.

She nodded once. "The Western Optymans are also treated horribly, even though they never sided with Jake Agnes. Those *Eastern* and *Western* identities died with the war. They are all *just* Optymans now. And why?" She paused, watching her breath fill the air before her. "Maybe it's because the surviving Optymans know too much."

Matt eyed her footing. "What...do they know?" he stuttered, his teeth chattering from the cold.

"My grandparents became billionaires during the war," Christine whispered. "Streak Corp supplied the American military with special weapons. Hidden...illegal weapons. But publicly, they're only known for providing the USS Callisto." She hovered her foot over the edge, and Matt's heart hammered. He reached for her arm again, but she ignored his touch this time. "My uncle has done everything in his power to protect his family's public legacy. So, as long as these secrets stay hidden, Streak Corp will continue to thrive."

"What illegal weapons?" Matt winced, keeping his hand on her arm.

Christine shrugged. "No one is allowed to know." She grimaced as the wind pushed her hair over her shoulders. "Instead, let's look at this 'campaign' of degrading the Optymans. The survivors. The sole people who know about those weapons and what truly destroyed Optyma." Her eyes followed the snowflakes, and her gaze rested on Matt. "First, let's target their 'evil' leadership and religion, which includes the *Rare*. Make everyone despise Lapaism and the concept of the Rare Souls. Then, let's condemn the people for following such demonic ideals. The Optymans were all to blame for their own civil war. So, of course, a man in Riverside gets away with murdering a family. Never mind the fact that the victims could have been Western Optymans."

Matt shuddered. "How could they target a whole demographic like that?"

"Come on," Christine scoffed. "We can't just eradicate a whole population because they *know* something." She shook her head with a half-smile.

"But they *can* be silenced." She lifted her head, finding the outline of the moon in the clouds. "They can be blamed for enabling a tyrant. And they will die off in time."

"I used to hear that a lot," Matt mentioned. "Down in Miami. People would blame the Optymans for Jake Agnes' actions."

"And that's the other thing," she sighed, leaning back. "President Jake Agnes spent months fighting a civil war with his sister before he decided to bomb *Baltimore*. Why is that?" Her head tilted slightly, and Matt kept his eyes locked on her every movement. "If you ask anyone, they will tell you Jake Agnes was simply insane. Which...to be fair, was true. But if you ask someone who knows..." She gazed at him over her shoulder again, and his eyes desperately met hers. "They will say the president was driven mad by something."

Is this a part of the answer? Matt wondered, his eyes following her drifting, auburn hair. *What did Streak do during the war?*

"And it's fitting," she continued. "Why wouldn't the Rare Sniper be an Optyman lunatic? That itself just gives people here an excuse to abolish a dying population."

Once again, the guilt followed him. The Rare Sniper was only "Optyman" because of Speedfire's theory.

"Christine...that was a lot."

"It's just a *theory*," she exaggerated, glaring at the dock.

"Yeah. So...do you think you can...maybe..."

"What did they say about me, Matt?" she demanded, staring across the bay. "After I left. What did my uncle say?"

Matt's heart dropped. "You don't want to know."

"I do."

"Really...no. I think your uncle was just upset," he said sheepishly.

The last thing Christine needed to know was the truth behind her parents' marriage. Matt could protect her from that secret, even if it was not his to share or keep. Instead, he could hold on to her. If she could climb back over the railing, he would hold her close and never let her go.

Christine didn't need to know she was an accident, nor any other dark details of her family's history. She just needed to know she was loved.

"He's always upset." Christine turned herself around, climbing back over the railing with ease. Matt flushed with relief as he reached over to help her balance. "I think no matter what I do, I'm going to end up as a stain in history. You can't make history when it's already been made for you—"

Matt cut her off, pulling her into a tight hug the second she let go of the railing. Christine tensed as he moved his hand to the back of her head. In seconds, her posture sagged, and she melted into him. He held her for another silent minute, ignoring the blistering cold as he did everything to keep her warm.

Three words. That was all he yearned to share with her now. But the words got caught in his throat.

Matt shivered as he slowly pulled apart from her. "I believe you can make a legacy for yourself. You don't use the Streak name, Christine."

Christine watched him shudder, then frowned. "I'm sorry for scaring you."

"It's okay...you didn't," he lied.

She slipped the sweater off and handed it back to him. "Thanks for listening. Again."

He faked a smile. "Always." Her helpless feelings, on top of Streak Corp's supposed "involvement" in the Optyman War, weren't exactly fun topics to discuss out in the cold. But he was here to let her talk. He was just grateful that she hadn't slipped into the water. Without a doubt, he would have jumped in after her.

She raised her hand to catch the snow. "I'm going to head home now," she said. "The party's scheduled to last until midnight. And I don't care."

Matt joined her as she strolled toward the front of the building. "And you shouldn't. It's your uncle's business. Not yours."

"Well, it'll be my 'business' tomorrow," she scoffed. "He has a big meeting with the mayor. I can't escape that." She stopped, holding his hand before moving on. "Will I see you tomorrow?"

"I hope so."

She nodded. "Good." She let him go, then backed away to the street. "At least I have something to look forward to now."

Christine stepped away to saunter through the snow, and he stood alone under the lamppost. His mind lingered on their trip to the Inner Harbor together, and he knew there were unspoken feelings between them. She gave him the most subtle hints of interest, and he took in every look, every word, every smile, and every little blush.

His ring felt cold against his skin in this freezing weather, but how she often complimented it made him feel a warmth he never experienced before.

"Christine!" he called after her.

She turned to face him with concern. The snow danced around them, and tonight, he was making no regrets.

"I'll wait for you," Matt promised. Her eyes watered, and he smiled softly. "When you're ready, if that day ever comes, I'll be there."

Her lips quivered, and in those seconds, she found the strength to return the gesture with a silent nod.

He wanted her to know he was ready for her. Even if her feelings remained unspoken tonight, he had given her the promise of a hopeful future. She deserved that much.

Chapter 41

Fire in Flight

At least I have something to look forward to now.

Christine wouldn't leave his mind, even when Matt had a million other thoughts running through his head. He would give anything just to take her hand and leave this place behind for good. But she was indebted to her uncle, and he was desperate to settle the greatest scandal in the city.

There wasn't time to run away.

"Thirty minutes," Madeline spoke up beside him.

Matt jolted at his desk. "What?"

"The conference with the Core Stone. It's in thirty minutes," she said. He stared at her, and she huffed. "Do you want to join me?"

"*Oh.*" Matt blinked, then nodded. "Is that okay?"

"I'm allowed to bring you along." Madeline smiled, then stepped away. "Figured you *might* be interested in the subject."

Matt watched his sister leave for the elevator, then turned his attention to the clock on his computer. Everyone was already preparing for the conference.

Xander was not at his desk, and Kylie had left her room twenty minutes ago. Considering all those two could talk about was the Core Stone, he wasn't surprised they would want to attend the conference. But he wondered if there was a reason behind their interest in the stones.

Matt snuck out of his seat and moved to Kylie's office. He opened the door and slipped inside, finding no one else in the room. The guilt of meddling through her property was already eating at him.

You are investigating, he reminded himself. *You're not stalking.*

Her purse sat beside her desk, and he opted not to touch it. He gazed at some of the files and articles on her counter instead. The papers contained information regarding Streak's stone, the Rare Sniper, and the newest weapons from the distribution center.

Matt picked up the article about the Rare Sniper and her attack on Harry Faresoul. He never realized Kylie had this much interest in the topic, considering her hesitance when discussing Noah Mallory's fate. According to Xander, however, she had told him all about that night.

His eyes shifted to another article.

The Mysterious Connection Between Damien Surtair and the Tyrant.

Matt reached for the paper, then heard Kylie's laughter outside. He gasped, ducking behind her desk. He squeezed himself between the counter and her chair, then peeked through a hole as Kylie entered the room with Xander behind her.

"Thirty minutes until showtime," Kylie breathed out, then leaned against her desk. "Are you ready?"

"Ready enough," Xander sighed. "Streak really loves showing off his stone."

"He's bold for that," she said. "But I suppose this conference counts as private this time. It's not a public showing."

"Private with outsiders," Xander murmured. "Still, Flyes wants to *hide* it because of situations like this."

"And hide it from who? The mayor?" joked Kylie.

Xander smirked. "Which mayor?"

Kylie laughed. "Good one." She pulled her phone out. "Speaking of…Genevieve just made it to the warehouses. We should be set."

"Smooth sailing from here on out," Xander said, taking her hand. "That's all I want to promise."

Kylie stepped closer to him, then kissed his cheek. "Keep that promise." She pulled away, then moved back to the door. "I'll see you on the third floor, love."

Matt turned away and covered his mouth as she opened the door. He steadied his breathing, hoping he was quiet.

"I'll be right behind you. I just need a moment," Xander replied.

She left the room and closed the door behind her. Matt peeked through the hole and saw Xander's back to him in the darkness. The room's only light source came from under the door.

"It's a wonder how you can feel someone's presence in the dark," Xander murmured, "despite how well they're hiding." He turned around to face the desk and crossed his arms.

Matt's heart pounded against his chest. He swore he had been careful.

"Why do you think that is?" Matt called back to him.

"Perhaps it's a spiritual thing," Xander suggested.

Matt stood up slowly from behind the desk. Xander was not in his usual business attire; his hair was down, and his glasses were missing as well. He wore a long black coat, a red shirt underneath, and black boots.

"Why spiritual?" Matt asked.

Xander strode over to the desk and relaxed his arms. "You tell me," he whispered. "You've had your fair share of supernatural encounters in this city."

Matt shook his head. "I've been tracking down a Rare Soul. But that's it."

"Still supernatural." Xander looked away. "I pray she's the most absurd thing you'll ever come across in your life."

"And I'm still getting nowhere with her."

"Well, clearly, you need a helping hand," Xander said. "And when there's an opening, you take it."

Matt furrowed his brows. "What opening?"

"A breach in the foundation. You can end the cycle if you make it through the gap," Xander uttered, keeping his voice low. "So...*take it.*"

Matt glanced at the closed door. "You and Kylie..." he said quietly. Xander raised a brow. "You're her fiancé."

Xander grinned. "I knew you'd figure that out. Eavesdropping is your specialty."

Matt tensed. "I don't eavesdrop that much."

Xander burst into laughter. "Really?" he mocked. "Eavesdropping is all you ever do, *Speedfire*. You only say you don't because you hardly get caught. But I know. I *always* know."

Matt held his breath. "Why do you two keep your relationship a secret?"

"For starters, I doubt Jason Streak would have hired me if he knew we were engaged," Xander explained. "I even used Kylie as my reference, so that right there would have been a red flag for him."

Matt stayed silent, his mind buzzing with more questions. And all of them had the same basis. *Why?*

"Anyway, Matthew, we have a conference to attend."

Matt exhaled and pushed past him toward the door. "You can just call me 'Matt,'" he muttered.

He could sense Xander straightening himself. Matt didn't care about anything else he had to say. He was tired of the secrets.

Matt followed Madeline down to the conference room. He had no idea what to expect from the meeting, but he was grateful for his sister. Even if they were still on sour terms, she knew him best.

When they entered the room, he saw Billy Flyes sitting closest to the door with the mayor beside him. Christine was seated beside Edward—much to her disliking—with Richard on Edward's other side. Matt hid his frustration and kept his eyes off Edward, following his sister closely.

Madeline pulled her chair out, then motioned for Matt to sit beside her and Billy. At the other end of the table sat Streak. Madeline picked the seat next to Xander, who sat beside Kylie, and Lorelei sat directly across from Kylie. Two bodyguards stood at the door, holding their hands behind their backs.

"I'm glad you all could make it today," Streak announced as he took a stand. "Especially the incredible Mayor Fare."

"It's an honor to be in your presence, Jason," the mayor said, wearing an all-black suit with a silver-winged pin. He had pale skin, gray hair, and a square chin with a long, elegantly trimmed beard.

"Now, I've received some complaints regarding the Core Stone," Streak started. He pulled the lavender gem from his pocket and set it on the table.

"Of course," Mayor Fare replied. "Sergeant Flyes expressed his concerns to me. He and his father feel it's not safe in your hands."

"I can assure you all, it has never been more protected," Streak continued.

"How?" Billy remarked. "If the stone is in the public eye, more people are prone to take it. Look at the incident with Surtair."

"Damien Surtair is *gone*," Streak argued. "The stone probably sent him to the bottom of the ocean, for all we know."

I've witnessed someone's power turn against them.

Her words echoed in the back of Matt's head.

Jade's words.

"Still, how many people have deliberately tried to steal the stone?" Billy interrogated. "My dad and I demand answers."

"Then why is your father not here? If General Wilson Flyes is so adamant about me losing the stone, why does he let *you* do all the talking?" Streak pointed out. "This is a *public* matter. The world doesn't revolve around his feelings."

"His residence is north of New Harbor," said Billy. "We have two stone-keepers in the same city. That itself puts the stones more at risk."

Streak shook his head. "No, Sergeant Flyes, you are missing my whole point. The stones belong to the people, through entrepreneurs like myself."

"It's not *safe*," Billy argued.

"Actually," the mayor cleared his throat, "Jason has an excellent point. New Harbor needs a good boost in morality."

Streak's smile widened. "Thank you, Mayor Fare."

"My father isn't giving up his stone," Billy replied bitterly.

"Then why does the hypocrite insist I give up mine?" said Streak.

The stone remained on the table, transparent and dull. All Matt could see was the glowing gem in the sniper's grasp.

"If I may point something out," added Matt. He caught the whole room's attention. "The Rare Sniper has a Core Stone."

The mayor gaped for a moment, then nodded.

"And what does that have to do with *my* stone?" Streak replied.

"The Rare Sniper is targeting *your* business," Xander spoke up. "And without Speedfire, no one would have even guessed the sniper possessed a stone." He turned to Matt with a smirk.

Matt shot him a quick glare. "Yeah."

"This doesn't mean she's a danger to my stone. She appears to be after my workers, not my possessions," Streak stated.

"Stop dismissing them!" Billy called out. "They have a point! The stones are in danger if they're in public hands. You know what happened to General Fren. He's still comatose."

Sudden laughter came from the right side of the room. Everyone turned to Xander, who covered his mouth. He looked around at everyone and stopped.

"Sorry," he excused himself and stood up. "I just think this is all hilarious."

Streak snapped, "You think this is a laughing matter, Mr. Salamar?"

"I do," Xander replied. "But bold of you to question *me* when you just blatantly dismissed the lives of your own employees."

Streak scowled as Xander strolled to the end of the conference table. Everyone watched silently. "This is my last straw with you, Mr. Salamar," Streak threatened him. "You're fired after this."

"What's going on?" Mayor Fare demanded. "We need to discuss the stone."

Xander's eyes flickered to the stone on the table. Streak followed his gaze. Without a second thought, he reached over and grabbed the stone, holding it close to his chest as he glared at Xander.

"We are, indeed, discussing the stone. James, you're dismissed," ordered Streak.

Xander shook his head and exhaled. "I think Sergeant Flyes is right. That stone needs a better home."

"It's fine where it is now," Streak commented.

Xander smiled. His whole demeanor made Matt feel anxious. He glanced across the table as Christine tensed.

"Alright then, *Jason*," Xander mocked. "Let's settle this. You want to keep that stone, but I need it." He extended his palm. "Hand it over."

Streak scoffed at him. "You think I would just give it to you? Security!" he called out. "Please escort Mr. Salamar out of the room."

Matt sunk with relief when the guards stepped forward. They pulled the guns from their belts, and everyone gasped. One of the guards aimed their weapon at Streak, and the other stood behind Christine. Matt pushed his seat out, ready to jump across the table, but was stopped by Madeline grabbing his arm in a panic.

Christine quivered, looking straight at her uncle. Streak glanced at his niece and the guards. "What is the meaning of this?" he demanded, facing Xander again.

"The stone," Xander insisted. "*Now.*"

Everyone around the table panicked. Edward reached for his father's shoulder, while Lorelei kept her posture hunched.

"You're not getting away with this," Christine hissed at Xander.

"At the rate your uncle is handling the situation, I doubt you'll live to see me win," he replied with a sneer.

Streak faced him, defeated. He dropped his eyes to the stone in his hand. Without a word, he placed the gem in Xander's palm.

"There we go," Xander whistled. He grasped the stone and lifted his hand. The guards lowered their weapons and stood back.

"There are security cameras in this room," Streak mentioned.

Xander glanced at the upper corner of the wall. "Oh, go ahead and share this with the world. I don't care." He opened his hand, and the purple stone glowed in his palm.

Matt watched him intently. He couldn't risk taking action with the guards still bearing their weapons.

Streak murmured, "This has to be an elaborate prank."

"*Really?*" Christine shrieked.

Xander clutched the stone and gazed toward his seated audience. "Yes, very elaborate. But unfortunately for you, not a prank."

Streak gestured to the guards. "Then what is this? What did you do with my actual bodyguards?"

"They are your bodyguards, but they work for me," Xander said. Streak glared at him. "Peter Fren even put up a better fight than you did, Streak."

His posture sank. "You..." Streak stuttered. "*You* attacked Fren?"

"At the end of the day, you and Sergeant Flyes are both wrong," Xander stated. "It doesn't matter where the stone is hidden. It's meant to fall into my hands." He held the stone close to his heart. "And now, I have two."

A sudden flame surrounded his fist. Everyone gasped. Matt's eyes widened, his gaze fixed on the power in Xander's hand. Streak stood back, his mouth hanging open.

"One day, the world will know the order's mission." Xander stepped forward, and blood began to drip from his nose. "Hiding the stones does us more harm than good. Dismissing the *Rare* will continue to ruin us."

The fire in his hand. Matt had desperately longed for that power, and Xander possessed it.

"No one is being dismissed," Streak snapped at him.

"What of the Optymans, then?" Xander argued. "Come on, Jason! *You* dismiss those in need! Every day, these people suffer on *your* streets. They are survivors of a war, yet they're dying of poverty. Because of false accusations, they are facing constant brutality—"

"Those people destroyed *my home*. Baltimore is no more because of them," Streak stated.

"*Those people* are innocent civilians," Xander hissed back. "And yet you sit back on your throne, encouraging the oppression. You play the victim to an 'Optyman Rare Soul,' and because *one* person fits that mold, suddenly, all Optymans are bad. All Rare Souls are evil. Lapaism itself is *demonic*. You make these claims, knowing full well you are wounding the Optyman population. But I will make a change. This world is shattered. And with my jurisdiction, I will bring its pieces back together.

"We're all fragments of this broken world. But under one rule, with the power of all four Core Stones together, we can be united. And no one will be able to stop us. Not even the most influential man in the world." Xander cast a shadowed gaze toward Streak.

"*Us?*" Streak echoed. "Are you Optyman, then? How many of you people are going against me?"

"Me? Optyman?" Xander laughed. His nose continued to bleed, yet he did nothing to wipe the blood away. "I don't have to be Optyman to empathize with them. But I can speak for them. They've been silenced long enough. And it's time to bring them home, to revive Optyma. To prevent this world from breaking itself down. *This* is The Centennial Order's mission."

Matt shared a glance with Madeline as the others in the room watched uneasily. Madeline had nothing but fear and confusion in her eyes.

Streak trembled as he stood up to Xander. "*The Centennial Order?* You think you can come in here, and take my stone?" He clenched his fists as his face twisted with rage. "You and your radical *cult* of Optymans will not get away with this. You're a maniac."

"No...I'm a genius," Xander preached with a bright smile.

As Streak glared at him again, Matt recalled the talks of changing the world he had with Xander. Even his talk with Christine last night felt reminiscent of Xander's speech.

A dying population...

Matt had no idea what to expect from Xander, that using the Core Stones themselves would be the leading source of the change—to reviving Optyma and controlling the world.

The last person to use all four stones together was Jake Agnes, Matt pondered. *And his country fell.*

"A *genius*...? You're a fool," Streak seethed. "Who do you think you are?"

Xander stepped back, his flames growing. "Xander Salus," he answered coldly. Streak's face dropped in an instant. Xander peered at the rest of his audience. "And you will know me as *The Tyrant*."

Xander's dismal gaze fell on Matt. They locked eyes, and Matt had no words to say. He felt stabbed in the back.

Xander charged his right fist and threw the fire at Streak. The swirling blast of flames struck the window as Streak jumped out of the way, and he collided against the table. The glass shattered behind him, and a gust of ash swept the room. Xander sprinted for the open window and leaped out. With the stone's power, he summoned wings of fire, and the encircling flames forced him toward the water. Matt, Christine, and Billy bolted out of their seats to the window. Xander fell into the bay, then disappeared under the waves.

Matt felt his heart stir with torment. This entire time, he worked alongside the one who had hired Damien Surtair, the man who had stolen the stone from General Fren. "James Salamar" was just a cover for the stone thief.

The Tyrant.

He turned to Christine and grabbed her shoulder. "Are you okay?" he whispered.

Her face paled, and her lost gaze was still on the water.

Streak stood up, already on his phone. "I need security, *now!*"

Matt turned around as Kylie left the room with the bodyguards. He moved past Christine and the crowd, then stopped before Madeline, who finally made her way to the window.

"Maddie, they're—"

"Go. Just go," Madeline urged.

She patted his shoulder, and he was off. He followed them out the door, finding Kylie slipping up the stairs, then sprinted toward the staircase.

Matt burst through the doors to the eighth floor and ran down the hallway. He slowed his pace as he passed the empty cubicles. All the workers were gone. He kicked open the door to Kylie's office, and she turned around from her desk.

"Is Speedfire coming to stop me?" she mocked him.

"You have a lot to answer for," he told her, taking a defensive stance.

"But I have nothing to say." She scooped a folder off her desk and ran toward him.

Matt moved to tackle her, but she swerved his attack. She whipped out a needle, then plunged it into his back. He slumped to the ground. His muscles tightened.

Kylie straightened herself as she stared down at him. His body felt numb, and his eyelids became heavy.

"You're lucky he doesn't want you dead," Kylie uttered. She strolled toward the office door. "At least...not yet."

Matt tried to push himself from the ground, but to no avail. Kylie disappeared as his vision fell into darkness.

Chapter 42

LOVE, THE TYRANT

"Matt!"

The nights in New Harbor were longer for everyone. That was all Matt could think about as he ran across the rooftops of Canton.

"Matt, please!"

He didn't know where he was going or who he was chasing.

The Tyrant...

Matt skidded to a stop at the edge of a building. He stared at the rooftop across from him, his heart racing with grief.

The sniper.

The wind howled relentlessly. The Rare Sniper gripped Christine's shoulder, holding a gun to her head. Matt wielded his fire dagger now, but he had no memory of pulling it out.

"Let her go," Matt demanded, his voice cracking.

I doubt you'll live to see me win. Xander's words to Christine rang inside his head.

Christine cried, "Matt, don't..."

The sniper locked her violet gaze on Matt.

"Hang in there," Matt begged. The fire along his blade slowly died. "I'm going to save you."

Christine closed her eyes. "Matt, don't let me go!"

A bullet fired, and a blaze of white light blinded him—

Matt breathed in, opening his eyes in a panic. He woke up to Madeline's face, and she lifted the back of his head.

"Matt, are you okay?" she asked. "Harry! He's awake!"

"Oh, good!" Harry shouted from the other side of the room.

Matt realized he was back home. Sweat covered his forehead, and he trembled uncontrollably.

It was just a dream…

Harry ran over with a glass of water, then handed it to Matt.

"What happened?" Matt murmured.

"Christine found you on the floor in Kylie's office," Madeline told him. "We took you back home."

Matt's eyes widened. Everything came back to him. Xander Salus. The Tyrant. Streak had lost the stone, and Kylie had drugged Matt with a sedative.

"Xander…Where's Xander?" he demanded, wiping his forehead. "I need to find him." Matt nearly rolled off the couch, but Madeline grabbed his arm.

"No! You need rest," she ordered.

Matt lay back and frowned. "He's the Tyrant."

"We know," she sighed. "Mr. Streak is looking for the stone."

"How long has it been?"

"You were out of it for a while," Madeline said. "It's morning."

"What? *How?*" he stuttered.

"I don't know what Kylie did to you, but the police stopped by. The detective said you'd be okay," she mentioned. "He even helped us get you home."

Matt turned to the television. *Breaking News.* He saw the footage from the security camera. He watched as Xander escaped the building with wings of fire.

The Centennial Order.

Matt wiped a tear from the corner of his eye before Madeline could notice. "How's Streak?"

"Holding up. He has a few cuts," Madeline replied. "He's mad, though. Most of his employees went missing during the conference."

"*What?*"

"All the weapons at the warehouses were stolen, and most of the workers in the headquarters are gone, too," she continued.

"People believe that 'The Tyrant' and his cult have been planning this for a few years," added Harry. "And Kylie was in on it. She's been getting more people to join their order, and most of the new hires in the main headquarters were working undercover for the Tyrant."

Matt trembled. "I need to go back and talk to Streak."

"Things aren't looking good for him," Madeline mentioned.

"I know. You just told me," he said. "But Xander being the Tyrant doesn't make Streak innocent."

"What?" Harry stammered. "What are you talking about?"

"I don't know anymore. I had a theory," Matt muttered as Madeline turned away. "I thought Streak was the mastermind behind the Rare Sniper. The one pulling her strings." He crossed his arms as Harry listened with concern. "But now I'm not sure."

Harry sat beside him. "You think Mr. Streak is the sniper's boss?"

Matt winced. "I *did*." His eyes moved to the floor, uncertain. "But we're dealing with a whole other faction now. The Rare Sniper, The Reapers, The Centennial Order, Streak Corp, and Sal-Tech. They're all tied up in this scandal, and we're no closer to solving it now."

"You forgot Whip-Master," Harry mentioned.

Matt exhaled, *"Of course."*

"Well, The Centennial Order sounds like the Rare Sniper. Maybe they're working together," Harry suggested. "They're Optymans looking for revenge against Streak Corp." Madeline sat back, listening quietly with a scowl. "Trust me, I've been going down a rabbit hole for the past twelve hours. The Tyrant and the Rare Sniper both have Core Stones."

"Xander has two stones now," Matt said. "So...one goes to the Rare Sniper...and one to him..."

And The Reapers? he wondered, leaning back. *How do they tie into this?*

"The Rare Sniper has been around for over two years now," Madeline interrupted. "Which means, she has had a Core Stone all this time."

"And?" Matt spoke up uneasily.

Madeline faced him, her eyes slightly watering. "We shouldn't jump to conclusions."

"Maddie, we're trying to figure this out—"

"And you're already jumping to *another* theory," she remarked, raising her voice. Matt sat back, stunned. "Just...*think*. Please."

"I am..."

"How can the sniper and the Tyrant be working together?" Madeline asked. "The Tyrant got his stone a few months ago. But the sniper has had hers for two years. Jason Streak has also carried a Core Stone for two years."

Matt's jaw dropped. "What are you saying?"

Madeline closed her eyes with a deep breath. "I feel like Streak showed a different side to himself in that conference."

Harry tilted his head, confused. "What happened?"

"Not that I'd agree with the Tyrant, but what he said about the Optymans..." Madeline sighed as she faced Matt. "Streak would blackmail them if he could."

Matt blinked. "By...using the Rare Sniper?" He frowned. "Maddie..."

"I'm not saying you're *right*," she insisted. "But you might not be wrong."

Matt shared this desperate glance with his sister. He was speechless.

And when there's an opening, you take it...

"Xander...he believes Streak is behind the Rare Sniper, too," Matt whispered. "I can't trust him, either, but I think he intended this."

End the cycle.

"This adds up, honestly," Harry mentioned. "The Streak family has been like this for *years*. Marissa and Jonathon blackmailed people all the time for threatening their reputation."

Matt added, "Xander wanted to get the Core Stone. That's all he needed. Besides, publicly accusing Streak with no solid proof would be pointless. No one would believe us."

Madeline crossed her arms and looked at the ground. "So, we have two leads. Either the sniper does work for The Centennial Order, or...she's Streak's assassin."

"We need proof. Something that connects the sniper to Streak or the Tyrant," Matt mentioned. "We have to use the Core Stones."

"Whoa, what? How?" Harry asked. "They're gone!"

"The stones *are* the proof," Matt explained. "The Tyrant has two stones. Billy's father, Wilson Flyes, has one. That leaves us with one stone remaining, which is still in hiding because the person keeping it, unlike Streak, is responsible. So, if I catch the Rare Sniper, and she doesn't have the Core Stone, it's obvious. She has been using Streak's stone this whole time. Like you said, Maddie. Two years."

"What if the Rare Sniper is secretly the last stone-keeper?" Harry said.

Matt bit his lip. "I...didn't think about that." His shoulders sagged. "But no matter what, if she doesn't have the stone, then she's with Streak."

"Okay, so, how do we accuse Streak?" Madeline asked.

"We need to lure the sniper out," Matt suggested. "I sometimes find her when I patrol the harbor. But I haven't seen her recently. So, Streak would need to send her out."

"We do what I did, except we're more prepared this time," Harry said, beaming with confidence.

"And how are we supposed to do that?" Madeline asked. "He's lost everything."

"Not everything. Just his headquarters," Harry noted. "We should contact the Whip-Master and see what they think."

Whip-Master. Matt pondered the alias. He realized the conflict between Streak Corp and Sal-Tech was due to the Whip-Master's manipulative actions, but uncovering their identity would be another obstacle in the way of finding the Rare Sniper.

Madeline frowned. "So, who's going to piss Streak off enough to get a target on their back?"

"I don't know. I guess I can try," Matt offered. "But I'm trying to keep my identity a secret, and I need to be in the area to catch the sniper."

"You need a diversion," Harry mentioned. "I could try again."

"Harry, you don't even work there anymore," Madeline groaned. She rolled her eyes. "I'll do it."

"Maddie..." Matt stared at her, bewildered. "You don't have to."

"If Streak is the face behind these assassinations, I want to see him burn," Madeline admitted. "And if he's not, well...I don't know. We'll at least be one step closer to saving other people."

"You're taking after me. Look at you go," Harry laughed, then patted her shoulder.

"I don't want to end up like you," she snapped. She turned to her brother. "Matt, if I die, I'm going to kill you."

Matt raised his hands. "Maddie, I won't let anyone touch you."

Matt, Madeline, and Harry arrived at the headquarters by noon. Several police cars were parked outside, and Streak spoke with the chief of police, Robert Grand.

"We need to find more evidence," Matt whispered. "But I don't know how."

"Do you think Lorelei might know anything?" Madeline asked.

"*Don't,*" Harry gasped. "She's probably in on the scandals."

Grand walked away from Streak, then stopped to look at the group of three. "How are you all doing?"

"A bit shaken," Madeline replied. "Is everything going to be okay?"

Grand shook his head. "We have no leads on the Tyrant. I'm pretty concerned for Jason right now."

Matt and Madeline both faked a sympathetic frown, and Grand continued on his way out the door.

"Mr. Streak," Madeline called over as she approached him. "I'm so sorry."

Streak crossed his arms and muttered, "If someone told me a terrorist organization was going to raid my company and steal my stone, I would have thought they were crazy." His gaze fixed on the entrance of the building, and he let his arms fall to his sides. "And speak of the devil."

Matt and Harry turned around as a young woman entered the building with a guest card, accompanied by three bodyguards and an older gentleman. She sported a blue jacket with a matching split skirt. Her long black hair flowed behind her, and her sapphire blue eyes flashed toward Streak. Matt could see the family resemblance now.

"And what does Kiera Salus think she is doing here today?" Streak mocked.

Kiera put her hands on her hips. "Jason. I came to offer my condolences."

"*Condolences?*" Streak hissed with gritted teeth. "You think you can waltz in here after everything Alexander did?"

"Now, let's not get so heated," the older gentleman said, cutting between Streak and Kiera. He held his hand out to Streak. "Sir Timothy Hardy, one of Kiera's supervisors and a member of Sal-Tech's board of directors."

Streak glared at the man's open hand, remaining silent.

"Mr. Hardy, I can handle this," Kiera said.

Mr. Hardy chuckled, then pulled his hand back. "Sal-Tech's reputation is at risk here, Kiera. I'm not taking any chances," he replied with a fake chuckle. "Anyway, Mr. Streak—"

"I doubt Sal-Tech's *mascot* needs anyone to speak for her. So, if you don't mind, Salus has some explaining to do," Streak clarified, shifting his gaze to Kiera. "If I recall, it was *her* brother who stole my Core Stone, not yours."

"Oh. Of course," Mr. Hardy said, backing away. He cleared his throat, then patted Kiera's shoulder. "I will be outside waiting. Please...don't screw this up."

Kiera remained fixed on Streak as Mr. Hardy departed the lobby. She seemed unmoved by Streak telling one of her own board members to leave the building.

Over this whole confrontation, Matt could not take his eyes off Kiera Salus. She was incredibly youthful for her position, striding with pride and masking any humbleness. Her skin and hair were flawless, and the colors she wore matched her hydro-powered ambitions perfectly. The young engineer was perhaps the most beautiful woman he had ever seen, and he wasn't alone in thinking this way. He saw posts all over Oracle and VisionHive regarding the Sal-Tech founder's impeccable stature. She was the stunning face of Earth Day, the attractive mascot that drew many eyes toward environmental protection. Yet even with her beauty, she still resembled Xander Salus too much.

"I'm not affiliated with my brother," she remarked. "He has nothing to do with Sal-Tech."

"Tell that to all the employees who have sold my property to your company," Streak snapped at her. "Your brother is masquerading as a tyrant. And no one is holding you accountable for some reason."

"Why?" Kiera shot back. "You're acting like *I* stormed your headquarters."

"You might as well have," Streak murmured.

Kiera glanced to the side, meeting eyes with Matt before returning her attention to Streak. "He's been missing for years. You just happened to bring him out of hiding."

"The bastard has a cult. He had someone hold a gun to my niece's head," Streak stated. "I had to give her the rest of the week off for the damage your brother has done."

"Just less than a week off?" Kiera remarked.

Another figure entered the building. Matt caught a new face—a pale man with light brown hair and eyes the color of ice. His cold gaze lingered on the young engineer, and between his sly smile, he showed off a silver tooth. Matt kept his eyes on the visitor for a moment longer before watching Kiera and Streak again.

"Why do I feel like you're lying?" spat Streak. "You're putting on a face."

"Oh, please, don't act like you're innocent," Kiera replied.

"I am," Streak hissed. "And your brother deserves the chair."

Kiera gaped, then closed her mouth firmly. "You would say something like that."

"What?" Streak spoke sarcastically. "Offended? Your brother is a terrorist. He's an endangerment to society."

"He's still my brother."

"And you're no better than him," Streak seethed. "If I had to say, you're hiding even more under your sleeves than he is. What are you truly intending to do with Sal-Tech?"

Kiera scowled. "The matters within my company are none of your concern."

"I've done my fair share of reading on you, Salus," Streak continued. "You're just a mascot. A fake CEO who's become some symbol for environmentalism. But what would your fans have to say when they find out who your board of directors are? I know who Timothy Hardy is."

Kiera glared at him. "As I said, it's not your concern."

"Hm." Streak smirked. "All names tied to the oil industry," he claimed. "Within the next year or two, you'll be nothing but a fraud. Miss Earth Day herself was never saving the world all this time. She was breaking it."

"And what about you?" Kiera uttered. "Are you not the mascot for modern warfare?"

Streak tensed, then pushed by her abruptly. "I don't have time for this," he insisted. "I have more important things to worry about. I want you out of my headquarters." He met with the silver-toothed man, and they walked outside together.

Kiera watched them for a moment and rolled her eyes. "Arrogant son of a bitch," she murmured. She looked over at Matt, Harry, and Madeline. "I can't believe you work for a man like that."

"I honestly hate it," Matt replied.

"You do?" Kiera laughed. She smiled and walked over to them. "What do you hate about the job?"

"I don't trust him," Matt told her. He wasn't sure if he trusted her either. All he knew was that she would agree with any horrible thing he had to say about Streak. "He's probably responsible for organized crime."

Kiera burst into laughter. "Wow, that's the first I've heard about that," she mentioned. "I like you. What's your name?"

"Matt."

"Matt? Nice meeting you," she replied, shaking his hand. "You already know, but I am Kiera Salus, founder of Sal-Tech."

"Your inventions are so cool," Harry added excitedly.

"Thank you. I know," she noted. She glimpsed the doors. "I might as well leave. I wanted to possibly help Jason because of what my brother did, but it seems he wants nothing to do with me."

"Your company has bought illegal information from his employees," Madeline mentioned quietly. "Just saying. You're not completely innocent either."

Kiera smirked. "Well, you don't see me going around *organizing crime.*" She winked at Matt. "Streak Corp will undeniably drown if Jason can't fix his main headquarters."

"It's not going well for him," Madeline said. "I'm concerned about my job."

"You're his general manager here, am I correct?" she asked.

Madeline nodded. "Have been since the summer."

Kiera grinned. "If you're concerned about losing your position here, I can always offer you three something at Sal-Tech."

Madeline's face lit up at the thought. Matt, on the other hand, wanted no part of it. Once Streak Corporation was down, he would be leaving the weapons industry for good.

"That...honestly," Madeline breathed out with a grin. "Ms. Salus, I don't know what to say."

"Here, send me your email over text," Kiera offered. She pulled her phone out and showed Madeline her number on the screen. "You can have no part of Streak's downfall."

Madeline added Kiera to her contacts. "I will," she promised with a nod. "Thank you!"

"My pleasure," Kiera said. "I will be going. But if you two are also looking for a position here at New Harbor, my doors are open."

Kiera turned toward the doors with elegance, meeting Mr. Hardy by the entrance. If their plan succeeded, Madeline would already have a secure position with Sal-Tech. But Matt wasn't sure how well Kiera could be trusted.

"Look at you go, girl!" Harry prodded her.

"Wait," Madeline stopped and looked at them, "what if I tell Streak that I'm quitting to work for Sal-Tech? Do you think that would piss him off enough?"

"Did I hear that correctly?" Lorelei strolled toward them with a notepad. "Jason has put all his trust in you, and you're going to leave us just like that?"

Madeline's face went red. "Um. No," she blurted out. "Salus was being nice."

Lorelei narrowed her eyes at her. "In the few months you've been here, you've benefited us more than any previous manager has. Your loss would be devastating to the company."

"As if the Core Stone wasn't his biggest loss?" Madeline remarked. "Look, some sketchy things are going on here. Like the Rare Sniper and, uh, I guess a terrorist." She paused as Lorelei sharpened her glare. That woman's gaze could cut through steel. "I don't feel safe."

"If you don't feel safe here, you're doing something wrong," Lorelei muttered. She continued her strides as she passed them without another word.

"Wow, that didn't sound threatening at all," Madeline mocked. "I should get up to my office. Harry, come with me."

"Yes, ma'am," he stammered, following her to the elevator.

Matt was left alone in the quiet lobby. Elaine no longer greeted everyone at the front desk, and faces he would see every day had vanished within an hour.

One day could make all the difference.

No one was left in the marketing department. Matt felt gutted as he walked through the desolate space.

He returned to his desk, finding a red letter and a small jewelry box.

To: Matt

He pulled out the slip of paper from inside, noticing it was a handwritten poem.

Meet me upon the moon tonight
And we shall dance away
This perpetual woe,
Through fire, we will become
The world's last paladins,
I will smite this tainted mark
To leave behind my own
For this shattered earth is ours,
But no matter how far
I stray from my heart
I will give you the world,
My everlasting word,
Love, The Tyrant

Matt caught his breath as he laid the poem down on his desk. His gaze shifted to the jewelry box in his other hand, and he lifted the lid. Inside sat a silver cross necklace tucked perfectly upon some foam. Tears formed in his eyes as he raised the chain, letting it dangle in his grasp.

The stone was gone, and so was the lie of James Salamar.

Chapter 43

Six Shots

Fatigue conquered Matt. Kylie's drugs were still affecting him, and he lay in bed at sunset, clutching the letter Xander Salus had left behind. The silver cross lay against his chest as he stared up at the ceiling, still in disbelief.

All these thoughts left him in a daze. Even Lorelei's remarks to Madeline kept his heart beating with worry.

Matt glanced at his bedside table, where he kept the circus roses. The flowers were wilting, and beside the vase were his zolpidem pills. He focused his attention on the half-empty bottle, ignoring the sounds of Kiwi grooming herself by his open window. Regretfully, he took the tablets, slipping two in his mouth, then forcing them down.

He closed his eyes, praying that his meds would set in quickly. Maybe Madeline would walk in on him, only to see the poem still resting in his hand. He didn't want her to read it, but he couldn't bring himself to care anymore.

He was too sick to care.

His phone buzzed in his pocket. Matt opened his eyes, scowling. He swiped his phone out, finding a text from Katelyn.

Katelyn:

Hey! These big guys are following me

I was kinda stalking them first haha

Okay, this isn't funny, though…

I'm in southern Canton; there's this alley across the harbor. Just cross Boston St, near the water-park.

Not to sound pushy but there are four of them, and they are SURLY.

"*Damn it!*" Matt hissed, throwing the back of his head against the pillow.

He exhaled, then sat up. He shut his eyes as he brought his hand to his mouth. The feeling sickened him, but the tablets had to come out. He shoved two of his fingers to the back of his throat, gagging instantly.

Another few seconds passed, and he kept coughing. He pulled his hand back as his heart raced. He couldn't throw the pills back up.

Regardless, Katelyn was in trouble. He had no time to lose.

Matt wiped his fingers against his shirt, then grabbed his phone.

Matt:

Hang tight, I'll be there.

Matt was out on the rooftops as night befell the area. He sped eastward, heading for the alleys close to the Canton Waterpark. Time teased him, and anxiety crept into his heart. The tablets were setting in, but despite the drowsiness, he pushed on.

Even if Katelyn helped him save that flower shop from vandalism, she still wasn't a fighter. Katelyn had no training, no proper skills. She only had her strong will and the determination to do the right thing, even if that meant picking fights with the wrong people.

Matt skidded to a stop as he spotted Katelyn peeking into an alley. She pulled back, then scampered across the street.

"Kate!" Matt called out to her. He reached her in seconds, kicking the dust up behind him. "Hey, what's going on? Are you okay?"

She nodded. "Yeah...yeah, I'm—"

A man cried out from the alley. Matt turned to the noise as he heard bones crunching. A body hit the pavement, and a woman screamed as another man sounded like he was choking.

Matt's eyes widened. "What—"

"Another vigilante showed up," Katelyn whispered, shaking. A snap came from the alley, followed by the thump of another body falling to the ground. "I don't know...I thought you were the only one who patrols this area."

Matt swallowed. "I am...but..." A woman's voice followed with the beatings. Matt crossed the street, holding his hand out to keep Katelyn behind.

Trix.

He didn't want to encounter her again, but she was the only other vigilante he had seen around Canton.

WHACK!

Matt peered around the corner, sneaking a peek at Trix's latest work. Instead, a figure dressed in all black pummeled the last thug, beating his head senselessly against the steel wall. His heart froze as he recognized the feathers instantly.

The man slumped to the ground in seconds, and the Rare Sniper stepped back. She clenched her bloody fists, then sauntered to the other end of the alley. Matt gazed at the remains of the four criminals, his heart racing as he stared at their broken limbs and the smeared blood across the ground. The men were still breathing, but they wouldn't be waking up for a while.

She's never done that to me...

Matt watched as she fell to her knees. The Rare Sniper slammed her palms on the sidewalk, trembling as she faced the harbor across the street. Her sudden sobs struck him.

The Core Stone.

Matt needed to see if she still had her stone. But the way she sat on her knees, shaking with her cape hovering across her back, prevented him from getting a view of the pouch she usually wore.

"Whoa," Katelyn breathed out, inching to Matt's side. Her face turned to awe. "Which one is that?"

Matt pulled Katelyn close as the Rare Sniper tensed. She lifted her head, then turned to face them. Blood dripped from her gloves as she stood to confront them. Her tears smudged the heavy layers of eyeshadow, and her violet gaze cut through Matt.

She still has those eyes, he thought fearfully. *With or without the stone...*

Matt released Katelyn slowly, then moved forward. The sniper stepped back. She grabbed one of the pistols attached to her belt.

Matt gasped, "Wait—"

The Rare Sniper aimed at him and opened fire. *One, two, three—*

Matt rammed back into Katelyn, tackling her to the ground as the bullets missed his head by a few inches. The shots kept firing. Katelyn winced as her back hit the sidewalk, and Matt rolled off her, finding six bullet holes in the stone building across the street. He jumped up, his head swarming from vertigo.

"Speedy!" Katelyn called out for him.

Matt darted into the alley, only to find the Rare Sniper was gone. He passed the unconscious criminals and stopped upon the spot where she had fallen to her knees. The blood from her gloves had smeared into the sidewalk. He glanced back at the six shots.

Katelyn crept through the alley, careful to step away from the men, then stopped at Matt's side. "Who was that?" she asked, still in shock.

Matt trembled, then dropped his gaze to the blood. "Just...another vigilante," he forced out, taking in the lack of wind tonight. "Night-Raven."

Chapter 44

STITCHING LIES

Matt was running out of time. Even if Madeline was willing to put herself up as bait for the sniper, he was worried. Anything could go wrong.

Now that he knew the sniper was still roaming the area, he patrolled the bayside rooftops. She hadn't given him a chance to see her powers last night. Instead, the sniper scared him and Katelyn off with those six shots.

He overlooked the harbor, shivering from the draft. He was still not used to the colder weather and the snow. As much as he admired the flurries, he missed the sunny beaches of Florida. He preferred it over this freeze.

Focus, he forced himself.

The sniper was still nowhere in sight. Perhaps he needed to scout out different locations. He traveled west along the bay, and up ahead, he saw Edinburgh Towers. One of Streak's apartment rooms was inside the silver skyscraper.

A chill ran through his spine. Matt turned around as he felt another presence in the area. He crouched, whipping out his knife. Someone was stalking him. He trekked back to the other rooftop where he saw the figure. He peeked into the alley below, his heart pounding against his chest.

Matt gripped his knife but ceased to ignite it. He didn't want to bring too much attention to himself yet and stayed in the shadows. He slipped down the fire escape, landing with a light thud.

He heard sudden footsteps approaching him from behind, and he swerved around. A black-masked figure thrust a silver blade toward Matt. He pushed himself back, steadying himself as the dark-clad attacker jumped him. Matt blocked the attacks with his dagger, then kicked his opponent away. He felt the gravel grind beneath his shoes as he slid back.

He took a quick breath of the musty air as the figure steadied themselves. They looked too familiar. The black skull mask and the spiked jacket—Matt recalled the memory of the night he got a concussion.

Victor. The leader of The Reapers.

"Stop!" Matt screamed, holding his knife out.

"What? Afraid of the dark now?" Victor laughed and lifted his weapon. "I can make this quick and easy for you. If the sniper wasn't such a bad shot, we wouldn't be doing this."

Victor sped ahead, his knife barely grazing Matt's stomach.

Matt slid across the gravel. Victor swerved, then thrust Matt into the side of the building. Matt winced. He turned around to block his attack—*SLICE!*

Victor's dagger swept against his stomach. Matt seized his arm, then jabbed the side of his head with his dagger's handle. He pressed the button, igniting the fire as he leaped onto Victor's back. He brought him down to the concrete with a slam.

Crack!

Matt forced Victor to the ground, holding the fiery knife to his throat. Victor gasped and pushed his head against the gravel, careful not to make any movements.

Matt winced again. His stomach bled from the slice. He gripped his weapon tightly.

"Who sent you after me?" he demanded.

Victor's eyes flickered back and forth from the fire to Matt. "You're good," he muttered.

"*Who?*" Matt gritted his teeth.

Victor snickered, but the second Matt plunged the knife into his shoulder, he howled.

Matt removed his mask with one hasty pull and held his breath. The pale skin, the ice-cold eyes, the silver tooth.

Victor visited the headquarters just days ago.

Matt blinked a few times and backed away.

Victor ripped the knife out of his shoulder, then swung at Matt again. Matt dodged and ducked. He tackled Victor to the ground, banging his head against the pavement and twisting his wrist. Victor screamed and dropped the knife.

Matt scooped his dagger up and ran further down the alley. His breath felt jagged as he grabbed the slice in his stomach. He lifted his hand, and blood drenched his fingerless gloves.

"You're...not getting away...Speedfire!" Victor screamed from the other alley. Matt bolted down another lane. He needed to escape.

Victor intended to kill him.

Matt ran across the street toward the harbor, where he leaped over the stairs and hid against the dock walls. He looked down at his bloodied orange shirt, biting his lip as he hovered his hand over the wound.

The hospital was too far, and he wouldn't make the trip. He peeked around the corner and stared up at the monumental apartment building.

Streak's apartment. Edinburgh Towers.

Christine.

There was a chance she could be home. At this point, he had no other choice. The bleeding wouldn't stop any time soon. He pulled his phone out and dialed Christine's number. He got up from his spot, stumbling, then perked at the sound of her voice.

"Matt?" Christine asked. "What's up?"

"I...I need help," he stammered. "So..." He grimaced. He didn't want to tell her what happened over the phone.

"Are you okay?" she spoke up. "Matt—"

"I, uh..." Matt stared up at the condominium as he quietly climbed the stairs. "Are you home? In your uncle's apartment?"

"Yeah, why?"

"Is it...is it okay if I stop by?" he winced.

"Uh...yeah, come over," she said. "My uncle's not home."

Perfect.

"Okay, I'm heading there right now," he breathed. "Which floor?"

"Eleven. Room one-fifteen."

Matt walked up to the doors. "Buzz me in?"

"Wait, you're here already?" she replied, confused. Within a few seconds, the doors unlocked. "That was fast."

"I know," he muttered, then sped for the elevator. He hopped into the lift, closed the doors, and slumped against the wall. "I'm on my way up."

"You don't sound okay."

"Yeah. Um, about that..." He bit his tongue, grabbing the side of his stomach. "There's something I need to tell you."

I'm Speedfire. I'm that guy you and your uncle hate, but it's okay. Maybe. I don't know. Nothing's okay right now.

He had no idea how to tell her. She was already going to see his outfit.

"Anything," Christine assured him. "See you in a minute?"

Time was ticking. His heart raced.

Less than a minute.

"Yeah." He took another deep breath, then pulled his mask down.

Once the elevator doors opened, he walked forward slowly, careful not to tear the slice open even more.

She's going to kill me. She's going to kill me. She's going to kill me.

Matt raised his fist and knocked on the door. He straightened himself, trying to cover the wound with his hand. Christine opened the door with a look of concern, which turned into a face of utter shock.

"Hey..." He flinched and waved.

Christine's eyes widened as she stared at him, from his neck gaiter to his blood-stained orange shirt. She stepped back in a daze.

"Don't freak out...please! I need help," he told her in a panic.

Christine glanced over her shoulder, then back at Matt. She took his hand, pulled him into the apartment, and shut the door. She turned around, facing him as he lurched over in pain.

"What the hell?" she cried, gesturing to his suit. She covered her mouth and looked away, trembling.

"Christine, I got jumped," he mentioned. He lifted the bottom half of his shirt to show her the slice. "I didn't have anywhere else to go."

She stared at the wound. Her hands tightened into fists.

"Over here," Christine said with a shaky breath. She took his arm and let him lean against her. She helped him settle down on her couch, then pulled over a blanket as he removed his shirt. "Keep this on the slice."

Christine ran to the bathroom, then shuffled through the cabinet. Matt kept the blanket on his wound, but his blood seeped through, dripping all over her couch.

She returned with stitching supplies, a trash bin from the restroom, and a first aid kit, already unpacking everything. "Hold still. This is going to sting," she said, then padded his wound. Matt gritted his teeth and flinched. "Sorry..."

"Don't be."

After she cleaned his wound and applied more alcohol, she took the needle and thread, pulling it through his skin. Matt closed his eyes tightly.

"I haven't done this in a while," Christine mentioned as she concentrated on the stitching. Matt peeked over and saw his blood on her hands.

"I can explain..." he stuttered. He clutched the blanket as she pierced the needle through again.

She carefully pulled the thread, then repeated. With each movement, the wound proceeded to close. Her eyes glimpsed the scars on his chest, as well as the graze on his arm.

"I owe you one, and I'm sorry," he confessed. "I didn't want to keep it a secret from you."

She continued to focus on his wound and remained silent.

"I've been investigating...a lot. And I don't know how to explain it all to you. I shouldn't have been hiding it," he continued. "I was patrolling the area, and then I was attacked." He debated whether he should tell her the whole truth. He waited for her to pierce the needle over his skin before continuing. No more secrets. "His name's Victor. The man who jumped me."

She pulled the thread through, then stared at Matt. "Victor?"

"He's the leader of The Reapers. They're this gang of hitmen," he explained. "And...and I think your uncle hired them to kill me...to kill Speedfire."

Her face dropped, and she focused back on his wound again.

"I believe he also controls the Rare Sniper," Matt added. He recoiled as she repeated her work; she pierced and pulled gingerly. "I was looking for her tonight."

He paused for a moment to let her steady the needle. Christine grabbed another pad and wiped away more blood. She cleaned his wound before she proceeded, but still did not reply. Instead, she closed the rest of the slice. She backed away, set the needle and thread down on the table, then tossed a bloody cloth into the trash. She stared down at her hands.

"I...I'll be right back," she choked out. Christine wiped a tear away with her sleeve as she returned to the bathroom.

Matt stared down at his wound with awe. It still throbbed, but it no longer bled out. He leaned back, sighing with relief. His eyes drifted to the nearby trashcan, where he found a rag with his blood mixed in with other ordinary things. An empty box of contact lenses, dead flowers, hair chalk, and a broken watch. He tried not to feel too disturbed by his own situation. Injuries like this were normal for vigilantes.

Christine returned with the blood off her hands. "Okay," she breathed out. She curled her lips and lifted a finger. "*Asshole.*"

His eyes widened. "Wait—"

"*Why?*" she screamed. "Why tell me *now?*"

Matt watched her tremble. "Now...?"

"You've been lying to me. After all this time...it was you," she stuttered. He nodded, shaking. "It was you watching over me."

"Christine, I didn't know how to tell you," he confessed. "I wanted to—"

"Did you think I was that clueless? That I never had a feeling?" She fought back her tears. "It's you. It's just...*you.*"

Matt sunk further back.

Christine stared at his stitched wound with a defeated sigh. "You could have died."

"No shit. That's why I came here," he said. "At least your uncle's not home."

Her eyes fell to his bloody shirt. "He hates you," she mentioned. "He hates Speedfire."

His heart sank. "I know." His eyes teared up. "And I know how you feel."

"You don't," she snapped back.

Matt frowned, hesitant to keep speaking. But he had to get his words through to her.

"I know why your uncle hates me," he said. "He feels threatened by me. And I'm this close to proving him guilty of the murders."

"With what proof?" she questioned.

"The Rare Sniper herself." Matt sat up slowly, careful not to bother his stitches. "She has all the answers. And I can wrap this up before anyone else gets hurt."

"Anyone else besides *you.*" She crossed her arms and looked away.

"I'll be fine," he assured her. "I've fought the Rare Sniper, and I came out alive each time."

"And what happens if you don't?"

"You know how I roll. I'll keep getting back up," he told her. Her lips quivered, and she kept her back turned. "I'm worried she'll target my sister next. The Rare Sniper is Streak's right-hand. If I stop her, he won't be able to hide anything from me."

"Lorelei is his right-hand," Christine corrected him.

Matt caught her gaze. "Right..." he muttered.

He remembered the snide comment Lorelei made to Madeline the other day in the lobby.

If you don't feel safe here, you're doing something wrong.

He continued, "I just want to help you. I want to save you from this."

"I don't need saving," she said.

"Your uncle might be working with criminals to end anyone who threatens his business," Matt said. "I don't want you falling into that." Christine's shoulders sank. He watched as a tear trickled down her cheek. "I'm sorry...I can't let anything happen to Maddie. I'm going to stop the Rare Sniper."

Her lips parted. "What am I supposed to say to my uncle?"

"I don't know, just..." He sucked in a quick breath. "Please, can you keep my identity a secret?"

"Did Victor find out?"

Matt shook his head. "No, but he almost did. Christine, I'm begging you. I trust you—"

A sudden knock erupted at the door. Christine's eyes shot open, and Matt held his breath.

"Christine!" Streak called out from the other side. "Help me get the door! My hands are full!"

"Shit," she hissed. Her gaze flickered back to Matt, who was still lying on the couch. "You have to go."

"Where?" he breathed out in a panic.

Christine ran over and lifted his arm. She helped him off the couch, then shoved his clothes into his hands.

"In the closet. Quick!" She pushed him toward an array of coats.

"How am I supposed to get out?" he whispered back.

"*Christine!*" Streak shouted outside.

She shoved him inside and shut the doors. He staggered, slipping his shirt and jacket on. Through the crack between the closet doors, he saw Streak enter the room with three boxes.

"What are these?" Christine asked and took a step back.

"Blueprints I salvaged from the warehouses." Streak set the boxes down, then stretched his back. "I'm taking these down to the office tomorrow."

"Oh." She glanced at the closet.

After his stretch, Streak looked over at the blood on the couch. Matt's heart skipped a beat.

"Christine," Streak spoke up. He took a long stride toward the couch. "What is this?"

Christine followed her uncle's gaze. "Um…"

"Whose blood is that?" Streak demanded, then faced his niece.

Christine froze. "It's my blood."

Streak's eyes darted to the first aid kit on the table. He then glared back at her hands, which were still stained with remnants of Matt's blood. "I'm not stupid. Where is he?"

"Who?" she gasped.

"You know who." Streak took his glasses off. "He was here."

"I didn't know what was happening," she replied.

"Speedfire," Streak fumed. "Where is he?"

"He's gone."

Streak stepped toward her, then grabbed the top of her dress. He pulled her close to him as she tried to push away. Matt's eyes widened. He moved forward but flinched at the sharp pain in his stomach.

"You saw him. Tell me, now," Streak hissed. "Who is he?"

"I don't know," she cried, struggling against his grip. "He came here looking for you."

"For me?" Streak asked, confused. "Why?"

"Because…The Reapers attacked him. Victor. He knows," she told him. "He told me that…that you hired Victor to kill him."

Streak tightened his grasp on her. "You have to know who he is. *Tell me.*"

Christine swallowed. "He never took off his mask," she lied.

Streak threw her down to the floor. She winced as she pulled her left wrist to her chest.

"Then what is this?" Streak grabbed the first aid kit from the table, slamming the supplies on the ground beside her. "You helped him!"

"He was hurt!"

Streak closed his eyes and faced the ceiling. Christine glanced toward the closet and shook her head slightly.

Don't come out.

Matt understood her cue, but he felt helpless watching her confront her uncle.

"No one's loyal to me anymore," Streak murmured. "Not even you. And now Madeline is even testing me."

Matt felt a rush of blood. He tightened his fists.

"You're just afraid of losing," Christine stated, crawling back from him. "Speedfire is onto you. You can't hide everything forever."

"Just tell me the truth," Streak seethed. "Who is he? Where did he go?"

She scowled. "He won't come back. As I said, he was looking for you."

Looking for Streak.

The lie fascinated Matt. In a way, he was looking for Streak. Regardless, she was trying to find a way to sneak him out of here after she faced her uncle's wrath.

Before Streak could reply, his phone vibrated in his pocket. He pulled it out and sighed.

"It's Lorelei," he mumbled. He turned his back on his niece. "I'll be back."

Streak walked outside, then slammed the door shut behind him. Christine exhaled. Matt opened the closet doors and rushed over to her.

"Hey, are you okay?" he asked. He checked her left wrist, and she flinched.

"I'm fine." She turned to him and frowned. "You need to go."

"He's outside."

She nodded toward the balcony. "I know we're high up, but..."

"I can do it." Matt opened the doors. He patted his wound lightly, and despite the pain, he needed to push himself over the ledge. He hung over, ready to jump down to the balcony roof below.

"Matt..." Christine walked over to the edge. "I'm sorry."

"Why?" he replied. "It's not your fault."

"No, really." She knitted her brows. "Please be careful. That was too close."

"We're just a little lucky," he joked. He looked back up at her, and his sarcasm fell in seconds. "Come with me."

"What...?"

"Please..." he begged. "I can't leave you here with...*him.*"

"I'll be okay," Christine repeated. "He's too busy now, anyway."

"He's abusing you." Matt's heart ached. "You never told me that."

"Between you and me, who do you think he'd hurt more right now?"

"Would he really try anything?" he asked, curious. "I know he wants my identity."

"And you can't let him have it. Your identity also puts your sister in danger," she said.

Christine made a point. To protect his sister, he needed to conceal his identity from Streak and The Reapers.

"Then I'll come back. I'll save you," he promised.

She forced herself to smile, to assure him that whatever he believed would come true.

"I'll save you, too," she whispered.

Christine pushed away from the balcony and returned to her room. Matt took a deep breath and stared at the apartment's layout. Without another word, he made his descent.

Matt returned to his apartment within the hour. He kept a slow pace to ensure he wouldn't tear Christine's stitching. After what felt like the journey of a lifetime, he opened the door to his room. Madeline sat on the couch in her robes, waiting anxiously. She looked over at him instantly as he stumbled in.

"Matt?" she spoke up. She glanced down at his bloodied shirt and covered her mouth.

He opened his mouth to reply, but no words came out. Instead, his tears blurred his vision as he fell to his knees. All he could hear was Streak mentioning Madeline's name. Her life was on the line.

But after everything, he did not want her to see him like this.

Madeline ran over and fell with him. She wrapped him in her arms, holding onto him as he sobbed into her.

"I'm sorry..." he stammered.

Her hand grasped the back of his head. "It's okay," she told him, pulling him closer. "It'll be okay."

Chapter 45

Envy's Harbor

Over the next few days, Madeline discussed her future role at Sal-Tech with Kiera Salus. She printed an application and showed it to Matt as he lay in bed with Kiwi on his chest.

"Wish me luck," she told him. "I'm filling this out, then handing Streak my leave notice."

"Wait, what? Already?" he gasped. Kiwi scuttled off him. "Maddie, this is a bad idea. I can figure something else out."

"Matt, I'm the only one who could lure the sniper out. You wanted this."

"I never said that!"

"But I'm doing it for you," she insisted. "I trust you. This could save so many people from Streak in the future."

Matt rolled over on his side. He thought about the comment Victor had made to him—about the Rare Sniper being a terrible shot.

"I'll be back later with the news," Madeline said, then patted his shoulder. "Keep resting."

She left his room, and he opened his phone. His eyes watered as he glossed over the last texts he sent.

He pushed his phone aside, then held his arms together before drifting off to sleep.

Matt woke up as Harry shook him gently. He turned and rubbed his eyes.

"What?" he yawned.

"Your sister wants you," said Harry.

Matt pushed the covers off and got out of bed. He nearly tripped over Kiwi as she zoomed between his legs, but he steadied himself by grabbing Harry's shoulder.

"Sorry," he stuttered.

Harry laughed, "Cats are crazy, man."

"Always," Matt sighed.

Madeline waved over to him as she sat on the sofa. "Matt, I did it!"

"No..." he whispered.

"It's official. I pissed off Jason Streak."

"Isn't he terrifying?" Harry said, sitting beside her.

Yes. All Matt could see was Christine holding her sprained wrist. He didn't want to say a word about it.

"He said he couldn't believe it," Madeline mentioned. "I felt a bit sorry for him, but at the same time, he's been secretly hiring hitmen to keep his business untouched." She shrugged.

"Did he threaten you?" Matt questioned.

"Well..." Madeline bit her bottom lip. "No? He was gutted, but he was nice about it."

"Maddie," Matt groaned and looked away. "I'm not feeling good about this."

"I have you," Madeline reminded him. "Trust me. He sees I've been talking to Salus. *Kiera*. Not the other one. So, let's see if he sends the sniper after me."

"Be careful. The same *day* I revealed that I was selling his info, I got shot," Harry added. "I can't believe no one has called him out on this yet."

"It's because no one wants to," Matt murmured. "And no one has been properly investigating him. He has the city wrapped around his finger. Just put the pieces together. He *knows* he can get away with it."

"Well, that was until all his employees preferred the Tyrant," Madeline huffed.

The colors of the sky darkened. Matt got up and walked back to his room, spotting his blood-soaked shirt on the floor. He grimaced, then saw his dark blue hoodie on the chair.

"I'm going out," he told them as he slipped into his sweatshirt.

"Where?" Madeline asked, confused.

"I need to see someone," he replied and paced toward the door. "I'll be back."

Matt fought against the gnawing wind and snow as he walked to Streak's apartment. He wanted to catch Christine alone, but if Streak was home, he would put on an act.

He just prayed she hadn't slipped his identity to her uncle.

Matt stood outside the room, thinking his words through. If Streak answered the door, he would beg for Christine.

Is she alright? I haven't heard from her after what the Tyrant did...

And if Christine was alone...he still didn't know what to say.

Matt knocked on the door three times, then shoved his hands into the pocket of his sweatshirt. Within a few seconds, the door opened, and Christine stood before him. She wore a purple tank top with black yoga pants. She took a step back, out of breath.

"Hey," she exhaled. Her eyes dropped to his stomach for a second.

"Hi, um..." He paused, and she stepped aside for him to come in. "I wanted to see you."

She nodded and closed the door behind him.

They stopped and stared at each other for a moment. Matt could tell she was still not okay, judging by her awkward glance to the side.

"I came to check up on you," he said, noticing the bruises on her wrist. His eyes then moved to her face, where he found another mark close to her forehead, several along her cheeks, and one under her chin. "Are you okay?"

Christine crossed her arms. "You're the one who got hurt the other night."

"And I'm doing better, thanks to you."

"I don't know what to say," she sighed. "Why did you come back?"

"Why wouldn't I?" he asked, concerned.

"You're putting yourself and your sister in danger," she groaned and walked away.

"She's doing that herself," Matt pointed out. "I tried telling Maddie to stay out of it, but she wants to make herself a target."

Christine stopped. "And who gave her that idea?"

Matt's gaze dropped. "I didn't mean to."

She peered around the room behind her. Her eyes settled on the balcony outside. "I need to cool off," she said. She rushed over to pick up two weights on the floor. Matt assumed she was exercising before he stopped by, judging by her attire. "Come outside?"

Matt nodded and followed her out to the balcony. The clouded moon reflected off the wavy water of the harbor.

Christine huddled her arms and frowned. "Speedfire."

"I didn't come up with that name," he admitted.

"Most vigilantes here don't. The public gives them a name, and they embrace it," she replied. "And you did, too."

"I'm not like them," he mentioned quietly.

She let go of her arms and grabbed the railing. "I know."

Matt could feel the warmth from inside the apartment. Even the concept of confiding in Christine warmed him, yet he still felt anxious. He just needed to push himself. "So, can you tell me now?"

"What?" she breathed out, confused.

"Since you know me—my secret—can you tell me how you feel?" he asked. "What are your feelings for Speedfire?"

Christine's face paled. "Why?" she stammered. "I can't say it."

"Christine—"

"I didn't mean to get close to you. I already know how my uncle feels about you, and just hearing your name made me upset," she admitted. "And it's hard to explain why *Speedfire* made me so upset."

"Do you want to talk about it?" he offered, trying to mask his confusion. "I don't want to make you feel that way."

"But it's not *you*," she exhaled. "It's *me*. I just feel..." She lost her voice in the cold air.

Matt wanted to be patient with her, but he was desperate to brace for whatever feelings she did harbor toward his alter ego.

"Then what is it?" he pleaded. "Christine, just let it off your chest. You can't—"

"Matt." She looked sick as she curled her lips.

"Please." He gripped the railing. "I want to help you."

Matt was desperate for an answer, yet he was concerned about her well-being more than his own. After spending these past few months lying to her, he needed to confront any other issues she had with his identity.

Christine stared off into the distance as her eyes watered. "Envy."

Matt blinked. "*Envy?*" he repeated. "What?"

"That's it," she confessed. "It's envy."

Of all the things she could have said, he was least expecting *envy* as an answer. His mind swarmed with questions. *Why? How?* His heart hammered as he stepped back a few inches.

"Why?" Matt stuttered. "Did I do something?" His breath faltered as he searched her face for an answer. She stared ahead, unmoving, as the wind wiped her tears. "You're envious of...*Speedfire*? Christine, you don't want what I have. I'm serious."

"No," she said, shaking. "But I want something similar."

"Freedom? Choices?" Matt questioned. He recalled the night he had taken her to the rooftops. He didn't think much of her eyeing the text he received from Katelyn, nor her questions about being a vigilante, but his stomach twisted with guilt. "You don't want to be a vigilante. Please don't say that."

"I can't be one, anyway," she replied, swallowing hard.

"It's too dangerous. Even for me," he told her. "You...you don't even like vigilantes." Her frown deepened. "There has to be more than that. Christine, please tell me why."

She shifted her tearful gaze to the streets. "I think I'm paranoid," she whispered. "How do I stop it? I don't want to feel this way. Because then I think about *you*. It's the thought of you getting hurt. You're diving into danger without thinking about the consequences. You got yourself invested in my uncle's issues. That..." She shuddered. "My uncle would always rant about you. Every time he mentioned you, it made me feel sick." Christine turned her gaze to him. "He's not who everyone thinks he is. Even without the Core Stone, he still has so much power over this world."

A barren truth. Even Matt knew Streak's impact on the world had changed it, for better or worse. After all, he hid behind too many higher powers.

"He always hated me," she muttered, crossing her arms to block the cold. "You saw it the other night, too. He never wanted kids of his own. And getting stuck with me really took a toll on him."

"But that's not your fault," Matt said. "That still doesn't give him an excuse to abuse you."

She grimaced. "You become numb to the pain after a while."

"Christine...no..." His shoulders sagged. "When I find the truth—"

"No..." she whispered. "It's not going to be that easy. Just get out of this city while you can."

Matt shook his head. "Even if it's a trial of fire, I'm willing to cross it for you."

She pressed her lips. "You're already playing with fire."

"Literally," he said. "This is who I am. I solve mysteries, I save people. And even if I get hurt—"

Christine wrapped her arms around him and cried into his chest. He froze as she caught him by surprise, then held her softly. He rubbed her back as she sobbed, her tears already staining his sweatshirt.

"Hey..." he whispered. "It's okay..."

"No. Not when you're going to get hurt," she choked out. "He's still looking for you."

Matt furrowed his brows. "Your uncle?"

She shuddered, lifting her head. "Victor came for me," she said. Matt tensed. "He's trying to get me to spill your identity. And my uncle...he's keeping me here. He took my phone, and they're both looking for answers."

He glanced down at her, finding more hidden bruises along her arms, her shoulder blades, and across her neck. Even as he held her, she felt slightly skinnier than before.

"What did you tell them...?"

She winced. "I'd rather die."

Matt loosened his hold on her. "Christine—"

"I don't want to lose you," she confessed. "You're my only friend. I can't live with myself if you just...if something happened. And if it's because of *me*."

Matt stared into her eyes, her gaze full of desperation. If he started panicking now, he would only make her feel worse. But he still had enough promises in his heart to give her.

"No matter what happens," he said as she let go of him, "they can't take *this* from you. These moments, and all these memories. The beautiful thing about friendships is that they last forever."

She leaned back, shivering. "I want to keep holding on..."

"Then embrace it. We'll run away together," Matt promised, taking both of her hands. "Maddie and I can bring you back to Miami with us. We'll take care of you, and I'll even save up money just to fly you around the world. You want Amsterdam first? Then we'll go there together. Fly away, and don't look back."

Christine's lips parted, her brows knitting, as she gazed up at him. His heart melted when she smiled. "Matt...you're everything."

Matt breathed in deeply, his next words getting caught in his throat.

I'm nothing...Nobody.

Even with all the confidence in the world, he still treated himself as "nothing." But in his lowest moments, the feeling only worsened.

The wind brushed against him, and a vague memory crept into his mind. A rainy night on the pier, and a ghost on the water. A space he could barely remember. *Nothing.*

"*Speedfire*," Christine emphasized, her lighter tone cutting through his thoughts. "Don't let what I said...don't let it get to you. Please. I admire what you do. It's just..."

"It's difficult." Matt glanced to the side. "I wish it didn't have to be. And I don't think you feel envy. You're longing for things you never had a chance of having. And you're wishing someone would finally give you *something*." He looked back at her, and she was blushing.

Christine hovered her hands over his chest and leaned closer. His heartbeat quickened. Before she could close the space between them, her expression dropped, and she pulled back.

"I don't know what I'm doing," she gasped. "You should be doing other things, right?" She glanced back at him. "You shouldn't be here."

Matt's heart sank. "I want to be here for you."

"And what about my uncle?" she stuttered. "You should be focused on *him*. Not me."

Matt exhaled and looked out toward the harbor. "It's not just your uncle. It's everyone else involved, too. That includes you. Even Victor and the sniper. And...I could talk all day about the sniper."

He wanted to prove a point to her. He had made these choices to be here for Christine. She was a part of his mission, and he needed her to come out of this in one piece.

"This one talk we had changed everything for me," he continued. "She wasn't doing anything but watching the harbor. She did that some nights—just watched the waves. And I think about how bizarre that is. To share something in common with the Rare Sniper."

He felt her gaze on him, but he continued to stare at the water. A pair of birds flew in the faint moonlight, their black feathers dancing in the air.

"She even had a name for herself. Night-Raven," he lamented. "I just thought that was..."

He turned to face Christine again, and she gaped at him, concerned.

"Tragic," he finished. The birds sang in the distance. No matter where he found himself, the sniper was always on his mind. "But I think about it a lot. Perhaps in another world, or another life, she would be *Night-Raven*. She could save more lives than all the other vigilantes in New Harbor combined."

Christine raised a brow. "So, you're dreaming about a better life for your nemesis?"

"Maybe I am," he confessed. "Or maybe I'm just crazy."

Christine's blush returned, and she looked away. "I think you have a good heart."

"I could be better..."

Christine leaned closer to him again. She reached up and placed her hand on his cheek. "You're good enough for me."

"I've lied to you," he whispered and held her other hand. "And you still let me back in."

Matt could feel her breath—chilled and soft—as a faint breeze brought them together. She pulled him closer, tilting her head as her gaze fluttered to his lips. He closed his eyes, and his heart felt like thunder in his chest.

Maybe this was something he still didn't understand completely, and perhaps he never would. But if he was meant to be lost, he wanted to be lost with her. Time around them froze as they inched closer, slowly filling the space between them—

"I hope I'm not interrupting anything," Streak's voice cut through the wind. They pushed apart and turned to face the balcony doors. Streak stood there with a stern look and his arms crossed.

Matt locked eyes with Streak in a panic. He had no idea how long he was standing there.

Christine gasped, "Uncle—"

"I didn't hear the whole thing," Streak brushed her off. He kept his attention on Matt. "But I got what I needed."

Matt trembled. "Wait—"

"So, *you* are the vigilante interfering with my business?" Streak continued. "This whole time, you've been working undercover."

"It's not what you think," he argued. "I'm not—"

"*Speedfire*," Streak interrupted coldly. "You're no better than Salus."

"I'm not affiliated with the Tyrant," Matt said with a glare. "And I know what you've been doing. This doesn't change anything."

"Really? Then I'll assume your sister is conspiring against me as well," Streak countered. Matt strained. "I want you to leave. Now."

Matt stepped closer to Christine. "She's coming with me."

Streak smirked. "We'll see what Chief Grand has to say about that," he remarked. "Speedfire kidnapping my niece? That would make an interesting headline."

Christine pressed her hand against Matt's shoulder. "Go. Just go," she whispered, trembling.

Matt reached for her hand, holding her lightly before letting go. Streak had too much power in these walls.

He moved toward the door, stopping as he passed Streak. "I know what you do to her." He glanced back at Christine.

"Well, now you're getting into personal matters, Matthew," Streak replied. "Leave *now*. Or else I will call the police."

One wrong move could ruin his plans entirely. Like a game of chess, Matt had to plan his choices carefully.

"You can't accuse him of kidnapping if I leave willingly," Christine interrupted.

Streak faced his niece and kept his arms crossed. "Go on, then. Leave," Streak insisted. Matt stopped in the apartment and turned around to watch. "But you won't. You know what will happen."

Christine clenched her fists, then locked eyes with Matt. He saw the darkness in her gaze, her hardened posture, and his heart ached with doubt.

You want to save the day, right? You want to be New Harbor's knight in shining armor?

Matt forced himself to turn away, finding that he was truly lost in envy's harbor.

Chapter 46

His Festering Greed

He knows now…

Matt entered the headquarters with Madeline, regret filling his heart with each passing second.

I screwed up…

The night left him vexed, sick to his stomach, but he suppressed the feeling from Madeline. He didn't want her to worry about him.

"Stick to the plan," Madeline cut through his thoughts. She took his hand and walked into the open lobby.

They came across an interview with Jason Streak and Natalie Tray, the most well-known journalist in New Harbor.

"This place is so quiet," murmured Natalie. She glanced over at Matt and Madeline, then pulled out a microphone.

"Ms. Tray, now is not the best time for an interview," Streak sighed, pinching the bridge of his nose.

"Mr. Streak, the incident regarding your company and the Tyrant is all the rave," she insisted. "We need your words on it. You've denied too many interviews this past week."

"Perhaps it's because I'm not ready, and I still haven't recovered from it," he snapped at her. Natalie stepped back, stunned. "It's a lot to take in."

"Kiera Salus has given her public statement already. The people of New Harbor need to hear from you," Natalie pleaded. "The *world* needs to hear from you."

"Damn the world," hissed Streak. "All I've ever done for this world is *given*. I need a damn break."

Natalie pursued him. "Mr. Streak, we need something. *Anything.*"

Streak glared at her. He then looked at the camera and gave the operator a single nod. "Make it quick."

Natalie smiled, then motioned to the cameraman. With a thumbs up from the operator, she straightened her posture.

"This is Natalie Tray reporting straight from the Streak Corporation headquarters in New Harbor. I am here with the esteemed Jason Streak on this lovely winter morning. Following the recent incident regarding the Tyrant, we are finally hearing a public statement from Jason Streak himself.

"Over a week ago, a man named Alexander Salus went undercover as an employee at Streak Corporation and stole the Core Stone from Jason Streak. After suffering a few minor injuries from the incident, Mr. Streak is ready to give us a statement on the matter."

Natalie and her cameraman turned their attention to Streak. He cleared his throat and straightened himself.

"Regarding the stone, the New Harbor police department is looking into the robbery. This is a public matter, so local investigators are currently involved, including Detective Hu Chen," Streak explained, then took a deep breath. "As for the company, most of the employees here in New Harbor worked undercover for the Tyrant and have stolen our weapons from the warehouses. Investigation teams are looking into that matter as well."

"Such a shame about the bad news, but don't worry. It'll all get better with time," Natalie said directly to the camera.

Streak scowled at Matt and Madeline before he returned his focus to Natalie. His eyebrows creased. "Don't give yourself false promises."

"Mr. Streak, this whole city looks to you for motivation," Natalie mentioned. "If you don't have hope, none of us will."

"Then that's their fault," he uttered with a glower. "Do these people not know the pressure I endure as the *face* of this godforsaken city? Do they not realize the troubles and turmoil I go through for them?"

Natalie caught a quick breath and leaned back in shock. "And they adore you for that," she stated calmly.

Streak shook his head and started to tremble. "I know they don't adore me. A lot of them hate what I do. They're just like the damn Tyrant! Targeting me because of my wealth, for the success I was born into. They blame me for their problems, yet they do nothing to get off their damn feet," he ranted. "And I'm talking about the Optymans. One of *their* assassins has been targeting me for *two* years, and suddenly, I'm the bad guy. What am I supposed to do for them? Their country was falling, and they abandoned it! *They* let it fall to ruin!"

Natalie gasped, then signaled the cameraman to cut the recording, but the operator must not have noticed. He kept the camera rolling.

The corner of Streak's eye twitched as he lifted a finger toward the reporter. "Yet they will get mad at me for turning them away. Their nation destroyed my old home. Damn you all for what you put us through!" he yelled. "And the Tyrant?" He chuckled. "I want to watch you burn, you bastard. When I find you, I'm going to end you."

Natalie groaned quietly, "Mr. Streak—"

"I want to see the fear in your eyes when you die," Streak added. "If you want any chance at a life sentence, give me back that stone. Beg for my damn mercy."

Streak left for the elevator without another word. The camera operator turned the device to Natalie Tray. She covered her mouth and stared at the floor, speechless. She blinked a few times, glanced at the camera, and fixed her eyes on Matt and Madeline.

"Cut the stream," she whispered and scowled at the operator.

The cameraman gasped and shut the device off.

Natalie yelled, "I told you to cut it!"

"I didn't hear you say anything," he replied with a shudder.

"I motioned it to you!" She made a "T" sign with her hands. "Idiot!"

"I can't help it. I'm sorry," he mumbled. He shuffled around to take the camera off the tripod.

"I swear to God..." she muttered. She took a deep, rigid breath and closed her eyes. "We'll just cut that last part out when we broadcast it. That's all."

Matt and Madeline watched in silence. Natalie had recorded Streak's rant, but she would let the world see only half of the truth.

"I guess someone's true colors show when they're under pressure," Matt added as he strolled by them.

"You think?" Natalie packed her microphone away. "That man is going insane right now. He's losing all his shares, too."

"All because of Xander?" Matt asked cautiously.

Natalie's eyes widened as she nodded. "He's losing it. The Tyrant hit the *main headquarters* of Streak Corp," she exaggerated. "If a nation can fall in one day, so can a business." Natalie flicked her bangs out of her eyes. "Streak's lucky he has a small chance to recover it all."

"Apparently not," Madeline whispered. "I'll check on him."

"Yeah, go ahead," Natalie scoffed. "I'm out of here. Let's go, Ben."

The camera operator picked up his bags and followed the reporter out the lobby doors. Madeline beckoned Matt up the stairs with her.

"So, what are you going to say now?" Matt asked her.

"Streak just killed his reputation in front of that reporter," she laughed. "After tonight, it might be easier to accuse him of organizing the assassinations."

"I hope so," he sighed. He grabbed his sister's hand, and she tightened the grasp.

"We can do it," she assured him.

Within the next few minutes, they made it to the top floor. Madeline led the way with Matt beside her. She opened the door, where Streak stood in the middle of his office. He faced the windows as he rubbed his temple.

"Mr. Streak?" Madeline said. Streak turned around immediately, and as he noticed Matt, his gaze darkened.

"What?" Streak snapped.

"I wanted to confirm my last two weeks with you," she mentioned. "I'm leaving to work for Sal-Tech."

"Of course." He tilted his head and glared at her. "Perfect time for you to leave."

"You know I've done all I could for this company," she argued. "For these past five years, I've done nothing but support you."

"And haven't I done the same?" Streak raised his voice. "I gave you a career. I valued your work. What more can I do to prove that to you?"

"You talked about refugees as if they weren't human," Madeline added, crossing her arms.

"That's an entirely different topic," Streak hissed. "Optyma deserved to fall. And it's a good thing that island is under quarantine. Let it rot, and make the world forget about its existence. I want nothing to do with that nation."

"You don't think we do, too?" Madeline clamored back. "Our parents died in that war, yet I still want to help everyone hurt by it. Those refugees had no choice. They either stayed and died, or they escaped to see another day. You can't blame them for what their leader did wrong."

"I can, actually," Streak replied. Madeline exhaled, irritated. "Who was Jake Agnes?"

"The president," sighed Madeline.

"Exactly. The president," Streak repeated. "And how does a president assume leadership?"

"They're elected," Madeline answered with a raised eyebrow.

"Precisely. They elected him. They chose him and let him fight a war that would change the world forever," Streak continued. "And when they had a chance to oppose him, half of them still sided with the lunatic. Now, tell me why they aren't responsible for that."

Madeline yelled, "I doubt they would have elected a madman if they had known a war would happen under his reign!"

"Wasn't Jake Agnes the vice president first?" Matt whispered to his sister.

Madeline rolled her shoulders. "He was, but jackass here doesn't care," she muttered.

"Waste your breath. Nothing will change the grudge I hold against the Optymans. They rebuilt this city, but they couldn't even call it *Baltimore* anymore. Bazyl just *had* to call it New Harbor," Streak seethed. "The refugees stole Baltimore from us. And now, I'm losing *everything* because some oaf from England wants to be a 'savior' for the Optymans. People like him are dangerous, and he will rot like the rest of Optyma."

"You're ignoring that your niece is Optyman," said Matt. "Where is she?"

"She's no longer your concern," Streak murmured with a glare. Matt curled his fists. "Trust me, you don't want to see her again. All she'll ever do is break you—"

"I'm not going to ask again!" Matt screamed. "What have you done to her?"

Streak narrowed his eyes at Matt. "You shouldn't even be here."

"Hey," Madeline stepped forward, "you're losing it. Don't think for one second that we don't know what you've been doing. You reek of *greed*."

"You have no proof," Streak said coldly.

"No proof?" Matt mocked. "Where is Victor? Why does he talk to you when he's the leader of The Reapers?"

Streak's eyes widened. "How do you know that?"

Matt shrugged. "I don't know." He smirked. "Something tells me I shouldn't be here. Don't you think?"

Madeline gave her brother a cautious glance, then fixed her gaze on Streak. "Sir, I'm afraid this will be our last day. I'm not waiting for two more weeks," she said. "I wish you luck in the future, but I think my brother and I should stay away from here."

"You truly think you're off the hook?" Streak said.

"I know we are," she replied. "I'll finish up my work here today, but after that, I'll be on my way home." She grinned. "Back to Miami."

"Wait." Streak slammed his hand on the desk. "Can we take a walk later this evening? Just the two of us, Madeline?"

Matt's heart beat faster. He looked over at his sister, who continued to stare at Streak with a straight face.

"Of course," she said. "But this is the end. I think it would be better for the both of us if we part ways after tonight."

Streak smiled with a sigh, "I would have to agree." He turned away from them and walked back to his desk.

Madeline tugged on Matt's arm and motioned him to follow her. Once they stepped outside the room and closed the door, Madeline pulled on two clumps of her hair.

"I'm doing it. I'm doing it," she stammered. "I can't believe it."

"Why did you accept that offer?" Matt panicked.

"What offer?"

"*The walk.*"

"Oh. I thought that was what we're doing."

Matt shook his head. "No, the plan was for you to be alone and for me to catch the Rare Sniper."

"And Streak?" she added.

"Streak being there is *not* part of the plan!"

"Shit! Just stop!" she groaned, then walked down the hall. "It's not going to make a difference. He'll just be getting a front-row seat of his downfall." They stepped onto the elevator. "Wait, what about those reaper guys?"

"Victor?" Matt thought for a moment. "I don't know. I gave him a bad head injury."

"Was he the one who gave you that concussion?" Madeline asked.

Matt smiled. "I gave him a taste of his own medicine."

"And that's what I'm about to do to Streak. You're my sniper, buddy," she teased.

"Please don't," he whispered. "I'm not the Rare Sniper."

"Okay, but you're my equivalent. Speed-Demon."

"You're embarrassing." The elevator doors opened to the lobby. "I'll get prepared. Just text me when you start heading out. I'll be stalking the area," Matt huffed.

"Stalker."

"Okay."

"I should tell Harry about this," she mentioned. "He might want to know."

"Then you do that," he told her. "Forget about working for Streak right now."

Madeline flashed a grin at him. "I'll see you later, Matt."

"I love you, Maddie."

"Love you, too."

Matt closed his eyes as the winter breeze drifted around him. He crouched on the rooftop across the street from the headquarters. Instead of his usual gear, he wore all-black tonight. He still needed to find a way to clean the bloodstain off his orange shirt.

As the night sky awakened, he wondered what was taking his sister so long to start the walk with Streak. He peered around the rooftops of the harbor and the streets below; no other shadow-clad figure in sight.

His heart raced at the thought of her—the sniper. Dread overcame him, but he focused his eyes on the fluttering snowfall. He had to win this last dance.

And Streak needed to lose the sniper tonight.

Chapter 47

As Justice Brings Blood

Matt heard talking in the distance and glanced over at the headquarters. Streak held the door open while Madeline bundled herself up in a black coat. They proceeded with their walk, following the pathway to the road, then turning eastward along the harbor. Madeline gazed toward the rooftops, spotting Matt instantly. She turned her attention back to Streak, and Matt followed them quietly from above.

The sudden breeze made him shiver.

The wind isn't hers, he reminded himself. *She shouldn't have the stone.*

Matt stopped as Madeline and Streak crossed the street. He could hardly hear what they were saying through the wind. Madeline glanced back over her shoulder as Streak strolled along. Matt nodded to his sister, and she bobbed her head back silently.

Streak turned away from the waterfront park up ahead, then beckoned Madeline. "A shortcut," he mentioned. "Takes us down a safer road."

Matt crept around the corner. The alley was narrow and opened into an area surrounded by four buildings. A dead-end.

"Shit," he hissed, climbing back onto the roof.

Madeline and Streak stopped in the middle of the dead-end. She looked around the area, confused.

"I thought this was a shortcut," she said.

"Actually," Streak spoke up, peering around, "that might have been the other alley down. My mistake."

Madeline wrinkled her nose. "Okay..."

"But we can still talk, of course. No one will be eavesdropping on us here," Streak assured her.

Matt crouched, stretching out on his stomach. He squinted through the hazy snow, spotting a dark figure on the building across from him.

"There you are..." he murmured.

He climbed down, then ducked under a nearby dumpster, sneaking to the other side as Madeline drew Streak's attention. Matt grabbed the windowsill, then pulled himself up. He rolled over quietly, sat up, and spotted the sniper at the other end of the roof as she prepared her rifle.

"Not this time," he whispered, barely making a sound.

The Rare Sniper took a step back and examined the alley below. She turned her head to the side as she heard footsteps, then whipped around.

WHACK!

Matt tackled her into the cement roof. She turned herself around, but he gripped her arms, pulling them around her back as she scrambled to escape. She kicked his stomach, then rolled away from him. He stumbled back but shot up, steadying himself as he faced her.

The sniper shuddered. Matt had the offensive.

He sped toward her, and she backed away. He swerved under her arm, kicking her hip. She flew to the other side of the roof with a yelp.

"Stop!" she yelled with a wisp in her voice.

"You're not touching her!" Matt shouted. He glanced back at the rifle. As he did, the sniper threw herself up and sprinted toward the edge.

She breathed deeply with her eyes set on her rifle. He launched himself toward her, grabbing her waist. She whimpered, then kicked him back.

Matt landed beside her, then scrambled back up. As she leaned away, he stood in between her and the rifle. He pulled out his dagger, igniting the flame.

She crawled back. "Matt, stop!"

Matt paused. His heart thudded.

The sniper pulled down her mask, and regret twisted inside him. Aside from the black eyeshadow, he recognized her face instantly.

Christine breathed out, "Matt..."

He stood back, stunned. Her braided hair looked darker at night, stuffed under the hood. The eyeshadow obscured her emerald-green eyes. And her skin—pale and bruised.

The air was windless around her tonight.

He shook fiercely. "It was you...It was really you—"

"Wait," Christine stuttered. She sat up and winced, holding her waist. "Matt—"

Matt raised his knife toward her. She eyed his movement, her lips trembling.

Trust no one.

He stared into her green eyes, noticing she had ditched the violet irises—or purple contact lenses. Her auburn hair, all those other nights, had been masked with plum-colored chalk.

She had planned to reveal everything to him tonight.

His heart beat faster with every passing second. He felt like he was going to be sick.

"You're not touching my sister," he said. He gritted his teeth. "I won't let you."

"No, wait," Christine pleaded. "I'm not—"

"Then what are you doing?" he cried. Tears streamed down his face. The person he had confided in the most was his greatest enemy. All those days and nights he devoted to her, everything they shared with each other—and *only* each other—was a fabrication destined to die. Christine Elerare was the Rare Sniper, and he never wanted to believe it.

"I can explain," she stammered, her black makeup following her tears.

"Explain *what?*" Matt demanded. "Why the hell were you mad at me for being Speedfire when you...you lying—"

"I didn't know what to say!" she confessed. "You were promising to take me down!"

"I didn't think *you* were the sniper!"

She covered her eyes and screamed. "I know! I'll tell you every-thing—"

"*Now.*" His fist tightened. "Spill it."

She trembled. "It's *him.* You were right. It's all Jason Streak."

Matt glanced down at her belt. *The symbol.* With no pouch attached, she hadn't used the wind against him.

"The Core Stone," he mumbled. He met her eyes. "I can't believe you."

"Then don't."

"No, I...I do. But I can't..." He gestured to her. "You're a..."

"Matt, I'm not..." She choked on her tears. "I didn't want to be."

Matt pulled his mask down, dropping it to the cement. She watched him warily.

"Okay..." he said quietly. He lifted his arm and extinguished the fire around his dagger. He dropped the knife, then held his hands up. "Let's just...talk."

Christine's eyes flickered to the rifle, then back to Matt. She nodded. "I've been trying to find a chance to escape," she explained. "My uncle has forced me to be the sniper for the past two years."

"Why?" he demanded.

"Victor Strage."

Matt raised an eyebrow. "What about Victor?"

"Victor and The Reapers...have been longtime hitmen for the Streak family. He used to work for my grandparents," she continued. "My uncle and mother had known Victor for a while, too. They mean it when they intend to kill any competition."

"That's why Streak owns the weapons industry," Matt contemplated quietly.

"And...it never stopped. Anyone who tried to double-cross the company would die. And he has so many dirty secrets. Intel from the war that could destroy his family's legacy. He can't afford to let anything slide," she said, holding onto her arm. "My uncle always framed the murders on other people. Sometimes The Reapers would even cause car accidents. And no one ever suspected the Streak family had anything to do with the deaths."

Matt listened to her carefully, but he trembled with anger. "And you knew about this...after all this time."

She curled her lips. "I didn't have a choice," she stuttered. "Victor wanted me to be a part of The Reapers. He's had his eyes on me since I was six."

Matt tilted his head. "And are you a Reaper?"

"Partially," she whispered. "After everything Victor did for the Streak family, they wanted to give back to him. My uncle allowed him to start training me when I was ten. And now...I'm still going through his test."

"What about Edinburgh? What's the deal with that?" Matt added. "How can you be a part of The Reapers but also carry the company on your back?"

Her gaze dropped. "You already know," she exhaled. "I'm a bad shot."

Matt kept his eyes on her as she looked away. "You never killed any of them. Victor always had to finish the job."

"Not this time. I have to do it, or else..." Her eyes returned to him, desperate and afraid.

He tensed slightly. "Christine...I'm not letting you hurt my sister."

She stood slowly. "You don't understand," she cried. "It's not her."

"What?" he stammered.

"Matt, you're my target," Christine confessed. "Maddie's just bait."

His shoulders dropped as she stood across from him. He could barely even catch his own breath.

"I'm supposed to put a bullet in your head," she said, shaking. "My uncle wants me to drop you down there...and he's going to force your sister to watch."

Matt shuddered as he wondered how this night was really going to end. The sniper always won their battles, whether he wanted to admit it or not. If Christine was intent on killing him tonight, he was screwed.

"You were supposed to kill me before," he said, rubbing the graze in his left arm. "And you didn't. You missed—"

"I don't miss," she snapped coldly.

"They say you do." Matt backed away.

Her eyes moved to the sniper. "They think I'm a bad shot. My uncle swears I'm useless." She balled her fists. "But I'm not." She ignored the snow sticking to her braided hair. "Not tonight."

"I believe you," he whispered. He lowered his hands. "Hey, Christine...we can figure this out."

"Matt, get out of my way."

"Christine—"

"I'm ending it all tonight. No one was ever going to believe us."

He shook his head. "That's not true. We have proof."

"Matt..." She tilted her head as another tear slid down her cheek. "Let me do it," she whispered. "I'll save her. Let me end him."

You can end the cycle if you make it through the gap...

Matt's breath stuttered. He glanced over his shoulder, back to the rifle. He then faced Christine, whose eyes also laid upon the sniper.

"Christine, stop. That's not—"

"You already know everything!" she screamed. "Get out of the way!"

Christine broke into a sprint for the sniper rifle and slid toward it. Matt jumped in the way. He grabbed her, pinning her to the ground.

"I can't let you do this," he sobbed, tightening his grasp. He believed Streak deserved a justifiable punishment, but he needed him alive to confess everything. And he could not let Christine do this to herself.

Once the blood is on your hands...

Christine kneed his stomach and pushed him away. He caught his breath as he attempted to catch up to her.

"You're not a murderer!" He leaped toward her, dragging her down with him.

She winced. "You always thought I was!" She elbowed his chest. He gasped for breath. "You wouldn't have believed me!"

"I believe you…I believe you now!" he begged her. "I don't want to hurt you!"

She dived for the rifle and gripped the handle. Before she could set her aim on Streak, Matt grabbed her calf.

Christine struggled as she kicked, and he pulled her away. He took her arm, then twisted her around. She yelped as he sprained her wrists, holding her in front of him. He seized her, his head inches from hers.

"There's another way," he whispered. "I'll help you. I promised you that, remember?"

Christine melted back into him. She trembled uncontrollably. "I don't deserve help," she sobbed, leaning the back of her head against his chest. "There's no saving me anymore! Just let me go!"

Her sobs sounded hysterical as she broke down in his grasp. He kept her arms clamped behind her back, but he wanted to let her go. He wished he could turn her around and hold her—to tell her everything would be okay. But he realized it now, with each passing second, she was slipping away from him.

"You're not a monster," he said. "Christine, you're not the monster."

She whipped her head back and cried, "Please…"

"Matthew!" Streak called from the center of the alley.

Matt and Christine turned their heads. Panic-stricken, they stared at each other, speechless. He kept Christine in his grip as they inched their way over to the edge. What Matt saw next caught him off-guard.

Streak gripped Madeline while he aimed a pistol at her head with his free hand. He stared up at them, his gaze stern.

"Matthew, if you come down here with my sniper, I won't shoot," Streak ordered brashly.

"Don't—" Matt's heart raced. He looked at Christine, who watched hopelessly. "Did you know he had a gun?"

"He never does," she stuttered. "I don't know what he's doing. He never…"

Matt glanced back at his sister in Streak's sway. Despite the distance, he locked eyes with her.

"Christine," Matt whispered, then stepped away from the edge with her. "We need to do something."

"I don't...he's never—"

"Christine!" He turned her around and grasped her shoulders, staring into her eyes desperately. "He's going to kill her!"

"Then go down with me. Take me." She unclipped one of the pistols from her belt and handed it to him. "An eye for an eye."

Matt held the gun unsteadily. "Are you sure?"

"Do it. This will get us close enough. He won't pull the trigger." She rested her hand over his. "Lock me up, take me down, and we can make an exchange."

Matt inhaled, then nodded. This was the only choice they had. If they refused, he didn't know what Streak would do to Madeline. He resumed his lock over Christine, gripped her arms behind her back, and trekked down the fire escape with her. Once they reached the bottom, he raised the gun to her head and walked into the alley.

"Well done," Streak whistled with a smirk. He moved the gun closer to Madeline's head. Her eyes widened with horror when she saw Christine. "So, you also had a plan tonight."

"Nothing that involves killing anyone," Matt retorted, then stopped with Christine. "We know you're behind all of this."

"I figured," Streak muttered. He glanced at Madeline before he returned his gaze to Matt and Christine. "What did she tell you?"

"Everything," Christine answered with a glare. "He knows."

"Well, that's a waste of your breath now, isn't it?" he chuckled. "We're not letting him out of here, especially now that he knows our secret."

"I'm not killing them," she hissed.

"No, not Madeline. Just...*Speedfire*." Streak's gaze darted to Matt, and Madeline closed her eyes, her brows furrowing. "Not that you've been able to kill anyone. Even with all that training Victor put you through, you still can't land a clear shot."

Christine's eyes darkened. "You shouldn't have done this to me," she replied. "You made me into this..."

"You say that, but I'm not the one holding you hostage," Streak pointed out. He nodded to Matt. "You chose to follow me."

"I never had a choice!" she yelled. "If I did, I would have disappeared like my father a long time ago!"

"Don't get me started on him," murmured Streak.

Matt glanced at Madeline while Streak and Christine confronted each other. His sister's tears stabbed at his heart.

An eye for an eye.

Madeline lifted her chin and mouthed "I love you" to Matt. His lips trembled.

"I want to make an offer here tonight," Streak sighed. "Since, well, all four of us are together, and the cat is out of the bag—"

"Let us go," Madeline interrupted. "We...we won't say anything. We'll leave for good, and you won't have to see us again—"

"Your brother's not going anywhere," Streak assured her. "Out of everyone here, Madeline, you've caused me the least trouble. If I were to let anyone go, it would be you."

"Then do it. Let her go. You can have me," Matt pleaded. "I'll let Christine go, too. I don't want anyone to get hurt."

"Yet look at what you've done to me," Streak argued. "I'm losing everything."

"You're blaming me for something the Tyrant did," Matt countered. "But this is your doing. No one told you to force your niece into being your failed assassin."

Streak aimed the barrel even closer to Madeline's head. "Don't test me."

"I doubt you could do it," Christine taunted him. "Look at you. You're trembling."

"We all are. You're a sobbing mess," Streak remarked impatiently.

"But you can't do it," she continued. "You don't have it in you. That's why you hire assassins to do the dirty work. You've never had to—"

"My dear niece," Streak interrupted. "You don't know me."

"I do," she argued.

Streak sneered. "Do you want to know what happened to your father?"

An eerie chill swept the area. Christine stiffened in Matt's grip.

"He disappeared..." she said quietly.

"He did," noted Streak. "He never came back for a reason, too."

Christine's shoulders sagged. "He's still out there."

"Your father and mother argued a lot," Streak continued. "He wanted to move to Optyma or Amsterdam. Amelia, bless her, she wanted to stay here with her family. But she was torn. The family business was hers to inherit one day, but she didn't want a divorce. And she didn't want him to take *you* away, either.

"My parents were grief-stricken at the thought of losing all contact with their only grandchild. We all hated your father, Christine. He was not like the rest of us. He often traveled the world and could never really stay in one place. We didn't want that for you or your mother. Something had to be done."

Matt hung onto Christine, but deep down, he regretted not letting her shoot Streak from the rooftop. He could feel Christine trembling, and there was nothing he could do about it. His eyes remained fixed on the gun against his sister's head.

"So, one night—a similar night like tonight, actually," Streak commented, glancing up at the dancing snowflakes, "I took your father out for a walk. I explained how important the business was to Amelia, and that we needed to stick together. But I guess he couldn't understand. He told me about how he lost his whole family to a train accident west of Amsterdam a few years back, but despite that, the city still felt like home. He also had one family member left in Optyma. A cousin or a brother, I forget. Your *other* godfather, Christine." He rolled his eyes. "But Issac didn't convince me. He wanted to break my twin sister's heart and take her only child away." Streak grimaced. "Do you want to know what I did next?"

Christine shook her head slightly. "You didn't..." she whispered.

"I killed him. Shot him in the back," Streak stated proudly. "And it felt refreshing, as if my problems were all solved with the simple pull of a trigger."

"You bastard!" Christine screamed. She struggled to escape Matt's grip. He wanted to let her go, but Streak kept his gun locked and loaded on Madeline. He couldn't risk it.

"Victor helped me hide him." Streak sighed, and his gaze dropped to the snowy pavement. "Your mother never got to grieve. She assumed he was missing, but she later learned the truth. The guilt of *knowing* ate her alive. You could even say it drove her mad. She would always tell me that looking at you, Christine, made her sick to her stomach. Everything about you reminded her of him.

"So, she visited me on her last day. She drank too much...and we talked about the future. Issac's death couldn't come out, and my poor sister...she was spiraling. But she said goodbye, then left my apartment with you...” He rested his eyes on his niece. “You just happened to survive the crash.”

“You can’t blame Issac for any of this!” Matt yelled at him. “You did this to them! You broke them!”

“He was an outsider. He had no ties to this family,” Streak argued.

“Tough shit,” Matt snapped. “You’re not getting away with this.”

“Boy, I already have.” Streak shot Matt a glare before he looked back at Christine. “This doesn’t have to be the end.”

“It is,” she murmured.

“Christine, we could still walk away from this. We have support from Richard and Edward. You can move on from being the Rare Sniper. And Victor will have no choice but to let you go,” he insisted. “My plan was to frame an Optyman for the murders. And thanks to Speedfire here, everyone would believe it—”

“You killed my father,” she spat. “I want nothing to do with you.”

Streak gripped his weapon. “And you’re disgraceful,” he remarked. “An arrogant, selfish—”

“She is nothing like you!” Matt cut in.

“And you,” Streak seethed. “None of this would be happening if *you* never got involved. This legendary kid from out of town, *Speedfire*, thinks he can save the day. Well, congratulations, Matthew. You’ve triggered the end.”

“Don’t talk to my brother that way!” Madeline snapped.

Streak stiffened and glanced at Madeline beside him. He pulled the gun away from her head, then aimed it at Matt. He smirked as he laid his finger on the trigger, and all Matt could do was take a quick breath.

His last breath—

Madeline launched herself toward Streak. She grabbed his arm and pulled him back. Streak turned as she attempted to rip the gun from his grasp, and all Matt could hear was the gunfire.

All he could see was the bloodshed.

Matt screamed.

He tore the pistol away from Christine’s head as his sister fell. All he wanted to do was catch her. Christine swiped the gun from Matt as Streak aimed his bloody weapon back at him.

Streak fired at his chest, and Christine pushed Matt out of the way, shooting back at her uncle. Matt fell, his head slamming against the steel building behind him. He sat up in time to watch Christine collide against the ground. She rolled away, followed by a crimson trail. Streak was already down, his chest drenched in blood.

Matt grabbed the back of his battered head. His eyes fell on Madeline, who lay on her back. She grimaced painfully, holding onto her stomach as blood poured through her hands.

He rushed over to her, then put pressure on the wound. Madeline grabbed Matt's wrists tightly. Her breath faltered.

Matt glanced over his shoulder at Streak. He lay there with a hole in his chest, choking on his own blood. His defeated eyes met with the cloudy night sky.

"Long...live...the legacy," Streak uttered with his last breath. His grip around the gun loosened.

Matt looked down at his sister as blood rose in her mouth. "Maddie..." he cried as he put more pressure on her stomach. "Maddie, stay with me—"

"Matt..." she breathed out. "We did it..."

Matt nodded. "We did it. You did it," he repeated, choking. He glimpsed Christine, who sat up slowly. He felt even more devastated when he noticed her blood-soaked waist. As she pushed herself to stand, she picked up the gun and limped over to him.

She peered at her uncle's body. "I...I have to go..." she said weakly.

Matt's eyes fell on her wound, which she quickly covered with her hand. "You're hurt..." he whimpered.

Christine lifted the gun with her other hand. "This...has your fingerprints all over it," she stammered, losing her voice. "Matt...I have to get far...away from here..."

She gazed down at him as he held onto his sister. She gripped her own wound tighter as the blood escaped her.

"I'm so sorry," she cried, and her posture sagged.

Matt's mouth fell open as he tried to register this reality. He knew what she was going to do. She was planning to escape and disperse any evidence of him committing the crime with her. He stared at his blood-stained, fingerless gloves over Madeline's stomach.

"Christine..."

She turned and limped toward the fire escape.

The back of his head throbbed. He wanted to cry out for her again as she left a trail of blood behind her. He peered down at his sister, noticing she had closed her eyes. Her breath had gone still, and the surrounding blood soaked her long brown hair.

"Maddie?" he choked out, shaking her. "No...no! Maddie! *Maddie!*"

Chapter 48

Long Live the Legacy

Matt sat across from the lead detective of the New Harbor police, Hu Chen, while Robert Grand stood close to the wall with a stern expression. A single lamp lit the room, and gray walls surrounded them, except for the one-way mirror behind the detective. Matt shuddered, staring at his blood-soaked hands in cuffs.

When the police arrived, they struggled to rip Matt from Madeline. All he could do was cradle her in his arms, lost in shock. He sat at the center of a crime scene, and even if he had not committed the murders, he felt responsible for them.

An accomplice.

"Matthew Ellis," Chen spoke up. "I know this is hard, but we need a lead."

Matt glanced across the table at the young detective. Hu Chen had beige skin, and his brown hair framed his narrow face with right-side bangs. Judging by the look in his onyx eyes, Matt read him as someone honest and sincere.

He then locked his gaze on Grand's blue eyes—the eyes of Jason Streak's closest friend. Matt's heart sank.

"Matt," Chen pleaded with him. "We need something. Can you tell us what happened?"

Matt focused his attention back on Chen and his desperation.

"We found you in an alley with the bodies of Jason Streak and Madeline Ellis," Chen explained. "There was only one weapon at the scene. An autopsy should report if this gun was used on them both—"

"It wasn't," Matt stuttered.

Chen tilted his head, confused. "Explain."

"The gun," he continued, finding his voice. "Jason Streak used it to kill my sister."

Chen nodded. "We found the gun in his hand—"

Grand cut in, "Wait until we get the autopsy report and the fingerprints. We can't accuse Jason right away."

"Chief, Matt is our only witness," Chen insisted.

"And our number one suspect," Grand muttered back.

"Listen to me!" Matt cried out. "Streak killed her!"

"Then who killed Jason Streak?" Grand demanded, striking Matt with a glare.

Matt knew what he had to say. He knew her identity, her motives, and what she did. Christine Elerare had killed Jason Streak.

"The Rare Sniper," Matt answered quietly. "She was there."

"Who is the sniper?" Chen asked carefully. "Take your time. Please."

"We need answers *now*," mumbled Grand.

Chen whipped his head around to face his boss. "He just lost his sister," he snapped.

"And the world lost Jason Streak," Grand replied, then stared down at Chen. "We need answers. Jason is not a criminal."

"You'll find his fingerprints on the gun," Matt choked out, his hands trembling. "He killed Maddie."

"And why did the sniper kill Streak?" Chen inquired.

"Because he was trying to kill me. The sniper stopped him."

Christine had dug herself into a hole. Now that she had killed her uncle, the man who forced her to become his assassin, Matt's evidence could hardly support the connection between the sniper and Streak.

No wonder she waited two years to end her pain and break the chains. She waited for the right person to help her end Streak's reign over New Harbor, and these burdens had fallen on Matt the first night he encountered the sniper.

"Damn it." Grand exhaled sharply and shook his head. "I don't want to believe it."

"We took an oath," Chen reminded him. "You're showing bias."

"No, I'm thinking about every possibility, detective." Grand stroked his beard and peered at Matt. "Keep the case private."

"What?" Chen gasped. "Why?"

"Until we can find a concrete answer, don't let any of this get out," said Grand. "Let the people grieve for Jason Streak." He faced Matt again. "We will let you go, Mr. Ellis. But you must sign an NDA."

Matt blinked. "*What?*"

"This is a confidential case," Grand emphasized. "For now, the Rare Sniper is responsible for the murders."

"And what if I don't sign the contract?" Matt asked.

Grand scowled. "Then *you* will be the culprit."

Chen guffawed, "*Chief.*"

"Jason Streak's reputation is at risk, and he's no longer alive to defend himself," Grand hissed. "I will not have his name tarnished over *false accusations.*"

Matt's mind spun in a daze. He glanced at his bloody suit, realizing they had never addressed him as Speedfire. He wore a black top instead of his orange gear and had also left behind his mask on the rooftop. In their eyes, he was just another victim.

"Please listen," Matt begged them. "Streak isn't innocent. His family has a long history with this gang of hitmen called The Reapers."

"The Reapers?" Chen repeated.

Matt nodded, somewhat relieved that the detective paid attention to him. "Victor Strage is the leader. Find him. They're stationed in New Harbor," he explained hurriedly. "Jason Streak has been using them to kill his competition."

Long live the legacy.

Streak's last words rang in his head. If Matt played his cards right, he could envision a world that would paint Jason Streak as the monster his parents raised him to be.

"We'll look into it," Chen promised him. He gave Matt a single nod. "Right now, you need rest."

"Wait, before we let you go," Grand interrupted and stepped forward, "you claimed that the Rare Sniper murdered Streak."

Matt caught his breath. "She did."

"So, tell me," Grand continued firmly, "who is the Rare Sniper?"

Matt knew this question was coming. This was the question he yearned to answer ever since he met her—an answer he wished he never knew.

Christine Lenore Elerare.

Jason Streak's niece.

The false assassin.

He clenched his bloody fists.

Night-Raven.

"I don't know," Matt confessed, staring into Grand's eyes. "She never dropped her mask."

Matt stood in front of Madeline's grave. The New Harbor Cemetery was north of Canton in the Berea neighborhood, a large field of quiet tombs. He crouched before her and placed his hand on the tombstone.

Madeline Ellis, beloved daughter and sister.
May 15, 2023 – December 15, 2048

His heart ached to look at the fresh dirt mound beneath the stone. He sat on his knees, and Harry placed his hand on his shoulder.

"She was incredible," Harry spoke up. "You two did so much."

"I wish we could have done more." Matt wiped away his tears. "I promised I would protect her." He trembled. "I couldn't even do that."

"She was protecting you, though," Harry mentioned. "She wouldn't want you to beat yourself up."

"I know..."

He swallowed his tears. *It's still my fault.*

As Matt peered down at Madeline's grave, he knew there was no need for vengeance. Streak was already dead.

The news talked about the disappearance of Christine Elerare, however. He hadn't seen her since the night she killed her uncle, and the police wasted no time in deeming her a missing person. Robert Grand had made a public statement regarding Streak's death and his niece's disappearance. He believed the two incidents were linked and that the Rare Sniper kidnapped Christine. No one had considered she was the sniper yet. Matt was the only one who knew the truth.

Grand had also refrained from mentioning Streak's intentions of murdering Madeline Ellis. The autopsies matched the bullets found in Streak's barrel, and his fingerprints were the only ones found on the weapon. Grand knew Streak was responsible for killing Madeline but had denied the public any validation.

The Rare Sniper is responsible for the murders—the only "truth" the public was given.

And from Grand's "testimony" came all the headlines.

Jason Streak, CEO and New Harbor Legend, Dead At 38

Rare Sniper Kills 25-Year-Old Daughter of War Hero Eveline Ellis

Jason Streak's Niece MISSING After Sniper Attack

18-Year-Old Survivor of Rare Sniper Shooting Remains Silent

The Rare Sniper—An Optyman Menace

The Optymans Are THREATS to New Harbor!

What Will Happen to Streak Corporation?

Since Christine had disappeared, Lorelei Modisette arranged Jason Streak's private cremation and carried his ashes. And with Richard Edinburgh's help, they revived what remained of the main headquarters of Streak Corporation.

"So, I'm still visiting my family in New York," Harry mentioned, kneeling beside Matt. "You're welcome to join me. I don't want you to be alone on Christmas."

Matt pulled his knees up to his chest as he stared at his sister's grave. "Thank you, Harry," he said quietly. "I think I'll stay here, though…"

Harry wiped a tear from his eye. "I love her, too," he sighed. "Keep in touch, okay?"

Matt sat with Madeline as the hours passed, and the snow drifted with the frigid wind. He never felt more alone.

Chapter 49

SPEEDFIRE

The Optymans faced even greater prejudice since the death of New Harbor's most beloved CEO. The public was only told that the Rare Sniper, an Optyman assassin, had slaughtered Jason Streak in the dead of night, and the city's rampage further grew when everyone learned that Madeline Ellis was the daughter of two war heroes. With the sniper missing, the people had to put the blame on somebody for their deaths.

The Optymans inspired the sniper! It's all their doing!

In reality, nothing could have prevented Jason Streak from taking his final breath. But Madeline would still be alive if her brother had made a different call.

Matt lay on the couch Christmas morning, stroking Kiwi as he stared at the tree. He could not bring himself to fall asleep this past week. Every time he closed his eyes, all he saw was his sister's blood on his hands. She was always there on the ground, lying dead in his arms.

This time, he closed his eyes and prayed. He prayed that he would see Jade standing before him instead of his sister's lifeless body. He prayed for forgiveness, for his own naiveté that had led Madeline to her grave. He spent so many years questioning his faith after mourning for his parents and his aunt. But today, he prayed to save anyone who would cross his path of misfortune in the future.

When Matt opened his eyes, he found himself on the shore. The sea of yellow mums swayed behind him, and before him was the ocean. Relief flooded him.

Matt's gaze flickered to the thunderous clouds above the horizon. A great eagle flew out from the storm, and its silhouette swerved through the lightning striking the atmosphere. Matt narrowed his eyes as he noticed the bird had not two but six wings. Before he could stand to get a closer look, a crackling bolt of lightning struck the water, and his vision went black.

Matt opened his eyes again. His heart raced as Kiwi reached her paw to his chest. He lay there on the couch, stunned.

I need to get my zolpidem refilled, he thought.

Matt glanced at a package he received in the mail yesterday, which sat on the table. The care package came with a blanket, groceries, desserts, cash, and a red wool sweater. He detached the envelope from the box and slid the card out.

Dear Mattie,

I'm so sorry for your loss, honey. You and Maddie are two of the sweetest kids in the world. If you ever need anything, give me a call. I'm traveling all over the place, but when I get the chance, I'll stop by New Harbor and shower you with gifts. Never stop fighting, baby.

Love you lots,

Beth C.

Ms. Beth. His mother's best friend.

She frequently visited him and Madeline after their parents died, and she provided for them when she was able to. Beth eventually had to travel overseas for a job, and since then, Matt hadn't seen her in person.

It also didn't help that the Tyrant had left her husband in a coma after stealing the Core Stone. Matt needed to wish her well at some point.

He picked up his phone to add Ms. Beth's number. He scrolled down, then saw Christine's contact. His stomach twisted.

She was still missing. Night after night, Matt feared she had fallen into one of the dark alleys of New Harbor. She was losing too much blood, and if she was unconscious and alone, no one could have helped her.

And if Victor Strage had found her, she was already lost.

The thought of her disappearing entirely made him sick, even if he knew whatever relationship they had was severed. Christine had kept her secrets, but so had he.

Christine was right when she warned him about revealing the truth. It only resulted in the spread of rumors. People like Chief Grand were hesitant to believe Streak was a murderer, and if word got out, everyone might paint Matt as a lunatic. But her secrets meant more than just avoiding rumors. Christine didn't want to lose Matt.

Even if she was gone, he couldn't get her out of his mind. He was the only person who knew the truth. And he had been forced to sign an NDA.

Matt got up to ease his thoughts and walked into Madeline's room. He didn't want to snoop around her belongings, but he needed to organize the apartment. He sat on the edge of her bed and stared at the drawer beside it, holding his breath as he opened it. A black box with a small note attached to it caught him by surprise.

For you to keep track of time while you're out at night.

Matt opened the box and saw a golden pocket watch tucked inside. He opened it slowly, hearing the ticking of a clock. The top half was a picture of him and Madeline in Florida a few days before their departure, and the bottom half was a clock, the center dial marked with a fire charm.

"Maddie..." he whispered, holding the pocket watch to his heart.

He then lifted the letter from the drawer.

Dear Matt,

Okay, so I'm terrible at explaining things out loud. And you know that. So, I wrote this for you, and you better not look at me like I'm the biggest dork in the world right after you read it.

I realize these past few months have been rough for you, and leaving Miami was a mistake for both of us. I never meant to hurt you, and I should have been keener on listening to you. You are right. We probably should have stayed down in Miami, and you should have looked for a college this year. But I was selfish. I didn't even think about my mental health. I just wanted to make our parents proud by honoring them with my choices. Instead, they would be ashamed of me.

I want to say that I am sorry. Ever since our parents died, I've been so hard on you. I was growing up. I already knew how to plan my future and what I needed to do. But you were only eight. You lived that first part of your life watching our parents take care of me and my depression, thinking I needed more attention than you. You grew up believing you needed to always do as I said, as long as I was happy. I feel so wrong for that. After Aunt Lizzie passed away, I started controlling you. I took advantage of you because I was scared of losing you, too.

Matt, I love you. You are all I have left in this family. And there is one thing I know for certain. Our parents would be proud of who you have become. Mom always said to put others before yourself because someone just might do the same for you. I remember when you were younger, after our parents died, you enjoyed volunteering, especially at pet shelters and retirement homes down the street, and you always helped those in need at school. I never even stepped outside to volunteer because I was worried my depression would get the best of me. But you were always out there, putting a smile on someone's face and just doing the right thing. Even when you were bullied in school, you still didn't stop. You fought back. And that's what I want you to do.

Keep fighting back.

You have every right to pick on me. I just needed to write this out. But I want you to know that no matter what, I'll always be there for you. Accepting the position at Sal-Tech was just my way of getting Streak on my tail. If I'm working there, it will have to be in Miami, because I'm following you now. It's time for you to stand up and do what you always wanted to do. I just hope that one day you will forgive me for my selfishness.

I love you, and don't you ever forget it.

Stay strong,
Maddie

Matt covered his mouth as he read the letter. He had no words to say.

He leaned back against her bed, held the papers to his chest, and cried. Kiwi hopped onto the mattress. She sniffed the area, finding Maddie's scent on the letters.

Her words meant the world to him, but there was still no going back. He only felt guilt.

The next day, Matt donned his Speedfire gear. Despite his efforts, the blood stains had stuck to his shirt.

He trekked along the rooftops of New Harbor in broad daylight, passing the dead-end. He climbed the building he had encountered the Rare Sniper on, then found what he was looking for: his mask and his dagger.

Matt crouched to scoop them up, stuffing the mask in his pocket and clipping the knife back to his belt. He then noticed Christine's sniper rifle on the other side of the roof. He kneeled beside it and held up the strap, recognizing the weapon as the SK–08. As he strapped the rifle across his body, he gazed around the rest of the city, contemplating.

He was free to escape back to Miami. He could leave...

Yet his time in New Harbor was far from over. He needed to avenge his sister's memory.

And if Christine survived, Matt would find her.

But she was not the only person on his mind. Matt gripped the silver cross hanging against his chest.

The sound of footsteps entering the alley echoed from below. Matt turned his attention to the dead-end. He crept toward the edge and found a familiar individual peering around the area. From afar, Matt recognized the black attire and the detective's cap. Without thinking, he pulled his mask up around his face.

Matt slipped down the fire escape and landed lightly. Chen turned to him immediately, then stepped back calmly.

"Interesting," Chen muttered. "Wasn't expecting *Speedfire* here."

Matt straightened his posture. "You recognize me?"

"You've been all over the news." Chen cocked his head to the side. "But just by hearing your voice alone, you don't even need to tell me why you're here."

His eyes widened. "Detective—"

Chen held his hand up. "Ellis. Don't."

"It's not what you think—"

"I'm not here to dox your identity. Whatever you're about to say, I believe you," Chen assured him. He sighed and took another step forward. "I came here to investigate on my own. *Again.* You and I both know there's more Chief Grand is hiding. More about Streak, even The Reapers."

"And the Rare Sniper..." Matt added quietly.

"I've been stuck on this case for years," Chen told him. "I'm ready to wrap it up."

Matt held back his tears as he nodded. "You're going to help me?"

Chen smirked. "I've worked with vigilantes before," he said. The detective held his hand out. "A case like this is something we can't crack alone. Even you know that."

"I do." Matt lowered his mask and gave the detective a small smile.

"Perfect." Chen winked. "Let's settle it, then."

Matt returned home to his apartment and realized he had more work to do—with Chen, with the Tyrant. If he and his sister had never gotten involved in Jason Streak's scandal, then perhaps he would be okay. Perhaps Madeline would still be here. But others would be facing his grief instead.

His phone buzzed, and he pulled it out to see a text from Katelyn.

Katelyn:

> I've been working on some upgrades to your attire! Want to see it?

Matt:

> I'll send you my address.

Matt waited for her arrival. He watched the time tick away with the pocket watch as Kiwi brushed up against his legs. He heard Katelyn knock on the door, then took a deep breath.

"Hello!" she squealed as he opened it. She held up a new black jacket with orange paddings, an ombre orange shirt, and a belt with an insignia in the center. The emblem was a metallic flame with a lightning bolt at its center. She also held a pair of folded dark pants with orange knee pads.

"You...you actually did it," he gasped. He stood back in shock. "I like the symbol."

"Felt it screamed *Speed*fire," she teased. She stared at his current clothes and bit her tongue. "Oh, geez. Yeah, buddy, you needed a new suit."

"I've been busy," he sighed.

"I can tell." She puffed her cheeks out and exhaled. "Wow."

Matt took note of her enthusiasm. He remembered the last time he had fought crime for her and stopped the robbery. He had caught those criminals *with* her. She had even saved him from getting bashed in the head that night.

"Kate..." he said as she placed his new suit on a chair. "I need to ask you something. Two questions, actually."

Katelyn smiled and nodded. "I like questions," she added excitedly.

"Okay." He breathed in anxiously. "Remember when you wanted to be my sidekick or something? I've been thinking about it."

"Oh, my gosh—"

"If I trained you, and you took it seriously, would you want to join me?"

Katelyn drew in a large breath. "Please!" she cried out. "That's my dream come true. I can't believe it—"

"You have to take it seriously!" he reminded her.

She shut her mouth and nodded quickly. "Oh, yeah. You know me," she prodded, then pointed to herself proudly. "I'm quite the serious person."

Doubt clouded his face, but he nodded.

"Okay, next question," Matt continued as Katelyn's grin spread. "Can you keep a secret?"

"Secrets are easy," she scoffed. She turned to him again, and her face dropped. "I mean...I definitely could."

Matt looked into her eyes. This could be another risk, but he was the king of taking risks. For as long as he had known Katelyn, he did trust her. She never took advantage of him and had always called him when there was an emergency. She was even on the lookout for crime herself. This moment would mean everything to her.

He took the hood off and lowered his mask slowly. Katelyn gasped. Her eyes widened as she covered her mouth with both hands.

"My name is Matt Ellis...I'm Speedfire."

Acknowledgements

First and foremost, I want to express my love and gratitude to my family. You have always been my biggest supporters in life.

To my mom, thank you for being one of my first readers. After watching me write for most of my life, I was beyond thrilled to finally share what I've spent all my time working on. You always gave me motivation to keep going.

To my dad, thank you for everything you have given me. I want to do nothing more than to give back to you after all these years. You're the hardest worker I know, and I have no idea where I would be without you.

To Isabel, my best friend and twin sister, whom I have dedicated my first book to. You mean the world to me, and this book would have never seen the light of day if it wasn't for your unconditional support. You've read this book countless many times, even when it was in its pitiful first draft. The draft I wrote in high school is nothing like the version it is today, and you helped this story grow.

To my cats, Edie and Adrien, who are no longer here today, but you were always present when I was writing this book.

To my other cats, Sparrow, Bumblebee, and Po—my biggest distractions. Bumblebee, you're technically a co-writer for all the times you've walked across my keyboard.

To my other best friend, Rachel Sergent, you always wanted to read this book. After all this time, it's finally ready. Thank you for being patient.

To Patrick McDonald, you're awesome for being my last beta reader. I'm lucky to have someone as supportive as you when I need a set of fresh eyes to look over my writing.

To Catherine Conrad, your critiques are super appreciated, and it's always a fun adventure when we swap drafts to read. Especially since we swap early drafts. I look forward to seeing what stories you come up with next.

To Evan Lydon and Tach Martinez, your words have always kept me going.

And lastly, I want to thank *you*, the reader. Thank you so much for picking up this book and giving it a chance. I don't know if you love it or hate it, if it made you laugh or cry. It has been my honor to be among the many authors you have read. Matt's story has been an emotional ride for me to write, and I am beyond excited to have finally shared this book with the world. From the bottom of my heart, thank you.

I hope to see you in the next book.

Also by Ariel Barbera

The Rare Souls Series:
Fire in Flight

Standalone Novels:
Moss and Stone

Ariel Barbera graduated from Penn State with a BA in English, and lived in southern Pennsylvania for most of her life. She currently lives in Virginia with her family and three cats. *Fire in Flight* is her debut novel.

Find her on Instagram and TikTok, and visit her website:
www.arielbarbera.com
@authorarielbarbera